THE SECRET
SAUCE

A novel by

ADAM PATRICK FOSTER

978-0-6486464-4-0 (paperback)
978-0-6486464-5-7 (hardback)
978-0-6486464-3-3 (ebook)

Dedicated to

My cousin, my best friend,
and my constant inspiration

Sabina

prologue

To know the story of the Plucky's Chicken Palace rise to fast food prominence, there are four books written on the subject. The most critically acclaimed is *"The Source of the Sauce: The Legend of the Plucky's Empire."* Then of course, there's the Houston Chronicle's best seller; *"What Came First, the Chicken or The General?"*

Those four books were, in some form or another, financed or supported by the Wallace Estate.

There is a fifth; *"The Rooster in the Hen House."* Independently published, it was pulled from publication two years after release following a lengthy court battle over its authenticity and claims of slander. Because a lot of the copies were recalled from stores, it has somewhat become a collector's item. And this publication is hailed in many circles as the closest account of the events leading to one of the world's most successful restaurant chains.

That publication is well written and detailed, but it can be summarized quite easily.

Franklin John Wallace was born in Chesterfield, Missouri, USA, in 1908. Frank to his friends. And later, "The General" to the public. Franklin was the son of a farming equipment supplier and was being groomed to take over his father's role. However, the farming lifestyle did not tantalize Franklin enough, he instead opted to join the military. While serving as an officer in Fort Leonard Wood in Missouri, Franklin met Marcy; a waitress and cook at a local diner. They married and had two children, Josie and Benjamin, and opened their own diner in the town of Dixon named "Marcy's."

When World War II broke out, Franklin was sent to fight on the front lines. He survived several battles and, as a result, gained a virtuous reputation among the ranks, earning him two promotions over 5 years and a Medal of Honor for his involvement in the Battle of Monte Cassino. There is a rumor that Franklin hid in a tool shed for the worst five days of this conflict. But the comrade who claimed this was killed four days later while urinating in the forest at night. He was shot in the back three times. His death was officially recorded as enemy fire. Even though no enemy forces were reported in the area at the time.

It is widely known that amphetamines were administered to soldiers to combat fatigue and boost morale in wartime. Franklin took quite a liking to a particular strand and, along with a few army buddies, took it recreationally. The top brass discovered his addiction right after his Medal of Honor was awarded to him. As a result, Franklin was secretly placed in a rehabilitation program where he kicked the habit.

After the close of the war, Franklin returned home a war hero. Marcy's Diner was turning over good business, prompting Franklin and Marcy to invest in a restaurant in St. Louis. In 1950 a third child was welcomed into the Wallace family – Reuben.

While giving a speech at a military academy in Louisiana, Franklin was taking a drive through the backwaters of the Kisatchie National

Forest, looking for an infamous peach moonshine he had heard about from a cadet at the academy. His car broke down on Dyson Creek Road, forcing him to walk on foot to the nearest establishment for a phone, which turned out to be "Herby's Cookhouse."

Franklin wasn't a fan of Soul Food, or what he referred to as "that colored junk." The mechanic was taking his time and Franklin's turning stomach was getting the best of him, so he ordered a plate of fried chicken which came with a side of dipping sauce. Not only was the fried chicken the best he'd ever had, the sauce was an intriguing blend of cocktail sauce, Cajun spices and curry infused Remoulade, and was so delectable that Franklin had the restaurant's proprietor, Herby, make him up a jar to take back to his wife.

Marcy was also blown away by the sauce and they both went to work to decipher the ingredients so they could replicate it and add it to the menus in their restaurants. This task didn't prove successful, so Franklin returned to Herby's Cookhouse and offered to buy the ingredients from Herby. The stubborn old Herby told Franklin that the sauce was a family recipe and was not for sale at any price. Herby claimed he had plans himself for distributing the sauce, now accelerated due to Franklin's dogged interest. But Herby's rejection was more about the fact that he simply didn't like the man and his condescending attitude.

Franklin's resolve to obtain the sauce ingredients only heightened by Herby's blunt refusal. He even offered him a stake in the sauce sales. When Herby wouldn't budge, Franklin resorted to intimidating his family with his military prowess. He even used the Army to try and gain the land on which Herby lived. Nothing worked. Old Herby wasn't caving.

Franklin learned that Herby was hiring a lawyer to patent the sauce. But old Herb never made it that far. On one of his regular fishing trips,

Herby was shot and killed on the side of the road next to his car. A young journalist named Charlie "Chuck" Ramsey tried to argue that the two fatal shots were by the hand of a trained professional, and the gun used was a Smith and Wesson SW Model 29 - a standard issue military sidearm in the early 1950's. His death was ruled as a robbery gone wrong by the authorities. The assailant was never found. Even though a military Jeep had been spotted in the area at the time of the shooting.

Chuck was found dead in his own swimming pool two weeks later. Drowned, as the cops said. Even though Chuck was a swimming coach at a local elementary school.

Franklin offered Herby's grieving family a settlement for the sauce recipe which included the recipe for the chicken as well. A particular clause in the contract stated that they are forbidden to make, distribute or discuss the recipes indefinitely. With nowhere else to turn, the family accepted Franklin's offer.

When the chicken and the sauce were introduced at Marcy's Diner, they weren't met with the enthusiasm that Franklin was hoping for. Customers liked it, but not enough to justify the price he paid for it or the amount of stock he had produced. As a result, the chicken and the sauce took a back seat in the menu and Franklin wrote it off as a loss.

The following year, Franklin was promoted to the rank of 'Brigadier General'. The new prestigious rank meant that he yielded more command over certain new military projects. One such project was a drug research program. An adjunct military research facility was experimenting with amphetamines which, in 1957, was nowhere near understood as it would later become. One thing they did know was it had strong addictive qualities. It was neither legal nor illegal, so Franklin took it upon himself to "borrow" the amphetamine and subtly lace the chicken sauce with it. The following year in the new restaurant he and Marcy purchased in St. Louis, Franklin re-released the fried chicken and sauce combo. It had a spectacular response.

People flocked from all neighboring counties for the addictive Southern grub. Word of mouth spread like spilled water on a varnished table top. Sales rocketed. Franklin and Marcy introduced the combo in their other two eateries, and the same thing happened. Demand was transcending supply.

The chicken and the sauce were so popular that the kitchens in their restaurants couldn't cope with the sudden influx of orders. Because of this, Franklin decided to open up a diner that specialized in fried chicken only. And so, in the summer of 1959, the first ever Plucky's Chicken Palace opened its doors in St. Louis.

The official reason for why Franklin chose to name it Plucky's was a nostalgic nod to his first pet chicken when he lived in the farmland as a child. Another, less popular reason for the namesake, was that Franklin named his male appendage "Plucky the Pecker" when he was a young Army cadet. Either way, the name and brand was enthusiastically embraced by the public. So much so, that another outlet was opened in Kansas City the following year.

Due to Franklin's military commitments, his ability to oversee the old and new restaurants were limited. Marcy ran the two older restaurants, while Franklin's son Benjamin was given the two Plucky's outlets to run. With the new McDonald's fast food outlets popping up all over America, Benjamin proclaimed to be their main competitor, and fashioned the menu so burgers, fries and shakes could be purchased along with the now famous chicken and sauce. They needed a mascot, so Benjamin's sister Josie came up with the now iconic Plucky the Chicken, and a fox character that sported a formal military outfit, called "General Fox."

By the mid 1960's Plucky's had expanded to 47 outlets from California to New York. Benjamin was CEO of the Plucky's Corporation, while Marcy and Josie were key board members. Although Franklin was officially a silent partner, he had all the control of the company and the brand. Because of his military status and his war hero history, he was the face of the company, and often attended media junkets and grand openings of certain outlets dressed in full Army uniform complete with medals and badges. The media dubbed him "The General", and this title was incorporated into all advertising campaigns.

Franklin reportedly once barged into a McDonald's soused with alcohol exclaiming; "Why buy chicken nuggets from a fucking clown when you can get 'em from a real life war hero? The sweat on my balls taste better than their fuckin' dipping sauce."

By the early 1970's Plucky's was now considered one of the main three successful fast food chains in America. Their brand and look were a household staple across the whole country. Well, until Vietnam.

The General Fox character had to be retired in 1968 due to mixed feelings over the Vietnam War. Some anti-war protesters and angry veterans gained media attention for vilifying the fox as a fascist war sympathizer. Plucky the Chicken then became the solo mascot for the franchise.

The removal of General Fox was a precursor for darker days to come for the Plucky's organization.

In 1971, the United States Department of Health and Human Services did a spot check on one of the core Plucky's factories, testing chemicals contained in the food. No surprise that traces of amphetamine were uncovered. The HSS ordered the Plucky's Corporation to cease with it immediately and pay a hefty fine. Franklin's lawyers beat the fine claiming it was not an illegal substance. But two years later, in 1973, it did become illegal under the Controlled Substance Act.

When the media were reporting on the new newly appointed illegal substance, a privy young reporter named Jake Wrigley did some digging and found that Plucky's had been using amphetamines in their Secret Sauce. The story erupted into a scandal, but the Corporation played it down stating that it no longer used the substance and that it was a mild strain that Franklin claimed was used in some of the army food in WWII, which was harmless. While this was partly true, it still didn't stop a media storm led by Wrigley affirming that Plucky's has been operating as a "drug peddler".

The Wallace Foundation found proof that Wrigley was a homosexual and released it. In those times it was not exactly an acceptable character trait. Wrigley was subsequently fired from his newspaper. They claimed he was a communist. Even though he had no ties whatsoever to Communism.

Despite that, it was too late. Wrigley's point made its mark.

Consumer paranoia had Plucky's in a bind. Sales dropped significantly. Several outlets across the country closed.

But it didn't stop the restaurant chain. Franklin and the board decided to expand their menu with healthier options, such as green beans, Cole Slaw, corn on the cob and broccoli. They packaged together "family friendly" meals and featured advertisements showing The General, his children, and their children sitting around the dinner table like regular folk. The Plucky's Corporation even went so far as to donate charitable funds to anti-drug campaigns.

Things were looking good for the chicken empire. They picked up the pace and put themselves back on the top of the fast food heap with their main competitors. But 5 years later in 1979, another dubious incident would put Plucky's back in the negative spotlight.

Benjamin Wallace was busted in a pedophile sting in Kansas City. The prosecutors had no real concrete evidence, but decided to push forward with a case against him regardless. Benjamin stepped down as CEO for the duration of the case. Franklin appointed his other younger son, Reuben, as the new CEO.

Reuben, a Yale business graduate, was the right fit to take over the organization. He even insisted on wearing a Southern Gentleman attire to reflect the roots of the cuisine, which helped the troubled image of Plucky's.

Benjamin winded up beating the pedophile charges. As a result, he expected to be re-appointed as CEO. Franklin told him despite his innocence, his reputation was still tarnished, and therefore he was unfit to act as the face of the "family friendly" restaurants. This kicked off a father/son legal battle that would last a few years. Franklin and Benjamin went head-to-head in the courtroom over the rights of the company and unfair dismissal. Things grew nasty and it tore the family apart, but Benjamin refused to give up. The media learned of this and became involved, much to the rage of Franklin.

It wasn't long after the media spectacle over the feuding family that Benjamin committed suicide. Authorities found him in a dingy motel room off an overpass in St Louis, his brains blown out and a gun in his limp hand. The police ruled it as a suicide, even though the coroners found defensive bruises on his wrists and hands.

With Benjamin gone, the scandal behind them, and Reuben officially at the helm, the Plucky's Corporation pushed forward, re-branded their image once again, and flourished through the 1980's.

Franklin Wallace passed away in 1991 from heart complications at the age of 82, leaving Reuben in complete control of the Plucky's empire.

By the mid 1990's there were considerably more fast food chains on the scene, and fierce competition was growing. To fight the ever evolving industry, umbrella companies were formed to buy out profitable chain restaurants and have more control over the capitalist marketplace.

Ever the shrewd businessman, Reuben bought shares in two up and coming franchise's, "Burrito Bell" and "Gobble Gobble Turkey." He helped shape them up to be successful fast food outlets. Reuben decided to strike when the iron was hot and facilitated a merger with Tasty Incorporated, allowing him a key position on the board and control over Plucky's interests, including the manufacturing of the famous General's Secret Sauce.

Reuben put into place a practice whereby only three board members of the Plucky's Corporation are allowed to know the exact ingredients of the Secret Sauce, and are not permitted to travel together, or all be in one location together at any given time. This is to protect the gold mine that Plucky's holds over many of the popular fast food chains. There is even rumor that Reuben added a touch of rare Polynesian wine vinegar to the sauce. The acetic acid dominates over some of the other ingredients, making it considerably difficult to uncover the total ingredients within a science laboratory.

The next ten years would prove to be a fruitful epoch for the Plucky's Chicken Palace organization and its constituents.

That is, until Reuben developed a coarse drinking problem and was in and out of rehab. A point was reached where Reuben retired from the mantle of Tasty Incorporated and an ambitious young woman named Jillian took over.

Reuben remains a silent partner and is currently one of the only three board members who knows the recipe for the General's Secret Sauce.

That's the basic summary of "*The Rooster in the Hen House.*" The writer of that book was Jake Wrigley, the same journalist who cracked the amphetamine scandal.

Jake died in 2011 from being beaten to death with a "Lovehoney Triple Tickler G-Spot Realistic Dildo Vibrator" by a junkie transvestite hooker he owed money to. They were well acquainted.

There was nothing mysterious about that one.

CHAPTER ONE

The Pit Stop

The mist is low and thick on the stone and yellow dirt desert floor. Cacti and agave plants poking through the ground clouds. A rare black coated coyote trots out of the darkness through the mist. Her big bushy tail swings behind her as she moves. She's alone and scared, not knowing where she's going. The two remaining members of her pack were shot and killed by a hunter several moons ago. Since then, she's been roaming the Arizona desert, looking for a new pack, a lover, or a place to call home. Right now she's starving, and she's been following her nose for a few miles now, the salty scent of cooked meat has been wafting through cold night air. The smell growing stronger now, she can almost taste it. She licks her muzzle. The last proper meal she had was a house cat several days ago.

She stops, seeing a light in the near distance. A lone light in an otherwise empty landscape. The occasional car and truck drive past. She sticks her nose in the air and smells the sweet scent of fresh meat. But there's something else in the air. Something she can't quite place. Tension. Anxiety. Some kind of trouble. She can't put her paw on it.

She decides to circle the area first. That hunter might be around. For some reason, she suspects he is. That white light in the sky is tempting her, and also vexing her. She moves on through the night with trepidation.

Hordes of insects frenziedly buzz around the large lit up face of the Plucky; the mascot for Plucky's Chicken Palace. Fashioned like a cartoon character, the white feathered chicken wears a red vest, a red baseball cap and gives the thumbs up with a toothy grin in his orange beak. What looks like food in his teeth are actually the splotched remains of dead bugs and dirt from the abrasive Arizona desert winds.

Sitting 50 feet in the air, the Plucky's sign is a shining beacon in the otherwise vast darkness of the barren plains. Eighty yards from the sign is a Plucky's fast food outlet, which looks like any other pop-up chain restaurant. Hospital-like white neon lights, a Drive Thru and cheap linoleum flooring with an uninspired checker pattern.

The spacious car park is empty. Not surprising, considering it's around 11 o'clock in the evening. The only real customers at this time of night are the passing truck drivers on a cross-country haul and stoners from the nearby towns of Holbrook and Chambers. Hence the reason for the car park being spacious; to accommodate the road trains, and the horrendous parking jobs of baked drivers.

The truck drivers are the cream of the consumers for this particular Plucky's outlet. That is because it lies on Route 66, a popular passage for many freight and transport companies from Chicago to Los Angeles. That, and there are no other 24-hour food options in Holbrook or Chambers. Even though this location is closer to Holbrook, people make excuses to drop in from a 60 mile radius, even as far as Chambers and Sanders.

The real excuse is they want a "Plucky's Mega Value Loaded Box Meal", their highest selling food kit, which contains 3 pieces of fried chicken, mashed potato and gravy, Cole Slaw, green beans, a biscuit, a medium drink, and of course, a side of the General's Secret Sauce. All for the value price of $8.95. How much value received is up to the individual. There's more Cole Slaw and green beans in the trash cans than there are gnawed chicken bones.

Two garbage bags are tossed into the dumpster at the back of the restaurant. Seth, the night manager, slams the lid of the dumpster shut and fishes in his pocket for a crumpled soft pack of Parliaments. He takes out the second last smoke, bent in three places, and straightens it out with his thumb and index finger. Seth is wearing the customary Plucky's uniform. It matches the cartoon mascot. Red vest, white long sleeved shirt and black slacks. Seth isn't wearing the customary baseball cap because it will ruin his black gelled rockabilly hair.

He lights up the crinkled cigarette and gazes around the empty parking lot. His eyes come to rest on a Vespa chained to a light post several feet away.

A restored classic. The 1968 Vespa VLB Sprint. Aqua blue and white. Stainless steel sport exhaust. Chrome rims and round hubcaps. His baby. Seth recalled seeing the same one a year ago in some 60's Italian movie at 3am, six bongs deep. It recently cost him over five grand. A hard stretch on his shitty managers wage, but he needs it for all that mad pussy he's going to get when the girls actually start paying attention. And they will. Especially that delicious pin-up girl goddess, Winter, who works at the bar down the road.

Seth's gaze shifts from the Vespa to a set of car headlights in the distance on the highway.

'Christ', he thinks. Another fucking asshole coming to stare at the menu too long knowing damn well what they want. Fuckin' stoners.

Seth watches as the car reveals itself out of the darkness under the bright Plucky sign's bubble of light.

A black stretch limousine.

About to inhale another drag, he stops the cigarette just shy of his lips. His eyes narrow. He knows that limo.

The limousine cruises past, then suddenly slams on the brakes; the rubber tires crackling loudly against the loose gravel on the well-worn highway. A moment passes as the car runs idle on the spot. The brake lights flick off and the limo speeds back several yards, coming to a crunching halt right next to the base of the Plucky's sign.

Seth sneers and angrily tosses his cigarette aside.

'Mother fucker', he growls under his breath, then turns and sprints back inside the restaurant.

The engine still running, the driver's door to the limo kicks open and a tall bulky black man in a shiny chauffeur's suit ambles out of his seat as quick as his 260lbs weight will let him. At 6'1" he's an intimidating sight. Dennis quickly rounds the front of the car to the other side and opens the back right door, a little out of breath.

'You sound like a dying buffalo', Reuben says as he climbs out of the back. 'And you smell like it too.'

Reuben Wallace, Ruby to his associates, exudes a guttural grunt as he heaves himself out of the limo, one arm on the door for support, the other supported by Dennis. Ruby finds his footing and peers up at the Plucky's sign towering over them. He whips out a silk handkerchief from the top pocket of his light cotton white suit jacket and dabs his sweaty brow and alcohol reddened nose. His suit is custom made.

White cotton pants, vest, shirt, and jacket, with a black string tie and polished black shoes. The Southern Gentleman getup. He bleached his mustache and goatee to perfectly match his thin bone white hair.

'Stay here, boy', Ruby says.

'Yessir Mister Wallace', says Dennis. He nods in compliance, pulling the bottom of his black jacket to straighten the creases over his bulging muscles. Dennis likes to think of himself as a bodyguard, but most of his days were spent driving the drunk old man around. Mostly hunting trips. Dennis is not by any means an action junkie, despite being a heavyweight boxer in his mid-twenties. Almost ten years on and he doesn't miss it at all. But working for the old man was mostly dull. Cracking a couple of heads would be nice once in a while.

Ruby ambles toward the base of the sign, tripping on a spiky agave plant. He tumbles forward and lands on his bloated Santa gut in the red dust with a loud 'oomph'.

Dennis sighs and shakes his head, going to Ruby's aid.

'I said stay by the car god-dammit! I got this!' Ruby shouts through wheezing breath.

Dennis halts in his tracks, looking down at Ruby as he struggles in the dirt to get on all fours, thinking he looks like a dog at the end of its life.

Ruby manages to get on his knees and catches his breath a moment. He reaches into his jacket pocket and takes out a sterling silver hip flask encased in crocodile leather, taking a lengthy gulp. He winces as the Makers Mark hits his lungs and flushes his face. He caps the flask and places it back inside his jacket, patting it gently like a good pet. Ruby, now filled with liquid courage, heaves to stand up. He thinks he does pretty damn alright for a man in his mid-seventies.

Ruby dusts the yellow desert dirt off his white suit and briskly waddles toward the base of the sign again. He reaches the metal pole and smacks his sweaty palm up against it for support. He uses his other hand to fumble around under his belt for his fly. With some difficulty he manages to unzip his pants, spraying forth a gushing deluge of piss. Ruby groans as the contents of his bladder pool around the base of the sign pole, floating the abundance of Cicada corpses once drawn to the heaven-like Plucky's sign above.

Ruby finishes, does his post-piss tugs, and starts to do his pants up. He stops. An idea hitting him. He takes his hand off the pole and frantically undoes his belt and drops his pants to his urine soaked shoes. He grunts as he turns around and squats his bare ass down toward the dirt.

Dennis grits his teeth and looks down, shaking his shiny bald head with dismay.

'Sweet mother of Jesus', says Dennis to himself, 'not again.'

Ruby is in full squat position, preparing to launch a number two on the side of the pole. His face twists as he begins to force one out.

Dennis glances up and notices Seth running frantically across the parking lot toward them. He's grasping a pressure spray bottle with both hands.

Dennis yells 'Mister Wallace, we gotta go!'

Ruby looks over his shoulders to see that Seth is almost upon him, leaping down a small incline from the car park to the dirt, kicking up dust as he sprints to Ruby.

Ruby grunts as he rises to stand, pulling his pants up with him. No time to fasten his belt, Ruby holds the front of his slacks together with a balled fist and rapidly hobbles back to the limo where Dennis has the back door open for him. Seth has caught up to Ruby and starts spraying grape soda at him, covering the back of his white suit with the sticky purple liquid.

'Next time you pull this shit I'm calling the cops again!' Seth yells, knowing that's a hollow gesture, because this rich asshole will just pay them off like he did before.

Ruby dives onto the back seat of the limo and Dennis slams the door shut. Seth skids to a halt and aims the bottle at Dennis, who gives him a look that foreshadows a hospital inducing punch. Seth gulps, then looks to the black tinted window of the back door.

'You hear me?!' said Seth, spraying more grape soda all over Ruby's back window. Ruby peering through the tinted window, his eyes glowering between the streaks of sticky liquid.

Dennis quickly strides to the driver's side and climbs in. He puts the car into gear and slams his foot on the accelerator.

The limo's tires spin on the asphalt creating rubbery smoke. The car rockets off down the highway.

Seth grips the spray bottle like he's choking it to death as he watches the limo roar away down the road. Angry and helpless. He looks back at the base of the pole.

'Well', he thinks, 'at least he beat him to it this time and won't have to clean up any shit'.

The back door window rolls down and Ruby pokes his head out, the wind whipping around his thin white hair.

'Eat shit like the kind ya serve, ya rotten dick cheese!'

Ruby flips Seth the bird and cackles, echoing in the otherwise silent desert plains as the limo speeds off into the night.

CHAPTER TWO

Sweetpea And Honeybee

The mid-afternoon golden sun softly beams through the front window of Helen's Dry Cleaning, highlighting the dust particles swirling through traces of light steam from the two ancient industrial multi-matic dry cleaning machines up the back. A dusty Thunder From Down Under calendar on the wall, which has been sitting on September for the past four years. An early 90's boombox by the front counter, the CD player part only works now if you perfectly balance a slightly heavy object on top of it while it plays.

Behind the front counter are two garment conveyor belt racks filled with plastic covered clothes on either side of the long narrow space. Two women sit between the racks on paint chipped stools, facing each other. The owner of the dry cleaners, Helen, early fifties with an 80's hair perm and a tanned leathery face, sits with her eyes closed as a make-up artist uses a blush brush to dab her cheeks.

'And a touch of toner to make those pretty peepers of yours really pop', says Winter Bloom, the make-up artist in her mid-twenties.

Winter's lofty Monroe-esque voice is to the ears what half melted whipped cream on a hot slice of apple pie is to the eyes. The porcelain pale white foundation on her face is to contrast the black winged eyeliner and natural puffy lips accentuated by bright red Velvetine lipstick.

Winter lifts the brush off Helen's face and leans back on the stool, taking a moment to study her whole upper body with one eyebrow cocked in a scrutinizing manner. Helen's eyes slowly flicker open.

'Bup, bup, bup', Winter exhorts, waggling her index finger at Helen, 'keep those eyes closed for now gorgy porgy. I need to see those pigments without pupils'.

Helen promptly closes her eyes again. Winter leans in again to survey Helen's face close up, using her ring finger to twirl the tip of a red and black bandanna tied around her plump raven hair. Along with her matching red and black short-cut polka-dot yarn dress, Winter has the 50's pin-up girl look down pat. To call her hot wouldn't do her justice. To call her cute would be short-changing her. She is the physical manifestation of Minnie Mouse having an orgasm.

Winter leans back on her stool again, nodding while a content little grin emerges.

'Okay, open 'em up', Winter says. 'Me oh my Helen. Don't you just look like the belle of the ball'.

Helen pats the bottom of her perm with a bashful smile. Winter wondering if the wrinkled flabby skin jiggling under Helen's skinny arm is the result of her genes, poor diet or too much sun. Winter's eyes dart back to Helen's face, squinting her eyes at something.

'Wait a...', Winter trails off into thought for a moment. She snaps back to focus and reaches down to a make-up kit next to her stool. A professional standard kit, red and black, and covered with stickers of kitty skeletons. Winter's hand rummages around the kit, her fingers feeling the shapes of nail varnishes, compact holders, blushers, until she touches what she's after.

'Everything okay?' Helen asks with concern.

Winter holds up a small pair of tweezers in her long fiery red coated fingernails. Now Helen's concern goes up a notch.

'Sorry sweetie, but I'm gonna need you to close your eyes and keep your face dead still, just for a milli-secci, that okay?' Winter says as she bats her long lashes.

Helen gulps, not sure what she needs to do with the tweezers. But how can anyone say 'no' to that face? Helen nods and gives her best fake smile, closing her eyes again.

A dry-cleaning machine hisses in the background.

Winter squints her eyes again, leans in close to Helen with the tweezers open. Like a cobra striking, Winter nicks a stray hair from Helen's left eyebrow. Helen almost jumps on her seat and flinches back. She blinks her eyes open to see Winter pucker lips and blow the hair from the tweezers like it was a smoking gun.

'There. That wasn't so bad, was it?'

Winter bends her neck slightly from side to side, surveying her handiwork on Helen's face. A smile lights up her face and she nods with satisfaction, dropping the tweezers effortlessly back into the kit.

'Now you're not just the Belle. You're the whole darn ball,' Winter says, handing Helen a little purple hand mirror.

Helen turns her head back and forth, adjusting her hair and staring at her reflection with astonishment.

'Oh wow, you really outdid yourself this time darlin'. Now I gotta get the right dress to match.'

'Has Cinderella got a ball lined up?'

'Me and Bill are going to the new Chinese restaurant downtown. On Navajo and Hopi. There's live fish in a tank, and you pick which ones you wanna eat. Supposed to be real fancy, y'know? It's the first date night we've had in months. The bastard better not take his eyes off me tonight.'

'Well if he does, I'll bet every other man, woman and fish won't,' Winter says with a wink.

Helen smiles bashfully and waves her hand at Winter as if to say 'oh stop it you'. She stands up and steps over to a small sewing table, picking up her handbag and rifles through it.

Helen says, 'Now I know you told me there was gonna be no charge-'

'And I mean it,' Winter cuts her off as she rises from the stool.

'Well Winter honey, I gotta give you something. I mean, for your materials, your time, or...,'

Winter steps over and puts her hand on Helen's, gently making her close the handbag with physical suggestion.

'Honestly Helen, it's fine. You give me the dandiest discounts for my dry cleaning. And besides, I'm gonna be in Broadway soon enough, makin' the big bucks. Which means I gotta get all the practice I can, to stay sharp. But what I will ask you to do, is if any ladies see you and ask who did your make up, you tell 'em it was little ol' me. Would ya do that?'

'Oh Winter, you got it.'

'Do you have Insta?'

Helen's face twists with confusion.

'Instragram. You know, the app?'

'No, I don't think so. My daughter Sue is into all that. I got Facebook though.'

'That'll work just fine', says Winter as she pulls a smartphone from a black frilly garter on her left thigh. She taps the screen a few times then loads up the camera function, lines it up, and takes a picture of Helen.

'Hmm, can you shift over here just a smidgy? The lighting's better over here.'

Helen shuffles a few steps to stand where the sun hits her face with a warm glow. The transparent plastic sheets covering dry cleaning behind her shimmering from the light.

'Lovely. Much better.'

Winter adjusts the phone to get the right angle. Winter is digging the pops of light reflecting from the plastic clothes covers. Better than any app she has on her phone. Click. Click. Click. Click.

'Aaaaand, one more for safety.'

Click.

'Perfect.'

Winter stares down at her phone and rapidly taps her thumbs on the screen.

'Now we gotta find the filter that's juuuusssst right.'

Helen watches Winter furrow her brows and curl the corner of her lips as she dresses up the picture with an app. She knows Winter isn't a church going kind of girl, and she's mixed up with that degenerate 'c-word' of a woman Rose. But with those looks and that thin body and long legs, those childbearing hips, thinking her and Bobby would make some damn good looking grand kids.

'You're a very gorgeous woman, Winter.'

'Why thankie. You're easy on the eye too, pumpkin.'

'You don't have any tattoos, not like most of the young women today. I think it ruins their bodies. Looks so unbecoming.'

Winter motions to her body in a sweeping arm gesture.

'My body is a blank canvas for all my pretty little outfits and accessories.'

Helen smiles broadly. Winter looks at her phone to pretend she's just received a message, not a fan of Helen's judgmental comments.

'Say Winter?'

'Uh-huh?', Winter doesn't look up from the phone.

'Bobby...you know my son Bobby right? My second youngest? Well, he just got back from deployment. Back for a while he reckons.'

Winter looks up and thinks hard, blinking as she tries to recollect anyone named Bobby. Helen watches her with anticipation. Helen seems so sure of it, and she's probably right. Helen's a nice lady, and, well, Winter doesn't want to disappoint her. Especially when she's got that yucky skin. Must be horrible.

'Why yes, I do remember Bobby!' she exclaims with a big assuring smile. 'I can't recall where we met, but he's a very nice boy.'

'Well, like I said, he's just got back from...usbe... usbek... oh I can't remember right now, something ending with -stan. Anyway, he's staying with us for a short while 'till he gets himself adjusted. I'm gonna have a little dinner thing, this Sunday night. Pork chops and mash. Nothing fancy. And I was wondering if you wanna join us?'

'Sunday? Hmmmm...'

Winter cocks her head up thoughtfully, pretending to go through her mental directory of people she's met. Looking at the ceiling, she notices green fungus in little splotches starting to form from the heavy amounts of steam used here. It reminds her of peeling paint on the roof of the men's bathroom at- oh. She's got it. She un-cocks her head and looks to Helen again.

'I think Rose and I are repainting the men's bathroom at The Glass Half Full in the afternoon. I'm not sure how late we'll be.'

'Bobby thinks the world of you. It'd mean a lot to him if you came by.'

Winter smiles, sucking a sharp uncomfortable breath in. Since she was around twelve, boys and men have lusted after her, and mothers have tried to set her up with their sons, and even daughters. She knows Helen's intentions. She's no fool. Even if she has an IQ of 68. Well, that's what they told her parents just before she dropped out of senior year to study at hairdressing school. Anyway, who needs to know which team won at the Alamo when you can make a housewife look like a movie star. It's what she does best. And avoiding sexual advances. Winter doesn't hate many things, but lying is one of them. As her Mawmaw always told her, "for a lady, a little white lie can sometimes avoid a very dark situation." And she has no intention of having dinner with Bobby. Or repainting the men's.

'Tell ya what. I'll work super-dooper fast, and if my job is done in time for dinner, I'll drop by. That sound good?'

'You got yourself a deal.' Helen smiles warmly. 'And I know you won't accept cash, but do you have anything you need dry cleaned? I can put in with a batch tomorrow. Easy peasy Japanesey.'

Winter thinks for a second, then shrugs and nods.

'Actually, I do have a garment that needs it. A corset if that's okay?'

'You've got yourself a deal sweetie.'

A car horn blasts from outside. Someone holding it down so it's one long continuous, annoying blare. Winter turns her head to spot a blue and white restored '67 Shelby Mustang parked across the street.

'Oop. My chariot has arrived.'

Winter stoops down and collects her make up kit, securing it shut. She steps over and gives Helen an air peck on each cheek.

'I'll drop by in the morning with my dry cleaning.'

'I'll be here.'

Winter slings the strap of the make-up kit over her shoulder and trots to the door in her red stilettos studded with silver ball bearings.

Rose sits slouched at the wheel of her muscle car, one arm flopped indolently out the window, the other hand planted on the car horn. She spots Winter exiting the dry cleaners and stops chewing gum to smile.

Rose has a chiseled jawline and high cheekbones to go with it. Her toned muscular 5'11" figure, tanned all over, give her a very masculine presence. If she put in any effort to act feminine she could be gorgeous. But it's Rose, so she doesn't. To emphasize that she's no lady, she wears a gray tank top, army green cargo shorts, mirrored aviator sunglasses, and has her short coppery brown hair pulled back tight into a little ponytail that borders on being a manbun.

Unlike Winter, Rose has several tattoos. Her left arm is a full sleeve of roses and thorns spiraling up from her wrist to her shoulder. Most of her tattoos are old now and could use a touch up. She doesn't care though.

Rose takes her hand off the car horn as Winter approaches, lowering her aviators slightly so her piercing blue eyes look just over the rim.

'Hey Sweetpea', says Rose.

'Hey Honeybee, lay some sugar on me!'

Winter reaches the car and bends down to the window with only her upper body, ass in the air, and plants a wet sloppy kiss on Rose's lips.

Helen watches them passionately kiss from the doorway of her shop; lips pursed in disgust. Rose tilts her head slightly in mid kiss to lock eyes with Helen and winks. Helen waves her off in repugnance and storms back into her shop.

Winter rises upright and swishes her tongue inside her mouth, using her fingers to withdraw Rose's gum.

'Cinnamon', Winter says with an air of contentment.

'I got a fresh pack of peppermint in the glove box, just for you.'

Winter shrugs and pops the chewed gum back in her mouth.

'This is fine', she says in her squeaky voice.

Rose grins and turns the ignition key and the engine roars to life. Winter scurries in her thick heels to the passenger side and climbs in. She reaches in her kit and takes out a pair of big black Jackie-O sunglasses and puts them on.

Rose puts one heavy foot on the brake, one on the accelerator. She revs the engine coarsely and stares over at the dry cleaners at Helen, who is now trying to stand hidden to the side of the main front window. Rose grabs the gear stick and throws the car into action, the wheels spinning on the spot creating a plume of dense rubber smoke. She slams the car into drive and spins the wheel sharply, skidding into a drift as the car swerves across the street, stopping briefly in front of Helen's shop with a deafening engine roar, and rockets off down the street.

Helen strides angrily out of the shop, waving the tire smoke out of her face. She watches the mustang speed off down the small-town street.

'Fuckin' kitty puncher.'

Rose's mustang cruises down Navajo Blvd heading out of Holbrook, past the cemetery and Dairy Queen, hitting the on-ramp to Route 66 behind a big white truck.

'Makin' that old witch passable as a lady must be like tryin' to make a turd look like a Twinkie', says Rose.

She smiles and swings her head to glance at Winter for a laugh, but Winter, sunglasses off, is busy applying eye liner using the little mirror on the back of the sunshade and didn't hear. Rose waits a moment then repeats herself louder. Winter shrugs, not looking away from the mirror.

'You know what they say. The fun is in the challenge,' Winter says with a distracted tone. She pauses, taking the eye liner pencil away to look at Rose. 'Or is it, the challenge is in the fun?' Winter blinks, then goes to put the pencil back to her eye and pauses again, her face strained with thought. 'No. That doesn't make sense does it?'

'That old battle axe doesn't know the meaning of the word fun.'

Winter doing her eye liner again, 'I think she's nice enough.'

'I bet Hitler's sisters thought he was nice enough too.'

Winter drops the eye liner pencil in her kit, fumbling around for something else. She looks over at Rose with furrowed brows.

'Hitler had sisters?'

Rose does a haphazard one shouldered shrug,

'I don't fuckin' know. I ain't a historian. But people liked having big families back then. So I reckon he did.'

Winter looks back down at her kit and fishes out a lip liner pencil and checks the color, dropping it back in the bag. Rose stares at her a moment, feeling like she might have been too rude to her Sweetpea.

'I'll Google it later. To be sure.'

Winter pulls out another pencil, this time happy with the color. She takes out her gum and sticks it under the side of the seat, adding to the collection of other previously chewed gum of all different faded colors stuck there. Winter looks back to the visor mirror and applies the maroon pencil to her outer bottom lip.

'Who is they, anyway?' says Rose.

'Huh?'

Rose adjusts her aviators a notch up her nose.

'You said, "you know what they say". Who the fuck is "they"? I mean, everyone says that before a popular, I dunno, phrase or some shit.' Rose, staring at the road, spots a pothole ahead. She glances to Winter and says, 'Pothole.'

Winter pulls the pencil away from her lip just before the car bounces from the tire hitting the missing chunk of the road. A moment later she resumes her lip liner.

Rose says 'What is there? A group of anonymous people sittin' around sayin' stuff 'till they all agree on something the rest of us can say they said?'

Winter finishes the bottom lip and tilts her head from side to side to check her handiwork. She's half listening and says 'Yeah, I guess.'

Rose is becoming agitated, drumming her fingers on the leather cased steering wheel.

'They could be anyone. I mean, the phrase you just said. "The challenge is in the fun". Shit. That could have been thought up by... I dunno. A pedophile. You know?' Rose clears her throat and speaks in a deeper tone, trying to emulate a man's voice. 'I'm gonna try and rape that nine-year-old boy. It's a challenge, but it'll be fun. Hey! The challenge is in the fun. I'm gonna start saying that. Maybe it'll catch on.' Rose finishes the statement by hitting the steering wheel aggressively with her palm.

Winter pauses doing her top lip and looks over with heartbroken eyes.

'Who's going to rape a nine-year-old boy?'

'The same sick bastard that said what you just said!' Rose looks at the road and sees another pothole ahead.

'Pothole!'

Winter quickly pulls the pencil from her mouth as the car shudders from the hole.

'Really?' Winter says with genuine concern.

Rose twists her lips and raises her stretched palms off the steering wheel, as if to say 'maybe'.

Winter frowns and looks out her window, shaking her head in disgust.

'That's horrible. That's really, really horrible.'

Rose nods in agreement with her, focusing on the road. Winter sighs, then starts to finish her lip with the pencil.

Rose says, 'Anyway, fuck it. There's just some things we shouldn't know the answer to.' She reaches to the compartment between the two front seats and grabs a pack of cinnamon gum, popping one stick of it in her mouth. 'Ignorance is bliss, right?'

'That's what they say,' says Winter aloofly.

Rose throws her head back and laughs. Winter finishes her top lip and looks to Rose, wondering what's so funny. Rose puts her hand on Winter's thigh and squeezes it affectionately while staring through the windscreen as The Plucky's Chicken Palace sign becomes visible ahead.

'So, how much did you make off that old witch today anyway?'

Winter, fishing through her kit, stops movement and remains silent with a guilty visage. Rose sighs. Her expression turns sour.

'Now Rose look, I-'

Rose spins the steering wheel and swerves the car to the side of the road and brakes hard. *Screeeeeeeeech.*

The mustang stops several yards from the Plucky's sign. Ahead, by the side of the road, a short young girl is standing clutching a home-made sign. A yard long piece of timber with a cardboard square that reads: 'IF YOU EAT AT PLUCKY'S, YOU ARE A MURDERER!' in red paint, with a badly drawn headless chicken; the head in a pool of blood at its feet. Crudely drawn crosses through its eyes. The girl is vaguely dressed like a Native American, wearing a long woolen poncho with Navajo patterns, ripped whitewashed jeans and a wide brimmed floppy sun hat. Under her hat she is wearing an American Indian inspired crocheted headband made from white and brown thin rope, two strands dangling down her frizzy brown hair to her shoulder, at the end of which are black Grackle feathers.

As the dust clouds around the mustang drift away, Rose spits her gum out the window, takes off her aviators and glares daggers at Winter.

'You did it for free. Again?'

Winter holds her hands up like she's surrendering to an armed robber and gives her best cute smile. Rose sighs and shakes her head, looking at the little hippie girl by the sign, then looks down at her lap. She suddenly pounds the steering wheel with her fist and leaves it there a moment. Then pounds again. And again. Thump. Thump. Thump.

Winter watches her with growing apprehension, twirling a curl of her charcoal hair with her pinkie finger. She reaches in a pocket on her dress, pretending to pull something out using her fingers, reaches her hand across and stuffs an imaginary object in Rose's defiantly closed lips.

'Take a chill pill Honeybee.'

Rose stops hammering the wheel. Winter picks up a bottle of half drunk water from the middle seat compartment and opens it, giving it to Rose, who takes it and sculls the rest, then languidly tosses the empty bottle over her shoulder to the back seat. She is visibly calmer now, taking controlled breaths.

'There. All better,' Winter says as she gently wipes Rose's lips with her thumb.

'How come you didn't make the bitch pay?'

'I'm sorry Honeybee. I... I just love it.'

Rose turns her body in her seat to face Winter, resting her elbow on top of it.

'I know you love it Sweetpea. And I love you more than a dog loves sniffin' assholes. But ya gotta grow some spine girl. In this world, you're either the lion or the gazelle.'

Winter blinks.

'What's a gazelle?'

'You know, they're kinda like, African deer, I guess. I watched one of those documentaries on Discovery the other week.'

Winter nods like she's understanding but her bemused facial expression says she's not. Rose picks up on that and looks around for a better example. She looks through the windscreen, at the little girl waving her sign to trucks and their disengaged drivers. Rose's eyes dart to the sign, then up the pole, locking on to the Plucky's mascot rooster giving the thumbs up. She turns her attention back to Winter.

'Okay. You're either the chicken, or the egg.'

Now Winter looks really lost, just scratching her head with a vague expression.

Rose looks down confused. She doesn't even know what she's saying anymore.

'Never mind. Look. We need every dollar if we're gonna make it Broadway. And I'm tryin'. I'm really tryin' here. I'm selling the bar. Moving to a big city. And you know how much I hate big cities.'

'I know Honeybee. But I keep telling you. Don't worry about the money. As long as we have each other, we'll be right as rain drops.'

Rose smiles endearingly and reaches over to stroke Winter's hair lovingly.

'Yeah, and it's a wonderful sentiment. But I don't wanna take any chances. I wanna make you happy, baby. And we're not happy here. So the sooner we get outta this shit hole, the better. Which means we don't owe anyone anything. Not even a smile, unless they pay ya for it. We gotta take, take, take.'

Winter nods, looking down at her lap and twiddling her fingers. Rose uses her index finger to lightly force Winter's chin up so she's looking her directly in the eyes.

'Say it with me Sweetpea. Take, take, take.'

'Take, take, take.'

Rose grins proudly.

'That's my girl.'

Rose grunts as she shifts in her seat again to face forward, putting her sunglasses back on. Winter puts on hers as well. Rose starts the engine and gives a few good revs, then leans over quickly and gives Winter a swift air kiss just shy of her lips, so as to not ruin her make up job, then turns her attention to the road.

Rose throws the car in reverse and speeds backward, swinging it around into the driveway leading to the Plucky's restaurant behind them. She slams the gear into drive and speeds back onto the highway, kicking up red dust that blows all over the protesting hippie girl. It doesn't phase the girl though. She starts performing a victory dance, thinking the mustang and its inhabitants decided not to eat at Plucky's because of her awesome sign.

The little girl yells as Rose's mustang speeds past her.

'Yeah! Good for you! You just saved an innocent bird's life!'

Rose adjusts the rearview mirror to get a glimpse of the girl and her cheesy dance as they hightail away from her.

'That little girl is too young to have any kind of opinion.'

Winter is using her middle and index finger to walk like a person across her dress, stepping only from polka-dot to polka-dot. She giggles, realizing that her long fingernails look like the little finger person has high heels on. She makes the little person jump, skip and twirl across the dots. She makes her fingers start to kick like they're doing the Can-Can dance and giggles again. She stops, bringing her hand up to her face to inspect her nails. There's a slight chip in the paint on her ring fingernail. It's something most people wouldn't notice. But it's all Winter notices. She curls her lips, thinking she ought to put a fresh coat of paint on all of them. Or maybe she should change it to purple so she can wear that fun new violet playsuit with the gold trimmings she made the other week. But which shade of purple would go with that better? Or would a coat of gold match? Subtly is often the key. But she won't know for sure. She'll have to do a test. Maybe even put a bunch of samples next to each other before she commits. Like people do when they're deciding what to paint their kitchen, or their bathroom. A lot of folk don't understand the compl- wait. Bathroom. Winter lingers on that a moment.

'Hey, I was wondering Honeybee.'

'Whatcha wonderin' Sweetpea?'

'I'm thinking we should repaint the men's bathroom at The Glass.'

'Why's that?'

'It could use a fresh coat. And with us selling soon and all. It's looking a little drab, y'know?'

'Well it wouldn't surprise me if the paint got stripped with what comes out of some of the fella's we serve. Especially after burrito night.'

Winter nods. Content.

Rose says 'Well, we gotta get the hooch out of the basement before the health and safety inspector comes next Monday. We may have buyers almost locked down for The Glass, but if we don't pass that inspection, we ain't sellin' shit. So we may as well do it all at once. Make a day of it. When were ya thinkin'?'

'I'm thinking Sunday afternoon.'

'Sunday afternoon it is.'

Winter nods again. She stares out at the desert terrain, the little patches of green plants littering the seemingly endless golden yellow dirt. The shiny mix of gravel on the side of the road glistening in the sun. Winter thinking about Helen's unappealing offer for Sunday roast with her dropkick son. A smile creeping onto her face. She's no longer a dirty little liar.

CHAPTER THREE

The Death
Of Katherine
Robicheaux

Rose flicks the clunky old metal pedestal fan on at the foot of her and Winter's rickety old double bed. Winter is passed out in the fetal position, still in her pumps. She's cuddling her Pikachu stuffed toy. A half smoked joint in a green glass ashtray on the bedside table that Winter couldn't finish. Rose tiptoes in her black Doc Martin boots to the door, stealing one more look at her sleeping beauty, then quietly slips out.

Rose ambles down the narrow stairs from the living area upstairs to the main floor of her bar through a locked door in a passageway. The small corridor leading to the main bar area. It's a large room with a high A-frame ceiling. The pillars are made from thick logs sanded down and varnished. Rustic tables and chairs scattered in the middle of the room. One side has a long mahogany bar that takes up the whole end of the room, with the front entrance next to it. At the other end, several private booths, and a small performance stage in the corner next to them. Lining the sides of the rooms are the odd corduroy couch here and there.   All wooden planked floors that have seen their fair share of scuff marks; table and chair scratches, and the odd old brown blood stain from that won't come out since the brawls they were created in. The walls are decorated with the usual saloon accessories. Two dart boards. A few taxidermy animal heads. A large moose head that Rose hates, but the customers seem to like.

Next to the end of the bar closest to the entrance is a single doorway leading into another corner room with two windows, one looking out to the parking lot and the other looking out the front of the building toward the highway. An old dusty TV set mounted in the corner, a wireless modem sitting on top used by gamblers to watch whatever sport they're betting on. Some tables and chairs neatly arranged, each table with tins of pencils and little pieces of paper. The massive gene-rator powering the whole building is just outside the window facing the car park.

Rose approaches the bar and rounds the side to stand behind it. She pulls out an empty milk crate from under the counter and starts peering at the collection of name brand liquor bottles up on the wall shelving unit. She looks for near empty bottles and places them in the crate.

There is a faint beep nearby, followed by the crashing sound of metal meets tiled floor, coming from the kitchen several feet away. Rose uses her whole body to sigh angrily, placing the crate at her feet. She marches to the kitchen swinging doors and bangs them open.

A tall skinny nineteen-year-old boy looks up from several metal trays scattered on the floor like a deer in headlights.

'What the fuck is all that racket Nick? You're gonna wake Winter!'

Nick wipes his long sandy blonde fringe from his face, swallowing hard.

'Sorry Miss Glass, I-I-I was loading the dishwasher, and I-'

'I told you to stop it with the "Miss" shit. I'm not a fuckin' school teacher.'

Nick clenches his eyes shut and faces down, clearly disappointed in himself. He sticks his hands in the pockets of his dark blue skinny jeans.

'Sorry Rose.'

'Clean up that mess, quietly. When you're done loading the washer, go and make sure there's enough toilet rolls in the shitter's. It's Mexican night.'

'Sure thing Miss Gl-,' Nick stops himself quickly, catching a mindful look from Rose. 'I mean, sure thing Rose.'

'Did you take the burrito's out of the freezer?'

Nick points to three large boxes of generic brand frozen burritos on the steel countertop on the other side of the kitchen.

'Yeah. Just like you asked. They've been thawing for a few hours.'

Rose glowers at him a moment, trying to think of something he missed. She can't think of one right now, but she bets there is. Rose looks past Nick to the window at the back of the kitchen. The sun beams coming in a soft orange, signaling late afternoon.

'I'm gonna hit the lights on.'

Rose steps back and lets the doors swing back into each other.

Rose strides across the bar's main floor to a small wooden box hanging on the wall. She opens the little door exposing a fuse box inside with several rows of switches. She uses the sides of both her hands to flick them all up at once. The lights in the room all come to life. All the globes are in gas lamps which hang from Ash wood wagon wheels. The bulbs are all environmentally friendly. Not because Rose is a climate change enthusiast. Environmentally friendly bulbs cast a duller amount of light, and therefore don't pick up the stains on the floors and couches.

Rose slams the fuse box door shut and meanders to the front doors, unbolting the upper and lower door latches. She grabs a yellow cord tied to her belt leading into her pocket and yanks out a clump of keys attached to it. A Swiss Army Knife dangles with the keys. She unlocks the main door and swings them both open to the outside world. The Route 66 highway a hundred feet away. A rolling landscape of dusty apricot colored hills on the other side of it. Nothing for miles except the Plucky's restaurant on the edge of town.

Rose takes a few steps out and puts her hand on her hips, looking to her right at the makeshift parking lot. The gravel and dirt space is large enough to fit the cargo trucks and road trains that often park for the night. No vehicles yet tonight. Most of Rose's clientele are from the Cholla Power Plant on the other side of Holbrook, and they won't be knocking off work until about now.

Rose's bar is spacious old weather worn saloon made from logs and timber planks. It resembles the ones from the Wild West, even boasting decaying oak alcohol shipping barrels around the front and sides. Above Rose on the porch roof is a lit up yellow sign lined with thick rope and containing deliberately bad calligraphy reads; "THE GLASS HALF FULL". A beer glass blinking on and off to the side, dipping back and forth with three phases; empty, half-filled and full.

Rose wanted to call it "The Glass Half Empty", but Winter thought that sounded too negative. Rose told her that most of the clientele wouldn't notice or give a shit. But Winter said it might be a bad omen. And this struck a chord with Rose.

Smashed mirrors, black cats, walking under ladders and all that garden variety superstition have her at the knees. Rose originally from

Baton Rouge, Louisiana. Her family was from old money, on her mother's side mostly, from a prominent trading company passed down through the family for several generations. Rose didn't get along with the other neighborhood kids or her siblings, opting instead to hang out with the hired help. Especially Beatrice, a 21-year-old Haitian kitchen hand. Beatrice went for trips to the fish market every Saturday and would take Rose with her. Rose loved picking out the crabs and giving them names.

Beatrice would sometimes take Rose to a relative's Voodoo shop that sold potions, gris-gris, powders and trinkets from the ancient religion. One time when Rose was fourteen, she stole a doll from there and hid it under her bed at home. She didn't like its outfit, so she took her mother's violet scarf and wrapped the doll with it.

When her mother caught a twelve-year-old Rose smoking a cigarette with Beatrice, she fired Beatrice and grounded Rose for two weeks. Filled with contempt, Rose pretended her mother was the doll and wished it dead. Nine days later Rose's parents were both killed in a freak car accident. Convinced she wished her mother dead using a Voodoo doll, Rose became forever wary of the occult and its superstitions.

Rose meanders down her bar's basement stairs carrying the plastic milk crate filled with assorted empty name brand alcohol bottles. The basement is large and dank, no windows and a single light bulb dangling from a long cord in the middle of the room. An air vent with a pipe leading to the back of the building.

Rose reaches the bottom and walks past three steaming 18-liter stainless steel alcohol distilling boilers with Turbo 500 condensers. Rose places the crate at her feet, pulling her phone from a side pocket of her cargo shorts. She checks the time, and the settings on the boilers. Satisfied, she stuffs her phone back in her pocket. She goes to pick the milk crate back up, when she glances over at a punching bag hanging from a chain to the rafters. The bag is old and seen its fair share of action. There are cracks on the vinyl surface, some so big they have duct tape stuck on them to hold it together. Rose approaches the bag, loosening the muscles in her neck, arms and feet in a little jig on the spot. She raises her clenched fists and focuses on the center of the bag, then begins hitting it with a left hook. Then the right. She dances on her feet around the bag, jabbing and ducking like she was in a live boxing ring with a real opponent.

Rose is an above average boxer. She had to be. Being the only wealthy kid in her class meant she was a perfect target for bullies. One day she fought back and smashed the nose of Charlotte Prichard. Rose was suspended for two weeks. Her mother was less than proud, saying it wasn't how a lady acts. Her father said that she's as beautiful as a blooming rose, but if you squeeze her stem, you'll get pricked by her thorns. Rose loved the nickname. After that she took boxing classes and became a solid fighter.

After five minutes of sparring the boxing bag, Rose feels sweat collecting in her armpits and decides to stop.

She picks up the crate and walks it over to a sturdily built hardwood shelving unit, containing thick plastic drums on all four levels. Every drum labeled with gaffer tape and magic marker handwriting. The top and middle shelves holding liquor. *Vodka. Whiskey. Scotch. Gin. Bourbon. Peach Moonshine. Pear Moonshine. Cherry Moonshine.* The two bottom shelves below containing beer. *Beer. Light Beer. Heavy Beer. Cider.*

Rose lightly drops the milk crate to her feet with a clinking sound of the bottles inside. She stoops down and grabs an empty Smirnoff bottle, uncapping it. She places the nozzle of the bottle to a tap in the drum labeled *Vodka* and presses the little lever until the bottle is full. Rose does the same thing for the rest of the bottles and her bootleg hooch. Gordon's Gin. Jack Daniel's Whiskey. Johnny Walker Scotch. Wild Turkey Bourbon.

She picked up the distilling skills from "Jumbo" Jackie Lamourex, an illegal gambling operator in Lexington, Kentucky, who took Rose in when she was on the run from the law as a teenager. She had just put her brother Martin into a coma when she found out he swindled their parent's inheritance from the other siblings. Rose didn't mean him to fall three stories off a balcony, but she did mean to punch him in the face, which sent him over the railing.

Her siblings ratted her out to the cops, so she had to flee. Right into the arms of a notorious criminal overlord.

Jackie liked Rose's spunky attitude and gave her a chance to work, having her make sandwiches for guests, wash glasses, wipe cigar ash off tables and sweep up around the poker players feet. It was Jackie that helped Rose change her name. Rose was sure the authorities would find her and arrest her for making Martin a vegetable. So, on her 16th birthday, Katherine Robicheaux ceased to exist, and Rose Glass was born.

Good thing for her too. Because her brother Martin died in his coma two weeks later and the police ramped up their hunt for a Miss Katherine Robicheaux, who in her own way, was just as dead as her brother. Figuratively, of course.

Jackie taught Rose to make hooch so good that no customer at the Glass has noticed over the years. And no one ever has. Except that drunk old asshole Reuben, who knows his Makers Mark like a dog knows the smell of piss. The one time Rose tried to pass off her home made bourbon to him, he took one sip and spat it on her feet. She would have given him a good backhand slap for manners, but the mean old bastard is her best customer and practically keeps the place open for business.

The only danger in making hooch, aside from breaking health and safety laws, are the highly flammable paint cans full of methanol in the opposite back corner covered with a large polyester canvas tarp is the real danger. But she is responsible with the stuff. Rose knows perfectly well that it's a toxic liquid, and if used too much or boils under 148 degrees, can cause blindness, a coma, or death when consumed. Not to mention the explosive fire hazard they are capable of.

Rose finishes filling the Wild Turkey bottle from her bourbon drum and places it in the crate with the other filled bottles. She cups her hand under the nozzle for the peach moonshine and fills her palm, slurping it all down her throat. She picks up the crate of hooch and heads toward the stairs.

Rose catches a glimpse of a corset on a hanger hooked onto a portable clothing rack in the side of the basement across from a stack of packing crates. The Victorian Gothic corset is purple with black lace trim, the torso covered with black flocking vines and leaves. The packing crates are full of Winter's dizzying array of outfits and accessories. Corsets, dresses, stocking, gloves, scarves, the list goes on. Winter crafted this particular gothic outfit herself from scratch. She usually does, using old outfits, butchering them and making new ones out of old parts. What Winter refers to as "Frankenstiening" her outfits. She taught herself sewing and stitching a few years back by watching Youtube tutorials. Rose is proud of her girl. Rose would never forget that day they met, when she was heading to-

THUMP. A noise upstairs breaks Rose's attention.

Rose strides from the basement stairs to the main bar and dumps the crate on top. She peers around for the source of the noise.

'Nick?!'

No answer. Rose hears another faint sound from the kitchen.

Rose mutters under her breath as she storms toward the kitchen doors.

'God damn it Nick, can't one minute go by without me having to-'

Rose bangs the doors swinging open and stops in her tracks. Standing several feet away from her is a coyote. A big skinny one with a charcoal black coat. A little tuft of white hair on her chest. The box of thawing burritos on the floor at her feet. She licks her muzzle clean after having already eaten a few of them.

Fucking Nick, man. Left the back door open again.

The coyote stares at Rose. Rose stares at the coyote. Neither know what to do next.

Rose slowly backs away from the kitchen, easing both doors to swing shut steadily, so as not to spook the animal. As soon as the doors are properly closed, she turns and dashes for the bar. She shoves her hand under the bar top where a holster is pinned to the underside of the bar top. The holster houses a .44 Magnum Revolver with an 8-inch barrel and stainless steel finish. Rose pulls the gun out of the holster and checks the barrel. Fully loaded. She snaps the barrel back into place and marches steadfastly toward the kitchen doors again.

BANG. Winter sits bolt upright. She blinks her groggy eyes and wipes a small leak of drool from the side of her smudged lips.

'Was that a gunshot?' she thinks.

Winter remembered that Nick would have started his shift by now. No. No, no, no, no, no, no, no. Not possible. Nuh-ah. But Rose *had* mentioned once or twice how much she'd like to shoot Nick. But if she had a nickel for every time Rose did something she said she was gonna do, well, she'd have enough to buy new name-brand bronzer. Rose didn't like the poor kid much, but they're so close to getting out of here she knows Rose wouldn't do something stupid. But it *is* Rose… so… she better go check.

Winter gently places the Pikachu on the pillows and pulls the covers up to tuck him in. She swings her heels off the bed and starts for the door, passing by her extravagant collection of wigs on old lamp stands by the window. She has every color imaginable; fiery red, raven black, incandescent white, hot pink, fluorescent blue. She passes her vanity dresser and catches a glimpse of herself in the mirror, noticing the smudged bit of lipstick on the corner of her mouth.

'Oh no,' she thinks, 'this will never do. What if someone sees me like this?'

Winter plonks down on her maroon velvet cushioned wooden stool and opens up her lipstick case filled with thirty different colors. She picks up a few wet wipes, crosses her legs, leans into the mirror, and starts removing the red from her lips.

CHAPTER FOUR

Checks And Balances

The twinkling building lights of the downtown Chicago skyline blend in with the soft luxury lamp lights on the wall to floor windows of the Ritz-Carlton 23rd floor penthouse on Water Tower Place. The doorbell chimes. A few moments later Lance, a beer bellied middle-aged man wearing a bathrobe, answers the door to find a pretty blonde girl in her mid-twenties dressed in a beige hotel room service uniform. She is carrying a metal ice bucket with a bottle of Louis Roederer's Cristal champagne and two champagne flutes neatly nestled in the ice.

'Mister Pyles?'

'That's me.'

'Here is your bottle of champagne sir. If you like I can bring it-'

Lance snatches the bucket from her grasp.

'That won't be necessary.'

Lance cradles the bucket with one arm, using his free hand to reach into the pocket of his robe and fumbles around a moment. The rigid movements of the robe loosen the poorly tied robe belt, inching the robe open a few inches, exposing part of his gut and his flaccid penis covered in deteriorating bubble bath suds. The girl's eyes unwittingly look down and come to rest on his appendage. She blinks and looks back up to lock eyes with him, her eyes widening with embarrassment.

'Oh my God! I-I-I'm so sorry Mister Pyles, I didn't mean to look there.'

Lance pulls out a money clip filled with a stack of 50-dollar notes. He hands it to her, and she gingerly takes it.

'Grab two bills. No, three.'

The girl clears her throat and counts three notes, removes them, and hands the clip back to Lance.

Lance winks and says, 'Who's servicing who, huh?'

The girl smiles awkwardly on her reddened face as she nervously pockets the money in her uniform jacket.

'Much appreciated Mister Pyles.'

'It's Lance.'

Lance winks again and closes the door.

The girl stands there perplexed a moment, then turns and strides down the corridor, muttering under her breath, 'I hate this job.'

The door to the ensuite bathroom whisks open and Lance barges in with the champagne in one hand, the glasses linked on his fingers in the other. In front of him, in a bubbly jacuzzi bathtub with gold taps, is a middle-aged chubby lady named Claire. She is resting against the back of the tub with her arms splayed out either side, one holding an empty champagne flute. She is dressed in a Xena: Warrior Princess costume. Her voluptuous breasts almost popping out of the brown leather torso corset with shoulder straps. She smiles seductively as Lance stares at her with a playfully mischievous sneer. Claire leans forward and glides through the bubbles toward him, holding out her glass.

'Hercules. I'm desperately in need of a top up.'

Lance places the champagne bottle and glasses on the marble sink counter top next to an empty bottle of the same champagne, then shimmies the bath robe off to his feet. He is also in costume, somewhat. Lance is wearing a loose fitted beige leather vest, stitched and patched to look Greek era. Other than that, he's naked.

'One top up coming, my warrior princess!'

Claire belts out the Xena war cry yodel at the top of her lungs. Lance snatches the champagne back up, trying unsuccessfully to rip the cork out of the bottle with his teeth as he steps into the jacuzzi. He gives up and pries it open with his hands. It's stuck tight in the bottle neck. He grimaces with strain trying to pull the cork out. He feels it slowly rising. Almost there.

POP.

The cork rockets free, hits the wall, ricocheting to a metal towel rack above the jacuzzi and hitting a hair straightener resting on top which is plugged into a socket nearby. Lance and Claire watch with frozen horror as the straightener falls to the jacuzzi and plops into the bubble foam. ZAAAAP-POP. Lance and Claire convulse in fried seizures as the bathroom lights spasm from the sudden electrical surge.

The lights in the penthouse flicker momentarily before the electricity on the 23rd floor of the hotel shuts down, leaving the whole level in darkness.

A latest model smartphone lights up with an incoming call and vibrates in silent mode on top of a glass top walnut wood coffee table. Half-eaten Chinese take-out and an empty Martini glass next to the phone.

The owner of the phone is Jillian, who is a few feet away in the middle of a spacious New York City penthouse apartment living room. She is in her late 30's, short with sharp facial features, high cheek bones and sandy chestnut brown shoulder length hair.

Jillian, wearing a blue silk pajama top too big for her and black panties, huffs and puffs at a large projector screen that beams an X-Box Kinect first person boxing game. Covered in sweat, she ducks and weaves like a pro boxer, laying hard punches on her digital opponent on screen. The phone stops vibrating and the screen goes dark.

'C'mon you pathetic little fuck, don't waste my time. Hit me faggot!' Jillian yells to the projector screen.

Jillian gives a left hook to the face, then a right, ducks, liver punch, right hook again, bobs and weaves, jab, jab, jab. The buzzing sound of the phone vibrating on the glass table again.

'Fuck's sake!'

Jillian delivers one last devastating right hook to her on-screen opponent resulting in a K.O.

'That's how we do downtown, bitch!'

Jillian gives the screen a gesture with her middle finger. She sharply blows strands of hair hanging over her sweat mottled face and picks up a bottle of Evian on the glass table, pops the nozzle open with her teeth and drinks almost half of it in one go. She looks down at the vibrating phone and sees the name of the incoming caller, Cassandra, her secretary. Jillian picks the phone up and takes the call.

'What?!'

She listens a moment, wiping the sweat from under her eyes with her thumb. Her face suddenly twists with confusion.

'Wait… are you serious? Both of them? How… I mean, what were they doing together?'

Jillian starts pacing, rubbing her forehead with her fingers as she listens to Cassandra. She wanders down the hall, past the private entry elevator doors, and without thinking turns into her ostentatious dining room that overlooks Central Park, thirty-one stories high.

'A convention? For what?' Jillian listens a moment, then says 'as in that shitty 90's show? Who the fuck even-'

Jillian stops mid-sentence to growl under her breath and smacks a heavy hand on her long twelve-seater antique mahogany dining table.

'Okay, okay, it doesn't matter for now. Fucking morons. We need to go into damage control. Get a hold of that security company we contract. Ask for the head guy. The one who installed our master safe.'

Jillian turns around and paces back and forth in front of the windows.

'I don't know, call them. I've had a few cocktails. I can't remember his name. All I remember is it sounds like a chick's name. You're the fucking secretary, do your job.'

Jillian hangs up on Cassandra with repeated aggressive taps on the 'end call' button. She looks around her lavish dining room and tries to remember when she last came in here. Fine China vases filled with fresh flowers. Antique clocks. Glass cabinets filled with commemorative plates. The extravagant dining table she never uses. She looks at the original Picasso pompously hung up with special little lamps on the wall. An abstractly painted man with weird triangles sticking out of his face. She doesn't even like the thing. Her imaginary guests would probably be impressed by it. Still, she'd rather have a Mean Girls movie poster up there.

She thinks perhaps she should do more entertaining. Have a dinner party. Invite important clients over. Act like the CEO of a forty-billion-dollar company for once. She sighs and rubs her hand along the top of a finely carved Chippendale dining chair. 'Nah, fuck that', she thinks.

She barely gets enough time for gaming as it is. And she just came hot off the heels of yet another scandal to boot. Jillian picks up her phone again, dialling her off-again-on-again shrink, Maxine Delonge. Jillian listens to the ringing sound as she makes herself a Moscow Mule at the wet bar in the corner. Jillian knowing she's going to answer, because she pays this woman a lavish fee for being available any time, any day of the year, regardless of whether it's Christmas day or if she is in session with another client.

'Hello Jillian. It's been a while.'

Jillian also likes her because she sounds like Bea Arthur over the phone.

'Hey Max. Good time?'

'I'm having a dinner party.'

'Is it fun?'

'Yes, it is actually. I have-'

'Great. Anyway, I've got a situation.'

'You're not smoking again, are you?'

'No, it's been three months and eleven days.'

'Good. And the drinking?'

Jillian finishes a gulp of her cocktail. 'That's not what I'm calling about. I've got a fresh scandal.'

'You have barely recovered from the last one.'

'And the one before that. The Souper Salad thing. It's mostly settled, but there's a few civil suits still ongoing. The chain is performing better, thanks to me.'

'You started using imitation bacon again.'

'They, the franchisee's, were using imitation bacon the whole time. The stupid fucks were using beef tallow to cook it in to save money. You should remember all this.'

'I'm at home, I don't have my notes. Plus, I've had a few. Anyway, I remember you said your accountant was going to smooth out the ledgers for that, didn't you?'

'Do we have a client, psychia-'

'For the hundredth time, yes I cannot divulge our discussions to anyone else.'

'Yeah, we did some, shall we say, creative accounting. But that's old news now. And no one found out, so who cares. No, there's a new Plucky's fuck up.'

'The pigeon thing again?'

'I'm still beating down media from that shit show. Y'know, if the reporters did their fucking job right, they would know we were using Damascene pigeons. They don't live in gutters, they live in Syrian mountains. They are fucking pedigree. The media would have you believe they were filthy urban birds. Fucking third world refugees sparking dissent led to this. And that asshole war correspondent with his breaking revelation. If the government over there knew the meaning of genocide, I wouldn't be paying through the nose to use real fucking chickens. I'm so under the microscope, I can't even use battery hens.'

'But PETA and the liberals are happy now.'

'Fuck those tree huggers and the libtards. Y'know, I'd actually like to be more involved in the business on a creative platform. Be involved in the menus, the branding, maybe even picking out colors for take-out cups. But no. Law suits. Always fucking law suits. Anyway, fuck it. That's not the current problem.'

A voice in the background on the other end. Max covers the phone and speaks to someone about not being much longer.

Jillian snaps her fingers. 'Hey, you're talking to me.'

'Yes, sorry Jillian. You were saying.'

'So I've got a problem with a bull headed old drunk.'

'By the tone of your voice, I'm going to assume it's about Reuben.'

Jillian gulps more Moscow Mule and wipes her mouth with the back of her hand as she walks round and round the table.

'I don't care if the mean old bastard's father came up with the Secret Sauce. It's mine now. I kicked him out fair and square. There's no room for nostalgia when billions of dollars are at stake.'

'You did get him drunk and trick him into giving you power of attorney. Then you sent him to rehab, knowing full well it was enough to convince the board he was a liability.'

'Well, he was. And y'know what, when the fucker took me under his wing after Yale, it was him who taught me to be ruthless. He's the one who told me the first rule of business is there are no friends in business.'

'Yes, but in your circumstance, it's-'

'He tried to kill me, remember that?'

'He showed up drunk to your apartment complex with a gun. Yes I remember you telling me.'

'Not just any gun, it was an antique hunting rifle. It was special. He was gonna blow my intestines out my back. Luckily I was skiing in Aspen.' Jillian lifts her head back and downs the rest of the cocktail, slamming the glass on the table. 'Here's the thing, *Maxine*. It always sounds like you're taking the other side.'

'I play Devil's advocate. You know that. I'm not a yes man. It helps us get to-'

'You're a fucking faggot!'

She hurls phone at the wall on the other side of the room. It hits a vase full of Australian opals and shatters it, spilling the hundreds of shiny colored gemstones all over the white tiled floor with a clattering of dull pinging sounds. One rolls to her feet, and she picks it up as she takes a seat at the table.

A smile creeps across her face. 'I'm coming for you Reuben.'

Jillian gently lays the opal down in the middle of the table, lining it up with the Picasso painting on the adjacent wall. She squints one eye as she leans in and flicks the opal hard. The rock shoots through the air and hits the forehead of the man in the painting with immaculate precision, bouncing off back to the floor.

In the middle of his ornate games room, Ruby sits in his throne seat. Six and a half feet high, finely carved hardwood lounge chair with a gold leaf cover and leopard skin print fabric. He is in a thick dark blue velvet bathrobe and has a black Sig Sauer SSG 308 rifle in his lap, polishing the scope lens with a goat skin Shammy. Ruby pauses to pick up his crystal lowball glass from a tall coffee table next to him and takes a long sip of Makers Mark, makes the 'ahhh' sound, then resumes cleaning his gun.

Hank Williams music wafts from the speakers from a vinyl record player at the back of the games room, surrounded by oak tables bearing chess, checkers and backgammon boards. Two large tables bearing battlefield miniatures of famous civil war era conflicts. The Battle of Pea Ridge and The Siege of Vicksburg currently on display. A few feet away from Ruby is a crackling fire in an old river rock fireplace. Above the fireplace is a large oil painting in a gold frame. The subject of the painting is a broad shouldered man in his 50's, wearing a military dress uniform littered with colorful medals, holding a Winchester rifle. He has the square jaw and stalwart posture of a hardened army man. The gold inscription on the bottom of the frame reads; 'Brigadier General Franklin Clancy Wallace'.

Several open cardboard boxes lie around Ruby's chair, filled with papers and files. An Avery yellow manila folder sits atop one of the boxes.

Ruby finishes cleaning the rifle and puts it back in its case. He takes another sip of Makers and starts pondering what went wrong today.

He was in the hills south of the Arntz Road freight train station twelve miles from Holbrook. Jagged shadows of mountain clefts in the distance that look like a drunken God took to them with scissors. A prime area to bag a coyote. The blue palo Verde trees and their thick clumps of needle leaves making for great cover. Ruby had a good position. He waited for an hour and forty-five minutes, and there it was. A healthy looking coyote. The dark coat immaculately glossy in the harsh midday sun. 'Is that a...?' Ruby had to pull his eye away from the scope and blink a moment, then look back again. Yessiree bob. That there is a black coyote.

What a beauty. He'd peel that coat off finely with his fillet knife, dry it out, clean it, and mount it on the wall next to the albino wolf coat he'd bagged in Alberta and the giraffe head he claimed in Africa.

Ruby sips his Makers again with a scowl settling on his face, resenting how he missed the shot and spooked the animal away. He'll go back to the same spot tomorrow and put a clean bullet through the neck of that son of a bitch. Finish it off. 'That coyote is mine', he mused as he throws his head back to finish off the last of the bourbon in the glass.

Ruby pushes out of his throne and eases up to stand, stretching his arms out to the sides with a guttural groan.

Ruby picks up a two-thirds filled bottle of Makers from the tall coffee table and pours a generous serve. He puts the glass to his lips, his eyes focus on an oil painting above the fireplace, then raises his glass.

'Cheers, dad.'

Ruby gulps his Makers and licks his lips.

'I'm gonna take that bitch down. Don't you worry. I'm not letting that conniving little cunt keep what you built, and what's rightfully mine.'

Ruby meanders over to one of the filing boxes and picks up the yellow manila folder sitting on top. His golden ticket.

When he read about Souper Salad's scandal in the news, he paid close attention to how it played out. Jillian handled it well publicly. She's good at that. It's her arrogance that is her weakness. He warned her about that when he was showing her the ropes. If you bend the rules, make sure you bend them back into place when you're done. That's the mantra he tried to instill in her. All it takes is one little loose screw to topple the structure. So when he read that not only did Souper Salad perform solidly the next financial year, it slightly surpassed earnings from preceding years. A tad suspicious, Ruby thought. Especially after such a scandal involving the imitation bacon. And those leaf munching hippies are a begrudging bunch. They took Tasty Incorporated to court and won millions. How can the franchise recover so quickly after they'd literally been feeding vegans meat? With that in mind, Ruby got to work.

Being on the board for Tasty Incorporated meant that Ruby has clearance to confidential accounts for all franchises under its wings. After months and months of searching through a giant haystack, Ruby found his needle. It turns out an account had overstated income, and understated expenses. A sneaky trick that recognizes revenue before it is earned. That's how the clever bitch bumped those numbers and didn't arouse suspicion. Not really that clever actually, because Ruby himself taught her that. However, in this instance, Souper Salad's numbers evened out the following year and all was back to normal. She got comfortable. Complacent. And that's how he caught her out.

Ruby opens the manila folder bearing just one piece of paper. This was the most important piece of paper. It has her signature. Which means she signed off on it, knowingly committing an illegal act.

Ruby wants to take his company back and head the board once again. But that's a complicated legal battle for another time. Right now he wants to watch Jillian go down in flames. He can't wait to go to New York in two days. Invite everyone to a meeting. Make Jillian feel comfortable. Then drop this bombshell and watch her shit her pants.

Ruby closes the folder and gently places it back on top of the box. He takes a sip of bourbon, then another, then sculls the rest down. His cheeks reddening as the alcohol hits his bloodstream. He wipes his mouth and places his empty glass on the coffee table.

'Time to hit the bar,' he thinks.

Ruby shuffles in his velvet slippers down the long wide corridor of his mansion. The ceilings high. Thick marble pillars. Trickling water features. Exotic plants in big clay pots. He passes through the expansive kitchen. His plump Mexican maid Karina is emptying the dishwasher and stacking dishes. She customarily says, 'Good evening misser Wallace.' And Ruby customarily ignores her.

Ruby ambles through the laundry, and into the back right wing of the property. As he nears closer to a door at the end of a long narrow hallway, he can hear music blaring. It's the soundtrack to the movie Cabaret. Ruby stops just outside the door, leaning his head close to the door. His eyes furrow in confusion.

Ruby raps on the doors with his fat knuckles. A moment later the music is cut off. There are frantic shuffling sounds for a few moments. Then the door unlocks and opens a few inches. Dennis's face appears in the crack.

'Yessir Mister Wallace?' His voice almost out of breath.

'What the hell were you listening to in there?'

'Ahhh, I was just doing some exercise. I left the radio on. Didn't really pay attention to it to be honest Mister Wallace.'

Ruby scrunches his face up.

'Sounds like some queer nonsense. I thought your kind listened to that rap shit.'

'They do sir.'

A moment of awkward silence.

Ruby says 'Well, I'm gonna shower and get dressed. Then we're going to The Glass.'

'You got it Mister Wallace.'

Ruby darts him a quizzical look, then turns on his slipper heels and ambles away down the hallway.

Dennis breathes a sigh of relief, pulling his hand from behind his back. He's holding a woman's blonde wig.

CHAPTER FIVE

Sex, Drugs And Candy Bars

Beep! A car horn sounds. Beat up old pick-up trucks, beefy motor-cycles and the odd few carrier cargo trucks are parked in the lot next to The Glass Half Full saloon. A long-haired trucker in double denim and wearing a Ford trucker cap is pissing on the giant rubber wheel of his semi-trailer as he sucks the last drops out of a Budweiser bottle. He burps, drops the bottle to his feet and shakes the last drops of piss out before zipping up. He pulls out a small glass pipe and takes a quick hit of meth from the dregs of bowl, then pockets it. The trucker moseys through parked cars toward The Glass when he steps out into a clearing and is washed over with headlights. A black limousine screeches to a halt and the horn blares. The trucker winces from the high beams and blindly flips off the driver of the vehicle, then languidly continues on his way to the saloon.

The limousine finds a spare park at the rear of The Glass. Dennis steps out, the front of the car rises slightly after being alleviated from his hefty weight. He rounds the limo to the rear door and opens it for a slightly soused Ruby. Dennis stands rigidly as Ruby eases out of the car, his muscles flexed in his black suit, peering around the vicinity with a steely glare like he was a Secret Service agent and Ruby the President. Dennis doesn't care much for the silly facade, but the old man likes it, and when the old man is happy, he talks less. And Dennis doesn't mind acting like he'd take a bullet for Ruby just to keep his mouth that little bit more shut. Of course, if anyone tried to shoot the old man, Dennis would gladly step out of the way. Maybe even buy the shooter a beer afterward.

Bing! The microwave announces that it's finished its run. Winter, in The Glass kitchen, is propped up against the adjacent countertop applying concealer to the edges of her hot red painted lips using a pocket mirror.

Winter is wearing her homemade purple and black corset with vine leaf cross stitching down the front and back and matching stitched fishnet stockings. Her hair sits in a big bouffant 1960's style beehive with excess hair falling down her shoulders and forming into curls just above her buxom breasts. A thin purple string bow nestled neatly in her hive.

Winter trots to the microwave in her deep purple stilettos and gently opens the microwave doors gingerly, grabbing a roll of paper towels and ripping off an unnecessary amount of squares to bunch in her hands to lift the hot plate inside filled with microwave burritos.

She dumps the freshly nuked burritos on a Mexican floral Talavera pattern plate which already has microwaved beef taquitos and Mexican hotpockets on it. She carefully places the plate on one flat palm and struts through the kitchen to the double doors, spinning around to use her back to open them.

Winter backs out the doors to the main bar and spins on her heels again to face forward at the busy scene in front of her. Truckers, bikers and locals mill around, swilling beer out of large glass mugs, trying to talk over the top of each other while the jukebox blasts the end of a Creedence Clearwater Revival track. Around twenty-five people. A decent crowd for The Glass. Three factory workers, still in their coal dusted overalls, play a sloppy game of darts waiting for the alcohol to kick in so their confidence grows. Two dental nurses from Winslow in their late 30's wearing booty shorts and tight tank tops play doubles at pool against two bearded Banditos Bikers in their early 40's wearing black leathers with their appropriate insignia; one of them fresh out of prison.

Nick ducks and weaves through the rough crowd collecting empty glasses and bottles. Ruby sits in his usual booth in the back corner, sipping his drink and watching everyone with a scrutinizing scowl.

Dennis stands rigidly against the wall nearby, a physical warning to anyone that Ruby's booth is a no-fly zone. He takes out a small notebook and scribbles for a few moments. Musical notes. He shuts the book and puts inside his coat, assuming his tough guy stance again.

Winter readies the Mexican plate on her palm and is about to walk into the crowd when Rose steps in front of her, in one hand holding a large metal German Stein mug that has "Tips" written on the side in red sharpie pen, and a double shot of Makers Mark in the other hand. She gives Winter the mug to her free hand and nudges the taquitos with the bourbon glass to make room for the drink on the side of the food plate.

'This is for the old fart when you get there,' says Rose.

She pats Winter on her bum cheek.

'You ready to shake that moneymaker Sweetpea?'

Winter smiles with all her teeth.

'I'm a ready teddy.'

The jukebox wraps up Credence and whirs as it changes records. Click. A new vinyl is in place and blasts the opening to 80's track "Love is the Drug" by *Roxy Music*. The needle inside the jukebox hits a scratch on the vinyl and stays in a skipping loop, the base guitar in the song crudely repeating over and over. Winter struts over to it with both hands full and swings her hips so her ass bumps the side of the jukebox, dislodging the needle and sending the song's opening drums into action.

Winter effortlessly shimmies into action, casting her lustful spell over the bar's patrons as she sashays her taut derrière from table to table, flashing her winning smile that makes every man and woman think they're the most important person in the world, while she hands out off-brand Mexican food. She places the fresh Makers Mark in front of Ruby. He elicits a trace of a grin as he stuffs the Stein mug with a generous tip. Winter leans down and pecks Ruby on the forehead. His face would go bright red with bashfulness if his face was not already flushed from the booze. Winter uses her thumb to wipe off the lipstick mark on his face. Her tone suggestive.

'Can't have these other girls in here get jealous now, can we?'

'Aw now, girl, you know how to make an old badger feel like a young buck.'

Winter smiles, then winks at Dennis as she swivels on her high heels and saunters back into the crowd.

Winter works the room from wall to wall. She throws a few darts that come nowhere near the bullseye while Bikers watch on, stuffing their faces with burritos. She interrupts a game of pool and doesn't sink a ball, the factory workers happy enough to watch her bend over to take shots. Rose watches Winter like a hawk while she dispenses drinks at the bar, waiting for some punk to cross the line with her Sweetpea.

She's wearing her hair down tonight, though greased back into a polished mullet. Her green tank top showing off her tanned biceps.

A group of truckers are hoarded around a vintage pinball machine a few yards from the main bar. The theme of the pinball is 'The Lone Ranger', the 1960s TV show. One of the truckers, the one with the Ford truckers cap, is vigorously pumping the buttons on the sides of the old machine.

Winter meanders past the pinball, Ford glancing at her ass.

Ford says, 'Now that's an ass I could sink my teeth into better'n a porterhouse steak,' Ford follows up by smacking Winter on her fishnet clad behind.

Winter spins around abruptly with big blinking innocent eyes, looking Ford up and down with pretend shock.

'Oh now, fella, my heiny is in a net to keep you animals safe,' says Winter.

Ford moves in close to Winter, so he is now intimidatingly towering over her.

'Well little darlin', you're in luck. I'm no ordinary animal. I'm a lion. King of the beasts! And you're a deer waiting to be ate.'

Ford tries to grab her ass again, but Winter shifts to the side quickly, bumping into a table which an empty glass falls from and smashes on the floor. Rose, cutting lemons with a small cleaver, sees the exchange and slams the cleaver into the wooden cutting board. She wipes her hands on a rag and storms down the bar toward Ford and Winter.

Winter stands her ground, gently placing the plate and tip mug on the table, standing stiffly with one hand on her hip.

'You mean a gazelle.'

'Huh?'

'They're African deer. That's what a lion eats,' says Winter matter-of-factly.

A wet rag hits Ford in the face, slipping off and drops to his feet. He looks over to find Rose hopping over the bar top using her backside to slide across and over.

'Touch her again and you'll be seein' all kinds of pretty stars.'

Ford huffs a chuckle, 'You're fit, but I ain't fightin' a girl, it's too damn easy. Why don't you get back behind the bar and use them muscles to make me a sammich before you forget how to woman.'

'Come on. I'll give you the first shot. By the looks of you, it won't be the first time you've hit a girl,' Rose says as a cheeky little lopsided smile grows on her face, 'I bet the first one was your daddy.'

The patrons around them erupt into laughter.

Ford bellows out a guttural roar and lunges a blind angry swing at Rose. Like a pro, Rose ducks his attempt and lands a swift punch in his side. Ford topples off balance and hits a nearby barrel table, using it to regain his balance.

Rose appears next to him.

'That was your first shot.'

Ford goes to punch her again, but she slams her fist into his gut making him bend over, then she uppercuts him on the chin and he flies back into a table, the legs snapping and crashing the whole table to the floor.

Rose is jigging a boxing dance on the spot, waiting for him to get back up. He doesn't. Rose lets out a long exhale. She stoops down to grab her polishing rag.

The crowd of onlookers around her don't applaud or cheer. They silently watch her, dumbfounded at the ease of which she dispatched the big trucker. Winter is seated at an empty table nearby, playing the Candy Crush game on her smartphone. Ruby shakes his head, chuckling under his breath as he ambles back in his booth, muttering to Dennis.

'Ass handed to him by a God damn girl. Fuckin' shit berg.'

Rose walks back over to the bar and tosses the rag over the bar top, grabbing a bottle of water. She downs the whole thing while the patrons still stare at her. She eyeballs all of them a moment, then announces-

'The fuck you all lookin' at?' Rose points to Winter. 'Tip the lady for Christ's sake.'

The patrons start rummaging through their pockets to find any loose cash as they all approach Winter, who looks up from her phone with a startled expression.

Rose looks down at the unconscious trucker and notices a glass crack pipe has fallen out of his pocket. She steps over and crushes it with her boot heel.

Nick, watching the commotion from the other side of the room, uses the opportunity to slip down the hallway.

Click. The cellar light bulb hums to life after Nick pulls the thin cord next to Rose's punching bag. Bubbling noises coming from the distilling boilers. Muffled sounds of music and voices come from upstairs. A little dust falls from the floorboards in the far corner. Drunk people stomping heavily as they dance.

Nick has never been drunk, nor even tried a drop of alcohol. Being a Mormon has a lot to do with it. A Mormon by default anyway. His parents are strict Mormons, but Nick is no longer a true believer. His new girlfriend, Sue, has opened his eyes. A spiritualist, she doesn't believe in one God, or any God for that matter. Karma is her true belief, the cycle of life. She was metaphysically reborn as "Star of the Sea", a title given to her by the Grand Elder in her spiritual society of "Lords of Light". A group of activists who proclaim to be more 'woke' than the sheep of society, and predominantly protest animal murder, sex slavery and all organized religion. The Grand Elders are also known as Eric and Reylene Schmidt, who both work part-time as cashiers at the Safeway supermarket in town.

Nick's parents still think he's working late shifts at the Plucky's down the road, not this sin encrusted bar. And if they knew he was dating Sue, an atheist in their eyes, they would disown him for sure. He hasn't had sex with her yet, but the very thought causes his horny condition to absorb him in ways he can barely control.

Nick stuffs his hand into his jeans pocket and pulls out a Milky Way candy bar, fumbling to open the packet with wild determination. He jams the chocolate into his mouth and it goes down his throat in two bites. The sugar hits his bloodstream and assuages his cravings. Chocolate is his cure, and even though he subconsciously knows it's a placebo, it still works.

Okay, time to focus.

Nick looks over to the cans of methanol in the corner. He is trying to figure out how to get a couple of them upstairs and in his car without anyone seeing.

Nick hears a flush of rabble noise from upstairs then it ceases. Someone opened the door to the basement. Darn it. If Rose knew he was down here to steal her methanol he would be a dead man. He scrambles to the corner where a bunch of dusty wooden flat crates are stacked and slips behind them.

'Hello? Is there anyone down there?' Winter's voice sings down the stairs.

Nick breathes a sigh of relief. But now he's hidden, he might as well stay hidden. Clomp, clomp, clomp. Winter's high heels loudly connecting with the wood slat stairs as she gingerly makes her way down into the basement.

She marches to her little clothes rack in the corner opposite the flat crates, an old wooden desk bearing a sewing machine, fabrics and sewing accessories next to it. She likes to work down here sometimes. Partly because there's no windows, and therefore fewer distractions. Partly because of the oddly comforting smell of the chemicals forming into alcohol from the distillers. But mostly because she feels like Rose's booze is her little creative outlet, and making outfits down here gives Winter a sense of connection to Rose's fruitful labors.

She flicks on a battered old desk lamp that warmly illuminates the corner she's in.

Nick breathes extremely controlled breaths through his nose, remaining dead still as he watches Winter remove her purple feather earrings and places them in a large jewelry box. She curls her calves up one at a time to unbuckle her heels to take them off. She looks around the room again, scanning to see if there's anyone around for sure.

Satisfied, Winter unbuttons the back of her corset and pulls the lace strings daintily until the bows are undone, then shimmies the loosened garment to her feet. Now standing in black lace panties and matching bra, Winter puts one foot on the desk chair and bends over and rolls her fishnet stockings down her leg. Nick's breathing intensifies, a mixture of fear for being caught hiding and the sheer exhilaration of Winter's breathtaking figure complimented under the soft yellow glow of the desk lamp, catching every smooth curve of her body.

Nick licks his lips, his eyes widening. He doesn't know exactly when he stuck his hand down his pants, but he soon realizes that he is rubbing his fingers up and down his erect penis and has no intention of stopping. Winter finishes with the stockings and lays them over the clothes rack. She reaches to her beehive hair and pulls a long pin from it, letting her silky hair collapse to her shoulders, and shakes it slowly to let the curls unravel. Then the unthinkable happens.

Winter releases the hook holding her bra in place, and gently pulls the strap so it swings slowly on the end of her index finger. This is too much for the young 'sort-of' Mormon. His penis is out and he is furiously stroking it with blind vigor. Nick's eyes clamp shut, and with a soft unwelcome whimper, he ejaculates.

Nick's eyes open again, looking straight down at the creamy mess he created. Oh God. Nick clamps his eyes shut again in horror. What did he just do? He feels defiled. Winter is such a nice lady. And here he was beating off to her in the shadows like a creep. Nick begins to wonder if she had been aware the whole time. The deliberate slow movements when she changed positions to take off another item makes him suspicious.

Nick slowly opens one eye and looks through the crates. Winter is gone from the clothes rack. Her purple ensemble outfit remains. He hears her faint footsteps going up the stairs, the door opens for a moment and closes again. He thinks maybe he should run away and never come back to this place. Keep himself, and his urges, intact. Train himself to be a better suitor for Sue. But, then, he wouldn't have Winter in his life. And he just cannot bear the thought of that. But most importantly, he needs that methanol to give to Sue for their plan to attack Plucky's. Too rattled to do the deed now, Nick does up his pants and slinks back upstairs.

Splotch. A steaming hot wet mop hits a puddle of vomit. The yarn threads soaking up the stomach bile mostly consisting of half-digested beef jerky and Makers Mark. Nick is steering the mop back and forth, gagging intermittently from the smell of the puke. The hour is late and The Glass has emptied of the patrons. Winter exits the ladies bathroom and immediately pinches her nostrils closed with her fingers as she passes Nick mopping at the entrance to the men's bathroom.

'Someone lost the race and couldn't save face,' she quips to Nick with a nasally blocked voice.

Winter peers at Nick's face a moment, spotting something. With her other hand, she reaches to the side of Nick's mouth and nicks a small smear of chocolate with her index fingernail, then sticks it in her mouth and sucks off the residue.

The intimate act of sharing his leftover sweet with Winter and the lingering finger suck she did only makes Nick crave more chocolate. A lot more chocolate. Right now, all he can do is stare at her, unable to mutter a word.

'Sorry about the mess Winter,' says Dennis, who is standing by the bar rigidly, 'again.'

Winter, now wearing a more comfortable getup of tight stonewashed jeans and a loose fitted white top showing off her shoulders, sails across the floor in pink Adidas sneakers and rounds the bar so she's opposite Dennis.

'Oh Dennis, I won't hear it. You and Ruby are always welcome here. Rain, hail or puke.'

The door to the men's bursts open and Ruby staggers out, one hand gripping the belt tightened around his bloated gut, the other using the walls for support as he ambles past Nick toward the bar.

'I ain't apologizing for shit!' Ruby loudly slurs, 'My very presence here is what keeps this shit heap afloat. And another thing. Only my friends call me Ruby. To the rest of you shit shovellers, I'm Mister Wallace.' Ruby reaches the bar, resting half his body weight against it, clearly exhausted. 'That shit clear to you?'

'Clear as shit Mister Wallace,' Winter says with a cheerful tone.

Ruby clears his throat, grunts, and pushes off the bar to stand on his own. He rambles drunkenly under his breath as he strides to the front door. Dennis purses his lips and apologizes to Winter with his eyes. She gives him a two-eyed wink back in understanding. Dennis turns and follows his employer out the door, closing it behind him.

Winter reaches under the bar and pulls out the Stein tip jar which is brimming with cash. She dumps it all out on the bar top and arranges it small piles according to numerical value. Winter is by no means a math wiz, but in her stripping days worked for tips and has become skilled at counting money quickly before management try to pilfer some. She looks around for Rose a moment, who last said she was going to sort out a rat problem in the pantry.

With no Rose in sight, Winter makes a new little pile of cash, skimming notes from the main stash to add to it. Nick picks up chairs and turns them over so they sit upside down on the tables one by one.

'Pssst. Nick.'

Nick whips his head around, startled, wiping his long fringe back into his hair. Winter is holding up the small stack of money, beckoning for him to come over to her. Nick swallows hard, and sheepishly drags his feet over to her with his hands stuck deep in his shallow pockets.

'For you. Tips.'

'Are you sure Miss Bloom?'

Winter giggles. 'It's Winnie. And yes, you earned it tonight. But let's keep it our little secret, okie-dokey?' Winter follows that with a suggestive wink.

Winter reaches over the bar and takes his hand in hers, then adds his tips to his open palm.

'I know Rose says you get your tips at the end of the week with your pay based on your performance, but I saw how quick you were bussing tonight, and I reckon you should go gorge on those candy bars you love so much,' says Winter.

She turns around and bends over to the small electronic safe under the liquor shelf, unlocking it.

'How is your studies coming along? You're in school to be a vet, aren't you?'

'Uhhmmm, yeah. Yes. Veterinary studies. Well, technically it's called a Doctor of Veterinary Medicine.'

'Uh huh,' Winter says, half paying attention.

Nick's eyes look everywhere in the room except for right in front of him, which is a full view of Winter's ass stuck up in the air, wiggling in those jeans.

The kitchen doors fling open and Rose barges in carrying a large dishwasher rack full of recently cleaned glasses, slamming it down on the bar top. Nick jumps with a spook, and quickly stuffs the tip money on his pocket.

'What the fuck do I pay you for Nick?!' Rose bellows out, 'I wanna hit the hay and the floors ain't even mopped yet.'

'Sorry mis-... I mean, Rose.'

Nick hotfoots it back to the tables and starts flipping the remaining chairs triple time.

Winter closes the safe and rises up.

'It was my fault Honeybee. I was asking him about his studies.'

Rose briskly walks behind the bar and pours herself some moonshine in a battered tin camping mug.

'He should be studying the third cubicle of the ladies room. What's left in the bowl takes the lady right outta that room.'

Nick has finished with the chairs and grabs the mop, dunks it in the soapy water, and starts mopping in the back corner next to Ruby's usual booth. He yanks the dish rag from his back left pocket and begins wiping the table, when he notices a white iPhone partially lodged in between the red vinyl seat cushions.

'Oh shoot,' Nick says as he snatches it up. 'Uh, Rose?'

'What is it now, Nick?'

'Mister Wallace left his phone.'

Rose snaps her fingers repeatedly until Nick dashes over to her. She plucks it from his grip, looking it over a moment to make sure it's not hers. She pats her pocket and fishes out her phone, which is identical. She is slightly repulsed for a moment, registering the fact that she and Ruby share the same aesthetic taste.

'He's the last customer to leave, and usually the first to show up. I doubt he'll miss it much until he's in here again tomorrow.'

Rose languidly drops the phone on the counter behind the bar. She picks up her mug of moonshine and heads back into the kitchen.

'Put some muscle in your hustle and finish up cleaning.'

Nick is focused on the hypnotic swathing of the mop head back and forth on the wooden floor, thinking about Ruby now, and how he actually has been here every single day and didn't realize it until Rose pointed it out.

'Miss Bloom? I mean, Winnie?'

'Yeah hun?'

'Why is Mister Wallace so rich he can drink all day and not have a job?'

'You know Plucky's Chicken Palace?'

'Of course. Just up the road. I worked there for a little while.'

'No, I mean, the company.'

Nick stops mopping, stiffening his posture and puffing out his chest.

'Their treatment of animals is appalling. They keep their birds in tight cages, so small they can't even move or stand up. And they've been using pigeons as chicken meat.'

'I thought I heard somewhere they don't do that anymore?'

'Maybe not the pigeons. But they have several poultry slaughterhouses, and most of them use free range. But they outsource to others that use those cages, all to save a dime. It's a sick state of affairs if you ask me. Awful. Just like their food,' Nick wrings the mop with both hands, a mixture of nerves and agitation, 'not that I, you know, have ever eaten it.'

'Well, whatever you think of it, they're one of the biggest fast food chains in the world for a reason.'

'The Secret Sauce?'

'Yahtzee,' Winter points at him with her fingers in the shape of a gun.

'What's that got to do with Mister Wallace? Does he own the one down the highway?'

Winter giggles, then accidentally snorts. She looks at Nick apologetically.

'Sorry, I'm not making fun. It's just, a little more than that. Mister Wallace's grandpa was the one who invented The Secret Sauce.'

The mop handle falls out of Nick's grip and hits the floor with a dull clack.

'No way! Really?' Nick ponders this a moment, then a piece of the puzzle falls into place. 'Wait. Wallace. As in, General Wallace, the founder? How do you know they're related?'

'Sometimes he drinks himself so silly he forgets who he is and who he's talking to. After a bottle of Makers Mark, you're either his best friend or his worst enemy. One night I was his BFF.'

Winter beckons Nick to come a little closer. Nick also glances at the kitchen doors in fear, then takes a few steps closer to Winter, who lowers her voice a little.

'That night he tells me that he knows the secret for their famous chicken sauce. There's two other people high up in the company who know the recipe as well. And there's a safe containing the original piece of paper General Wallace wrote the recipe on. And the three of them know that safe combination as well. The three of them are never allowed to travel together, or even be in the same vicinity if it can be helped, so as to avoid an accident, or have anything happen to them, or the recipe will be lost forever.'

Nick looks up from the floor, scratches his head, and wipes his fringe out of his eyes.

'But, can't they just test it in a lab? Break it down or something like that?'

'All their competitors have tried that. Even Plucky's themselves. But The Secret Sauce is made in four different locations, and all combined at a factory, so none of the employees can figure out the precise combination of ingredients.'

Nick's eyes are darting all around the room as he takes this newfound knowledge in.

Winter throws one arm up in the air, for dramatic effect.

'Anyhow, who knows, right?'

Winter struts over to the now empty dishwasher rack, picks it up and heads toward the kitchen, spinning around to face Nick as she approaches the doors.

'Ruby is a drunk, and drunks tend to say drunken things. And drunken things are usually porky pies.'

With that, she winks and pushes backward through the doors. Nick stands there alone for a moment, trying to process what he would do with all that money if he were Mister Wallace. Not drink it away, that's for sure. No. He knows exactly what he would do. Pluck Winter from this place and whisk her to a better life with him. Nick smiles at the thought, dunking the mop in the bucket with a messy splash, knowing he's got a plan in motion to do just that.

CHAPTER SIX

The Chubby Moron And The Oatmeal Giraffe

A motley crew of seven inductees sit at second hand high school desks in a tight little lecture room under thrumming white hot fluorescent lights. The walls and ceiling are all painted a sterile white, and the cheap corporate felt carpet is a dull light gray. The only color in the room is a collection of faded light green post-chewed Doublemint gum; stuck under one of the desks seven years ago by a high school student in Albany New York named Debra Massey. Debra is currently in Los Angeles and yesterday robbed her third safe. But that's another story.

Sitting at Debra's old desk now is a plump Indian woman wearing a security guard uniform, a light blue shirt with a 'Duke Security' badge emblem on the top left, navy pants and a black tie. At the behest of the Human Resources department to avoid another Fair Employment

Practices probe, these new employees at Duke Security range from a gay Latino man to a disabled colored lady whose pinkie and ring fingers are webbed together. They may all be different in appearance, but one thing they all have in common besides the uniform is the disenchanted visages they cannot hide from wanting to be anywhere but here. The only thing keeping them awake is the overly bright fluorescent lights.

They are intentionally at maximum brightness because Marion, the tall beanstalk of a man in his late 30's at the front of the room, wanted to make his new employees as uncomfortable as possible so they pay attention to his droll, deep voice. His black hair is short flat-top military cut, his pupils as dark as his hair. His suit is also black from top to bottom with a white corn starched shirt underneath, and a thin black tie. Stitched on the breast pocket of the suit is the Duke Security emblem, an eagle with its wings open and the letter 'D' in gold, outlined in the shape of a police badge. Marion is slowly pacing back and forth in front of a white board where company rules are listed in black marker with precision handwriting. Marion taps the marker in his hand as he talks, the way a policeman would repeatedly smack their baton menacingly in their palm to a crowd of oncoming rioters.

'When you wear the uniform, you wear it with pride. You are not just protecting the client and their interests, you are also protecting the values of Duke Security. We treat every job just as important as the last. You could be protecting the president, or the corridors of a shopping mall. It doesn't matter.'

'Do we get to protect the President?' says Felipe, the gay Latino man, stopping Marion in his tracks.

'No,' says Marion with a deadpan expression, then continues pacing. 'If you're sitting at the front desk of a corporation signing people in, every man, woman, and yes, even child, are a possible threat to the organization.'

The slightly overweight Indian girl, Anaisha, raises her hand stiffly in the air. Marion glances over, sighs dispassionately under his breath and tilts his head back slightly so his square jaw is pointed at her.

'Yes?'

'Excuse me sir, but how is a child a threat to a Fortune 500 company?'

Marion rubs his chin a moment with his long spindly fingers. He looks down to his black almond-toe shaped shoes, polished to a shine every morning before breakfast. A memory is being conjured up.

'A lack of discrimination can cost lives. I've seen it with my own eyes. When I was stationed in Kandahar, Afghanistan, I was with my unit when a nine-year-old girl approached us with a basket of fruit, asking if we wanted to buy anything.'

He steps forward and eyeballs everyone in the class with a cold hard sentiment.

'By the time my ears stopped ringing, and the smoke cleared, most of my unit was either dead or severely injured. A-', he uses physical quotation marks, '-pineapple... in the girl's basket was a type 314 cluster bomb.'

Marion now stares at the back wall of the room, blinking as if remembering every one of his fallen comrades. He looks down at his shoes again for a moment, saddened, keeping everyone in suspense, then looks back up with conviction.

'Had we taken the proper discrimination initiative, lives would have been spared. Lives that once had wives and children. Mikey-O. Jimmy Jeepers. Tomahawk. Randy. They'd be on vacation in Florida with their families right now. So the next time you let a minor slip into a corporate office without signing the guestbook, you put the lives of every soul in that building at risk. And you have to live with that the rest of your life.'

Marion scans the room.

'Have any of you seen any front line combat?'

The class all look up one by one with vacuous expressions.

'Have any of you seen any combat, at all?'

There is a deft silence in the room as they all look at each other gingerly, expecting someone to hark up and take one for the team. A guy in his mid-twenties shifts in his seat, using his hand to wipe flatten his badly combed mop of blonde hair that used to be dreadlocks.

'I ah, I used to work, like, at a paintball range. For, like, a year. Maybe 8 months?' he says with modest pride.

Marion sucks a lung full of air through his wide nostrils, trying his damnedest not to let his new recruits get a glimpse of the seething rage welling up inside of him. The only giveaway is a slight twitch in his left eye on his otherwise stony face.

The door to the classroom suddenly opens and a stocky short older man in good shape for his age marches in with a robotic military discipline to his gait. He approaches Marion and whispers in his ear a few moments.

Marion turns to address the class.

'You'll have to excuse me. I have sudden and urgent business with a high priority client. My associate Mister Kemp here will take over in my absence.'

Marion briskly strides out the door.

A dark blue Lincoln company car pulls up at the curb to a shiny glass windowpane skyscraper on Front Street, just off Maiden Lane in the Financial District of Lower Manhattan. Marion steps out of the backseat onto the sidewalk next to Amin's Halal Food stand.

Marion pulls his suit cuffs to straighten his jacket and marches in the 41-level building through brass gold revolving doors.

Marion walks up the lobby escalators, having to stop behind two women in activewear carrying coffees. Marion grits his teeth, the jaw muscles poking out as he does, battling the urge to tell these insensitive gas baggers that it's a universal unwritten rule to stand on the left side of the escalator so people with impetus can move past. They reach the top and Marion passive aggressively pushes through them to let them know they inconvenienced him. He marches up to a long thin pallet wood security desk. A fit young man wearing a Duke Security uniform rises up behind the desk to greet Marion with a smile.

'Good morning mister Delaney. They're expecting you on level forty-one. You're good to head on up.'

Marion looks the Guard up and down with scrutiny, not being coy about his disappointment. He reaches in his coat pocket and pulls out his Duke Security laminated identification card, holding it out for the Guard to take.

'Where's the guestbook?'

'Excuse me sir?'

'I sign the guestbook just like everyone else, after you check my ID.'

'But... I know you. I work for you.'

'I could be an impostor. Have you seen the masks 3D printers can make these days? It's uncanny. Show me the book.'

The Guard sheepishly takes the ID and pretends to look it over, then picks up the guestbook on his desk and slides it across the marble desktop to Marion. He promptly signs it and slides it back to the Guard with a knowing glare. The Guard offers him back his identification card. Marion snatches it and slips it back in his coat pocket, glancing at the Guard's name tag. He'll write him up for this mistake.

Marion looks over his shoulder at the halal food stand outside as he approaches the row of elevators, and wonders what the men cooking in there are really up to. He'll run a background check on them later.

Ding. The elevator doors open and he steps in, pressing the button for the top floor which has a plaque next to it that reads; '*Tasty Incorporated*'.

The penthouse CEO office takes up a whole third of the 41st floor. The floor to ceiling windows curve around the entire office and face south west, overlooking the East River and the Brooklyn Bridge. The carpet is an inviting warm blue contrasting effectively with the gun metal-colored walls. A psychologically confusing choice which makes the business prey feel welcome and simultaneously intimidated at the same time. The large space is sparsely decorated, with a mahogany desk to one side, a glass coffee table surrounded by cream fabric armchairs in the center, a wet bar with large tropical plants either side and a treadmill by the windows. A boxing speedball mounted in the back corner, for stress relief. One of those wooden birds that dips back and forth into a glass of water sits on the edge of the desk.

Jillian, dressed in a slick pin striped blazer and matching tight knee length skirt, sits in one of the armchairs with her black pantyhose legs crossed, facing across the coffee table to Peter Kane, a medium built slightly chubby man with neatly combed thinning blonde hair and piercing blue eyes. For the past hour they have been discussing what legal options Reuben would have to sue the company once they file a claim to the board to call for a vote to oust him. Jillian wants all her ducks lined up. This is a big move she's making. The biggest of her life.

Peter, Tasty Incorporated's chief in-house legal adviser, has said earlier that they are protected as long as they can prove Reuben is a danger to the values of the company. Impeachment won't be a problem. She needs the vote to go two thirds her way, and that's a walk in the park, especially with the two Xena Warrior nitwits out of the picture.

They were Reuben's closest allies, the ones he picked to be the protectors of the recipe. Lance and Claire's untimely deaths have ultimately benefited Jillian in profound ways.

Jillian says, 'Peter, the board will be at their knees under my reign. I can squeeze their votes in my favor. Alter their stock value on Wall Street. Buy into rival companies. Buy out smaller chains. Be the queen of the fast food industry. End up on the cover of Forbes. Become an industry hero. Drop large donations on local political campaigns. Even become a politician. Maybe Mayor of New York? Yeah. Kiss babies and cut ribbons for all sorts of shit.'

Peter, sitting stiffly and smiling politely, says 'Sounds great Jillian.'

'And then pay my way into congress. Become a senator even? Jesus fucking Christ. The sky is the limit.'

Jillian swallows and rubs her neck feeling a slight glaze of fresh sweat. Was the air conditioner having issues, or is she getting flustered? "Fuck", she wonders, "am I horny?"

She quickly realizes that indeed she is. She uncrosses her legs and crosses them again tightly, trying to subdue her relentless barrage of high blood pressure. She exhales slowly, looking at Peter in a different light other than colleague while he thumbs through legal documents. She is unwittingly scratching the sides of her armchair with her sharp nails. Her eyes drop to his waistline. He's getting out of shape. His waist looking like a roll of raw pizza dough. She looks up to his wispy hair, combed just the right way to cast an illusion that his scalp follicles have a few more years left to give. She reckons more like eight months before he starts to research plugs and rugs. He has nice eyes, but his jowls are starting to bloat.

Peter looks up at her a moment, sensing she's been silent for too long.

Jillian gives him a forced smile. He grins awkwardly and looks back down at his paperwork. She gives him one more look up and down, surmising he hasn't been laid in a while. Well, without paying for it. That could work in her favor. He might be so desperate that he gives her a good hard pounding. Raw and dirty. Or he's a one pump chump. She figures the latter. He used to be a good looking man, but he's become complacent. And that is not attractive to her one bit. She needs confidence. She needs a man. An asshole. And this limp dick won't fit the bill.

A little rap at the office door. Jillian sits up rigidly in her chair, her posture stiff and commanding.

'Yes?'

The door opens and Jillian's pretty personal assistant Cassandra pokes her head through the door, her short black bob cut hair styled rigidly in place. She's in her mid-twenties and already had work done on her face.

'A mister Marion Delaney here to see you.'

'Send him in.'

Cassandra opens the door wide and stands aside so Marion can enter. Jillian plants her hands firmly on either arms of the chair and rises up gracefully. Marion strides into the office, Jillian matching his gait to meet him halfway. She holds her hand out, his hand almost twice the size wraps around hers to give her a soft but firm grip of a handshake.

'Welcome back Marion.'

'Glad to be of service, ma'am.'

Cassandra closes the door behind him and he glances over his shoulder a moment at the sound. Jillian using this opportunity to give him a quick up and down appraisal. Still a little horny, she wonders for a moment if she'd bang this tree of a man. He's got a good handshake.

Looks like he throw you around the room like a limp puppet. His neck is a little long and skinny like a giraffe though, but she could work with that. Then he looks back to her and they lock eyes. Deal breaker. His dark dull pupils show him for what he really is. A selfish arrogant prick who wouldn't ever go down on a woman, or even know how to.

'Thanks for coming in at such short notice.'

'My pleasure,' says Marion, feeling like her tone is insincere.

'Come, have a seat with us.'

Jillian steps to his side and gestures over to the table and chairs. Peter now standing with hands loosely clasped at the bottom of his stomach, grinning widely to show his freshly whitened teeth.

'This is our head of legal, Peter Kane,' says Jillian.

Marion accepts Peter's outstretched hand. Both of them squeezing a little too hard to assert dominance. Peter gives in and withdraws, not wanting to ruin the manicure he had this morning.

'Pleasure to make your acquaintance Mister Delaney.'

'Just Marion will do fine, thank you.'

'You recognize me, don't you?' Peter says, reading Marion's curious raised eyebrow.

'I've seen your billboard coming off Queens Bridge on 3rd street. I pass it on the way to work every day.'

'You have the power of persuasion!' he exclaims boisterously, giving Marion a finger gun point with his other hand.

Jillian rolls her eyes and looks at the floor, sighing.

'Oh, right, that Tony Robbins stuff,' Marion says drolly, picturing the loudly colored yellow and red advertisement that he sometimes is forced to look at while sitting in gridlocked traffic. Peter pictured in the middle pointing at the viewer with confidence, "YOU HAVE THE POWER OF PERSUASION!" in big bold font. A self-proclaimed life coach dolling out confidence tips to poor saps down on their luck with just enough money scraped together to hand over to this guy in hopes of learning to become the next successful business entrepreneur.

'Correction. That Peter Kane stuff.' Peter zealously quips. 'I'll send you a copy of my latest book, "The Perception of Intention".'

'I found a copy of a book like that on the subway once. I read a third of it from Franklin Avenue to Penn Station. Not one of yours, but the same concept. Telling people they can make up lies and end up believing them.' He pauses a moment, looks at Jillian and remembers she's a top client, then looks back to Peter. 'No offense.'

'None taken. But I will say, believing is the foundation of personal security. There is an art to self convincing. Consider me Rembrandt.' Peter caps it off by making brush strokes in the air with his finger.

Peter grins, accustomed to people like this. Non-believers. But he thinks of them as a challenge.

'I'll have a copy of my book sent to you. There's a great section in it, about body language. A man in your profession can never know too much about that.'

'Oh yeah? What is my body language telling you now?'

Peter takes a step back, looking Marion up and down.

'You're agitated.'

'I am?'

'Well, your constant frowning when you're not talking is obvious. But you keep rubbing the tips of your left fingers together.'

'My left hand is in my pocket.'

'Yes, but I noticed movement in the fabric, at the base of your pocket where your fingers rest. It's a common sign of agitation. I may not see it outright, but if you know what you're looking for, it's not hard to find.'

'So you've been clocking me?'

'Since you walked in the door.'

Peter grins proudly.

Marion breathes loudly through his long nose, staring at Peter with cold eyes.

Jillian's heard enough.

'So, Marion. How's the...' she pauses and scratches her head. 'I'm sorry, I haven't seen you since the, ah, installation. The Plucky's thing. When was that?'

'Three years ago, ma'am.'

'There's no formalities in this office. Jillian is perfectly fine. Three years huh? Time flies. So, how's the wife?'

'I'm not married.'

'Oh... um, my condolences.'

'I was never married.'

'Well then. Congratulations.'

Jillian flashes a cheesy grin and pretends to sock him in the arm playfully. Peter busts out a forced hearty chuckle. Jillian darts him a look that shuts him up.

She says, 'Let's get down to business. Can I get you something to drink?'

'No thanks,' says Marion as he takes a seat.

'Are you sure? My assistant Cassandra can fetch anything you like. We've got four types of coffee. A great one from Argentina. Any tea you can think of. A killer hot chocolate. Juice. Red Bull. Hell, even a cocktail if you're in the mood. It's five o'clock somewhere after all.'

Peter leans forward to the glass coffee table and lifts a glass of light red liquid in front of him, holding it up for Marion to see.

'You should try this stuff. Agave juice with carrot and ginger. Like nectar of the Gods. Flown in from Peru. Is it Peru?' Peter looks to Jillian.

'Bolivia.'

'Close enough. Have Cassie fix one for our friend here.'

'I'm fine, thanks.'

'You sure? This stuff is like a party in your mouth.'

Marion looks at Jillian then back to Peter, their earnest expressions suggesting they are desperate to be good hosts, which means he'll seem like an asshole for rejecting their stupid juice. He sighs quietly to himself. He hates explaining what he's about to explain, because you can't just say it and move on. People always ask questions.

'I have a rare oral condition called Ageusia.'

Just as he predicted, Jillian and Peter stare at him with beguiled visages. Marion explains that his tongue has the inability to detect sweet, sour, salty, bitter, or basically anything that has flavor.

It annoys him that all his life people seem fascinated by his condition, and then ultimately feel pity toward him like he's been bestowed with a horrible curse. Since he has never been able to taste anything, he's never known any different. It sickens Marion that people become inherently concentrated while consuming food and drink. A distraction. Marion pities them. They have the curse, not him.

Peter says, 'Okay, so if you can't taste anything. Everything you eat or drink must have the same taste. So, what does everything taste like to you?'

'How would he know, Peter, if he doesn't know what anything tastes like?' Jillian's tone turning annoyed.

'You could say everything tastes like oatmeal to me,' Marion says to placate them.

Peter raises his brows and settles back into his chair, somewhat satisfied.

'So no parties in your mouth?'

'No parties. Ever.'

Peter takes a sip of his juice and makes an 'ahhhhh' sound. Marion wondering if he is rubbing it in in or if he genuinely makes that sound after quenching his thirst.

Jillian looks at her watch.

'Can we move on? I've got a twelve o'clock meeting I can't push back.'

Jillian doesn't have a meeting at all. When the chubby moron and the oatmeal giraffe leave, she plans on chugging a couple of martinis and rubbing one out in her private bathroom.

'Let's cut to the chase. That safe you designed and installed for us. I'm gonna need you to open it.'

'Ah. Okay. Sure. I'll need you to get one of the three assigned trustee executives to come in.'

Jillian shifts uncomfortably in her seat.

'Two of the said executives perished, just last night.'

'At the same time?'

'They both happened to be at a...' Jillian clears her throat, 'Xena convention, in Chicago.'

'Zee-na?'

'Xena. Warrior Princess,' says Jillian.

Marion creases his brows in confusion.

'You've never heard of Xena?'

Marion shakes his head.

'It's a TV show. From the 90's. Greek stuff. Like Hercules. Except with a chick.'

'There was a bathtub incident,' says Peter.

Jillian growing impatient.

'They were having sex and got electrocuted. The point is, they're as dead as Harvey Weinstein's cock. Which means we have to open the safe, reset it, and appoint two new executives. And we have to do it now.'

'What about the third executive?'

'He'll just make things very difficult for us.' Jillian's tone now very matter-of-fact. 'You're the one who installed the safe. You can open it for us.'

'Well... no.'

'What do you mean, "no"?'

'I mean, I can't.'

Jillian leans forward with a menacing, teeth gritting face, gripping her talon-like nails into the sides of her chair.

'What, the *fuck*, do you mean you can't?' Jillian is on her feet, pointing at him accusingly. 'I paid your faggot ass company handsomely for that installation. And if memory serves me correctly, and it serves me like Novak Djokovic on a fucking set point, I gave you a fat bonus out of good faith. Because I'm real fucking sweet like that.'

Peter feigns a laugh in an effort to defuse the tension. 'Marion, what I think Jillian is trying to say here, is that-'

'Shut your fucking mouth Kane.' Jillian's eyes stay focused on Marion. 'What I mean is, open that fucking safe cheese dick, or I'll have my lawyers open you a new asshole for me to personally fuck you in with a strap-on at my wistful leisure.'

Marion's jaw physically drops.

'Hey, hey, now, you just hold your horses a minute, would you? Jesus Christ.'

'Jesus Christ could walk on water and heal the sick. But there's no mention of him opening safes. That's what you do. Apparently.'

'It's not that I don't want to, you have to understand.' Marion, now a little scared of this woman, places his hands together on his lap sheepishly. 'Didn't you read the paperwork?'

'No, I did not read the fucking paperwork. I pay people to do that for me.'

Marion is about to say something along the lines of, "well, that's your own fault", or "maybe you should hire better readers", but he doesn't want the Baccarat crystal vase on the coffee table smashed on his skull, somewhat believing she might actually do it.

Jillian takes her hands off her hips and folds her arms against her chest, under her petite but rock hard fake breasts, looking smarmy now.

'So, tell me, why can't you physically open the safe? Is it being guarded by a giant fucking cyclops? Or the fucking eye of Sauron?'

Peter fake laughs again, cut short by the daggers Jillian's eyes dart at him.

Marion says, 'The original contract for the safe stipulated very clearly that the safe be opened only if all three executives perish before they can open the safe. With Reuben Wallace still alive, he could sue me, you, everyone involved for astronomical financial proportions, and possibly even grand theft, if he wanted to, and we would serve jail time.'

Jillian's head snaps to Peter.

'Is that true?'

'Actually, he's right.'

Marion says, 'On top of that, the safe I designed has a fail-safe mechanism. If anyone tries to open it without the password, or the facial and fingerprint recognition, it triggers a device that fills it with an acidic jelly that dissolves the contents.' Marion raises his hands out defensively. 'It's why three people are trusted with the password. Who are never to interact. That was the deal they wanted.'

'Well, two of those idiots broke that deal and are now dead. And the third one hates me. So much so, that he once tried to kill me. Ergo, he's not really an option.'

'We could stage a personal intervention. Get him to answer to reason.'

'You've got more chance ordering a shrimp cocktail at a Bar Mitzvah.' Jillian sighs and puts her hand on her forehead like a headache is coming. 'Just... okay. Surely you had a fail-safe built into it. In case of an emergency. Like now.'

'Sure. There's a dead man's switch.'

'What the fuck is that?'

'It's a mechanism that is designed to deactivate the safe if all three have perished, or become incapacitated in some way.'

'What if it can be proven an old drunk like Reuben is incapacitated?'

Peter chimes in, 'That's where Reuben's power of attorney comes into it.'

'The old fuck entrusted a power of attorney to the dead man's twitch, or whatever it is?'

'Afraid so.'

'Well call them right now.'

'I've tried. They are denying any contact with the company.'

Jillian growls and rubs her hands over her slick hair.

Jillian looks at Marion. 'There has to be a back door. This is a billion dollar recipe we're talking about here!'

'The engineer did ask me. But I decided against it.'

'Why?'

'The client brief stated there was to be no back door.'

'There's always a back door.'

'Not this time, I'm afraid.'

'Not this time, is not an acceptable answer, you useless faggot.'

'Would you not call me that. I'm not gay.'

'You don't have to be gay to be a faggot.'

Marion rises up from his chair briskly, adjusting his jacket and buttoning the second one down.

'I don't have to sit here and be spoken to like this. I'm a contractor, not one of your employees. Now, you-'

'You don't have to be an employee for me to fuck you in the ass until it bleeds. Do you know how much I'm worth? Quite a fucking lot. I can take you to court at the snap of my fingers.'

'What for?'

'Gee, I dunno. But I'll have my legal team find something. I mean, not building a fail-safe option could be considered, I dunno, what?' She darts her eyes to Peter. 'Negligence?'

Peter shifts in his chair uncomfortably. 'It's a far reach, but we could make Negligence Tort stand up.'

'But you had the paperwork. And you signed off on it,' says Marion.

'Yes, yes. Blah blah blah. The point is, I have more money than God. I'll just keep slamming you with civil suits until you run out of money to defend yourself. It's not rocket science, hun.' Jillian pauses to look away in thought a moment, then looks back at him. Her tone bitchy. 'And, say, doesn't Tasty Incorporated contract Duke Security for all our office's? It would be a shame if we had to cancel that agreement and find some other security company to give our business to, wouldn't it?'

Jillian's tone turns soft now. She uncrosses her arms and assumes a relaxed posture.

'I don't want us to be enemies, Marion. I want us to be friends. And friends help each other out. And once we clear this mess up, I'll be sure to help you out. I've got friends in high places that could use a new security detail. You'd have to double, no, triple your staff of course. But it would be quite lucrative for you.'

There is a twinkle in Marion's eye. He doesn't want to show it though. He puts his hands on his hips, pretending to be semi-interested. But he's very much interested.

Marion says, 'Look. You have two options. There is a retinal scan and a fingerprint scan. You can get a hold of the remains of the two perished executives and it can be opened via one or both of those means. I would be happy to foster the process myself.'

Peter stands up to join the conversation.

'There was a small fire in the hotel bathroom. Their forearms and lower legs were charred. And as a result of the extreme electrocution, their corneas have been damaged beyond what we would need for them to do. I, ah, already looked into that.'

'What's the other option? You said there were two options,' says Jillian.

Marion shrugs. 'You gotta talk to the remaining third party. Or, get his fingerprint at the very least. Which, you know, is not in any way legal.'

Jillian spins around to look over at Peter, who is already preemptively shaking his head.

'I know what you're thinking, and no. Marion is right. Even if we could somehow acquire a copy of his fingerprints, open up that safe, there's a chance it could be found out what we did, and we lose all the grounds we have against him, leaving us in a lot more trouble than we are already in.'

Jillian swallows hard, looking down at the coffee table in thought. Marion and Peter share quick worried glances. Jillian slowly closes her eyes, concentrating on her breathing. Slow. Concentrated. Zen. Jillian's eyes suddenly snap open. She half screams half roars through clenched teeth, picks up the Baccarat crystal vase from the coffee table and pitches it across the room, missing Marion by a foot. It smashes on the opposite wall.

Marion's body betrays him by a knee-jerk reaction to plant his ass back on his seat. He looks over at Peter, who has done the same thing. They both look up at Jillian. She calmly wipes a loose few strands of hair hanging down the side of her face back into place on her slicked hairdo.

'We've got a phone call to make.'

CHAPTER SEVEN

Moose Knuckle

Rose steers her speeding mustang off Route 66 and comes to a crunching halt on the dirt outside the entrance to The Glass. She slams the driver's door shut, and opens the back door, grabbing a brand new paint can. Rose in good spirits. She's done a lot already today and it's still early. Visited the real estate to talk about the final papers for handing over the bar. Dropped off Winter's purple outfit to the dry-cleaning witch. Paid some bills at the post office. And ducked into the hardware store to get paint for the men's bathroom; Pale Buttercup, the color Winter picked out.

Rose spins her keys around her index finger using the main keychain ring, swaggering toward the saloon entrance. She looks over to the parking lot and notices two cars parked there. A boxy yellow 2002 hatchback Mazda mottled with dents and scratches. She recognizes Nick's shitbox easy. But the other car several yards away, a navy blue BMW M4, clean as a whistle, Rose doesn't recognize. Rose continues her swagger into the bar through the wide-open doors.

'Nick! The front door's wide open. Damn coyotes get in here all the time. And you ain't started on the tables!' she says, laying the paint can down.

Rose ambles to the bar, placing her phone next to the cash register. On the other side of the register is Ruby's phone. She fixes herself a glass of moonshine with a handful of ice cubes.

The kitchen doors open and Winter appears, wearing a red and white high waist halter top bikini and a large brimmed red sun hat. She takes off her white bold rounded sunglasses and removes one ear pod, smiling at Rose. Her eyes a little bloodshot from smoking one of her pencil thin joints.

'Hey Sweetpea.'

'Honeybee. Gettin' some sun?'

'You know it. My skin's a teensy weensie on the pale side. Gotta jack it up with some of that Sunny D.'

Rose snorts a laugh.

Winter cocks her head. 'What's funny?'

'Nice pun.'

'What is?'

'Sunny D. The orange juice. The sun is vitamin D...'

Winter looks to her feet a moment, processing. Then she looks up and laughs. 'Oh yeah!' A moment as Winter contemplates this further, then looks confused. 'Wait. The sun is a vitamin?'

'It sure is, muffin.' Rose notices a folded magazine tucked under Winter's left arm. 'Wha'cha readin' there?'

Winter pulls it out and unfolds it, holding it out for Rose to see. It's a copy of an old Hustler magazine.

'I found it next to one of the trash cans outside. It's got a naughty crossword puzzle.'

'If there's any pages stuck together, don't try and unstick 'em.'

Winter opens it up to stare at the crossword puzzle that has been a third filled in already by the previous owner.

'Hey, what is a two word slang for a protruding body part, featuring an animal? Twelve letters.'

Rose looks down at the bar counter, thinking. She whispers 'camel toe' under her breath, then slowly counts every letter. She shakes her head 'no'.

'Can I Google?'

Winter waggles her index finger side to side.

'Nuh-ah. That's cheating.'

Rose has had enough of this little game.

'Oh, hey, I got that paint you wanted. Pale Buttersnap. Buttercup. Whatever.'

'Yay!'

Winter pushes her feet to stand on her tip toes and claps her hands together excitedly.

'We could get started on it today if you want?'

'No. It has to be Sunday.'

'Why Sunday?'

'Just... because.'

Rose shrugs and sips her 'shine.

'Oh, ah, would you be a doll and turn on the back generator. Seems like shit for brains forgot to do it, among other things.'

'Don't be so hard on the kid. He's just young. He'll pick it all up soon.'

'You seen him?'

Winter shrugs haphazardly. 'Nuh-uh'. She puts her sunglasses back on. 'I'm gonna have some Jell-O.'

'Don't eat too much. We're having lunch soon. You'll ruin your appetite.'

Rose turns her back a moment to put the moonshine bottle back on the shelf, and Winter pokes her tongue out at her while she's not looking. Winter sticks earphones back in, tucks the magazine back under her arm, and moseys back through the kitchen toward outside. Rose peeking through the swinging doors for glimpses of Winter's booty before the doors fall back into place. Rose thinking it funny that Winter is attempting a crossword puzzle when she suffers from dyslexia. That girl is an ever growing mystery. Rose looks down into the beer fridge.

'For love of... the beers aren't stocked either. Fuck's sake. Nick!'

Rose takes another sip of her drink and licks the cold liquid from her upper lip. She slams her glass down on the bench.

'Nick?!'

Nick stands next to Rose's distillery at the back of the basement with his hands deep in his pockets, nervously rocking back and forth on his heels. Standing across from him is a portly bald man, wearing pressed black pants and a light blue business shirt. He is furiously scribbling on a clipboard. He stops writing a moment to scratch the back of the horseshoe patch of hair running around the back of his head.

Nick says, 'Look mister, I don't think Miss Glass would be happy if we-'

'Nick?! What are you doing down here?' Rose calls out as she trudges down the stairs. 'The beers need re-stocking, the chairs...'

She stops on the bottom step, frozen in her tracks, staring at the new visitor in front of Nick, writing away on his clipboard.

'Okay. Who the fuck is he?'

Nick goes to answer but the man cuts him off without looking up from his writing.

'He, is Ned Collins. And you, must be Rose Glass.'

'I must be. But that don't clear much up,' says Rose as she charily steps over to the methanol cans and pulls a sheet over them.

'What the fuck are you doing down here, *Ned*?'

Ned clicks his pen and sticks it in the metal clamp holding the paper on the clipboard. He turns to address Rose, his manner cordial. Somewhat condescending.

'I am hereby shutting this establishment down temporarily, pending an investigation. All business and trade must cease henceforth.'

'You can't do that,' says Rose in a flat uncompromising tone.

'First of all, the kitchen upstairs is in violation of several health and safety guidelines, and I didn't even make it to the back pantry. Nothing too serious, but you'll have to bring it up to speed.'

Ned unlatches his checklist from the clipboard and holds it out for her to take. She snatches it and starts skimming over it.

'Secondly, and much more importantly, this private alcohol distillery you've got going on here is not only illegal, but a brazen health risk to anyone who steps foot in, or even close to, this establishment. The carbon emissions you would be producing are not authorized by the Arizona Department of Environmental Quality. And, not to mention the beyond considerable fire hazard those tins of methanol behind you.'

Rose scrunches up the yellow checklist and balls it in her fist.

'You can't just walk in here willy-nilly. You need a warrant, or, whatever it is you government pricks need.'

'An Administrative Warrant for Health and Safety Inspections? Yes, indeed I do. Holbrook Realtors sent me a notice that your property has been on the market and is in final stages to closing a deal. It's standard practice to review hospitality establishments prior to sales that an inspector such as myself carries out. I wasn't scheduled to have the warrant finalized until Friday and for the inspection on Monday.

However, I was passing through from an inspection in Ganado, and I recognized the name of the saloon, so I thought I'd drop in to casually touch base with you regarding next week.'

Ned motions to Nick.

'This helpful young man was kind enough to show me around. And, well, there was staunch evidence of health and safety violations for me to make a formal inspection. You are breaking laws here, and that's grounds enough for me to make an unscheduled inspection.'

Rose's eyes shift to Nick, who is still rocking back and forth on his Converse shoes, staring at the cement floor, his long hair covering his face.

Rose says, 'Why. The fuck. Did you. Let. Him. In.'

Nick scratches his head. 'He had a piece of paper.'

'A piece of...' Rose can't finish the sentence out of fury. She pitches the ball of paper in her hand at him as hard as she can. But it merely bounces loftily off his head and lands at his feet.

'I thought he was a cop or something. The way he spoke,' says Nick.

'A cop? Why would you let a cop in? You don't just let cops in, Nick. They're like vampires. They gotta be invited in.'

'I don't... I don't know much about vampires. Or cops.'Cept on the TV.'

Nick swallows the lump in his throat and backs up as Rose gets closer. His back hits a wooden foundation pole, and he stiffens up against it as she approaches his personal space.

'He's a health inspector, Nick.'

Rose suddenly thrusts her arm out and clamps her fingers around his neck, starting to squeeze tight.

'He's worse than a fucking cop!'

Nick's eyes are widening as Rose's grip around his neck strengthens. The sound of clomping feet on the wooden floorboards above. Rose whips her head around to find that Ned is gone. She whips her head back around to bore her eyes into Nick's.

'I'm not done with you. Not by a long shot. You stay right here, boy.'

Rose turns and runs up the stairs.

Nick rubs his neck and lets out a long breath of relief.

Rose dashes out the front door and peers at Ned's BMW, the engine just started up. Rose hotfoots it over to Ned's car, planting her hands on the hood.

'Wait! Just, hold on a second.'

The driver's side window whirs down and Ned sticks his head out.

'What?'

Rose scuffles around to the driver's window and grips the window-sill tightly with both her hands.

'Can it wait? Just a few days. I'll get rid of all the booze. And the methanol. I'll fix up the kitchen like you asked. And when you come back Monday, it'll be spic and span. I promise. Cross my heart and hope to die.'

'I can't just unsee what I've seen. I could be held liable if something happens to someone as a result of the infringements I've witnessed. It's my duty as an employee of the state of Arizona. I have to process this report.'

Rose's jaw clenches in anger. Her mind is racing.

'Can you please take your hands off the car. I've got business to conduct.'

'Okay, okay. Listen. I need to sell this bar. I need to get me and my partner out of this shit stain of a town. And I'll be willing to do anything to achieve that. So, perhaps we could, ah, work something out. Off the books. Know what I'm sayin'?'

Rose rubs her fingers together making the international sign of 'cash'.

Ned looks at her gesture, then back to Rose's face. He looks mildly disgusted.

'Get your hands off the car, or I'll add bribery into the already long list of offenses against you.'

Rose holds his gaze a moment, gripping the windowsill so tight her knuckles have turned white. She lifts her hands from the car and steps back, resisting the urge to break his face. Only because it would upset Winter.

'We'll be in touch,' Ned says as the tinted window closes.

The BMW drives away, and Rose watches it, her eyes falling on Nick's car several yards away. Nick getting in quickly and slamming the door shut.

'Hey! Where do you think you're going?! You get outta that car right now Nick!'

Rose starts jogging toward the beat up old Mazda as the engine splutters to life.

'You little weasel! Stop the car now!'

The tires of Nick's car spin into action, kicking up a large cloud of dirt and sand into Rose's face as she reaches the side, making her shield her face with her elbow, coughing and spluttering. Nick slams the car into gear and it rockets off toward the highway, spinning the wheel to the left, swerving sideways onto the road. He narrowly misses a 1968 Vespa VLB Sprint which is zooming past the opposite lane, causing the driver, Seth the Plucky's manager, to wobble and almost lose control. He manages to get it back on track, turning to give Nick's Mazda the middle finger.

Nick's car swerves across his lane until he manages to get it on track and zooms off down the highway. Rose has reached the side of the highway, out of breath from running.

'You're fired! You hear me shit for brains! I see you here again I'll set you on fire!'

Rose watches with heaving breaths of fury as the yellow dot of the Mazda is consumed by the heat waves rising from the asphalt concrete road and vanishes from view on the horizon. Rose violently kicks an agave cactus sending pieces of it into the air. She growls under her breath and marches steadfastly back to the saloon. She walks up the stairs to the main entrance and stops, noticing a piece of white paper stuck to the door. It reads; "CLOSED. BY ORDER OF THE ARIZONA DEPARTMENT OF HEALTH SERVICES."

Rose sneers and rips it from the door, scrunches it up and tosses it over her shoulder. She storms behind the bar and downs a glass of moonshine. She pours another. She looks at the edge of the bar to notice that Nick has left his trucker hat behind. Nick was too much of a hurry to leave to grab it, the little shit. Rose storms over and balls the blue and white hat in her hand with rage and throws it against the wall.

Winter in the kitchen doorway holding the swinging doors open. 'What was all that ruckus? I saw all the dust come around the building and went to take a peek-a-boo, and saw you yelling at cars on the highway.'

'Our trip is gonna have to wait a little while longer, Sweetpea.'

Winter makes a little girl pouty face.

Rose says, 'Don't worry. I'll work something out.'

'So how long we gotta wait?'

'I dunno. Six months.' Rose pauses, looks down at her feet with dejection. 'Maybe a little longer.'

'A little longer?!' Winter scoffs. 'You said we were leaving in a few weeks!'

'I don't know what else to tell ya. Look, sugarcane, I..'

Winter stamps her foot hard on the floor and runs to the hallway and up the stairs to their bedroom, whimpering all the way up.

Rose's fists tighten. She looks down at her left hand to see she is still holding the glass of 'shine, almost busting it to pieces in her hand. She lifts it to her mouth and downs the whole thing.

Rose looks over at a moose head on the wall a few feet away. She balls her fist angrily and strides over to it, and punches it hard in its fat nose, making a little dent. She studies the dent a moment. Is it noticeable enough to let it be, or will she have to get it fixed? The alcohol in her system starting to take effect now. She punches the moose again. And again. Each pound harder than the last. Thump. Thump. Thump. Now she uses both her fists and growls with aggression as she lays into it with all her might, pummeling it almost flat. She grabs an antler and pulls so hard the whole head comes off the wall and lands with a thud at her feet. Rose stomps it into a furry unrecognizable heap. One of her feet connects awkwardly with an antler and she loses her balance, toppling backward and landing hard on her back.

Rose lets out a few exasperated breaths. She groans and rolls over to get to her knees and uses one of the tables to hoist herself up. Rose looks at the mess that was once a moose head. She never liked that thing anyway. She looks at the back of her hands. Her knuckles red raw, a few of them even bleeding through broken skin. Rose looks back at the moose. She blinks. A thought hitting her like a bolt of lightning. Rose points her finger in the air, counting imaginary letters under her breath. Then she smiles ear to ear proudly.

'Moose knuckle,' says Rose out loud. The two words Winter was looking for in her naughty crossword.

'What in the name of baby Jesus's unwiped asshole happened here?'

Rose turns to find Ruby standing in the doorway, in his full white suit with black ribbon tie, hands on hips, staring at the remains of the moose.

'How long you been standing there?'

'About five seconds.'

'One of the punters last night got in a fight with this here moose.'

'He sure fuckin' won and wanted everyone to know it.'

Rose nods stiffly. 'You left your phone here last night. Again.'

'Yeah, goddamit. That's why I'm here. I'd normally wait until night, but I kinda need it. Goin' to New York this afternoon to take care of some business.'

'Everything okay?'

'You bet your ass it is. I'm gonna go make a certain little bitch sorry she was born.'

'Good for you Ruby.'

Ruby ambles toward the bathrooms.

'Alright. I gotta use the pisser. Then I'll grab the phone and be on my merry fuckin' way.'

Rose stares at the remains of the moose head as Ruby disappears inside the men's.

'No problem.'

Rose saunters toward the bar to pour herself another drink. The sound of heavy shoes on the floorboard. Rose looks over to find Dennis standing on the doorway as she rounds the bar.

'Hey Dennis.'

'Rose.'

Rose grabs the bottle of moonshine and holds it up suggestively toward Dennis.

'You wanna sneaky one?'

Dennis grins mischievously. 'I'd love to.' He tips his head in the direction of the men's room. 'But it'll only loosen my tongue.'

Rose smiles, and nods in understanding and drinks her 'shine. A phone next to her starts ringing. She's a little beyond tipsy but not yet full-blown drunk. So when she picks up the phone thinking it's hers, despite the ringtone being a little different than her own, she doesn't realize it's Ruby's phone as she presses the green answer button without really looking at it. If she did pay more attention, she would have seen the incoming caller ID says "COCK SMOKING WHORE". Rose gulps the remainder of her moonshine, the bitterness hitting the wrong part of her throat causing her to cough. She clears her throat and puts the phone to her ear. Her voice low and gravelly from the 'shine.

'Yeah?'

CHAPTER EIGHT

With Whom Am I Speaking?

Jillian is leaning against her two-tone plum brown mahogany desk with leather trimmings. She has a crystal low ball glass in her hand, swilling around a generous serve of 25-year aged Laphroaig Whiskey as she waits impatiently for the other end to pick up.

Marion and Peter sitting in their seats watching Jillian with anticipation.

Phone ringing. Click. A course sounding voice answers.

'Yeah?'

That's bourbon breath right there Jillian assumes. It's almost lunch, so Ruby would be well on the sauce by now. Hopefully the booze has softened him a little. No time to fuck around, she thinks, let's get this ship sailing. She sets her glass down and pushes off the desk to stand rigidly with her game face on.

'Alright Reuben, listen carefully. It's Jillian. And before you say a single word, it will be worth your while. I'll be as blunt as a butter knife. I need your help. The company needs your help. And if you play ball nicely, consider yourself a hundred percent back on the board. We'll double your salary. You'll get your own private jet. Fuck it, I'll even thrown in a boat if you like. A good one. Like one of those big fuck off yachts that you can park other boats inside.'

Jillian pauses, hearing just breathing on the other end of the line, and continues.

'Anyway, shit went down. We lost Lance and Claire. And by lost, I mean they're dead. My condolences and all that. It's a long story I can fill you in on later. But the crux of the situation is, we can't open the safe containing The Secret Sauce recipe. Now, you could come in and open it, which is the optimal solution. I know we have our differences, so I'll stay clear while you do that. The second option is, you just dole out the recipe. Email it. Post it. Hell, give it over the phone right now. I know you know that recipe like the back of your hand. So, yeah. I need you, and I don't care what it takes. Name your price.'

Silence on the other end. The faint sound of breathing. Marion and Peter still in their seats, both ogling her for a reaction. Still silence. Jillian looks at them and shrugs.

Jillian blurts out, 'As I said, I know we had our differences. I'm sorry about the whole buying you out thing. You must understand I was pissed you, y'know, tried to kill me and all. But I know you were hammered, and we all do stupid things when under the influence, so it's all bourbon under the bridge for me. I'm prepared to-'

'Who's talkin' here?'

Jillian stiffens. Was that a woman's voice?

'Come on now, we're above playing games. You know it's Jillian. I just want you to name your-'

'My price? Well Jillian, I haven't decided yet. But you can bet your bottom dollar it's gonna be somewhere in the six-figure department.'

Jillian freezes. That most definitely is a woman's voice. Marion and Peter watch the blood drain from her face. Jillian downs the rest of the whiskey and clears her throat elegantly.

'With whom am I speaking?'

Rose walks through the kitchen doors to get out of earshot of Dennis. She takes a sip of her moonshine and runs her tongue slowly clockwise around her lips.

'Oh now Jillian, you really think I'm that dumb I'd give you my name?'

'I was kinda hoping you were, yeah.'

'You can just think of me as the thorn in your side for now. Because I have your man Ruby here. And I'm willing to bet you want him back safe and sound. Well, you don't get your butter until my bread is lathered.'

A loud sigh on the other end of the phone crackles through the speaker.

'And how much exactly are you willing to bet?'

Rose lightly touches a metal strainer ladle hanging from a hook next to other various kitchen accessories. The ladle swings gently back and forth, Rose playing with it.

'I'll call this number again after I've spoken to my associate, and we figure out the price tag. So until then, read a magazine. Have a cocktail. Dance in the fuckin' rain. I don't care. But if for one second you give me reason to believe you've called the cops, I'll execute your dear Ruby. And your precious chicken empire dies with him.' Rose uses all her finger to stop the ladle swinging, holding it firmly in place. 'Do we understand each other?'

A few moments. No answer. Rose thinking it sounds like Jillian has cupped a hand over the phone speaker and talking to someone else.

'Do we fucking understand each other Jillian, or do I have to kill the old prick right now?'

Jillian sounding flustered. 'I... yes. Fucking yes. Jesus. No cops.'

'Good. I'll be in touch soon.'

Rose ends the call. She looks at the phone in her palm. Her hand is shaking a little from adrenaline. Her life is screwed either way. What happens if she gets caught? A few years in the clink. What does she get if she succeeds? A few million dollars, an open road, and Winter. Yes, Winter. It's a no brainer.

Rose pounds her fist on the steel counter, shaking all the loose utensils violently on their hooks. She strides rigidly through the swinging doors to behind the bar.

Rose fishes her keys out of her pocket and unlocks the padlock on a rusty old toolbox. A hole in one end of it covered in duct tape. She pops the lid of the box. A 12-gauge sawed off shotgun. For emergencies. She's only ever had to use it once, a couple of years ago.

It was late afternoon and Rose was doing maintenance. She was on a ladder replacing light globes when a former plant worker, turned desperate crackhead, came rushing in holding a shitty ass Colt Viper .38 revolver. Yelling at Rose to open the safe. Rose coolly telling him that the safe only has liquid asset bonds in it. 'Why you keep drinks in there?' he said. The dumbass misinterpreting liquid assets.

She calmly climbed down the rungs, telling him she keeps all her cash in a toolbox under the bar, and there's a lot in there, can he please not take it all. The guy getting excited now. Letting his guard down. Rose got behind the bar. She grabbed the toolbox and gently placed it on the bar top. Slowly opened the lid. Before the guy knew what happened she spun it around to face him and fired a blast right through the side of the box. Lucky for him the guy was short and the pellets hit him in the shoulder. Rose had the shotgun out of the box before he hit the deck. She jumped over the bar and was considering a second, fatal blow to his face. Winter came running in, screaming at the scene in front of her. The guy yelling in pain. Rose had no choice but to drag his bleeding ass outside and dumped him on the side of the highway. Rose threw the revolver on the other side of the highway in the dirt incline. She was in a good mood and called an ambulance. She didn't know if it came or not. One thing was for sure; no one ever tried to rob The Glass Half Full ever again.

Rose now looking at her old friend in the toolbox. She grabs the shotgun by its wooden coated butt and immediately racks the pump as she rises to stand. The noise of the pump causing Dennis to look over. Rose has the gun pointed at him as she rounds the bar to the main floor. Dennis grins playfully, sticking his hands in the air.

'Should I stick 'em up?'

'No, you should sit 'em down.'

Rose flicks her head to the side, motioning to the nearest table. The chairs still upside down on it.

The smile on Dennis's face slowly fading as he realizes she may not be joking.

'Now Dennis. I ain't kiddin' around.' Her voice cold.

'Sh... should I keep my hands up?'

'No Dennis. Just have a seat.'

Dennis slowly lowers his hands, eyeing off the crudely sawed end of the barrel. He walks to the table and picks up a chair, gently placing it on the floor. He sits down, putting his hands stiffly on his knees.

'Now look here Dennis. This ain't personal or-'

'Hot damn! I dunno what you put in those God awful burritos, but comin' out it's like shittin' through a screen door,' bellows Ruby as he bursts through the men's room door, adjusting his belt. He stops dead in his tracks, staring at the shotgun, then looks up to Rose's stone cold face.

'Take a seat next to Dennis.'

'What the hell is this shit?'

'Hurry up Ruby. I won't count to three or nothin' fancy like that. Just do as you're told.'

'Have you lost your fuckin' mind?!'

Rose nonchalantly half turns and swings the gun around in one hand and aims it at the pinball machine. BOOM. The kickback jolting Rose's arm as she fires a shot, hitting the top facade of the Lone Ranger pinball machine and shattering it to pieces. Not missing a beat, Rose turns back around and swings the shotgun back into her waiting palm, racking the pump again.

Ruby's eyes are wide with a mix of awe and consternation as he watches an empty shell pop out of the shotgun chamber. Ruby takes a deep breath and half power walks, half waddles to the table next to Dennis and grips the bottom end of an upside-down chair, pausing to look at Dennis, who is in the process of rising up to help his employer.

'Stay down Dennis,' says Rose, 'he can do something himself for once.'

Dennis shrugs and sits back down. Ruby exhales irritably and drags a chair over to Dennis like a pouting child, then flips it over so it's upright, and plonks himself down on the chair. Ruby folds his arms tightly on his chest with a cranky expression.

'This better be joke with a damn good punchline, or else you'll be seein' the business end of my wrath, woman.'

'You know my name. Call me woman again you chauvinistic prick, and your face becomes a pinball machine. Got it?'

Ruby doesn't respond. He just frowns at Rose and grits his teeth.

'I'm gonna need you both to turn your chairs so you're both back-to-back,' says Rose as she steps backward toward the bar. 'Don't ask questions, just do it.'

Dennis stands up to shift his chair around while Ruby stays seated, shimmying his seat so he scrapes the wooden floorboards until he and Dennis are back-to-back. They both look over to find Rose re-emerging from behind the bar. Shotgun in one hand, a large roll of duct tape in the other.

Marion stares at Jillian, watching her talk on the phone in a cool and calm fashion with her back to him and Peter. She suddenly turns around and cups her hand over the bottom of the phone, speaking to Marion with a sense of urgency.

'Can you trace cell phones?'

'Uh... the police have-'

'No, I mean you, personally.'

'I, I don't think-'

Jillian shushes him with a stiff index finger, talking back into the phone speaker. Her voice flustered. 'I... yes. Fucking yes. Jesus. No cops.'

Marion looks over at Peter, who in turn looks at him with an equally confused expression. Peter shrugs. They both look over to find Jillian has ended the call and is staring down at the phone in the palm of her hand with a blank expression.

'Ji... Jillian?' says Peter, sitting forward in his chair.

Jillian doesn't respond. She gently places the phone on her desk next to the wooden bird, staring ahead to the window in deep thought.

'Jillian? What was that about the police?'

Jillian rubs her left arm, feeling the bumps of three nicotine patches under the fabric. Really feeling like a Marlboro Light right now. But she needs to stay strong.

'Shhhh. Just... you shoosh now,' says Jillian.

Peter loosens his salmon pink tie, unable to sit still with agitation.

'I'm sorry Jillian, it's just that-'

'I said shut the fuck up Kane!' Jillian's face now red with rage.

Peter gulps, sitting back in his chair again, tightening his tie back into place.

'I'm trying to think. Your voice is like a, a, fucking squeaky toy being dragged across a grater.'

Marion says, 'How much did they ask for?'

'They haven't made up their minds yet.'

'Minds?'

'She has an associate apparently.'

'Another female?'

'I don't know. I don't think she said.'

'You should have recorded the call.'

'Hey, I didn't know I was going to get fucking blackmailed.'

'Extortion.'

'Huh?'

'It's not blackmail, it's extortion.'

'Pot-ato, pot-ado. The point is, someone is using this opportunity to shake us down.'

'Blackmail means they have damaging information. Extortion is demanding money by threat or force. In this case, they have Reuben Wallace and are threatening to kill him. Likely someone who is familiar to him. Does he have close friends where he lives?'

‎

'No, Reuben's only friend is Makers Mark. Probably got too drunk and flapped his trap about his position to someone in that dinky shithole town he's living in.'

'They said they're going to call back with a monetary figure?'

'That's what the bitch said.'

'Good. Record that call.'

Peter moves to sit on the very edge of the chair, leaning into the conversation.

'Wait. Someone has kidnapped Ruby?'

Jillian nods, pouring herself another scotch.

'Holy Mackerel!' Peter looks to Marion, eyes wide with shock. 'Shouldn't we be on the phone to the police?!'

'No, we shouldn't.' Jillian takes a dainty sip of her scotch and walks to her chair, easing to sit down gently.

'But... Ruby's life is in danger. We can't just sit here. They threatened to kill him for Pete's sake!'

'Who gives a shit about that miserable prick. It's the company I'm concerned about. And you should be too. It's why you can afford to get your nails done on Fifth Avenue while all the other lawyers actually do work. If the cops are involved, it gets messy. The media will get wind of it and stick their beaks in, and then it's a fuckin' free for all. After that chicken nugget scandal recently, which almost ruined us, I can't risk any more negative publicity for Plucky's. Not right now.'

'We can spin it in our favor,' Peter pleads. 'A poor defenseless old man is taken hostage by cutthroat thieves. It'll play out like a movie of the week. The media will eat it up like a swarm of pigeons.'

'Peter, that better have been a pun. Because the last time the media dealt with us, they said we were serving pigeons.'

'I read about that. Is it true?' says Marion.

Jillian waves him off.

'Oh for Christ's sake. They were pure bred Damascenes. Royalty in the pigeon world. Probably a damn sight better than the processed chicken we're forced to use now. But the media will have you believe we were serving up those feathered street rats.'

Jillian downs the rest of her scotch, playing with the empty glass with her dangling fingertips.

'No, fuck the media. And no cops. The Secret Sauce is what is keeping us happily afloat right now, and we've gotta protect that at all costs. I mean, that bitch said she would kill Reuben if she thought cops were involved. And if Reuben goes, we're all fucked.'

'What if these people don't know Reuben? They could have found his phone somewhere. Stole it, maybe,' says Marion.

'They know him well enough,' says Jillian.

Marion cocks his head slightly. 'How can you be sure?'

'She called him Ruby.'

Peter turns to face the window, wiping his hand down his face in dismay. Marion noticing his reaction.

'What's that got to do with anything?'

'No one calls him Ruby unless they're very familiar with him.'

Peter turns back around. 'So you're going to pay their demand?'

'I'd rather take it in the ass by a donkey in Tijuana cheered on by drunk frat boys than hand over any money to these bribing assholes. Hell, for all we know the cocksucker Reuben is in on it.'

Peter saying, 'You and I both know he doesn't need the money.'

'I'll go,' says Marion.

Jillian and Peter both look to Marion with confused expressions.

'What? Go where?'

'To the place. The dinky shithole. What was it called again?'

Jillian's back stiffening, leaning forward and placing her free hand on the arm of her chair. A smile almost breaking out on her face.

'Holbrook. Arizona.'

Peter places his hands on his hips, looking back and forth at the two of them with an incredulous expression.

'What in jumping jacks are you going to do in Holbrook exactly?' Marion's face full of determination.

'I'm a security expert. With precision military training. I can locate the enemy.'

'And what? Infiltrate them? Holy Mackerel. Listen to yourself. Locate the enemy. You sign people in at lobbies and escort hobo's out of bathrooms.' Peter huffs and indignant chuckle, looking to Jillian. 'Where did you find GI Joe here?'

Marion clenches his fists by his sides, glowering at Peter with contempt.

Jillian stands, saying, 'He's right. If we find out who we're dealing with, it gives us the upper hand. We can threaten to expose them. Make them back down. Look like heroes to Reuben. Threatened by mortal danger, he might just spill the beans easier than we could have hoped. Yeah. We could actually come out of this with a better deal than we could have hoped for.'

'But you don't know who you're dealing with,' pleads Peter.

Jillian marches over to Peter, getting right up in his personal space.

'I've spent most of my life in boardroom's flaying corporate sharks down to pet goldfish. I know how to separate the players from the punters. And the person I spoke to is not a player. For a start, she said seven figures. Pffft. Of course you want seven figures bitch. A player knows immediately how much they want. An exact amount. You make a deal without giving the other party time to think. Time to react. You don't go pandering to your associate. That's a rookie move right there.' Jillian takes a step back, not taking her eyes off Peter's eyes. 'No, she's a punter. And I've had time to think. And now I'm going to react. All of us, are going to react.'

Peter gulps like he's swallowing a watermelon. He loosens his tie again.

'What do you mean all of us?'

'You're in this now too Petey boy.'

Jillian picks up her glass. Peter frowns. She's never called him that before. He watches her as she strides over to the wet bar and pulls out a bottle of Grey Goose vodka, using one hand to open the bottle with her thumb. The cap falling to her navy blue Jimmy Choo heels.

'You're going to Holbrook with Marion. Anyone want a vodka soda?'

Peter blinks rapidly.

'Wait, what?'

Peter starts nervously rubbing his left arm at the elbow.

Jillian pours a generous amount of vodka in a tall glass.

'You know Reuben, Petey boy. Marion doesn't. It would be better if you're there.'

'I'm a lawyer. Not a private detective. And when this whole fiasco goes to court, and it will, how do you think it will look if the head legal counsel is a suspect in an elaborate scam, or whatever the dang thing this is?'

Jillian crudely digs her hand in an ice bucket and grabs a fistful of cubes, dropping it into the glass, some spilling on the carpet.

'I couldn't think of a better way to use my legal counsel than using it to negotiate with criminals if the situation requires it.'

'Negotiate? Jillian, I'm a desk jockey. I have no experience playing hardball with kidnappers, or would-be murderers. This is insane.'

Marion shifts uncomfortably in his chair, eyeing Peter with trepidation.

'I agree with Peter. I think I'm best handling this on my own.'

'Yes, let the professional deal with it,' adds Peter.

Jillian says, 'You're a motivational speaker, no? Well motivate these assholes into not being assholes.'

Jillian fills the rest of the glass with soda water, then holds it up toward Peter like she's giving him a cheers and winks.

'You have the power of persuasion.'

'I can't. I won't. I have a career. I... I mean, what if they kill him? I can't have that on my conscience. Nope. No way. I won't do it.'

Peter folds his arms on his puffed-out chest in defiance.

Jillian takes slow deliberate steps toward Peter, sipping on her drink. Her glowering eyes fixed on him the whole time. Peter anxiously unfolds his arms and straightens his jacket around his plump torso. Jillian stops right in front of him, removing the glass from her lips, making an exaggerated 'ahhhh' sound. She dangles the glass to the side loosely in her outstretched hand, staring into his eyes without saying a word.

Peter begins to panic now, stealing a few glances at Marion, who watches on with vague disinterest, then looks back to Jillian.

'You are my number one client Jillian. Always have been. But what you're asking me to do is-'

'Tell me again, Petey boy, who your main sponsor is for your previous publicity tours of your book. And your upcoming one at that. And, gee, who buys all those Instagram followers?'

Peter clears his dry throat, straightening his posture, knowing what's coming next.

'You see, Petey boy, you don't just work for me. I own you and your stupid used car salesman act. Now, I need you on this. Reuben knows you. The old dick bag actually likes you. That could help us considerably. And when this is all over, Tasty Incorporated will continue to help feed your faggot ass books to those grass chewing fucktards who lap it up like its God's ball sweat.'

She pauses, to fix his shirt collar. She smooths it out with her palm and smiles.

'If you can't help, I guess, well, we'll have to re-evaluate our donation scheme. We might have to redirect your grants, if you know what I'm saying. I hear there's kids in Africa who need food and shit.'

Peter sighs. Defeated. He purses his lips. 'When do we leave?'

Jillian smiles devilishly.

'I'll have Cassie book you both on the first available flight to Holbrook. Or wherever the nearest airport is to that dump.' Jillian taking another hefty sip of her vodka drink. 'Actually. Fuck it. Take the private jet. This is important. Are you both ready?'

Marion rises from his chair and buttons his jacket up, standing stiffly to attention.

'I was born ready.'

Peter gives a skeptical look to Jillian. She rolls her eyes, waves him off and brushes past him toward the bathroom office ensuite.

'Call me when you land.'

Marion says, 'When the kidnappers contact you, don't forget to record the call. I'll need it to analyze the voices and tones, and any background noises that may give clues as to where they are based.'

Jillian nods her head and gives him a thumbs up, unable to speak because her mouth is busy gulping the rest of her drink. She disappears into the bathroom and slams the door.

Peter points a finger gun at Marion.

'Howdy partner,' Peter says with a cheesy smile and a bad Southern accent.

Marion swiftly turns on his heel and marches for the door and exits. Peter sighs and collects his notes, stuffing them in his brown briefcase, running after Marion.

Chapter Nine

Total Control

A strong gust of westerly wind kicks up a cloud of dirt from the desert floor and sprays Rose in the face. She snorts some more dirt out of her nose as she reaches the side of the highway leading to The Glass, placing a makeshift sign in a good visible spot for any vehicles thinking of steering in toward the saloon. Made from a broken table leg, a cheap painting from the wall in the bar and a red Magic Marker, it reads; "BAR CLOSED UNTIL FURTHER NOTICE." Rose uses a hammer to pound the stake of wood until it's nice and snug in the earth. The .44 Magnum Revolver tucked into the back of her belt. She stands up and tests the durability of the sign, giving it a good kick either side to make sure this heavy wind won't dislodge it. She doesn't want any unsuspecting visitors tonight. Or else they'll become unsuspecting prisoners.

Rose parks Ruby's limo around the side of the building, covering it with a sheet of tarpaulin and weighing that down with loose bricks. She ascends the eight steps up to the saloon front porch, then reaches behind her back to grab the butt of the revolver as she cautiously enters through the main doors. Dennis is a big guy, and she wouldn't be surprised if he was able to bust out of his duct tape shackles in the ten or so minutes she was gone. She steps in and looks to her right, easing her grip on the gun.

Both still bound with tape back-to-back on their chairs without a hint of struggle. She did go a bit overboard. The tape has mummified them completely from ankle to shoulders.

Ruby says, 'You wanna rob me, there's better ways of goin' about it. That's all I'm sayin'.'

Rose casually saunters to the bar, lifting herself up to sit on it, her legs dangling. Her Doc Martin's lightly hitting the front wooden panels of the bar as she sways her legs back and forth slowly. She places the revolver gently on the bar top next to her.

'I'm not robbing you, Ruby.'

'I told you. Only my friends call me Ruby.'

'Well old timer, we're about to get a hellava lot better acquainted. And since I'm holding the gun, I get to call you what I damn well please.' Rose flicks the tip of the gun barrel sending it into a little spin on the wooden counter. She looks up at Reuben with a playful grin. 'Ruby Tuesday.'

'All my money is tied up in offshore company accounts. You're wasting your time.'

'I'm not interested in your money. It's the teat from which you suck I am to milk.'

Ruby creases his brows in confusion. 'You mean Plucky's?' He bursts out a guttural laugh, throwing his head back and knocking the back of Dennis's skull lightly. Ruby looks back over at Rose. 'Aw hell lady. You really are wasting your time. You think kidnapping me is gonna get you anywhere with them?'

'It's not really kidnapping if you already spend most of your time here. Think of it, more like, spending extra time with your friendly neighborhood bartenders.'

'And how long do you suppose that's gonna be?'

'I'm thinkin' a few hours. I'm calling your pal Jillian back in a bit and demanding a few million dollars, and she's gonna wire it to me, and I'll turn you loose. Then I'll be outta here faster'n a chicken running through Ethiopia.'

'She's not even gonna give you the sound of a penny dropping.'

'I Googled Tasty Incorporated. She's got money to spare.'

'Well now, see, money isn't the problem here. Jillian is more stubborn than a cat on a leash. She has to get her way. Trust me, it's the reason I'm living in this piss ant town instead of running my own damn company that my father built.'

Rose folds her arms defensively.

'She ain't dealt with the likes of me.'

'Rose, you're a tough bitch, I'll give you that. But people like her, and her little corporate army, they're smart. And smart begets cunning. She was the top of her class at Yale Business. It's why I chose her to be my protégé. She's sharp, and worst of all, she'll step over morals and ethics to get what she wants. Now, you could kick her ass in a fist fight, I've got no doubt. And you run a good bar. But she's a neon light and you're a dim bulb.'

'Are you calling me stupid?'

Rose unfolds her arms and steps toward him, slowly clenching her fists.

'I'm not saying you're dumb. I'm just saying you and your pretty girlfriend couldn't organize a fart in a bean factory.'

Rose standing over him now. She leans down, placing her hands on her knees. Her face mere inches from his.

'You can insult me 'till the cows come home. But you say anything disparaging about Winter again, and I'll feed your own shit to ya with a steak knife. You got that padre?'

Ruby maintains his glowering stare. He knows she would actually be capable of that. And she knows he knows that. She slowly rises up to tower over him again, not breaking eye contact.

'You think I care what college they went to, or their lack of morals?' Rose turns and strides toward the bar. 'I was living on the streets as a teenager, begging, borrowing and stealing. I worked for degenerate gamblers, loan sharks and the best thieves in the South, since I was fifteen. I can handle a couple of silver spoon Ivy League pansies in suits.'

Rose is behind the bar. She pulls down a bottle of Makers Mark and swipes a shot glass from the counter, heading back to stand in front of Ruby. She pours a shot and knocks it back, licking her lips.

Ruby eyes the bourbon bottle like it was the elixir of life.

'Well, sounds like you got it all under control. I'll do my part and sit tight. You collect your haul and hit the road to Timbuktu to for all I care. Thing is, missy, I was on my way to fleece those assholes too. I found a way back in. And I'm gonna come down hard on all the fuck knuckles who voted against me.'

'Good for you Ruby Tuesday. But I go first.'

Rose has another shot poured and downs it.

'Deal.' Ruby licks his lips at the bottle. 'So how about we drink to that?'

Ruby watches as she carefully places the shot glass on the table in front of him.

'Sure thing Ruby Tuesday. Get it yourself.'

Ruby scowling again.

'Why do you have to be such an asshole?'

'Because I've had to put up with your cranky bullshit for too long. Placating you so you wouldn't find another bar to drop your cash in. But that's not my life anymore.'

Rose picks up the glass and necks the shot. She makes loud "woo" noise. Ruby watching on, helpless in his duct tape cocoon.

Dennis turns his head to the side, calling out to Rose.

'Is that offer still on the table for that sneaky one?'

Rose tips the bottle and fills the glass. She struts past Ruby and rounds to face Dennis. She gently places the small glass to his thick lips.

'Chin chin,' says Rose.

She tips the glass, letting the bourbon flow into Dennis's mouth. He collects it all in his mouth and gulps it in one go, then winks at Rose. She winks back.

'You're wasting good bourbon on him. Niggers only drink cheap shit.'

'Enough!'

Dennis yells so hard that Rose cops a light spray of spit and Makers in the face.

'I've had it with your verbal bile and dinosaur mentality.'

Dennis looks at Rose with pleading eyes.

'Hun, since he's the one you need, what say you let me go? I won't tell a soul.'

'You backstabbing shit kicker. I'm gonna ruin you for this,' says Ruby.

Dennis talking now with an effeminate voice.

'Oh shut your fat trap you limp dicked old clit wart.'

Rose covers her mouth with the back of her hand, trying not to laugh.

'You'll never drive again. I'll ruin you nigger.'

Rose steps to the side, stooping down to grab the roll of duct tape lying on the floor next to Ruby and Dennis.

'Hey. Watch it. Sticks and stones will break my bones, but racist names will make me hurt you.'

Rose strips off a piece of tape and severs it with her teeth. She plants the strip firmly over Ruby's mouth. He stares at her with seething resentment.

'Oh let him think what he says means anything worth a damn. It's cute,' says Dennis.

Rose stepping around to face Dennis again. Dennis cocks his head and gives her puppy dog eyes.

'So how about it Rose?'

'I'd love to Dennis. But this is, well, kinda my first time extorting a massive corporation. I can't leave anything to chance.'

Dennis sighs, reluctantly nodding slowly in understanding. A dull thud in the background makes them all look in the direction of the kitchen. Winter is standing stiffly by the swinging doors in her swimsuit, her sunglasses low on her nose showing her aghast expression. Her open make up kit spilled on the floor next to her.

'What in hells bells is going on here?!'

Rose's face changes to panic.

'Babydoll!'

In all the excitement she forgot to tell her Sweetpea about the unfolding situation.

Winter's eyes dart around the room in bewilderment. The busted-up pinball machine. The .44 lying on the bar top. The shotgun sitting on a nearby table. The prisoners tied up. Rose charily steps toward Winter, like she was subduing a bull about to charge.

'Now baby, I know this looks bad. But there's a good explanation.'

'I may not be the sharpest penny in the shed. But I know an explanation always follows a situation. That there is a loaded gun. And when there's guns involved, the situation usually has a bad explanation.'

Rose has reached Winter now, and carefully takes her hands, massaging her thumbs on Winter's palms.

'Look me in the eye, cherry pie.'

Winter does.

'You want out of this place, right?'

Winter nods slowly.

'And you wanna leave next month?'

Winter nods again.

'Then how about tomorrow instead?'

Winter blinks in confusion, looking away a moment in thought. Rose gently takes Winter's chin in her fingers and guides her face back to look her dead in the eyes again.

'Sounds much better, don't it?'

Winter nods again.

'Our good friend mister Wallace over here is a big fat sack of juicy lemons. And when life gives you lemons, you make lemonade.'

Winter's bottom lip turning into a pout.

'That's what they say.'

Rose takes her fingers from Winter's chin and strokes her cheek affectionately, smiling fondly.

'Yeah. That's what they say.'

Winter suddenly knocks Rose's hand away from her face, her eyebrows furrowing.

'Are you out of your mind Rose?!'

Winter clomps on her pumps toward Ruby and Dennis.

'Lemonade?!'

She reaches the two and starts clawing and pulling at the duct tape to free them. Also trying not to ruin her nails.

'I'm sorry boys. My other half appears to have half a brain. I'll get you fellas out of this in a jiffy-wiffy.'

Dennis turning his head to Winter.

'Actually Winnie, maybe it's best to let this-'

Winter squeals as Rose locks her arms around her waist from behind, trapping her arms to her sides, and lifts her up. Rose carries her back toward the kitchen. Winter kicking her feet in the air and struggling to get her arms free. They reach the swinging doors, Rose continues to carry Winter down the hallway to the basement door.

Rose gently sets Winter down in front of the open door. Winter turns and shoves Rose out of defiance. Rose grabs Winter by the shoulders and ushers her backward through the door to the top of the stairs. Winter blindly hitting her with flimsy wrists, trying not to break a nail. Rose quickly grabs the door handle, pushes Winter softly back on the chest so she doesn't lose her footing on the stair top, and slams the door shut.

Rose holds the knob tightly in one hand while she fishes in her khaki pocket for her keys. The doorknob jiggling from Winter aggressively trying to open it from the other side, yelling muffled cries of protest. Rose finds the right key and jams it in the lock, sealing it shut. Winter now using both fists to pound on the door.

Rose places her flattened palm against the door, a sadness washing over her.

'I'm sorry baby doll. But this is for your own good.'

The pounding starting to subside.

'This is for both our good, Sweetpea.'

Sniffling coming from the other side of the door now. Oh jeez, here come the waterworks.

Rose places her forehead up against the basement door, talking softly.

'I can explain all of this Sweetpea, but first I'm gonna need you to calm down. I got everything under control. No one's gonna get hurt. I promise. We're gonna be rich in a matter of hours. You gotta trust me on this. We're into it now. There's no turning back, and I can't do it without you sweetie. I just can't. You know why? Because it's all for you. I love you, and we're gettin' the fuck outta here. We're startin' a new life. You and me. None of this will matter.'

There's silence on the other side now. The odd sniffle. Rose's lips curl into a weak smile. She's gonna be okay.

Heavy banging coming from the main room in the saloon. The sound of feet stomping on the floorboards. Rose exhales sharply through gritted teeth.

'I'll be back in a minute Sweetpea.'

Rose marches down the hall to the bar. She finds Ruby pounding his polished brown leather Oxford shoes on the floor. Grunting through the tape across his mouth. His face red from being forced to breathe through his nose.

Rose glances over at the bar, noticing the revolver still sitting there, thinking it was a sloppy move leaving a weapon in plain sight in front of her prisoners. And the front doors are still wide open. Any jackass could have waltzed on in. Damn it, she's gotta pick up her game.

Thump-thump-thump. Ruby's incessant stomping snapping Rose out of her little funk. Rose growls under her breath and strides to the gun on the bar, sticking it in the back of her belt again. She quickly moves to the front doors, closing and locking them. Rose treads over to Ruby, still with his childish stomping, and rips the tape off his mouth acrimoniously.

'What the hell do you want?' Rose barks at him.

Ruby splutters and licks his dry lips.

'Am I supposed to piss my goddam pants?'

Rose sighs and looks away a moment. When she Christmas wrapped these two, she didn't count on potty trips. Again with ignoring the small details. Get it together girl.

Dennis says, 'The troglodyte does have a point Rose. I mean, I'm really all for this, don't get me wrong. But I kinda need to pee as well.'

'Alright, alright. I'm thinkin'.'

Rose turns and marches to the bar. She grabs the cleaver stuck in the cutting board and yanks it free. She strides back and begins slicing the duct tape, getting the cocoon open in four neat strokes. She stands back, pulling the gun from her back. She uses the revolver to motion to the bathrooms at the side of the saloon.

'Ruby Tuesday. You've got the men's. Dennis, you're in the ladies.'

'Suits me fine,' says Dennis as he frees one arm from the tape and carefully pulls the rubber adhesive cocoon off his suit with a satisfying peeling sound.

Ruby begrudgingly yanks it off him in short angry bursts.

'You ruined my fucking suit.'

'I'm sure you've got plenty more.'

The two of them scowl at each other as they make their way to their respective bathrooms and close the doors. Rose uses her set of keys to lock them both.

Dennis's voice shouting from inside his new prison.

'Holy crap! And I mean that literally.'

'Sorry Dennis. I fired my cleaner today.'

Rose meanders over to the jukebox and flips the 'on' switch. She sorts through a few pages of albums, stopping at an album called *Motels*. She selects the track "Total Control". Rose sticks the gun in the back of her belt and heads down the hall to the basement door. The song starts up in the background. Rose takes out her keys and unlocks the door, swinging it open.

Winter is sitting huddled against the wall at the top of the stairs. She looks up with post-crying Panda eyes. Rose offers both her arms down to her. Winter sniffles and wipes her nose with the back of her hand. She raises both arms up. Rose grasps her hands and pulls her up to stand, guiding her into the hallway. They stare into each other's eyes, holding their intense gaze, until Winter smiles.

'Our song, Honeybee.'

Rose smiling now.

'Sure is, Sweetpea.'

Rose lets go of her hands and gently places her hips on Winter's, pulling her in so their bodies are pressed together. Winter putting her arms around Rose's neck, resting the side of her face on Rose's shoulder. Her mouth a few inches from Rose's ear. Winter speaking softly.

'I thought you were going to hit me.'

'Hit you? Darlin', remember what I said to you the day we met?'

Winter nods slowly on Rose's shoulder. Her black curls rubbing Rose's cheek.

'Rose... petal... I...'

'Shhhhh,' Rose coo's as she strokes Winter's raven hair tenderly, kissing the top of her head. The two of them slow dancing with their song playing loudly down the hall.

The noise of Ruby's pounding on the toilet door and yelling obscenities in the background, drowned out by the music.

CHAPTER TEN

Do You Feel Lucky, Punk?

Peter and Marion made good flight time, just under five hours. Their private jet just made the restrictions for the small airport that only services light aircraft. Peter leaving a Burger King outlet, crossing the road toward the rental place across the street as he inhales a burger. A few faint stars starting to glisten in the clear dusk sky.

Peter wearing a matching navy plaid suit he had tailored for him in Naples last year. Nicely contrasting with the plaid Burberry boasting several crisscrossing shades of blue. He walks into the car rental lot next door, a large white sign that reads; "Way Out West Car Enterprises".

Peter spots Marion talking to a customer service guy outside a small guest center. The rental guy handing Marion a set of keys and shaking his hand. Marion turning and briskly striding toward a maroon Tesla double parked on the gravel lot.

Peter steps up his pace to try and catch up with Marion, scrunching up the empty burger wrapper and tossing it aside on the ground.

Marion at the car now, opening the trunk. Peter's Luis Vuitton travel bag with Marion's military navy blue duffel next to the back wheel of the car. And another sleek long black case Peter didn't notice earlier. Looks like a briefcase, only triple the size. Marion putting his military bag in the trunk first, then the Luis Vuitton. Peter coming up to the car, wanting to help, picks up the black case. Heavier than he thought, he has to pick it with both hands.

Marion aggressively snatching it from his hands. 'Hey, don't touch that!'

Peter raises his hands defensively. 'Sorry partner.'

Peter giving him a peacemaking smile, walking around Marion to the other side of the trunk to unzip his bag. He rummages through, his hand finding what it's after. Peter pulls out a copy of his book, "The Power of Persuasion", and zips the bag shut.

'I'll be back in a minute.'

'Keep it brief, we're on the clock.'

Peter nods stiffly and marches over to the rental guy, who is savoring a cigarette with every puff. Marion watches Peter engage the man, then turns to his black case, now sitting in the trunk between the two other bags. Marion dials the security number locks either side of the handle. The latches pop open. He looks over his shoulder again, making sure Peter is occupied. Peter holding the book in one hand, forcefully pointing his finger on the book cover. The rental guy looking like this man in expensive shoes just ruined the best part of his day.

Marion lifts the top of the case open. Inside is a collection of weaponry, each in their own fitted hole in black Styrofoam. A standard military Beretta m9, two shades of brown. A Colt Model 1903 Pocket Hammerless .32, two shades of black. An M4 carbine assault rifle, 370mm barrel. It's accessories in neat little pockets around it. A telescoping stock. A laser pointer. Night vision scope. Suppressor.

Two full 30 round bullet magazines. Marion softly touches the rifle. He almost smiles with admiration. Letting his fingers drag over to the accessories one by one, stroking them with benevolence.

Peter's voice behind telling the rental guy not to worry, this one's on the house. The website details are inside the cover. He'll be doing a seminar in Phoenix in the Fall, and that he should definitely be there. Footsteps now getting closer. Marion pushes the gun case lid down and snaps the latches back in place.

Peter now standing behind him, asking if the car needs gas. Marion pushes the trunk shut, telling him it's got an electric motor switch if the need arises. Peter asking if it charges like an iPhone. Marion not answering as he rounds the car to get in the driver's seat.

Marion sits behind the wheel of the car staring intently at the long stretching Route 66 as they drive away from the airport, scores of headlights passing them as they head into downtown Holbrook. Peter in the passenger seat, looking restless. Drank too much coffee on the flight. He opens up the glove box, rifling around a moment. Marion's eyes darting over to watch what he's doing, then realizing he doesn't care and looks back to the road. Peter pulls out a remote.

'Hey, it's one of those keyless remotes. The ingenuity of these smart car manufacturers I tell ya. Holy mackerel.'

'Just makes it easier to steal.'

Peter shrugs and puts the remote back in the glove compartment. He looks out the window as they take an off-ramp, spotting a Dairy Queen on the other side of the highway. All of a sudden feeling like a milkshake. Telling himself 'no, gotta watch the old tummy'.

'So, a Tesla. Environmental supporter. I dig it.'

Marion's voice flat. 'It's all they had.'

Peter starts fidgeting with the dashboard control panel.

'Shall I turn on the radio?'

'I don't care for radio stations. Those loud disc jockeys annoy me.'

Peter nods reluctantly and eases back into his seat. He peers down the side of the seat. He sticks his hand down there and starts playing with the seat controls. Unlatching a lever that sends the seat rolling back. Peter pushes his hip forward to bring the chair back into place next to Marion, whose cheeks are moving from his jaw gritting teeth together in annoyance.

'Marion is an interesting name.'

Marion's eyes stay on the road.

Peter following up with, 'For a man, I mean.'

Again, no response.

'Not to say there's anything wrong with that. It's just... interesting.'

Marion makes a sound that Peter can't quite place a meaning to. It could have been a 'mmm-hmmm'. Or clearing his throat. Peter takes it as a form of agreement.

'My name isn't actually Peter Kane.'

The car stopping at a set of lights on Navajo Boulevard leading into the main part of town.

'My name is actually Lars Gronholt.'

Peter looks to Marion for a reaction. He glances at the cemetery on the left as the pass it. Peter disappointed his bombshell has no effect on Marion.

'My father is of Nordic descent.'

Marion internally rolls his eyes. This guy isn't giving up. 'Why did you change it?'

Peter, finally getting a reaction, shifts in his seat to talk more eagerly.

'I have two successful businesses. I'm an attorney. And a motivational speaker. The first thing about you people hear or see, is your name. It has to carry power. Respect. Image is everything. Peter is derived from an apostle in the Bible. Saint Peter. A best friend of Jesus. You could say they were BFF's.' Peter laughs boisterously. 'Anyway, the etymology for the name Peter is Latin. Petra. From a Greek word meaning rock, or stone. Tough. Resilient. Unbreakable.'

'You can break a rock with enough force.'

'Well, yes, but what I-'

'What other unbreakable things can you name?'

'Okay there big guy. Unbreakable is maybe a poor choice of word.'

Marion steals a glance at him, wanting to tell him not to call him 'big guy'

Peter saying, 'And Kane. What can you tell me about the word kane?'

'Bamboo. Sugar. Sweet.'

'No, that's not right at all.'

'You asked me what I thought, and I told you.'

'Yes, I did. But... okay, you're right about the bamboo part. Have you ever tried to snap a fresh bamboo cane in half?'

Marion shakes his head.

'They're strong suckers. They bend but don't break easily. That's why Kane. I don't break easily. And Peter. Strong as a rock.'

Marion noticing a motel on the right. El Rancho. Wanting it so badly to be the motel they're staying at so he can end this car trip. Looking at the satellite navigator. Their hotel is not for another eleven blocks. Damn it.

Marion says, 'Wouldn't being yourself, even with an odd sounding name, be an indicator of honesty? Make you more respectable?'

'Did the name Marion garner much respect in the service?'

'My father named me after John Wayne. His favorite cowboy actor. Wayne's real name was Marion Morrison.' Marion shifts in his seat, wriggling his shoulders higher with a sense of pride. 'John Wayne was the archetypal tough guy.'

'Okay. But, you see the irony right? He changed his name.'

'I have no problem with my name, Lars.'

'Neither do I Marion. I did some marketing research and Peter Kane seemed to be a clear winner for my intended audience.'

Marion sighs, waiting on a red light. Only six more blocks to the motel now. The light goes green and Marion accelerates.

Peter grins to himself, slowly turning in his seat to face Marion, holding his hand in the finger-gun pose again, speaking in a raspy voice.

'Do you feel lucky, punk?'

Marion blinks slowly. Four more blocks. Shit. Another red light. He slows to a stop, glancing to Peter, still holding a finger-gun at him. A proud grin on his face. Marion faces forward again.

'That's Clint Eastwood.'

Peter furrowing his brows. Not understanding.

'Different cowboy actor. And that line is from Dirty Harry. It's not a western.'

Peter shrugs and chuckles. 'I don't watch many movies.'

Marion leans forward and pushes a button to turn the radio on. A loud and annoying DJ voice blares through the car. Marion not minding it at all.

Peter briskly walks across the parking lot of the Holbrook Best Western Adobe Inn. A 90-degree right-angle two-story building, the reception at the front next to the driveway into the car park. Marion waiting in the Tesla which is parked next to the small swimming pool in the middle of the car park.

Peter reaches the covered carport leading into the motel reception. He pushes the door with confidence, almost bashing his face into the glass when it doesn't budge. Realizing it's a pull door, he yanks it open, the cold blast of pumped-up air conditioning hitting his face.

Peter strides through the moderately sized reception to the front desk, passing a magazine rack holding Arizona state publications. Peter reaches the main desk where a guy in his early 20's is fastidiously typing on a computer keyboard, his pale white face staring at the screen with a concerned look, playing a PC first shooter game. His hair is jet black and spiked at the back, pasted down and combed in one direction in the front. A small bandage on one of his eyebrows. A hole in his lip from another big stud piercing. His Best Western name tag reads 'Pete'.

'Great name you got there,' says Peter as he places one arm on the counter and leans his body weight on it, trying to be cool.

'Welcome to Best Western, how may I help you?'

Peter not a fan of the droll delivery. This kid works in customer service for Pete's sake. Peter finding it amusing for a moment that the phrase 'for Pete's sake' actually applies to this situation. Peter lifts his arm off the desk and places both outstretched palms on the counter. A body language technique to make the person on the other side completely attentive to his presence.

'I said nice name, because mine is also Peter.'

'My name's Pete.'

'An abridged version of Peter, no doubt.'

'I guess.' He steals a glance at the TV nearby, then back to Peter. 'Do you have a booking, or, like, you looking to stay?'

Peter sliding his palms half an inch closer to Pete.

'I do have a booking. It's under Peter Kane.'

Pete taps the keyboard a few moments, his pale face catching some of the colors coming from the screen as it jumps from software to software.

'Nothing here under that name sir.'

'Try Marion Delaney.'

Pete taps away at the keyboard again. Blinking stoically.

'We do have a booking under Marion Delaney. It's fully paid for, by, um...Tasty Incorporated.'

Peter is a little annoyed that Jillian's assistant Cassandra used Marion's name instead of his. Marion is a contractor. Peter is an actual employee for Pete's sake.

'A little mistake there, it should be under my name. Peter Kane. I'm head of legal for Tasty Incorporated.'

'I'm going to need identification.'

Peter starts pulling his wallet out.

'Not yours sir, from the name of the booking. This Marion lady.'

'Marion is a man, and he's in the car outside.'

'Okay. Well, he'll need to come in to complete the booking.'

'I'll go get him.'

Pete looking at the screen again. 'Oh, and there's a change to the booking. There were two adjoining rooms booked, but now we only have a double suite available.' He pauses, his voice monotone and forcing the next part. 'Sorry for the inconvenience, sir.'

'Wait, what do you mean? We have to share a room?'

'It's a large room with two double beds. It's all we have.' Pete sighs silently. 'Sorry for the inconvenience, sir.'

'How did this happen? Why didn't you say something when the booking was made?'

'I only clocked on an hour ago. I guess the person before me didn't flag it.'

'This is unacceptable. I want to speak with a manager.'

'The manager is out to lunch.'

'It's past six o'clock. How could he be at lunch? You mean dinner.'

'It's a she, and she starts at two o'clock and finishes at ten o'clock. It's technically her lunch break.'

Peter's eye twitches. Hating being corrected. Especially by a little punk emo kid like this.

'Did you come to know anything in the past hour you've been working? As to why our booking is changed?'

'As far as I know, several rooms were shut down late this afternoon. One of our guests is a health inspector in town to check on a property. He did a spot check here, and now some rooms need to get back up to standard.'

'What was wrong with those rooms?'

'I don't know.'

'I'm not sure.'

'Huh?'

'I'm not sure is a more polite, customer service friendly way of saying I don't know.'

Pete flicks his eyes to the TV again. A commercial for Geico. That little CGI lizard running around. Pete looks back to Peter.

'Do you, like, want the room, or should I cancel the booking? There's a fifteen percent fee for late cancellations.'

'Where else would we go?'

'There's a whole bunch of other motels that might be able to give you two rooms. There's one a block just down the road. Wigwam Motel. The rooms are inside teepee's.' Pete motions to the magazine and brochure rack. 'There's a flyer for it over there.'

'This is really unheard of. An employee for a motel is telling me to go stay at another motel. Holy mackerel.'

'It's a bit of a tourist attraction. And I'm not telling you to stay there, I'm telling you about it. The room in your booking is available. Just get this...' looks at the computer screen, 'Marion Delaney.'

'I will take the room. It's getting late and we have important work to do.' Peter leaning on the desk again, eyeing the kid mindfully. 'I work at one of the most successful fast food companies in the world. I'm not staying in a teepee.'

'No problem sir, like I said, I just need you to get the-'

'Do you know what the problem is with your generation?'

Pete staring at him vaguely, not giving anything.

Peter reaches in his coat to the inside pocket, withdrawing a brochure. He slaps it on the counter, nodding his head down to it for Pete to look at.

'You young people these days lack responsibility. You're withdrawn. Insipid. You're missing out on all the opportunities out there.'

Pete's eyes flick down to the yellow flyer. A picture of Peter Kane, both his hands holding onto the bottom of his suit jacket. Chest pumped, looking proud. A teethy smile. A text that reads; "Peter Kane invites you to learn the 'Power of Persuasion'. See him in person and buy the book. Start your journey to success – today!"

'I can give you the ability to be more than a receptionist at a second rate motel. Under my tutelage, you can be the manager on a lunch break. You can even own your own motel. Darn it, you could own the whole chain. The world is yours, you just need to learn how to take it.'

'I'm studying engineering.'

'Well... engineer your life... first....'

Peter pushes off the counter, apparently lost for words. He points at the flyer, giving Pete an assuring nod. He backs off several steps, not breaking eye contact with Pete. He turns and marches steadfastly for the door. Peter grabs the handle and pulls it hard. The door not budging. Peter realizing he needs to push, not pull. He turns around to take a glance at Pete, who is in the middle of scrunching up the flyer. Peter exhales loudly through his nostrils. His eyes angry.

'I'm a lawyer you know. Big company.'

Pete is frozen mid scrunch, staring back with a vacuous expression. He watches as Peter pushes the door so hard, he almost loses his footing and clomps angrily out.

Marion presses the plastic keycard on the reader above the handle. There is a mechanical buzz sound as the door unlocks. Marion pushes the door open, looking over at a portly bald man two doors down. He's wearing a white robe and carrying a bucket of ice. Marion wonders if this is the same guy who belongs to the navy blue BMW M4 downstairs. He also wonders if he should tell the guy he left his lights on, it'll drain the car's battery. The man regards Marion with an insipid look as he enters his room and slams the door shut.

Marion steps in the motel room, holding his gun case in one hand, jamming the keycard in the slot by the door that sets all the lights and power into action. A plain, typical motel chain room. Two double beds four feet apart, thin blue duvets. Framed water paint art on the wall, looking to Marion like scribbles a five-year-old did. A bar fridge, no doubt filled with overpriced brand names you can buy at the 7/11 for half the price. A polished wooden desk, a flat screen TV on a set of drawers next to it. Four remotes on the desk, lined up neatly next to each other. One for the TV, one for cable, one for the air conditioning unit, and one for... who the hell knows.

Marion picks up his bags by the door and sets them on the bed furthest from the door. Peter bustles in carrying his designer bag in one hand, two cans of soda in his other upturned palm.

'I got you a soda. Watermelon flavored. Never seen that before.'

'I can't taste anything, remember?'

Peter thinks a moment.

'Oh right. Ag.. agg.. asiezure...'

'Ageusia.'

'Yeah that's it.'

Peter cracks open his can and takes a sip, studying the can.

'Not bad.' Peter motions with his head toward the door. 'Hey, there's a car downstairs with the lights on. Do you think we should find the owner?'

'We've got much more pressing business.'

Marion opens his duffel bag and begins to arrange his neatly folded clothes on the bed. Two pairs of everything. Neatly folded to Marine standard. Two pairs of shoes tied up in plastic bags. Peter telling Marion on the plane he packed light. He only brought one suit. 'Why?' Peter asking himself on Marion's behalf. Because Peter believes packing an extra suit is setting himself up for failure. If he brings only one suit, he leaves himself no other option than to succeed. If he has a spare suit, he's got that to fall back on. And you should never have a Plan B. Go for the gold or nothing at all. It's all in his latest book, which Peter intends to give him.

Peter looks around the room again, this time with impetus. He strides in the bathroom to inspect it. Running a finger across the white shower curtain, looking for some kind of flaw. Looking at the mini shampoo bottles and mini soaps. Turns the taps on and off. Even checking the hinges on the door. Peter now walking with purpose back into the room, looking at the lamp on the desk. Checking the drawers in the dresser under the TV. Marion wondering what's he up to. Is he looking for a hidden bug device? If he is, Marion just might start to give this guy a little credit. Taking these kidnappers seriously.

Peter places his hands on his hips, ogling the walls and ceiling. He steps over to one of the "art" pieces on the wall. Three water painted tulips, each bulb a different color. Peter staring at it. Marion opens his gun case. He lifts the Beretta m9 out of its foam hold and grasps it tightly in his hand, slowly extending his arm to point the gun at the back of Peter's head. Lining up a shot. 'Perchoo.' Marion making a shooting sound under his breath. Imagining Peter's brains splattering all over the cheap beige wallpaper.

Peter steps back from the painting, starting to turn around. Marion puts the gun back in its place, out of Peter's view. He closes the case, snaps the latches in place and locks it.

Peter moseys over to the edge of his bed, putting his hands in his pockets.

'I think we should stick together. Y'know, so we cultivate our information.'

'I was thinking of exploring around town tonight. Try to turn up some leads. Go to a few key places. Check out Reuben's house of course. You need your rest. It's better if you're vigilant tomorrow. You have to be in a good place to converse with these criminals. Negotiate when it's time.'

'But… what if you uncover something, while I'm here?'

'I'll handle it.'

Peter glances over at the cheap wooden oak nightstand between the two beds, bearing a lamp, a little plastic "no smoking" sign and a snack menu.

'I think Jillian would prefer we stick together."

Like Hell, Marion thinks.

Peter approaches the nightstand and opens the drawer. 'A-ha!' A big smile on Peter's face now, motioning to the empty drawer. Marion wondering if he found a bug.

'No Bible,' Peter announces proudly.

Marion confused.

'You don't strike me as a man of God, Lars.'

Peter's eye twitches slightly.

'It's Peter. And you're right, I'm an atheist. But that's beside the point. This drawer should contain a Bible.'

'Why do you care?' Marion starts placing his clothes and shoes in open shelves in the closet.

'It's a matter of principle. All hotels and motels should contain a Bible.'

'It's an old tradition. It's not a law.'

'Yes, but what if I were a practicing Christian?'

'But you're not.'

'You're missing the point.'

'And what is the point exactly?'

Peter takes a deep breath, then waves Marion off with his hand.

'Never mind. You don't get it.' Peter closes the drawer. 'I'll sort this out.'

Marion wondering what the hell his problem is. He thinks about asking more, but decides he has bigger fish to fry. Or rather, a chicken. Marion zips up his empty duffel bag and places it on the floor of the closet. He picks up his gun case from the bed. Time to go to the first place on his list.

CHAPTER ELEVEN

Star Of The Sea

Band posters all over the bedroom walls, a couple of basketball posters, and one Sports Illustrated swimsuit poster, featuring a buxom girl standing seductively in front of a waterfall. This poster Nick had to fight to have up on his wall. His mother Evelyn not a fan of that "smut". Nick protested that since he has been working, he's contributed to rent. She went on that whole 'if it's under my roof, it's my say' racket. Nick's father, Spencer, chimed in on this one. A rarity. He usually let Evelyn deal with the boy. Spencer reasoned that it's healthy for a boy Nick's age to be focusing on women in the eventual pursuit of obtaining a wife. And it's a good thing he's not gay, and encourage him to keep it that way. Evelyn seeing logic in that, let the issue slide.

The room is neat and tidy like a boarding school room. His wide dark brown three draw dresser filled with immaculately folded laundry, courtesy of Evelyn. At the moment, the dresser is pushed a few inches to the side to block the bedroom door from suddenly opening. A black and white Fender Standard Stratocaster guitar sitting on a stand next to his desk. The desk drawer is filled with candy bars and an abundance of empty wrappers. The top of his desk displaying a MacBook Pro, a lamp, an old Ovaltine tin filled with pens, pencils and random stationary, a copy of the Book of Mormon, and stack of books on veterinary studies.

Evelyn is always snooping in his room. Looking for reasons to bitch him out. That's why he kept his weed in a hollowed out part of his Book of Mormon. She would never look there. Too obvious. Hidden in plain sight. And Sue. His girlfriend. Sort of. She acted like a girlfriend. They always hung out. Smoked weed together and discussed thoughts on the Multiverse. Make out on the hood of his car under the stars in the rocky clefts of the hills north of Holbrook. Gave him neat blow jobs. Like right now.

Nick is lying on his bed. His skinny jeans bunched at his Converse shoes. Propped up slightly on his elbows. His head arched back. Eyes closed. He licks his lips, bucks for a few moments, then lets his elbows slide out from under him.

A mop of frazzled hazelnut hair flicks up from his crotch. The face of Sue Smith. Her big brown doughy eyes watching him wipe his hand over his face from post-orgasm fuzziness. Sue's plump freckled cheeks puffed out like a squirrel with a mouth full of nuts. She languidly pushes off him and the bed, trundles over to the plastic wastebasket next to his desk, picks it up and spits out the congealed contents of her mouth into it. Nick looking over, wishing she used a tissue. There's a box of them on the dresser. She could've... never mind. He was lucky enough having her over tonight.

She had spent the afternoon doing her usual protesting outside the Plucky's restaurant and was supposed to meet her Lords of Light friends to go over plans for setting free oppressed animals from a ranch the next town over. But a couple of them pulled out to take an extra shift at the Safeway in town. She called him to come get her, which was perfectly fine considering he was now unemployed as of today. It was easier when he actually worked at the Plucky's restaurant. He used to just finish his shift and they would leave together. He loved the way they met. Him being an employee of the chain, her out in the hot sun every day, wearing her poncho and her brown straw floppy sun hat. Holding her homemade 'IF YOU EAT AT PLUCKY'S, YOU ARE A MURDERER!' sign.

Nick used to stare at her from the shade of the building when taking the trash out. One time finally working up the courage to talk to her. Taking a soda cup full of ice water down to her by the towering sign, telling her to keep hydrated. Her asking him if it was tap water. Him nodding, then her lecturing him on the amount of Chromium-6 carcinogen in the Arizona water and its links to poor health and even cancer. She told him to subscribe to her 'Unknown Health Risks the Government is Hiding From You' blog. And her corresponding YouTube channel, where she spouts conspiracy theories on the government's cover ups on the raping of the land, and cutting corners on health and safety standards, all from a webcam in her bedroom. He did tune in. And fell for her in the process. She convinced him that Plucky's was a corporate devil and opened his eyes to the disgusting treatment of animals. So he quit. She even persuaded him to become a vegan like her. Well, a part time vegan. There's no way his mother would condone that diet. So he eats her dry meatloaf's and Sloppy Joe's. And occasionally, when he's upset at Sue, Nick will sneak off to the Burger King by the Holbrook Municipal Airport for a Whopper.

Sue plonks down in his swivel desk chair. Nick watching as she rolls herself a cigarette from a pouch of tobacco. She doesn't like tailored brand name smokes. Too many chemicals, she says.

Sue finishes rolling and licks the paper, sealing it shut. She puts in her mouth, looking at him with the big brown eyes while she lights up, heavily sucking the first few drags to get the thing going. Nick loves those eyes, even when they're staring at him dully like this. She has attitude, which is sexy in a girl. Most of her friends in her tribe were guys. That's what they call it; a tribe.

Sue does have Native blood in her, a quarter Navajo from her dad's side. But that's not what she means by tribe. Sue and her environmental activist friends call themselves "Lords of the Light". They say it's a religion, but Nick is not aware of any God they worship. They talk about Gaia a lot, one of the mythical names given to Mother Earth. But they don't pray to her or anything. Nick isn't sure at all what they do. He knows they all get stoned and take acid often. Light bonfires in the desert and dance around banging sticks together. The guys are stand-offish to him. Sue must have told them about his Mormon family. Nick just wants her to look up to him the way she looks up to those complacent assholes. Which makes him feel like he should be an asshole too. To make her respect him.

'Y'know Sue. For a vegan, you sure know how to suck meat.'

Nick points to his crotch to make sure she understood his meaning. Sue stares at him passively, taking another sharp drag of her smoke.

'You got any beer? I need to wash the taste of this spunk outta my mouth.'

'I told you Sue, my mom doesn't allow alcohol in the house.'

'It's Star of the Sea from now on. I'm fucking serious. The Tribal Elders deadass picked it for me specially.'

'Sorry. I...,' Nick sitting up, starting to tug his pants back up, '... can I call you Star for short, or something?'

'No, *Nick*.' Emphasizing his name, like he's beneath her. 'The Elders honored me. Gave me a ceremony and everything. Clam shells, and...,' she trails off, smoking her cigarette.

Nick fixing the pants around his waist, doing up his fly.

'The Elders. You mean Eric and Raylene Schmidt?'

Star rolls her eyes, reaching over to the Ovaltine tin on his desk. She empties the stationary out like it was garbage, spilling it all over his neat desk. She picks it up daintily with two fingers and ashes her cigarette inside.

'We don't go by those oppressive names anymore, asshat. We serve our supreme goddess Gaia to ensure the…,' she takes another drag, exhaling the smoke with a bored sigh. 'Where's your weed?'

'I'm out.'

Star clenches her eyes shut a moment with disappointment. The cute little black freckles moving around her button nose, accentuated by her olive skin.

'I'm sorry Sue, I mean, Star of the Sea. My guy went to Flagstaff for a few days to restock.'

'You only have one guy? Fuckin' casual.'

'Hey, could you smoke by the window? The smoke might get under the door. You know how my mom is.'

Star rolls her eyes again, slovenly getting out of the chair, the Ovaltine tin dangling loosely from her two-finger grasp. She places one knee on his bed, then the other, dragging herself on her knees to the window next to the bed and unlatches it, pushing it open. She takes a drag of the smoke and blows it out the window, looking to him after with raised eyebrows as if to say, 'you happy?'

She says, 'You don't have anything? Like, at all? I'll even settle for bush skunk.'

Nick shakes his head, looking away, ashamed.

'I deadass didn't come here to smoke your cock, Nick. Christ, I thought… never mind. I'll get some off Jared.' She stops, putting a hand through her grossly under-washed thick, messy hair. 'Shit. I mean, Bear Claw.'

'I'm sorry Star…. of the Sea. I wasn't expecting to see you tonight.'

She motions to the empty cat bed in the corner of the room.

'Where's Rupert? I haven't seen him the last couple of times I've been here.'

'He's dead.'

Her eyes turn crestfallen.

'Oh no. How?'

'He just disappeared. Dad figures it was coyotes. He was getting pretty old.'

Star sighs heavily, pouting her bottom lip. She leans over and rubs his knee affectionately.

'I'm sorry. He was a chill cat. Cute little guy.' She blows a stream of smoke out the window. 'The Tribe are planning to liberate a breeders house. There's plenty of cats I believe. I can grab you a kitten if you want.'

Nick smiles at her. It's a nice sentiment, but he has his own plans of liberating himself from this town. Only without Star of the Sea. He's taking his true love. Winter.

'Thanks, but I'll take some grieving time.'

'Speaking of plans, tell me you got the chemicals.'

Nick's eyes widen. He stands up, doing that thing where he scratches his head nervously.

'Nick. Tell me you got the fucking methanol.'

Nick busies himself organizing the spilled stationary on his desk. Star sighs dispassionately.

'The Elders were trusting me. I trusted you. If I can't lace Plucky's chicken with methanol to close them for good, then the Elders won't promote me to the inner circle. It's hard enough to be taken seriously when I'm twenty-three and I look fucking twelve. This is important!'

Star, a strong-willed woman in every sense, has one major insecurity. Growth Hormone Deficiency. A rare disease where, as a child, Star had a weak kidney that affected the body's chemical messenger system, the endocrine system. As a result, Star's body stopped developing for the most part, around the age of thirteen. She stands at a height of 5-foot 1 inch. Which is two inches above what classifies being a dwarf. It doesn't help that she still carries baby fat on her face, making her actually look like a young teenager. Nick wasn't attracted to her physically at first. It was her maturity that hooked him.

Nick looking at Star apologetically. 'Okay, just listen. I was going to stick it in my car when I got to work today. But this guy shows up, with, like, a clipboard. Looking all official and stuff. I thought he was a cop. But he was some health inspector. He found Miss Glass's secret alcohol stash. And he, like, shut her down.'

'Wait, what?'

'And, well, she kinda, sorta, fired me.'

'She fired you?! Fuck, Nick. The plan's ruined.'

'No, just listen, I-'

'You don't have any weed. You didn't get the methanol. You've got no job.' She makes an 'ugh' sound, throwing her hands out either side of her dramatically. 'What the fuck did I come here for?'

Star realizes that was too harsh of a comment. He's a good kid at heart. She wants to apologize but stops herself. She needs to administer a little tough love, to keep him focused on their mission. If she's too soft on him, he'll falter.

Nick slumps his shoulders and sighs heavily through his nose, sticking his hands in the pockets of his jeans and swaying on his heels uncomfortably. His feelings for her have been waning. The main reason he still sees her, aside from the kickass blowjobs, is to get an audience with the Lords of Light Elders. Star of the Sea and Nick were getting super high one night, and she told him offhandedly about how one of the Tribe members spends his weekends exploring abandoned copper mines looking for leftover minerals with a metal detector. Apparently, this kid, Pete, stumbled on a collapsed shaft and found a lump of raw gold bigger than a football. Star telling him that they estimate it to value at near half a million dollars. Enough to buy them a plot of land to set up their official Lords of Light compound where they can worship and entice new members. The Elders too paranoid to move it from the mine in case people find out. Apparently, there's a map showing where it is at their secret headquarters. Star won't tell him where that is, until they trust him. And Nick wants that map. Star was so high she doesn't remember telling him about it. Nick thinking that the Elders are full of shit, and probably making it up to give themselves more credence to their flock of sheep. Still, if it's true, it could mean a new future for Nick and Winter. So Nick figures he better let Star of the Sea be a bitch to him if she wants. If he acts the loyal pup, she will be none the wiser to his plan.

Nick pulls a set of keys out of his jeans pocket, jingling them at her.

'I still have the keys to the bar. I'll go in tonight. She's closed until further notice anyway. I'll get it. I promise.'

'I hope so for your sake. The Elders will be very disappointed if you don't come through.'

'It's all good, babe.'

'I hate it when you call me babe. Sounds too try-hard. And I think we should do it tonight. The whole plan. We can go to Plucky's right after you get the methanol.'

'What? I thought the plan was for next Wednesday. That's when the oil man comes.'

'You said they come Friday mornings as well.'

'Four in the morning, yeah. The dead zone. The only two times a week the restaurant shuts down for thirty minutes.'

'Let's run through the plan again. Like I'm hearing it for the first time. We can't have any room for error.'

'Frankie cleans down the grill at three-thirty. The oil truck comes. Frankie deals with that. Seth locks the front doors and walks over behind the hill to have his winding down doob.'

'What if he doesn't?'

'He will.'

'But what if he doesn't?'

'Plan B. We'll be one down, but it'll be manageable. You distract him. Like we talked about. Have your anti-Plucky's sign. Make a stir front of house. When Frankie goes to deal with the oil man, I'll slip in the back. Turn off the cameras.'

'How much time?'

'Five minutes, no more. I know where they keep the prepped chicken for the coming day. I'll douse it methanol. It'll be easier if we had both of us, but it's still gonna work.'

'And what happens if you get caught?'

Nick looks around. He bends down and opens his yellow and black backpack, rifling through it. His manner becoming more manic. He starts looking frantically around the room. Star watching him, holding back a smile.

'Looking for this?' she says, holding up a mace cannister.

Nick snaps his fingers and points at it.

'If I get caught, I spray them in the face.'

Star raises her eyebrows at him to show she's vaguely content. She drops the canister back in her bag.

'Anything else?'

Nick scratches his head a moment, racking his brains. His eyes suddenly go wide. He snaps his fingers again. He opens one of the drawers in the chest blocking the door. He pulls out two ski masks, holding them up for her to see. Star nods with approval.

Star pushes off the bed, grabs her hemp satchel, and starts for the door blocked by the dresser. She heaves all her little might and pushes the dresser back into its place, freeing the door.

'You better get the chemicals tonight, Nick. Or else you can kiss these magic lips goodbye.' She air-kisses at him with pouted lips as she walks out the door.

Nick quickly pushes the stationary together on the desk, looking over at the Ovaltine tin on the bed, carelessly tipped over putting ash on his starch white sheets. Man, he could really go for a Burger King Whopper right now.

Rose sits on the shiny metallic kitchen bench top at The Glass, legs crossed with her hands in her lap. A few pharmaceutical boxes sitting next to her on the bench top. Ativan. Halcion. Valium. All heavy-duty sleeping pills.

Rose watches Winter pace in front of her, waiting for her to say something. Winter wearing a hot pink velour velvet matching track-suit. Her shoes hot pink Adidas runners. A hot pink ribbon tied around her head, a big bow tied and sitting on the left side of her hair. And of course, her nails painted hot pink. She's holding her Pikachu stuffed toy tightly to her chest.

It's been about ten minutes since Winter has said anything. The last thing was that she's concerned about someone getting hurt in this sting.

There's a lot to process, Rose gets it. But she's had a couple of hours. Winter took a warm bath. Rose having to use old thick black curtains to cover the front windows of The Glass. Also having to going through the closets, taking out what she's going to need for when they hit the road. Packing light, because she knows Winter will want to bring as much as the mustang will fit. Winter is attached to all her outfits and accessories, having made most of them herself. Rose figuring that with all the money they'll have she'll go on a shopping spree at Old Navy or Kmart when they reach New York. And she'll have to buy them both new identities. New licenses. Passports too, just in case shit gets hot and they need to abscond.

Winter finally stops, right in front of Rose. Burying her face in the top of Pikachu a moment. Looking up with those puppy dog eyes and pouty red lips.

'So, you promise?'

Rose holds up three fingers stuck tightly together.

'Scouts honor.'

'You can't Scout's honor. You're not a boy.'

Rose shrugs.

'Well, Girl Guide's... cookie... honor. Whatever. Look, I swear Sweetpea, no one is gonna get hurt. Promise.'

Winter looking away toward the window a moment, then back to Rose, then down to the top of Pikachu, noticing she got some lipstick smudged on the yellow fabric between his pointy little ears. She licks her thumb and scrubs the red mark with it.

'What happens if they don't pay?' says Winter.

'It's the Plucky's General's Own original thirteen herbs and spices Secret Sauce. It's literally their gravy boat. They'll pay alright. And they'll pay big.'

'You kidnapped two people. We gotta go on the lam no matter what now. Let's, just for the sake of it, be hypothermia.'

'Hypothetical.'

'Huh?'

'What you just... never mind. Okay, let's be hypothermia.'

'Let's say they don't pay. Hypothermilly.'

'Well, then, I'll set this fucking place on fire and we'll collect the insurance.'

'My God Rosie, you're adding arson and insurance fraud to the growing list of bad things we're doing?!'

Rose wondering for a moment how the love of her life can be so stupid and smart at the same time. She's an anomaly, that's for damn sure. It reminds her of the time they met. When Rose was sitting-

'Rose?'

'Yeah babe.'

'You're not going to set this place on fire, are you?'

'No Sweetpea. I was being hypothermia.'

Winter nods slowly, trying to be convinced. But still not sure. Her eyes falling on the revolver sitting on the bench just behind Rose. Her eyes drooping with a mix of sadness and anxiety, rocking Pikachu in her grasp like it was a baby. Her breaths becoming shorter and sharper through her nose. Winding up with emotion. Winter starts pacing on the spot again, one finger playing with a loose curl in her hair.

'We're gonna get caught. I just know it. We're both gonna go to jail. I'll be there for the rest of my life! I won't ever get to see the big city lights. The Statue of Liberty. Central Park. Broadway. And having to wear that prison jumpsuit. One outfit, the rest of my life? Oh Rose, I'm so scared!'

There's a banging sound coming from another room. Rose uncrosses her legs and pushes off the bench. Rose grabs Winter's hips, making her stay still. She reaches in her khaki pocket and pulls out an imaginary medication bottle, pretending to uncap it. She holds out her other palm and pours a bunch of imaginary pills from the bottle. She puts three of her fingers together and selects one imaginary pill, holding it up in front of Winter's eyes.

'Chill pill.'

Winter purses her lips tight, like a child not wanting her medication.

'Hey. Come on. All the cool kids take their medicine.'

Winter eyeing the imaginary pill in her fingers with a pout. Rose slowly guiding her fingers to Winter's tightened lips. Winter accepting her fate. She swallows, arching her head back and her neck out to show Rose she's being a good girl and taking her medication.

Winter now coming back from her anxiety, looking visibly calmer. Rose leans in and they kiss passionately.

Rose steps back and holds her arms out, indicting she wants to hold Pikachu. Winter handing him over. Rose stroking the felt fabric.

The sound of pounding still coming from the next room.

Rose says, 'You're not gonna go to jail, alright? If the cops do get involved, which they won't, I'll say I made ya do it. This time it's me workin' the floor, collecting the tips. And baby cakes, we got millions in tips coming our way.'

Winter folds her arms, thinking it over. Tapping her foot. Her gaze finds itself on the boxes of medication on the bench top. Winter frowning a moment, looking back to Rose.

'What's all those pills for anyway?'

Rose glances at them, then back to Winter, shrugging.

'My insomnia has been particularly bad lately. All this stress with selling The Glass. Y'know.'

Winter nods slowly in understanding.

The banging sound has finally got to Rose.

'For fuck's sake!'

Rose spins around on her heels, snatches the gun from the bench and strides through the swinging doors, through the main bar area, to the bathrooms. Rose places one arm against the door frame and talks with her head down.

'What's the problem now? You got a place to piss and shit, don't ya?'

Ruby's blustering voice booming from the other side of the door.

'I haven't eaten a goddamn thing all day. I got nothing to shit!'

Rose takes a long breath in, sighs, and wipes her face with agitation. She looks over at Winter, standing in the main saloon room. Arms folded.

Winter saying, 'He's right Honeybee. We have guests. We gotta feed our guests.'

Rose throws her arms up and steps back from the door.

'Fine!'

She whips the gun from her pants and kicks the chair away from the door handle, clattering it across the floor just shy of Winter's feet.

Rose opens the men's bathroom door to reveal a red, sweaty faced Ruby.

Rose says, 'But first, you're gonna tell me all about Plucky's.'

'I'll tell ya anything. Hell, grab a pen and paper. I'll give you the fuckin' recipe if it means we can end this shit.'

'I don't want your stupid recipe. What am I gonna do, open up a chain of fuckin' chicken stores?'

'They're restaurants.'

'Whatever. No, I don't wanna know about the links, I wanna know about the whole damn chain. Shares, liquid assets, silent partners, offshore accounts, you name it.'

'You got it. I'll tell you all I know. But first, you get me some food. Good stuff, not the microwave shit you cough up in this joint.'

Rose knocks her knuckles against the door frame, looking to her feet and shaking her head incredulously with a clenched jaw smile.

'You're a piece of work old man.'

An idea hitting Rose like a sucker punch. A smile creeping on her face.

'You want some grub huh? I got just the thing for you Ruby Tuesday.'

The three-quarter moon hangs over the desert terrain in the cloudless night sky. The Glass Half Full a dark silhouette on the vast plains behind. No visible lights coming from inside the saloon. The headlights from Rose's mustang peeking around the back of the building, then turning to drive around the side, hitting the main driveway then picking up speed toward the highway. She punches the gear, skids left onto Route 66 and rockets off out of sight down the highway.

Nick is at the wheel of his old yellow Mazda, parked in the bushy shadows on the dirt tip of an incline across the other side of the highway from The Glass Half Full. Nick watching Rose's mustang slip off into the distance, drumming his fingers nervously on the steering wheel.

'Well, she's gone. What the fuck are you waiting for?' Star of the Sea says with a mouthful of raw carrot. Bits of it spitting onto her tatty poncho.

Nick is peering at The Glass through a pair of small binoculars stolen from his dad's amateur bird watching kit.

'I dunno...'

Nick adjusting the settings on the binoculars, trying to focus on the building about a half mile away.

'The lights are still on inside, I think. I can't tell, it's like the windows are blacked out with something. I can see a tiny bit of light coming through gaps... I think.'

'So what,' a chunk of carrot falling onto her chest and rolls down to her lap, catching it just before it gets there and popping it back in her mouth. 'So she's put up some curtains and left the lights on. Big fuckin' deal.'

'It's not like her to do that. And what about Winter?'

'Who? Oh, that stripper chick. What about her?'

'She's not a stripper. She's a performer. And I only saw Rose in the car. That means she'll still be in there.'

Star points the stub of a half-eaten carrot at Nick.

'That dumb bimbo's a push over. She shops at Safeway. The Elders see her come in all the time. They say she's got the IQ of a picnic table.'

'I dunno.'

'I dunno,' Star repeats his words intentionally sounding like she's got Down Syndrome. 'Look, don't be a pussy Nick. Just go in and get what we came for. You got the keys, you know where it is. Just sneak in, grab a couple of cans of the stuff and get the fuck out. If you run into miss pin-up girl, just make up something. Like you forgot to take some stuff. Anything. This is our only chance. If Rose remembers you got keys, she'll change the locks. If she hasn't already.'

'Alright, I'm going. You better wait here.'

'I was going to anyway.'

Nick swallows hard, then leans over, his lips puckered. She turns her head, looking at him like he's crazy.

'What the fuck are you doing?'

'I thought maybe, I dunno, I could get a kiss. You know, for luck.'

'I'm eating Nick.'

She looks at his disappointed face a moment, then leans over and gives him a quick peck on the lips, then continues chewing.

Nick smiles, then turns and pulls the small car door handle, having to jerk it a few times, the car nearly as old as him. The door creaks as it opens, Nick getting out and slamming it shut. He looks at the darkened saloon with uneasiness.

Here goes nothing.

Nick half runs half jogs down the small incline toward the highway. Almost tripping on the .38 revolver encased in a hard crust of dirt from being there a couple of years. The same gun Rose threw there when her would be robber tried to stick her up.

163

CHAPTER TWELVE

Queen Bee

Jillian sits cross-legged on her white Italian top grain cowhide leather sofa, a tall glass filled with a Tom Collins next to her. This is her fifth this evening, not counting the other drinks she had at the office.

Jillian has her gaming headset on. Microphone in front of her mouth. She is wearing a white fine wool business shirt from Naples, three times too big for her. One side hangs down exposing her shoulder just showing the tip of one of her Nicotine patches. And a pair of cheap black cotton panties, bought at K-Mart. Her face glossy from sweat, her chestnut brown hair pulled up in a messy bun.

Jillian mashes her fingers over an X-Box controller tightly grasped in her hands. Her eyes full of ferocious tenacity as she focuses on the projection of a game on the adjacent wall. The projector unit fitted on the roof above her head, spilling out the visuals to a first-person combat game. Her avatar is running through what appears to be a war-torn Middle East country, shooting other online players. On the side of the projection is a separate screen showing Vanessa, a 14-year-old Cambodian girl playing from her home in Phnom Penh. Jillian jibes into the mic on her headset.

'What's it like living in a low income country? Do you enjoy being all poor and shit?'

Vanessa's voice half Asian, half British sounding.

'My dad's a company director at a major textile firm, asshole. I go to school in Europe.'

Vanessa's avatar shoots at Jillian's avatar and misses.

'Well, I hope the education there is better than your gaming. Fithly fuckin' casual.'

'I'm fourteen. What's your excuse old lady?'

'Come on you little faggot. Where did you learn to shoot? Faggot-ville?'

'How can I be a faggot? I'm a girl you dumbass.'

Both of them tapping frenziedly on their controllers. Not taking their eyes off their respective player.

'Girls can be faggots. The worst kind.'

An explosion in the game. Vanessa just launched a missile from a bazooka, almost taking Jillian's character out.

'Boom bitch. And if you read a book, you'd know that a faggot is technically a pile of sticks. Find a better word, asshat.'

Jillian turns her character around, and with quick precision, she changes weapons to a flamethrower and charges at Vanessa's avatar. She sprays forth a wave of fire, roasting Vanessa out of the game.

'Well I just set this pile of sticks on fire. Sayonara faggot.'

Vanessa flips Jillian off with a sneer then disconnects, leaving a black screen where her face was.

Jillian puts her controller to the side on the couch next to her Egyptian cushions, then leans forward and grabs her Tom Collins and necks the rest.

Jillian slides her legs out from under her and plants them on the thick carpet, wriggling her toes to get the blood running back in her legs. She moseys around the couch and walks up the three steps to the elevated room behind her that houses a casual glass dining table with oak legs, past that and into the expansive kitchen. She owns every cooking device known to man, or woman. Stainless steel pots and pans hanging on one side. Slow cookers. Espresso machines. Bread makers. Granite mortar and pestles of differing sizes. Pasta making machines. She's never used any of these things. Apart from the espresso machine. To make espresso martinis of course.

Jillian steps to the double door stainless steel refrigerator and opens one side. Three shelves are taken up by plastic jugs, all with different colored liquids. Brown, turquoise, clear, pink, red. All of them have neat little white labels stuck on them. One reads 'Mojito'. Another 'Shirly Temple'. 'Mint Julip'. 'Bloody Mary'. 'Manhattan'. She reaches in and grabs the one third filled jug of 'Tom Collins' and refills her glass. She sticks the jug back on the shelf and pivots on one foot to use the side of her other foot to slam the fridge door shut.

Jillian is heading back to her spot on the couch when the sound of a phone ringing reverberates around the apartment via Bluetooth. She stops in her tracks when she sees the incoming caller alert magnified on the projecting screen over the top of her game. It reads 'CUNTY MCCUNTFACE'. Reuben's number.

Jillian sighs. The stress taking its toll. Time to break a three month pledge. She goes back into the kitchen and hooks her toes under the metal handle of the bottom drawer, pulling it open. She dips her toes in the drawer, using her foot to rearrange all the random stuff inside. Power cords. Instruction guides to all the appliances in her kitchen. Take-out menus. Travel power adapters. Batteries. And there it is. Just what she is looking for. A packet of Marlboro Lights hidden under the mess. Jillian stoops down and pulls it out. She lights up as she rounds the table to the balcony sliding door and pulls it open, stepping onto her curved balcony overlooking Central Park. She sucks in a long drag and exhales into the wind. Jillian presses a button on her headset.

'Yessum.'

'Hello Jillian. It's the thorn in your side.'

'I've been waiting for your call.'

'I bet you have.'

'I bet you bet that I have.'

'That didn't make sense.'

'I've had a few drinks.' On cue, Jillian knocks back a gulp of her cocktail. 'So. Talk to me. What's your price tag?'

Rose speeds down Route 66 talking into her hands-free cord. The mustang's headlights illuminating a buckshot '55 speed limit' sign as it speeds past. She's doing nearly double that.

'Your man Reuben told me that not all your company's earnings are public. The haul from Plucky's alone is close to half a billion annually. Now, add that to Tasty Incorporated's other franchises, like Taco King, Gobble Gobble and...'

'Hey!' Jillian angrily flicks ash over the balcony rail. 'You leave the other feeding troughs out of this. Plucky's is your only bargaining chip. You want a taste of the whole pie, you can go fist yourself.'

'Alright, alright. Keep your pants on.'

'I wasn't wearing any pants to begin with. And don't tell me how to dress, fuck-knuckle.'

'You got some sass in your britches girl.'

A playful little grin forms on Rose's face, recalling the photo of Jillian on the Tasty Incorporated website. Rose thinking she looks like a cute little pocket rocket.

Rose says, 'And I got no problem with you wearin' no pants.'

Jillian frowns.

'You a dike or something?'

Rose purses her lips, realizing she's saying too much, and changes the subject.

'Twenty million is my price tag.'

Jillian spits out a fat mouthful of Tom Collins. Little does she know that in nineteen seconds, the mixture of her cocktail and her saliva will land on an infant's face on the corner of West 60th and Columbus, Upper West Side Manhattan. The mother pushing the pram not noticing the light spray of sticky alcohol on her two-year-old baby girl. Jillian wouldn't care anyway.

Jillian manages a chuckle at Rose's offer.

Rose says, 'To your company, that's chump change.'

'The company has board members. Employees. Equity investments. Stock points. Taxes. Labor and legal costs. And that's just the tip of the iceberg.'

'Well boo-fuckin'-hoo. I run a business of my own ya know.'

'What kind of business?'

'The kind that's none of yours.'

Jillian smiles despite not being successful in her attempt to weed out information.

'Well, you're dealing with me alone. If you want the cops out of this, there's a huge price to pay for that pleasure.'

'So what's your offer?'

'Five hundred thousand.'

'You think I was born yesterday?'

'I think your plan was.'

Jillian leans to the side, poking her ass out. She winces. *Brrrrrpppppp*.

Rose hears the noise and furrows her brows.

'Did... did you just ...'

'Yeah, so what. Suck it up princess. This isn't a courtesy call. You're trying to steal my hard earned money. So fuck off with your judgments. My only regret is that you're not here to smell it.'

Rose shrugs. The girl has a point.

Rose says, 'Can I ask you a question?'

'You just did.'

'You know how black cats are bad luck? I mean, when they cross your path?'

'An old superstition, yeah.'

'Does that rule only apply to cats?'

'Huh?'

'What if another animal with black fur, say, a badger, or a coyote. Does it mean the same thing?'

'Well, as far as I know, the black cat thing is of pagan belief. I think, because of witches or whatever. Like when they rode with their black cat on a broomstick.'

'Okay, I get that. But, let's say, a black coyote crossed your path. And you killed it. Would that be bad luck?'

'Is there such a thing as a black coyote?'

'There sure is.'

'Well, I'm no authority. But a coyote is like a dog. And cats and dogs are opposites. So, it's not the same thing.'

Rose lets out a sigh of relief.

Jillian frowns, then says 'But, thing is, you said you killed it. I haven't ever heard of a black coyote, but I imagine they're pretty rare. So, killing that would maybe be some kind of bad luck. Probably in some religion. Like Indian or some shit.'

Jillian's cigarette has died from the dense wind up on the 31st floor.

Rose hears the noise of the lighter on the other end of the phone.

'Smoking's a bad habit. It'll kill ya.'

'Yeah? So will a speeding bus. But I don't hold your hand crossing the street.' Jillian sucks in a lung full, then exhales long and slow. 'You got a family?'

Rose eases up on the acceleration pedal as she spots the lit up Plucky's sign ahead in the darkness.

'Why do you care?'

'You've committed at least two federal crimes. It's a huge risk. And people usually do desperate things for the ones they love. I guess I just wanna know who I'm dealing with.'

Rose spins the steering wheel and directs the car into the driveway leading to the Plucky's car park.

'You're fishin' for information baby bitch. Not gonna happen. Let's just say, life came up and stung me in the ass like a wasp.'

Jillian exhales a plume of smoke through her semi closed lips and murmurs, 'Yeah, it'll do that.'

'You got kids?'

'Fuck no.'

Rose smiles as she steers the car past a vintage blue Vespa chained to a light pole, then into a parking space in front of the entrance to the Plucky's restaurant.

Jillian tosses her cigarette butt over the side of the balcony, even though there's an ashtray on the patio table.

'And talk about being stung. You have a kid, you either get, well, a bee or a wasp.'

Rose shuts off the engine.

'Just how many drinks have you had?'

'Shut up and listen. Bees pollinate flowers. Makes nature happy. Keeps the world turning. Wasps don't contribute anything. They sting. That's it. They're assholes.' Jillian aggressively lights another cigarette. 'See, when you have kids, you either get a person that's going to be useful to society, or you get a troll. Worse yet, you could end up raising a murderer. A rapist. A serial killer. A Westboro Church picketer, or even...'

'-a pedophile,' Rose cuts in.

'Yeah, sure, whatever.' Jillian shrugs and takes a sip of her cocktail. 'So I guess that makes you a wasp. Cause you're not being useful to anyone except yourself. You come into my life and sting me in the ass for your own selfish reasons.'

'Takes one to know one.'

'I'm no wasp lady. I run several successful food chains. I feed the public. I oversee meal deals, promotions, and the dollar menu. Organize charity events and shit. I bring joy to their miserable lives while they toil their little jobs to contribute to the world. The hive, so to speak. So you see, I'm the queen fucking bee.'

A set of headlight flashes into Rose's car as a Tesla pulls into the parking bay next to hers, making Rose shield her eyes momentarily. The car parks and shuts off its engine. Rose looks over and sees a portly looking blonde guy in the passenger seat talking to the tall driver with animated expressions. The driver looking ahead, not enthused at all. Rose turns to look straight ahead through the glass doors to the restaurant.

'Well Queen bee, you go back to your hive and make me some honey. All five million of it. I was gonna play the whole negotiating game. I say twenty, you say five g's. I say fifteen, you say one mil. Blah blah fuckin' blah. I'm done. Five million, that's it. I ain't a corporation. I'm a desperate bitch with a shotgun and a mean old bastard who's starting to get on my nerves. So you get the money together or your special sauce will end up nothin' but pieces of brain sprayed all over my wall. You got eight hours from now. I'll call you with the bank account details first bark of the rooster. You better be ready.'

Jillian goes to say something, but the line goes dead. She takes a deep, angry puff of her cigarette, flicks it over the rail and marches back inside the penthouse to grab her phone.

CHAPTER THIRTEEN

For Your Eyes Only

Winter sits on the bar top, her legs crossed daintily, her hot pink runners dangling loosely as she carefully sands the edges of her fingernails with a nail file. She blows on a finger gently, takes a hit from her pencil thin joint and puts it back in the tin ashtray, then starts on the next finger.

The sawed-off shotgun sitting on the bar next to her thigh. A half-eaten cup of Jell-O on the other side of her. A box of shotgun shells sitting open next to the duct tape in front of the cash register. Winter has never fired a gun in her life. Rose said she's just gone down the road to Plucky's and won't be gone more than twenty minutes. Twenty-five, tops.

'Alllll I want, is a room somewherrrre. Far away, from the cold night air. With one enormous chair. Oh, wouldn't it be loverlllllllyyyyy.'

Winter stops filing her nails and cocks her head. Listening to a high-pitched voice singing "Wouldn't It Be Loverly" from *My Fair Lady*. Winter's eyes shift to the jukebox. It's off.

'Lots of chocolate for me to eat. Lots of coal, makin' lots of heat.'

Winter now pinpoints the crooning voice coming from one of the bathrooms. She pushes off the bar. Winter turns and picks up the shotgun, cradling it to her tummy. She slowly steps toward the bathrooms, listening to the singing with a growing smile on her face. Winter now between the two bathrooms.

'Who's heavenly voice is that?'

'Mine. Angel's blow me until my voice is melted butter on God's toast,' Ruby's gruff voice coming from the men's bathroom.

Winter turns and steps over to the women's bathroom door.

'Dennis, I had no idea you could sing!'

'Honey, I don't just sing. I write my own music as well.'

'Oooooh. No way! You're a proper musician.'

'A musician? Pffft. Sweetie, I'm a God damned Broadway superstar. They just don't know it yet.'

'Broadway?! That's where I'm going!' Winter looks at her feet in despair. 'Well, I will be going… when this boo-boo of a situation is over.'

'Chin up girl, you'll be taking Selfie's in Times Square before you know it. And I'll be busting out my tunes on stage nearby.'

'I wanna hear one of your songs!'

'If I had music to accompany me, and a little make up, I'd make Doris Day look like Doris Yesterday.'

Winter pushes off her feet to stand on her tippy toes and claps her hands excitedly. A new project.

Ruby's voice coming from the adjacent door, 'Holy shit Dennis, you're a goddamn faggot too.'

Winter ignores Ruby's remark, and lightly puts her hand on the door handle.

'If I open this door Dennis, are you going to be a good boy?'

'If you can turn me into a bad girl, then I'll be sweet as brown sugar.'

Winter's red puffy lips turn up into a wicked smile, thinking, oh golly gee whiz, Rose is gonna love it when she sees Dennis gold eyeshadow and a strawberry blonde wig.

Winter pushes down on the chair top holding the door handle in place, unfastening it. She pushes the door open to find Dennis sitting on the floor, his back up against the drywall.

'This is gonna be so much fun! Yay! Oh, but we gotta hurry. Rose will be back in around twenty minutes. I wanna surprise her when she walks in.'

'Let me get my keyboard from the limo.'

'Why do you carry a keyboard around?'

'Why wouldn't I carry a keyboard around?'

Winter pushes off the frame and makes a happy chipmunk 'eeeee-ekkkk' sound.

The dull golden brown glow of a half expired light bulb shines above the stoop of the backdoor to The Glass. Nick shivers from a chilly wind creeping in from the southwest winds as he fumbles in his pocket for the keys to the bar.

Nick raises his shaky hand to slip the key in the lock. Not shaky from the bitter desert air. Shaky because he is dreading Rose coming back anytime soon.

As soon as Nick enters the long kitchen, he can hear muffled music wafting in through the swinging doors at the other end. A both low and high voice crooning a song. The kitchen is dark, but moonlight and neon light from the glass door fridge allow him to vigilantly creep through.

Nick approaches the swinging doors and gently pushes one open just a crack. Nick squints through the small gap to the main area of the bar. He can just make out someone on the stage. A blonde, black woman sitting in front of an electric piano keyboard. She's wearing a long pink sparkly gown too small for her big frame, with shiny light purple sequins dotted all over it. The song she's singing is… wait. Nick pushes the door open a little more, peering intensely at the person on stage. That's not a woman. That's a man in drag.

It's a little hard to tell with the gold makeup caked around his eyes and lips, but it kinda looks like Mister Wallace's driver, Dennis. He flicks his curly blonde hair back as he belts out the chorus to the *Sheena Easton* song "For Your Eyes Only".

Nick's gaze falls on the back of Winter, watching the stage act. He can tell right away it's her by that rockabilly quaffed hair. She's dressed in a black and gold stitched corset. A golden glittery bow just above her butt. Fishnet stockings all the way down her legs to the gold stilettos on her feet. She's clapping her hands excitedly as Dennis makes a dramatic gesture with the piano at a poignant part of the song. Nick swallows a dry lump after noticing the shotgun in Winter's lap.

A dampened thump sound from somewhere behind Nick, making him spin around at breakneck speed. His heart almost jumping into his throat, thinking Rose has come back.

There's no one there.

Nick steps forward, peering into the shadows around the fridge. The shelving unit. The industrial oven that never gets used. Nothing. Nick's shoulders drop a little as he relaxes slightly. Nick wipes his hand down his face and breathes a quivered sigh of relief. He'd better get the methanol and get the hell out of here. He turns toward the swinging doors and hears another sound, this time sounding more like whimpering. Then scratching.

Nick's eyebrows furrow as he turns and starts toward the rear of the kitchen where the pantry is. There's nothing really in there, except piles of old tax related forms, giant packs of disposable hand towels and Costco boxes of Jell-O. Winter's favorite.

More faint scratching sounds.

Maybe those damn raccoons snuck in again. He better let them out.

Nick unhooks and swings open the door, pulling the hanging cord next to the entrance, clicking on the light inside. Nick freezes in terror. Standing five feet away from him is a coyote.

The animal's piercing yellow eyes, shining brighter from the glow of the light bulb above it. Nick not wanting to make any sudden movements.

Nick's first cohesive thought after imagining this thing mauling him to death is, 'why in the hell is this wild animal being kept prisoner in here?' He winces from a pungent smell hitting his nostrils. Nick noticing the floor now. Urine and feces splashed around. The Jell-O boxes have been ripped open, the colors everywhere mashed in with torn paper towels. Ripped up boxes of mash potato powder. The animal's black coat mottled with colorful Jell-O powder.

The coyote takes a wary step, placing her front paw forward, wanting to run past him.

Nick's mind assumes the worst scenario is about to unfold. So, he responds with what he thinks is the most logical and carefully constructed counter move his veterinary studies have taught him.

'Only for yoooouuuu..... for your... eyes... onnnnlllyyy.'

With a smooth run of the back of his hand across all the piano keys, Dennis ends the song. He stands up from his wooden chair and bows in different directions as if the bar is packed out with a big audience, then proceeds to curtsy, lifting the sides of the pink gown.

Winter gushes an exuberant smile and applauds enthusiastically on her stool. She sticks two fingers in her mouth and jets out a loud whistle.

Dennis says, 'Thank you... thank you. You're all so kind. What a wonderful audience. That was Sheena Easton's delectable classic, For Your Eyes Only. For my next performance, I'm going to re-'

Before Dennis can finish there is the sound of clattering metal in the kitchen, followed by screaming. Winter jerks half her body around to gawk at the kitchen doors just as Nick comes bursting through them, flailing his arms in panic.

Winter watches, frozen in her seat, as Nick skids on a little puddle of melted ice. He almost slips over but manages to grab the bar counter for support, pulling himself back up quickly. Nick looks over at the kitchen doors still swinging, the coyote on the other side timidly coming through. Nick screams again and dashes to the nearest saloon table, grabbing a chair and hurling it blindly in the air to what he thinks is the direction of the coyote. It soars and hits the wall between the two bathroom doors, falling and hitting the chair holding the men's bathroom handle in place - dislodging it slightly.

Nick runs to the main doors and grips the handles, pulling with all his might, shaking the doors with frustration when they won't open. Nick unaware that Rose has put a chain around the handles on the outside of the door with a padlock. He turns his head at near breakneck speed to ogle back at the kitchen. The coyote standing in the saloon area now, tail between its legs, looking around and sniffing the air. She looks over at Dennis on the stage, jaw dropped and staring back at her, then to Winter, with the same visage.

Winter gripping the shotgun in her lap now. She blinks her doe-eyes, looking over to Nick who has his back pressed up against the main doors, staring at the coyote like it was the Grim Reaper.

'Nick?!' Winter calls out. Not knowing what question to ask or where to begin. Her eyes darting back and forth between Nick and the coyote. The coyote now backing up into the hallway to the basement, her yellow eyes staying on all of them. Winter slowly rises up from her stool, making no sudden movements.

'Look at the poor thing, it's scared as heck. We gotta let it outside where it belongs.' She looks over to Nick as she moves toward him. 'What on Earth is a coyote doing in here Nick? Did you let it in?'

'N-n-no Miss Bloom. I swear. I came in the back door, through the kitchen, and I heard something in the pantry. I opened the door and there it was, right in front of me.'

Dennis is slinking carefully to the kitchen doors near the end of the hallway, keeping a steady eye on the coyote which is backing slowly down the narrow corridor. He's having no trouble walking on the size 13 leather diamond colored glitter pumps. The salty sour smell of coyote urine now reaching Dennis's nose.

'Peeee-yew!' Dennis waves his hand in front of his face. 'That is one smelly pooch.'

Winter glances at Dennis a moment, then back to Nick.

'What are you doing here Nick? Rose told me you don't work here anymore.'

'I-I, just... forgot something.' Nick scratches his tilted head. 'My, ah, phone charger.' He forces a little laugh, painfully fake. 'You know how expensive those things are, right?'

Winter noticing Nick's shaking hands as she nears closer.

'Nick, petal, are you okay? You're a big ol' sack of shake'n'bake.'

'Yeah Miss Bloom, the coyote startled me is all.'

Winter places her hands on her hips.

'Oh don't let that little guy worry you. It's just a big scaredy-cat. We used to have coyotes come on my grandaddy's farm. They're more afraid of you than you are of them. Come on. I'll show you.'

Winter beckons over to the hallway with her head.

'Come on.'

Nick momentarily hypnotized by the gold butt bow on Winter's outfit.

Nick sticks his hands deep in his pockets and follows Winter to the hallway, stopping near the end by the bar. The coyote in the shadows at the end of the hall in front of the basement door, cowering in the corner, watching nervously as Winter stoops down to one knee next to Dennis. She starts gently cooing at the animal, sounding like she's humming a lullaby. Nick takes a few safety steps back, still afraid of the animal. What Nick should really be worried about is the fact that during the recent chaos, Ruby had managed to dislodge the chair from its feeble hold after it was jolted by the chair Nick carelessly hurtled in the air.

Ruby steps carefully and quietly behind the trio in the hallway, stopping at the end of the bar a few feet behind Nick. He desperately looks over the bar top to the preparation counter behind, trying to locate some kind of weapon. He spots a chopping cleaver impaled into a wooden cutting board. As Winter continues to sing to the frightened coyote at the end of the hallway, Ruby painstakingly reaches over the bar, trying to stay silent. The odd little grunt forced out the side of his sealed lips as his rotund gut presses into the bar top counter forcing air out of him. His fat fingertips now touching the cleaver handle, sliding down the handle slowly as he struggles to hold in his breathing. Nick not hearing Ruby right behind him; too mesmerized by Winter's enchantingly sentimental croon to the coyote.

Ruby now has a firm grip on the handle and lets out a relieved wheeze of air as he rips the cleaver from its wooden hold. Nick hearing the sudden expel of breath behind, but he's too late – Ruby steps back from the bar and swings around, grabbing Nick by the collar of his shirt and yanking him backward and swiftly brings the cleaver up to Nick's neck.

'No sudden movements or I end this boy here and now.'

Ruby noticing Dennis's flamboyant attire and cocks an eyebrow, then shakes his head.

Nick manages a little whimper as the cold steel presses into his Adam's Apple. Dennis turns to find his ex-employer holding the frightened teen hostage with the large blade. Dennis tapping Winter on the shoulder. Her long black lashes popping up as her eyes widen with shock as she rises to stand with Dennis's help. Winter just stands motionless with the heavy-duty firepower dangling loosely in one hand. Dennis looking at the shotgun in her grasp, then up to her face.

'Winnie honey?'

'Uh-huh?'

'Shotgun.'

'Oh.'

Winter quickly fumbles the gun so she's gripping the barrel with her left hand and pointing it in the direction of Nick and Ruby. Her hands shaky. Rose promised she wouldn't have to use this thing. But she's in charge here, she's got to do something.

'Let him go… please and thank you.'

Ruby's reddened face half poking out from behind Nick as he starts to back off, pulling Nick along with him.

'Alright Jezebel, put the gun down.'

Winter raises the gun slightly higher, showing her deft resolve. Her hands still quivering. She's trying to come across like a badass, but it's a hard look to pull off in a corset with a bow.

'I mean it girl. Or I'll bleed this kid like a Halal pig.'

Ruby has backed up five feet with the still frozen Nick, staring Dennis and Winter down, eyes darting intensely between the two. He is now in the main saloon area in front of the bar, motioning with his head toward the stage.

'I want the both of you to move over there. No sudden movements, or I'll hack his head off.'

Nick saying, 'M-m-mister Wallace, p-please don't hur-'

'Shut your damn mouth boy!'

Nick clenches his eyes shut as Ruby digs the blade a little deeper into his neck.

'Move it!'

Winter, shotgun still trained on Ruby, sidesteps with Dennis out of the hallway, past the kitchen doors and into the maze of tables.

Ruby says, 'Dennis, get up on that stage where I can keep an eye on you.'

Dennis hesitates, glancing to Winter.

'Now nigger, I'm not playin' around,' says Ruby.

Dennis sneers at him, then clomps on his pumps to the stage, stepping up next to the keyboard.

Ruby staring at Dennis until he's stopped, then his eyes fix back on Winter.

'I've been in two wars. I've had bigger guns pointed at me, with meaner people behind them. And I can tell that you, my dear, have no intention of pullin' that trigger.'

Ruby shoves Nick prompting him to step forward. Another little push and they both take another step toward Winter.

'And I'm certain, deep down, you know if you do, a pretty little cream puff like you won't last two square meals in maximum security.'

'Don't listen to him honey. It's called self-defense. Shoot his fat ass.'

With a quick sudden movement Ruby withdraws the knife from Nick's neck and cracks the base of his skull with the cleaver handle. Nick sprawls forward into a table, bounces off it and falls to the side into two wooden chairs, clattering with them to the floor in a heap, groaning and rubbing his head.

Ruby now six feet away from Winter. She goes to rack the pump on the shotgun, but her hand slips and she almost loses her hold on the gun. Ruby silently chuckles under his breath. Winter regains her posture and whips her head up with a serious expression and aims the gun at him again. A cute little sneer on her face. One eye squinting. She grips the pump harder and tries a second time. The gun makes the dull metallic racking noise. Got it.

'I'll do what I have to Mister Wallace.'

'Oh, we're past formalities now. You can call me Ruby.'

Dennis covertly moving past the keyboard in an attempt to get behind Ruby's line of sight so he can step off the stage and attack him from the rear. Ruby speaks to him without taking his icy glare off Winter.

'Take another step Dennis, and I'll launch this knife into your thick skull. I'm dead sober and you know my aim is pretty fuckin' good.'

Dennis halting in his tracks, having seen the man play darts in the parlor room at home.

Ruby is only a few feet in front of Winter now, his arms stiff by his sides. His thumb running anxiously up and down the handle of the cleaver. Watching Winter act like a cornered street cat. Eyes wild with adrenaline.

Winter thinking he's getting too close for comfort. But she can't shoot him, or else the whole blackmailing thing is over. And Rose would be mortified. Do something Winter. Say something. What would Rose say?

'Right now you're probably going to give me some little speech about how I've never fired a gun before. Blah blah blah. Well you know what? I haven't. But that doesn't mean I don't want to. An opportunity just never came up. And lookie here. Now one has.'

'Aw now, doll face, there's a big difference between firing a gun and shooting someone.'

In two quick moves Ruby pelts the cleaver toward Winter; it lands with a *thonk* into the wooden wall behind, narrowly missing her head. Ruby launches forward and snatches the barrel of the gun, yanking it from Winter's grip entirely.

Ruby grips the shotgun with both hands. Looking like it's at home in his grasp. He uses the tip of the shotgun barrel to punch her in the stomach. Winter loses her footing on her heels and tumbles back into the wall letting out a loud "oomph!" She slides down the wall and lands on her butt. Slightly winded, she looks up to find Ruby towering over her with a wicked grin, the shotgun barrel pointed at her face.

'Here. Let me show ya how it's done sweetheart.'

Ruby wraps his index finger around the trigger and goes to squeeze.

Dennis leaps off the stage to intervene but trips and falls to the floor with a loud thump.

Nick hysterically cries out, 'NO!'

Winter blinks helplessly, staring into the barrel inches from her face.

BANG.

CHAPTER FOURTEEN

Extra Creamy

Marion sits at the wheel of the Tesla parked out the front of Plucky's next to a green mustang that just pulled up. He just spent the twenty-minute trip from the motel to Plucky's listening to Peter rambling on about how Fenway Park is becoming less affordable, and as a Red Sox fan, it's an outrage. Peter getting out of the car now, Marion about to do the same when his phone rings. It's Jillian.

Marion says, 'You go ahead. I have to take this call.'

'Okey dokey, Thor and Loki,' Peter says cheerfully as he closes the door.

Marion rolls his eyes and puts the phone to his ear.

'Marion Delaney.'

'I just got off the phone with the bitch.'

Marion watches Peter approach the front doors to the restaurant, his eyes flick a burly redneck woman in khaki pants who just got out of the mustang next to the Tesla. Peter opens the door for the woman. She gives him a greasy look and walks past him into the building.

'Did she give you much?' Marion rubbing his thin protruding chin in the rearview mirror.

Jillian sighs. 'Not really. She owns a business.' Jillian racking her brain for anything else. 'Oh, I think she might be a rug muncher. Can't be sure though.'

'Rug muncher?'

'A fuckin' dike.'

Marion looks back to the restaurant. Peter is inside now, approaching the counter behind the redneck woman.

'We'll just stick with what we do know for now. This is a small town. If we have it narrowed down to a woman who runs her own business, that's something. Did you record the conversation?'

'Shit. Mother fucker. Shit. Sorry. I'm a little soused.'

Marion wipes his face slowly with agitation.

Jillian says 'I've spent some time in the South. She sounds like she's from the South. Originally, anyway. If that helps.' She slurps a drink. 'Look, she didn't give up anything about location or her personal life. I tried.' A moment as she thinks. 'We talked about wasps.'

'Wasps?' Marion's bushy eyebrows both turn inward. 'As in the insect?'

'As in the insect.' A pause, then Jillian says, 'And coyotes.' There is a pause on the other end. And what sounds like liquid being poured into a glass. Then Jillian says in a lighter tone, 'Marion. If you come across this person, are you prepared to use... force?'

Marion sits up stiffly in his seat, licking his lips. His heart racing. This is just the question he has been waiting to hear from her. He can tell by the tone of her voice that she wants him to use force. Like a twelve-year-old girl sheepishly asking her parents if she can go to her friend's sleepover.

Marion being coy now. 'What kind of force are we talking here?'

'The kind that makes this problem go bye-bye for good. If you know what I mean.'

'I think I do ma'am.'

'Call me Jilly.'

'Thank you,' Marion says pretending to be grateful.

'Would you take a life... if you had to?'

'I was a Navy Seal. I've taken many lives on missions. And I consider this task at hand a mission.'

'Y'know, it would be a real shame if Reuben... ahem... met his end as well. If he, I dunno, fell down some stairs. Or got killed by the kidnappers while you were trying to rescue him. Or at least... make it seem like they did.'

'Ma'am?'

'Jilly.'

'Jilly. Are... are you suggesting what I think you are?'

'Maybe I am, and maybe I'm not. I have to know, though, is if you would or wouldn't be open to such possibilities. For a handsome price, of course.'

'How handsome are we talking?'

'Marlon Brando in his prime.'

Marion grins. 'Maybe I would, if the opportunity presents itself.'

'That's very comforting to hear.' A pause as she slurps her drink. 'Marion, let's keep this conversation between you and I, okay?'

'What conversation?'

'Atta boy.'

Peter just finished ordering a Plucky's Mega Value Loaded Box Meal with a side of three-piece chicken wings, a tub of sweet potato and gravy and a Diet Mountain Dew. He removes his Plucky's Platinum card in his leather wallet and gives it to the cashier. He looks over at the woman standing nearby at the end of the counter, her arms tightly folded, tapping her foot anxiously in her Doc Martin boots. Peter thinking she's got a "manly" vibe about her. Especially the way she has her hair pulled back in a tight ball on the crown of her head. Still, she's attractive in a rough kind of way.

'You eat here often?'

The woman looks up at him with a glowering stare. Her thick jawline clenched.

Peter saying, 'Sorry, I'm just wondering...'

'Why the fuck would you wonder that?'

Peter sucks in an uncomfortable breath of air. He's going to tell her he's high up in the very franchise they're standing in. She's beneath him anyway. She looks uneducated. Probably one of those feminists. Screw her. He's got work to do. A top secret mission to find kidnappers. Peter smiles and waves her a 'sorry' gesture, stepping a couple of feet back.

A teenager boy in the Plucky's getup with bad acne scarring approaches the counter from the kitchen holding a bag with four take out boxes.

'Rose?'

The woman marches over and snatches the bag from the counter, walking past Peter without looking at him. Peter turns to watch her leave, getting a look to see if she has a nice ass. Instead, he finds Marion briskly walking through the doors toward him.

Marion says, 'Did you order this garbage? Knowing what crap they put in it?'

'I get it for free.'

Marion shakes his head. Disappointed. The mustang roars to life outside and reverses with speed into a 180-degree spin, screeching on the asphalt, then rockets off out of the car park toward the highway.

Peter looks at Marion's hand, clasping his phone.

'Who called?'

'Personal matter.' Marion sniffs the air and twitches his nose. An overpowering smell of bleach on the tiles. 'Let's talk to the manager. See if he's got any leads.'

Marion approaches the counter. The acne kid coming to life out of the 'robot staring into thin air' mode. His name tag reads "Chester", and it's pinned on lazily, hanging lopsided. A fake smile as he says 'Welcome to Plucky's Chicken Palace. What can I get you?'

'Hello Chester. I'd like to speak with the manager.'

'Is... is there a problem sir?'

'There's no problem. I just need to ask them a few questions.'

'Are you police?'

Marion stares at him deadpan a moment, then says, 'Military.'

Chester's eyes widen slightly. In the space of a few seconds his mind races from terrorists to aliens.

'I, uh... I'll go get him... sir.'

Chester disappears out the back. Marion leans over the counter, eying off the back food prep area. He spots an overweight Latino guy in his mid-twenties in a line chef uniform, standing next to a bubbling deep fryer. Staring at his phone screen and picking his ear. He pulls out a lump of ear wax, looks at it a moment like he's thinking of eating it, then flicks it on the floor. Marion's face one of disgust.

Seth appears, adjusting his bouffant hair, smiling his best manager smile.

'Hi. I'm Seth, the night manager. What can I get for you?'

'That man over there by the deep fryer.'

Seth looks back, then to Marion. 'That's Freddie. He's our night shift cook.'

'Freddie needs some serious training in health and safety. He was just picking his ear. Right by the food.'

Seth swallows, nervous, and says, 'Really? Well, that is unfortunate. I'll speak with him personally. In the meantime, I can offer you a fifteen percent discount on any food or beverage purchases.'

'Fifteen percent? To eat this shit you call food with a side of Freddie's bodily discharges? Why don't you throw in a cockroach to sweeten the deal?'

Peter stepping in, smiling and saying, 'We don't need a discount. We already get it free of charge.'

'Free? I can't really do that I'm afraid.'

Peter reaches into his back pocket and withdraws his wallet, taking out the platinum card and waves it in front of Seth.

Seth furrows his brows and says, 'What's that?'

'It's a Plucky's platinum card. You're a manager, how could you not know what this is? As a branch manager, you should be aware of every and all coupons, vouchers, memberships and accounts. This is a Plucky's Platinum card. The most important-'

Marion overtly sighs.

'Okay, enough of this. We need information.'

Seth scratching his head. Thinking these guys are both well dressed. They're definitely not from around here.

'I'm sorry, but, I don't know who you guys are. Are you some kind of police?' Looks Marion up and down. 'FBI or something?'

Marion says 'We work for Plucky's. The headquarters in New York City. I'm Marion Delaney, security. He's Peter, legal.' Motioning to Peter like he's an afterthought. 'We're wondering. Do you know who Reuben Wallace is?'

'Yeah, I know who Reuben is. He's an asshole.'

'What?!' Peter blurts out.

Marion staring at Seth intently. Thinking that this might be a good thing. If they have a tumultuous relationship, this man might be privy to Reuben's other enemies.

Peter shakes his head in bewilderment.

'Do you know to whom you are referring? Reuben Wallace made this company what it is. You wouldn't have a job if it weren't for that man. He's a living legend, show some respect, young man.'

'The dude pisses on the sign out on the highway, all the time. Sometimes takes a shit too. And I always have to clean it up.'

Seth digs in his polyester black pants and whips out his smartphone. 'I got footage on my phone. Wanna see?'

Peter waves both hands out in front of him and crossing his arms.

'No, no. That won't be necessary.'

'I will.'

Marion has his hand out to take the phone.

Peter looking over with consternation as Seth hands him the phone, telling him what button to press.

Peter doesn't need to see the video. He's known Reuben for fifteen years, give or take. Peter, then going by Lars Gronholt, met Ruby at a bar after a game between the Red Sox and the St Louis Cardinals; Ruby's team. Ruby was in a good mood because his team won. Peter looking dejected at the end of the bar. The two got chatting about their love of baseball and hunting. Peter was actually never really into hunting. His grandfather was, and would sometimes take him out to Maine in the spring to shoot deer. Peter knew enough to talk the talk. It wasn't long before Peter joined the legal team at Tasty Incorporated. Ruby taking Peter on the odd hunting trips. Peter not doing any actual shooting. Acting more like an assistant, cleaning his guns and getting him snacks. Peter making Ruby think of him like a son he never had, or wanted.

It was out in the New Hampshire wilderness one time when Ruby was refused service at a local bar due to his intoxication. Peter was forced to watch while Ruby climbed onto the bartender's pickup truck and took a dump on the hood. Ruby managed to climb back down and run back to their car. The bartender ran out with a softball bat. Thinking Peter was the culprit behind the truck stunt, he laid into Peter several times. One of the blows cracking a bone in Peter's elbow joint that forced him to wear his arm in a sling for months. The breaking of the bone doing lasting damage that Peter feels in the dense cold on occasion. Or when he's stressed.

Peter looks over at Marion, about to witness what Ruby is capable of on Seth's phone.

Marion stares at the phone screen in the palm of his hand. Brows furrowed. He watches as Ruby in his white suit hastily emerges from a limousine stopped on the side of the highway. The camera jump zooms in awkwardly to the base of the Plucky's sign as the figure reaches the thick red pole. Marion watches as Ruby unbuckles his pants and drops his pants, doing his number two's right then and there.

Jesus.

Marion looks over to Peter, who is staring at the ground with a traumatized visage, rubbing his elbow.

'Order up!' Freddie blandly calls out and sets a bag of food in the metal delivery slot.

Marion turns to Seth who has his hand out, waiting to get his phone back.

Marion saying, 'What are your intentions with this footage?'

'My intentions? Dude, I tried calling the head office. Multiple times. I tried to tell them one of their main guys was coming and pissing and taking dumps on his own company sign. I normally wouldn't care. But locals have been complaining. Families don't wanna see that kinda shit,

y'know? Like, literally don't wanna see shit. The crazy midget girl who
protests out there. We can all deal with that. But not some old guy
squatting one out on the busiest road this side of the country. And you
know what happened? They didn't want a piece of it. Didn't return my
calls. Or emails. I sent them the footage and they didn't reply. So I said
to hell with 'em. I'll deal with the old bastard myself. Now can I have
my phone back?'

Marion holds onto the phone, his manner and visage resolute.

'If you have no use for this footage, then why is it still on your
phone?'

'I was gonna upload it on YouTube or something. If he did it again.
Use it as a deterrent. I dunno.'

Marion presses the phone screen, lighting it up again. He taps the
screen a few times until he finds the delete option, then deletes the
clip. He navigates to the video collection library and starts scanning for
similar video clips.

Seth careens over the counter, trying to see what Marion is doing.
Concern growing on his face.

'Hey, what're you doing?'

Marion ignores Seth and continues scrolling down the screen with
his thumb, peering at the little thumbnails. Mostly videos of Seth using
a selfie stick as he drives different places on his Vespa.

'Hey, buddy, I said give me my phone back.'

Seth tries to reach over and grab it but the counter is too wide. He
slaps his hand angrily on the counter and strides around the side of it
to approach Marion. Peter watches on with growing agitation. His eyes
flick over to the bag of food sitting in the ready slot. His jowls fill with
saliva, wanting this conversation to be over so he can devour it.

Seth approaches Marion and swipes his hand out to grab the phone
from him. Marion stiffly turns away as he does.

'It's my phone asshole. Give it back!'

'I cannot allow you to have compromising footage of the company's oldest and beloved founders.'

'Then maybe he shouldn't compromise himself on his own beloved company.'

Seth tries to grab the phone again, but Marion swiftly turns away again. This is repeated a few times until Marion has almost done a 360 degree turn on the spot. Peter thinking that the both of them looking like siblings fighting over a toy.

Marion reaches the end of the video library. Satisfied, he holds the phone out. Seth snatches it angrily.

'I don't care who you are dude, you can't go through my phone like that. It's illegal.'

Peter steps over to join them, his arms out in an apologetic manner.

'Technically it is considered trespassing among other crimes under the Information Privacy Laws. However, under the Electronic Communications Privacy Act, there is, unfortunately for you, a loophole that caters for consent to be implied to any reading of materials correlating to any and all electronic communications once you accepted the employment with Tasty Incorporated, a company that practices surveillance of its employees relating to work practices. You are… were, in possession of electronic material that could be damaging to the organization, and such material was taken without consent of the party involved, who happens to be a high ranking board member. That, and you gave initial permission to my colleague here to look at said material when you willingly handed your phone to him.'

Seth looks up from the screen.

'He deleted my video.'

'My finger slipped. Sorry about that,' Marion says without a hint of apology.

'Perfectly admissible in court,' Peter adds.

Seth scoffs and shakes his head, walking back behind the counter, sluggishly grabbing the bag of food from the delivery slot and turns to dump it on the counter with repugnance.

'Here's your food.'

Seth looks in the bag. Two take out containers featuring Plucky the chicken logo. And a medium tub of sweet potato mash. Seth grabs the tub and holds it up.

'The potato mash is getting a little cold. Let me get you a fresh one.'

Peter smiles.

'Now that's the Plucky's attitude I've been looking for. Thank you.'

Seth walks swiftly to the back of house and puts the tub on the edge of a steel food preparation counter, motioning to it as he calls out to Freddie.

'Hey Freddie. Would you be so kind as to prepare a fresh mash for our guests from head office. Make it extra creamy.'

'Sure thing.'

Freddie rips off the lid and dumps the potato out into a trash can by his side. He takes a large metal scoop and digs it in to a large batch of fresh mash and dumps it into the tub. Freddie silently extracts a huge gump of saliva and lung butter from his jowls into his mouth. Hocking it up makes too much of a sound, so Freddie has acquired this skill when retribution is required for difficult customers. He lets the gooey bodily fluid mixture fall from his puckered lips like a giant water drop into the mash. He uses his finger to stir it in, then places the lid back on.

Seth walks back to the front counter and places the tub neatly back in the plastic bag.

Peter nods thankfully at Seth, who returns the gesture.

Marion steps closer to the counter, his hands clasped together formally.

'It appears you have somewhat of a problem with mister Wallace. That's perfectly understandable based on what I just saw. We're simply looking to resolve the issue permanently, so you won't have to deal with his...'

'Eccentricities,' Peter cuts in.

'His eccentricities,' Marion repeats. 'You have my word on that. So any information you may have on Reuben would help us considerably to reconcile it. Such as, does he have any associates you've seen him with, or that you know of? Do you know any locations he frequents? Does he have any enemies?'

'Yeah. Me.'

For about four seconds Marion does wonder if this man is involved in the extortion sting in some way. But a quick glance up and down of him for the tenth time, the acne faced Chester, the disgusting cook Freddie, and the state of this Plucky's outlet tells Marion this guy can't even manage a small take out joint, let alone a kidnapping plot.

'Once again, I'd like to reiterate that we're here to help you. So any information you give us will benefit you.'

Seth's eyes dart between the two men a moment. He could tell them that Reuben hangs out mostly at The Glass Half Full down the highway. But damn it if he's going to help these two assholes who come in swinging their dicks like they run the place. Deleting stuff off his phone without permission. Fuck these asshats.

'Look, guys, I wish I could help. But honestly, I know nothing about the guy. He always has a driver with him. But I bet you already know that. I've never really spoken to him. So, yeah. Sorry, wish I could be of more help.'

Peter watches Seth talk. The lack of body movement being one give-away he's lying. When engaging someone in a conversation it is natural to move your body around in a relaxed way. The only movement he made was he kept touching his mouth, another telltale sign. When people touch their lips, it means they're not disclosing everything they have. Peter bets he has more information. But for now, it's time to eat.

'That's okay Seth. Thanks for showing us the video. If we need to chat further, we'll be in touch.'

Peter grabs the plastic bags of food and turns to follow Marion out the door, then stops. He can't help himself. He turns to look back at Seth.

'Hey, Seth? Why are you not wearing your full uniform?'

'Huh?'

'Your hat. Where is it?'

'Oh, I ah… it's in the back. Why?'

'You are a representative of Plucky's Chicken Palace. It is a company requirement that you wear the full uniform while working.'

Peter lays a brochure to his Power of Persuasion master class on the counter, tapping his finger on it.

'Take a read of this too. If you sign up for the monthly newsletters, I might just forget about this uniform infraction.'

Peter winks at him with a grin, then turns on his heels, making a squeaking sound on the overly bleached tiles, and strides to the door.

Seth watching Peter walk out the door, illuminated by the headlights of the Tesla as the car engine comes to life with Marion now at the wheel. Seth scrunching up the brochure and pitching it like a baseball into the deep fryer. It sinks into the bubbling oil and begins to disintegrate.

CHAPTER FIFTEEN

A Casual Sit Down With Gentleman Wallace

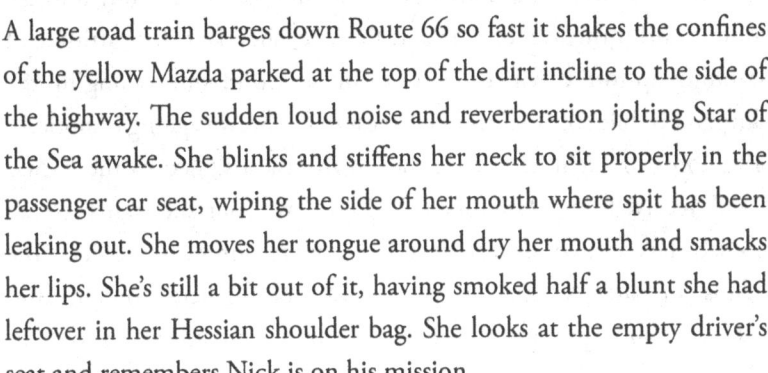

A large road train barges down Route 66 so fast it shakes the confines of the yellow Mazda parked at the top of the dirt incline to the side of the highway. The sudden loud noise and reverberation jolting Star of the Sea awake. She blinks and stiffens her neck to sit properly in the passenger car seat, wiping the side of her mouth where spit has been leaking out. She moves her tongue around dry her mouth and smacks her lips. She's still a bit out of it, having smoked half a blunt she had leftover in her Hessian shoulder bag. She looks at the empty driver's seat and remembers Nick is on his mission.

Star looks down at her late 1980's Casio digital watch on her left wrist. 'Damn it Nick', she thinks. He's been gone twenty-five minutes already. He should be back by now. Star shivers from gusts of cold desert wind penetrating the old car, folding her arms into her chest, wrapping her poncho around her tighter.

Star kind of feels bad the way she is stringing Nick along. It's for a good cause she reasons. If they can get the Holbrook Plucky's shut down due to food poisoning, Star and her Lords of Light tribe can move to the outlets in Flagstaff. Create an epidemic. The media will cover it. She can see the headlines now; "Plucky's Chicken Palace Poison Scandal!", "The Bird Flu is Back at Plucky's!", "Poison Scandal Pecking Away at Plucky's!" She giggles at that last one. Man, she would have made a good journalist if she wanted. That's where she met the Lords of Light elders, Eric and Reylene. The University of Arizona in Tucson, while she was in her final year of the Bachelor of Arts: Journalism: General Journalism Emphasis, she met the couple who were Teaching Aids in the College of Social & Behavioral Sciences.

Star desperately wanted to be a part of a club. A society. Always an outcast in her school days for being bullied about her height and her ancestry. And while Star didn't exactly a hundred percent buy into the more colorful theories of Eric and Reylene, she liked their attitude of standing up to the evil corporations in the world and waking up the dormant public spiritual consciousness to the horrors going unnoticed. The Lords of Light each have their own task assigned to them. Star hasn't received her "Assignment of Light" yet, but she wants it bad. So bad she's created one for herself in order to impress the Elders. The demise of Plucky's Chicken Palace. And it begins here. Tonight. And if Nick is but a pawn in the chess piece of her mission, then so be it. She plans to cut him off as soon as she gets what she wants. Nick isn't strong enough for the Lords of Light. He's a nice enough guy. But that's his problem. He's too nice. What would be nice is if he told her to shut the fuck up once in a while. Tell her not to smoke in his car, because he doesn't like it. Pull her hair when he's going down on her. Take charge for once, and not be such a sap.

Jeez, what is taking him so long? Another gust of wind cuts through the weatherworn rubber seals of the door making Star quiver again. That's it. Enough of sitting in this shit heap. She's going to have to handle this herself. Star angrily shuffles in her seat and picks up her shoulder bag, sticking the knitted strap over her shoulder. She pulls the old metal door handle down and pushes the creaky door, kicking it all the way open with her stubby legs.

Her worn out old New Balance sneakers with holes in them hitting the dirt next to a clump of hairy cacti. Star grabs the shoulder bag strap with one hand and strides down the small but steep dirt incline. Her right foot catches a mound of loose dirt and rocks, sending her foot slipping up into the air, and the rest of her body to fall back, landing on her ass and sliding several feet before managing to use her hands to stop herself. She sits a moment, looking at her now dirt covered hands.

A truck zooming past with high beams on making Star shield her eyes a moment, looking to the side. Her eyes fix on a lump in the dirt next to her. An unusual, shaped lump. Star leans over and pokes it with her index finger. The caked dirt breaking a little. Something cold and metallic under it. She uses three fingers to prod it again.

It's a gun.

Star dusts of the grip and picks it up, all the remaining dried dirt crumbling off it. Star studies the weapon under the moonlight glow. She recognizes it as a Colt .38 of some type. Her father and brothers avid gun enthusiasts.

One of her brothers, Bobby, a Marine, just got back from a deployment in Uzbekistan. Her favorite out of her three brothers. The one that picked on her less anyway. He used to take her out to the north of the Apache-Sitgreaves National Forest, right by Wiggins Crossing, to shoot cans and bottles with his different arsenal of handguns.

Star brushes off the excess dirt caught in the trigger loop, bullet chamber and top of the barrel. She pops the chamber open and more sand falls out. She shakes the bullets free. Four of them. She sticks them back in their little slots and clicks the chamber shut. Star stuffs the pistol in her bag and pushes off the incline to stand. She runs down the remaining decline to the side of the highway and toward the saloon.

Star carefully slinks up the stairs of The Glass, trying not to make any noise. When she approaches the door, she can see that a chain is wrapped around the old brass handles, padlocked shut. When she turns to leave, she can hear what sounds like shouting coming from inside. Star descends the stairs and dashes around the side of the building, past the big generator and to the back. The rear entrance is slightly ajar. She can hear more shouting coming from inside. Sounds heated. Maybe Nick is in some real trouble.

Star reaches in her bag and digs around a moment through the mess inside. Chapsticks. A frayed knitted scarf. Her rolling tobacco pouch. Himalayan prayer beads. Muesli bar wrappers. The canister of mace. A diary she rarely writes in, old, clipped news articles on Plucky's tucked in the back of it. A small tortoise shell she uses as an ashtray. There it is. The .38 revolver. She grips it tight in her right hand and steps through the door into the kitchen.

She looks down the long kitchen, past the industrial dishwasher, the fridge and the large chest freezer at the end next to the swinging doors. The shouting has stopped but she can still hear voices. She steps measuredly towards the doors to the main saloon. The sound of crashing furniture. Raised voices. Then someone says something about the difference between firing a gun and shooting a person. Star now at the swinging doors. She takes a deep breath and slowly pushes one of the doors open.

Star steps into a dimly lit hallway. She looks to her right, down the hall. Holy shit. Is that a coyote? Looks scared as hell. Poor thing. Star slowly puts the gun behind her back out of view of the animal, to not scare it.

Wait.

Why is there a fucking coyote in here?

Star turns and steps toward the main light source. She steps closer to the alcove leading to the main floor of the saloon. There's a scantily clad woman in heels holding a shotgun and a fat old man approaching her brandishing a meat cleaver. The girl must be that one Nick goes on about. Summer or whatever. Dressed like a glitzy prostitute. Ugh. She spots some big ass black dude in bad drag standing on the stage. Where is... there he is. Cowering on the floor, of course. Fucking Nick. Star sighs internally. The old man suddenly snatches the gun from the jazzed-up hooker and hurls the cleaver into the wall. Star watches from the shadows at the end of the bar as the old man slams the barrel of the shotgun into the girl's guts. Star stifles a laugh. The girl tumbles into the wall and falls to the floor. The old man points the gun right in her overly made-up face.

'Here. Let me show ya how it's done sweetheart.'

Christ, the old man is actually going to off this bitch. Better do something. Star doesn't want to be witness to a murder. She's got a fast food chain to destroy. She steps out and raises her arm in the air, pointing the revolver at the ceiling.

Nick yells out 'NO!'

Star squeezes the trigger.

BANG.

All eyes on her now. Except the hooker. She's still staring blankly into that shotgun barrel like she's waiting for the light at the end of the tunnel. The drag queen has fallen off the stage during the commotion. The coyote has seen and heard enough, the gunshot scaring her enough to bolt down the hall, through the kitchen doors and out the back.

Star's eyes flick to everyone in the room.

'What the shit is going on in here?!'

Nick grapples furniture to stand up quickly.

'Sue! Thank God you're here.'

'It's Star of the Sea idiot. And I came to see what was taking you so fucking long.'

Ruby turns toward Star. She drops her arm down and aims the revolver at Ruby.

'Drop it, dickwad.'

Ruby frowns. To him she looks like a little girl. Standing there in her Navajo poncho and wearing the woven headband with dangling black feathers. Her hair a huge, frazzled mop like she's been electrocuted. Her plump baby fat cheeks perfectly rounded on her olive skin face. Ruby looks her up and down like she was a circus clown, still moving to aim the gun at her.

BANG.

A bullet from her gun hits a wooden beam next to Ruby's head chipping off a little spray of wooden chips. Ruby looks at it then back at her, somewhat startled but still not lowering the gun.

'I'm not kidding around grandpa.'

Ruby glowers at her a moment, then starts to lower the shotgun aim to the floor.

CRACK. Ruby cops a piano keyboard to the back of the head and drops stone cold unconscious to the floor. The shotgun clattering across the old wooden floorboards. Dennis standing behind, holding the keyboard like it was a baseball bat.

'Been wanting to do that for a looooong time.'

Star twists her face with confusion, not expecting this tank of a man to have such a campy sounding voice. Well, he *is* wearing pink and gold make-up and sparkly high heels. But still.

'Put the… um… put the keyboard down.'

Dennis gently lays the keyboard on a table next to him. He immediately goes to Winter's side and strokes her hair.

'You okay sweetie?'

Winter looks up to him with her doe eyes, blinking slowly. Still in shock. She nods her head giving the indication she's somewhat okay.

Star watching them for a moment, then lowers the gun. Nick now by her side, placing a kiss on her mess of hair.

'Talk about lucky timing.'

'Lords of Light doesn't deal in luck. We are one with the Universe, and the Universe places us where we need to be.' Star motions to Ruby. 'Who's the douchenozzle? Why was he gonna kill her?'

Nick scratches his head with his long finger, giving a string of 'um's' and 'ah's', trying to figure out where to start. Star already becoming impatient. She steps over to ogle Ruby as he rolls over onto his back. Her strained expression starting to smooth out to a look of vague recognition.

'Wait a minute…', she reaches in her shoulder bag a moment, fumbling around, pulling out her journal. Star places the .38 on the table next to her and begins sifting through the cut-out articles on Plucky's until she finds the one she's after. It's a torn out magazine article. A 2011 New York Times piece about the history of the Plucky's empire. The main photograph accompanying the text is a big picture of Ruby, sitting in a throne-like Peacock wicker chair, dressed in his white suit and holding a fashionable white walking cane. A big hearty smile on his face. Star holds the glossy piece of paper out in front of her, eyes darting back and forth to Ruby and the article picture. A caption on the picture reads; "A Casual Sit Down with Gentleman Wallace." Her eyes starting to widen.

'Holy shit. It's... it's actually him.'

Star turns to look at Nick with a jaw dropping smile.

'Dude, it's the fucking man himself. Reuben Wallace. Lying right there. On the fucking floor in front of me! Can you believe it?!'

Nick is arching back and forth on his heels, his arms stiff by his sides and hands deep in his pockets.

'Yeah, I know.'

'Wait, what?'

She stuffs the journal back in her bag and picks the revolver back up from the table. She steps toward him with slow measured steps.

'You mean to tell me, that you've known about this guy being here this whole time?'

'Well, no. Not really. I mean, yeah I knew, but only until, like, yesterday.'

'And you didn't think to tell me? After all I've told you about my plan to take down Plucky's. And the head honcho himself is in town. It just, what? Slipped your fucking mind?'

'Look. I didn't think it, y'know, necessary?'

'Necessary? It's Reuben fucking Wallace!'

'What good does it do? Knowing he's here. What, you gonna kidnap him?'

Nick makes a pfffft sound, waving her off like she's crazy.

'That's exactly what I'm going to do.'

Star turns swiftly on her heels and marches over to the shotgun lying on the floor. She stuffs the revolver in her bag and stoops down, snatching up the shotgun.

Nick swallows hard, taking a step toward her.

'Are you crazy? I mean, lacing food with chemicals is one thing. But kidnapping? You've never kidnapped anyone before. That's, like, a major crime and shit. We could both go to jail for, like, life. I think.'

Dennis has helped Winter to her feet. She's still looking a bit dazed but coming back around. Dennis watching Star with trepidation, now that she has ownership of the shotgun.

Star says, 'Fuck putting that measly little backwater outlet out of business. Like it would really make a difference. No. Now we got General Wallace. The big cheese himself.'

Dennis giving her an impassive look. 'That's not the General. That's his son.'

'The fuck cares. He's my ticket to the inner circle. I'm gonna finally be a legit Lord of Light. Shit. This is big. If I deliver this animal torturer to the Elders... well, shit. They'll make me a fucking Elder too. They damn well should.'

Dennis frowns.

'What the hell are the Lords of Light?'

'You'll hear about us soon enough.'

Winter, now with some color coming back into her cheeks, clears her throat daintily.

'Listen Sweetie, I'm awful sorry, but Mister Wallace right there... well, he's in our care. My partner Rose will be back soon, and she made a deal with-'

'Fuck you and your deal rockabilly skank.'

Winter's lips part open and eyes crease, offended.

'Well now. That's just rude.'

Groaning. Ruby sits up, blinking erratically. He looks around at everyone. Dennis with his arm around Winter protectively. Star holding the shotgun with a determined expression. Nick standing behind her looking increasingly worried. Star turning the aim of the shotgun to Ruby.

'Nick, tie that fat asshole up,' Star says while using her head to motion to the roll of duct tape on the bar counter.

Nick looks over at the tape, then steps next to Star, talking in a lowered voice.

'Look, Star of the Sea, I think we should-'

'Don't think Nick. It's unbecoming of you,' Star's tone exhausted.

Ruby now using one of the chairs to pull himself up. Everyone watching with vacuous expressions as he struggles, grunting and groaning. Finally standing upright, red faced, Ruby looks to Star the shotgun in her possession. Looking silly to him. A little hippy girl with a weapon way too big for her.

'You ever shot anyone before, little girl?'

With an indolent expression, Star slightly adjusts her aim next to him and fires. The chair Ruby is leaning on explodes, sending wooden shards flying in all directions. The near deafening shotgun blast making Winter squeal and cover her ears. Dennis squeezes her into a protective hug. Nick steps back sticking his fingers in his ears even though it's too late. Ruby tumbles back down to the floor again. Yelling out in pain, as he writhes around in the fresh wood chips.

Star racks the pump, sending a smoking empty red shell out of the chamber and bouncing off the floor. She looks back over at the duct tape, and the box of shotgun shells next to it.

'Nick, I won't ask again. Get me the duct tape. And that box of shells while you're there.'

Without hesitation Nick spins on the balls of his feet and launches himself to a jog toward the bar. Ruby groans on the floor, propping himself up with an elbow, staring balefully at Star over his heaving stomach.

'You crazy little bitch! You could'a shot me!'

'I used to shoot pigs on my uncle's farm, old man. And they're harmless creatures.' She steps forward, pointing the gun down at him with one hand. 'So I got no problem shooting an animal like you.'

Star takes a step back, glancing at Winter and Dennis, and waves the gun in their direction.

'Same goes for you clowns.'

Nick returns with the tape and the shells. Star snatches the box of bullets and dumps them in her bag.

'Tie the bastard up.'

Nick looks at the tape in his hand, then to Ruby, gulps, then looks up to Winter. Those big puppy dog eyes. Looking so fearful and anguished right now. Poor thing. He wishes he could hug her. Tell her how-

'Nick! Fuck's sake. Tie him up!'

Nick skips to attention and lurches forward, stooping down by Ruby's side. He uses his fingernails to dig into the end of the tape and unsticks a little corner of it. He pulls a long strand off, looking up at Winter again.

'I'm sorry Miss Bloom.'

Winter manages a weak little grin.

'That's okay sweetie. You gotta do what you gotta do. For the ones you love.'

She follows that up with a suggestive little wink. Nick wondering what she meant by that wink. She's winked at him before. She winks at everyone. But this felt different. Like she was trying to tell him something.

Star stamps her foot aggressively on the floorboards. Nick jumps and takes the strand of tape in his teeth and bites it off. He leans over and takes Ruby's wrist, helping him to sit up.

'I'm gonna have to tape your hands now Mister Wallace, if that's okay.'

'It's not fucking okay.'

Nick looks at Star, who motions for him to get to it, snapping her fingers and pointing to Ruby. Nick sighs and starts to wrap Ruby's wrists together.

Star stands at the foot of the stairs leading to The Glass Half Full. Shotgun dangling loosely in her grasp. Ruby stands next to her, once again wrapped in duct tape. Two strips across his mouth, formed into an 'X'. Ruby is red faced and trying to talk to her through the tape.

Headlights from Nick's Mazda light them both up at the car speeds toward them and skids to halt. Nick jumps out of the car and rounds the vehicle to the back, opening the trunk. Star nudges Ruby in the back with the barrel of the shotgun. He doesn't move out of spite. Star rolls her eyes. She nudges harder, the blunt metal digging into his spine. Ruby starts to walk toward the car, muttering all kinds of obscenities under the tape. Ruby stops at the trunk, standing stiff with defiance. Star pokes him with the gun. He shakes his head 'no'. She shoves him harder. He eyes her with contempt, unmoving.

'Get in the trunk. I don't have time for this bullshit.'

Ruby tries to tell her that he absolutely will not stand for this kind of treatment. He has never, and will never, climb into the trunk of a car. Especially a piece of shit car like this. All Star hears is 'mmfffmm-mfffmmffmfmfmf'.

'I'm guessing you have a problem with getting in the trunk. Which is fine. I get it. But the thing is dude, I have a shotgun, and you don't. And yes, I'm smart enough to know that you know that I know that it would be perfunctory to kill you to achieve my goal. And you'd be right. But, here's the deal bro. I can hurt you, and that won't affect shit. Except you'll be walking around limping the rest of the short time you have left on this planet. A limp that occurred when I take the barrel of this shotgun in my firm grasp, and swing it like a baseball bat, snapping your knee in three different places with the wooden handle. Additionally, since your company productively engages in the slaughter of innocent animals, I have a pertinent disdain for you and what you represent. So, the longer we stand here, the more I fantasize about putting you in indefinite pain for your twilight years.' Star flicks the dangling string from her headband back over her shoulder. 'Get in the fucking trunk.'

Ruby looks at her for a brief moment, then turns and climbs in the rubbery carpet smelling space. He sits on the edge of the trunk, then shimmies backward inside, arms bound, getting into the fetal position. Star doesn't wait for him to get comfortable and slams the trunk shut, marching to the passenger side.

Nick is looking at the saloon with a sense of longing. Hoping that Winter will forgive him. If only she knew the bigger picture. The statement they're about to make to the world. The fight they are bring to-

'Nick, we gotta go!'

Nick nods with compliance and dashes to the driver's side and hops in. He tugs the rigid gear stick into second drive and floors the accelerator. The car tires spin on the dirt and the car shoots off down the dirt driveway toward the highway.

The coyote sits in the desert darkness, watching the yellow car zoom down Route 66. She sniffs the air. A familiar scent drifting in the wind. The coyote sticks her nose in the air and breathes in. The scent stronger now, she can recognize it. She looks over to find the human who trapped her in the pantry. She's running through the cold desert air toward the saloon. The coyote sticks her tail between her legs and scampers off into the darkness.

CHAPTER SIXTEEN

Sounds Of A Dying Cat

The salty pungent aroma of deep-fried chicken and sweet potato mash linger heavily in the small Tesla. Peter sucks the meat off the bone with a slurping sound, eyeing it off after every attempt to make sure he's getting every last square millimeter of meat. He occasionally dips the bone into the tub of mash and uses it like a spoon to stuff it in his mouth. Bits of it smeared around his lips and mouth, along with chicken grease. Marion can't help but occasionally side glance at him, further feeding his disgust of this man.

Peter scrapes the remaining mash out of the container using his index finger to wipe around the inner sides, collecting all that's left and sticking it his mouth, sucking it all off. Peter then licks all his fingers clean, leaning forward slightly to wipe whatever grease is left from his fingertips onto the underside of the passenger chair, pretending to scratch his leg, thinking Marion didn't notice. But he did.

Peter closes the takeout box in his lap with several chicken bones inside that have been stripped of any semblance of flesh. He places the container in the plastic bag with the other containers. Marion watches with his peripheral vision as Peter presses a button on the side of his door, the window whirs down, strong gushes of air whipping around the cabin of the car, Peter's tie and hair flaying around wildly. Peter languidly tosses the Plucky's bag out of the car. The containers all fly out of the bag and land all over the highway behind them. The sudden move making Marion do a double take. Peter puts the window back up returning peace back inside the car, flattening his tie back into place.

'Did you have to do that? Toss your garbage out the window like that.'

'I thought you said you weren't an environmentalist.'

'No, I didn't say that. I said the Tesla was all the rental company had.' Marion wincing from a set of high beams from the inconsiderate driver of the pick-up truck cruising past on the other side of the road. 'I'm no environmental crusader. But there's a difference between being lazy, and there's being an asshole, Lars.'

Peter shrugs carelessly.

'My name is Peter. And we're in a Tesla, so-' Peter's eyes widen, and he sits forward in his chair, the seatbelt stopping him tight across his torso. 'Pull over! Quick!'

Marion looks ahead through the windshield trying to see whatever it is he's spotted but can't see anything. Could be a lead, better safe than sorry. Marion jerks the steering wheel and the car cruises off the road onto the crunchy gravel dirt and hits the brakes.

Marion peers around through the windshield again. Nothing except for... wait. What's that? It looks like a building about 25 yards from the road. A little dirt track leading to it, overgrown with cacti and pink and yellow Dudleya plants. Marion can see it better now. It's a near dilapidated old chapel. Chipped white paint barely clinging on to weatherworn planks of wood. Not a very large building. Maybe enough to fit about fifty to sixty people in there on a good day. But this chapel hasn't had a good day in quite some time. It looks abandoned. The steeple is battered. Half sunk into the structure, the cross at the top lopsided and pointing at a 30-degree angle to the left side. Spray paint graffiti on the sides and on the crudely boarded up door. Marion looks at Peter, who opens his door to step out.

'I don't get it. It's just a rundown old chapel.'

'Just wait here a minute.'

Peter is out of the car and slams the door. Marion watches him trudge through plants into the headlights and toward the deserted structure, then looks at his watch impatiently, wanting to get to Reuben's home as soon as possible. Jillian told him that he gets around in a limousine. He has a driver named Dennis Coleman. Dennis apparently also acts partly as a bodyguard. Marion reviewed his file on his way to the airport. Former boxer. Six foot one. Too big for a woman to overpower.

Marion looks through the windshield toward the chapel again. Peter is now at the front door using his hands to try and pry off the planks of timber nailed to it.

Marion now wondering if maybe this guy Dennis had a plan like this brewing for a while. Reuben isn't known for his generosity. And if he's willing to defecate on public property, then he's likely not the best employer in the world. Which means Dennis more than likely has it in for the old coot. With his... girlfriend? Yes, that works. That's why she does all the talking. Dennis's voice would be too recognizable. Well played. If he has a girlfriend, even a business partner, there will be evidence of that in Dennis's lodgings. That's where they should have gone first. Not that Plucky's diner. That was a big waste of time. Just like right now. What the hell is that moron Peter up to?

Marion peers over the headlights toward the chapel. He can see Peter in his navy plaid suit examining a dirt stained window on the side of the chapel, hands on his hips. Marion watches as Peter takes a couple of steps to his left and picks up a large rock, gripping it in his hand tightly. He steps back over to stand under the window, maybe a few feet higher than him. What's he going to-

Smash! Marion watches with stupefaction as Peter launches the rock into the window, shattering the thin glass into pieces. Peter picks up another rock and uses it to smash off the remaining jagged glass pieces off the bottom of the windowsill. He grips onto the window ledge and clambers up and through the window.

'To hell with this,' Marion mutters under his breath as he slams the auto gear box into reverse and stamps his foot down on the accelerator. Marion throws the gear stick into drive, and the car hurtles off down Route 66 in the direction of Ruby's home.

The interior of the chapel is dark and dusty. Ten pews, five side-by-side from the door to the altar, all covered in red dirt and dust from windstorms that have infiltrated through two broken windows on the other side of the building. Sand all over the old creaky wooden floorboards. The front door partially obstructed by broken shards of wood sticking down from the ceiling from the half-concaved steeple above. The altar nothing but a cheap wooden podium with a bong sitting on top made from a plastic soda bottle and six inches of garden hose. A window above overlooking the podium, caked in dirt.

Peter now inside the chapel, dusting himself off and looking around through the soft moonlight coming through the windows. He takes out his cell phone and presses the home button, lighting up the screen. He uses the phone as a makeshift flashlight, stepping carefully through the dust coated pews. He walks over what looks like a trap door, kicking it a few times.

Peter walks up to the podium, Pabst beer cans littered around it. Peter shines his phone light on the homemade bong. The Mountain Dew ribbon still on it. The inside covered with a thick layer of black smoke tar. Peter holds his illuminated phone over the podium top. Next to the bong are clearly legible words scraped into the wood. It reads; "LORDS OF LIGHT WILL TAKE BACK THE NIGHT."

Peter lowers the phone down the length of the podium, lighting up a shelf under the top of it. There's a thick book inside covered in folded towels. He reaches in and pulls it out. It's covered with dust and dirt, but it's just what he's after.

A copy of the Bible.

A nice brown leather bound one. Peter grins with satisfaction. He dusts it off with his hand and puts it under his arm, making his way back to the broken window he came in from. He tosses the Bible through the frame and onto the broken glass covered ground outside. He makes a few false starts to climb through the window, realizing it was easier to get in than to get out. He marches over to the main doors, kicking the one accessible side a few times. No luck. He pulls out his cell phone again to call Marion. Standing in the pale lit room, in near darkness as the phone rings out, twice. Whey isn't he answering? Peter strides back to the broken window and peers out. The car is gone. What the bejesus? Where is Marion?!

Peter remembers the little trapdoor. He dashes over to it and digs his fingers in the little hole and unlatches it, pulling the door up. He shines his phone light down into the darkness. Shrubs and grass. Peter doesn't want to dirty his suit, but he has no choice. He places his phone on the floor as he carefully climbs down into the hole, his torso almost too big for it. Peter thinking that he should watch his diet more.

The trapdoor slams shut, the latch locking back into place. Peter, now on all fours under the chapel, crawls toward the moonlit ground several feet away, pricking himself on a few cacti on the way. He makes it out from under the structure and dusts himself off. Patting himself down, he realizes he left his phone in there. Darn it. The trapdoor won't open from the outside.

He looks back up at the broken window, contemplating climbing back in to get his phone. His joints sore now. His back now harking up with fresh dull aching. No, the phone is not worth it, he muses. He'll just buy another one tomorrow.

Peter marches around the building to the other side and leans over to grab his Bible from the bed of broken window glass on the ground.

Peter looks around the dark moonlit landscape for the Tesla. Nothing except a light mist blanketing the dirt. A mixture of dead and flourishing trees.

Peter looks to the highway as a truck roars past. The side of it bearing an advertisement for Papa John's Pizza, the text "Are You Hungry?" over pictures of pepperoni pizzas. Peter thinking he could definitely eat a pizza right now. Bible in hand and a pout on his face, Peter starts trudging toward the highway.

Peter reaches the edge of the road, looking both ways. A few cars and a truck zoom by. Peter watches as a 1960's aqua blue Vespa cruises by. He waves his arms for the driver to pull over, realizing as he goes by that the driver is Seth, the Plucky's manager. Peter now excited, thinking he'll stop because they're acquainted. Seth turns his head and regards Peter with an impassive look and keeps on going.

'I'll have you fired you little twerp!' Peter calls after him.

Peter sighs and rubs his face. He looks in the direction of Holbrook. He can see the lights from town softly touching the night sky in the distance. Maybe ten miles, give or take. He would call a cab or Uber if his phone wasn't in the dusty confines of that ratty old church. Darn it. He decides to start walking back toward town, sticking his thumb out in the air, hoping a good Samaritan will come his way and give him a ride in that direction.

The small mansion is an impressive looking property. Situated on the outskirts of Holbrook on the cusp of a large sprawling desert, it's a steep cut alongside a granite cliff. A mixture of smooth light brown sandstone and granite blocks. The Tesla cruises silently up the cobblestone driveway winding up to the mansion. Marion cruises into a car parking bay and parks in the shadows. He slinks around the house looking for an inconspicuous way in.

Eventually he finds a way in.

Marion steps quietly through the sleek modern kitchen. Stainless steel stove and marble counters. Clean as a whistle. Four different newspapers from different parts of the country neatly arranged on the main counter.

Marion wears black leather gloves, tightly fitted on his long skinny fingers. He has his Beretta pistol in one hand, his arm stiff and ready to bring up to aim and fire quickly, should he come across the kidnappers.

It wasn't difficult to gain access to the mansion. He picked the lock of a back door to the laundry using his leather cased 32 tool pick set. After entering Marion dismantled the alarm keypad and tripped the wire, rendering it useless. He quickly located the source of the CCTV camera connection and switched that off as well, deleting the last hour of footage while he was at it. No sense in anyone knowing he was here. When he kills these kidnappers there's more than likely going to be a follow up. Unless he can erase all evidence of it. Do it nice and quiet.

No witnesses. Even Peter. Marion especially looking forward to taking him out. But he's got to do the kidnappers first.

Marion slinks down a long open corridor, the floors and pillars white marble. The house separated in parts, the passage spaces drift from indoor to outdoor to indoor, bridged by trickling water features and medium sized banana trees. The furniture in most rooms old world Mexican themed.

The house is silent. Not a trace of anyone here. Marion ascends the infinity stairs up to the next level. Marion reaches the master bedroom on the second floor, carefully opening it, dramatically creeping in with gun at the ready, feeling like an FBI agent in the movies.

No one up here.

A king size bed sits at the end near a door to an ensuite. A sparsely decorated room. Old framed paintings of the American Civil War battle scenes. One big table featuring a large miniature Civil War battlefield. A prized piece at the hands of Ruby. The Battle of Fredericksburg. Marion can't help but admire the craftsmanship and dedication this must have taken.

Marion checks out the ensuite and walk-in closet, then the rest of the second floor which consists of a billiards room with a spacious curved balcony looking out onto the sprawling desert plain.

Marion makes his way back downstairs, keeping close to the walls and shadows as best he can. His adrenaline pumping being out in the field like this. He passes a large oval mirror with intricate carved gold metal framing. He watches himself with his gun drawn, looking all cool, like he was CIA on a mission to save the President. He stops in front of the mirror a moment, looking himself up and down, admiring his look and demeanor, then moves on.

Marion is in the back wing of the house, two tucked away rooms which he figures are for employees. One is basic. A punching bag in the corner and a weight set. A few framed posters on the wall of old Hollywood starlets, the likes of Grace Kelly and Ginger Rogers. There's music instruments in the other corner. A stand for paper music notes. A large wardrobe. He opens it to find a neat collection of dark suits. This must be the driver, he thinks. He goes through Dennis's drawers. Nothing of real interest. No weapons. Every item of clothing immaculately arranged and folded. Marion is curious that there's are some large women's clothes. Cocktail singer dresses. Even wigs of varying colors arranged neatly on foam mannequin heads. Likely belongs to his girlfriend. Must be a big lady like him.

Turning up nothing, Marion moves on to the next room. The Maid's. Plain. A few Mexican decorations and trinkets, but otherwise bare and tidy. Marion is disappointed after he cases the four guest bedrooms on the other side of the house and turns up nothing, or rather, no one. Leaving him to the last room. The huge reading room.

Marion stands in the middle of the ostentatious library, clicking on a lamp stand by pulling the dangling lace cord. His gaze falls on a mahogany coffee table stand next to the gaudy leopard skin armchair. Cardboard boxes all around the chair filled with files and folders. What has Marion's newfound interest, is a manila folder resting on the table stand, a printout on top. Marion moves over to the little table to have a gander, thinking it odd to have boxes filled with folders, and this is the one that has been selected. A special one. Marion picks up the piece of paper on top of the folder. It's a printout of an airplane ticket. United Airlines flight 230 from Flagstaff Pulliam Airport to John F. Kennedy Airport New York. Flight time was for 630pm earlier tonight. The date of purchase was two days ago. Before Lance and Clare died in the bath incident. Marion very much intrigued now that Reuben was on his way back to New York and Jillian had no idea.

Marion opens the manila folder and looks it over. He's got the mind for numbers, and it doesn't take him long to figure out that figures have been toyed with, and the main linking factor on these pages is Jillian's signature. Marion realizing now that Reuben has Jillian on the ropes, and he was just about to go take her down of her high perch. Marion becoming somewhat impressed by Reuben now. He thinks about the ramifications of this new information. If Jillian goes down, then Reuben will no doubt take her place at the head of the company. Based on what Marion has seen and heard of this man so far, he is a cantankerous callous fellow filled with spite and alcohol. The guy shits on the side of the road after all. What kind of a man sees that as any kind of justice? He doesn't sound healthy, and he's old, which means he won't likely be alive for too much longer.

Jillian, who Marion believes is a psychotic bitch, is at least straightforward. She's ambitious and loyal if you are on her side. Marion now weighing up his options. If Reuben is head of Tasty Incorporated again, he will clean out anyone who has any agreements or attachments to Jillian's regime. Just out of pure spite. If Jillian remains in her spot, she will honor her agreement to him and boost Duke Security's interests. Marion figures it's a no-brainer.

Marion closes the beige folder and tucks it under his arm as he briskly exits,

Walking down the long marble hall, past a giant stone ball on a pillar, and enters another corridor that takes him to a patio area overlooking a long black pebble tech pool below. The water shimmying from the bright patio lights. Marion didn't turn them on. Maybe they're on a sensor, he figures.

Marion takes the manila folder from under his arm and sparks a BBQ lighter from the patio table. He holds it to the corner of the folder, the flame licking the thin cardboard. Marion snaps the lighter shut and pockets it, not taking his eyes off the burning folder he's holding by the top corner in the pinch of his fingers. The folder now completely consumed by fire. Marion holds it by his fingertips as long as he can before he feels the stinging heat of the growing flame. He holds it over the twisting iron patio railing and lets it drop down to the pool below. Marion watches the fireball sail loftily through the air into the pool, the water quickly consuming the fire until all that's left is the soft floating black remains of what used to be cardboard and paper. Marion stays there a moment, momentarily drunk off his pride. Knowing he did a good thing here. Jillian will be pleased.

Marion turns to leave and then stops in his tracks. He hears something. Like a cat. A dying cat in some trouble. It's coming from over the edge of the patio balcony on the other side. Marion walks past the wooden four-piece outdoor table and chair setting to the side of the patio and grips the railing, looking down.

The pool is attached to a jacuzzi by a thin passage. The jacuzzi partially covered by an alcove. Not covered enough for Marion to see two people inside. A man, mid 40's, in good shape, and plump woman in her late 30's. Both Hispanic. She's naked, on her knees gripping the sides of the jacuzzi while the man, also naked, has her waist in his grip and is penetrating her from behind. The water rippling around them. The loud moans are the source of what he thought was a dying cat, no doubt.

Marion watches curiously a moment. Are these the kidnappers? It doesn't fit with his theory, about the driver and his girlfriend. But he could have been wrong. This is Reuben's home and these two are screwing in his pool. The woman looks up and locks eyes with Marion and screams. The man stops thrusting and looks up, also spotting Marion. They both awkwardly grapple around to hide themselves under the other side of the alcove.

Marion runs down the corridor, finds the stairs leading to the pool area and barges out next to a glass table and cast-iron chairs. He withdraws the Beretta from its holster and grips it with both hands as he approaches the jacuzzi. The couple are now wearing towels, frantically cleaning up take-out food, wine bottles and glasses. The woman turning around as Marion approaches, her eyes going wide noticing the gun in his hands.

'Is okay, is okay! I work here!'

The man now coming to her side, also ogling the gun. Both of them wearing light green towels and looking afraid.

'We are employee's here, sir. I can show you proof,' says the man.

'Are you police?' says the woman.

Marion aiming his gun in their general direction. His eyes steely and all business.

'Where is your employer?'

'Misser Wallace? His gone to New York. He fly out tonight. He say he's no back for a few days,' says the man.

'What do you do here?'

'I clean,' she says.

'I do the garden. Cut the grass.'

Marion realizes they may be just that. The maid and the landscaper getting their rocks off while the big cheese is out of town. He lowers his gun, though, still slowly stepping toward them.

'You haven't heard from him?'

'No. He lef today. He go to New York citay. Say he get back Monday.'

The maid now a little more relaxed and curious.

'Misser Wallace okay?'

Marion eyes them circumspectly. Two clueless dolts whose only thrill in life is to fornicate in their boss's pool, which he probably never uses anyway. It's best they not know the situation. They might make phone calls. To friends or family. The media might get wind of it. The police will then get involved. Jillian will be displeased. They are now officially witnesses. Can't have that. He did take out the CCTV. He's left no fingerprints. He didn't tell anyone he was coming here. No trace of him here at all.

'S'cuse me sir, is Misser Wallace in trouble?' says the landscaper.

Both of them pulling their towels tighter, growing uncomfortable.

'I am the police. Mister Wallace is fine. I was in the area and I got a call. One of the alarms was triggered here and I came to check it out. I think it was a… coyote.'

The landscaper seems to visibly loosen up. The maid remains a little skeptical. Her eyes still strong on the gun. And his gloves. She's wondering now why a cop would be wearing a JC Penny black suit and tie, and leather gloves.

'Can I see your badge, sir?'

The maid sounding reluctant to say that. Her landscaper lover looking at her like she shouldn't have said it. Marion knows they are both very suspicious now.

The landscaper says, 'Is okay sir. We don need to see you badge. All is good here. We have everything in control. Thank you.'

He follows that up with a big smile and puts his arm around the maid.

Marion takes a sharp breath and exhales loudly through his long narrow nostrils.

'Have either of you seen anything suspicious around here in the last twenty-four hours?'

They both look at each other quizzically a moment, then they look back to him.

'No sir, nothing.'

The maid adding 'We will let you know if we see anything.' Wanting him to leave now. Her eyes still flicking uncomfortably to the gun.

Marion says, 'We have reason to believe that there are criminals in the area. Keep inside as much as possible. We'll let you know if anything happens.'

'Criminals?' The maid already regretting asking. The landscaper darts her a quick mindful glance.

'Nothing too serious. Opportunistic burglars. That's all.'

They both nod slowly and rigidly.

Marion holsters his gun slowly, eyeing them down. Playing the cop part well, he reckons. He scratches the light stubble on his chin slowly.

'One more thing. Do either of you know if Mister Wallace has a place he likes to go? Any places he frequents?'

The maid looks to the landscaper. He looks at her helplessly. She shrugs and faces Marion.

'Yes. He always at The Glass Halve Full.'

Marion takes his fingers away from his chin. A spark in his eyes.

'The... Glass Half Full?'

The maid nods enthusiastically, eager to please.

'Yes, yes. It is a bar. Misser Wallace always there. Almos every night. He sometime go hunting. But always at the bar.'

Marion takes a deep breath, trying his best to not let them see how excited he has become. Finally, something he can work with. A bar. Of course. A known boozer.

'Does he go to any other bars, or just that one?'

The landscaper wanting to seem helpful too.

'Always that one.'

And there it is. Bingo.

'You've both been very helpful. Thank you. Have a nice evening.'

He nods to them cordially, then turns swiftly on his heels and marches away. He wonders if he made a convincing cop. Their expressions were somewhat fearful. People generally are afraid of the police, even when they haven't done anything illegal. It's a common reaction. He noticed the maid kept looking at his gun. Like she didn't trust him. They know he's heading to this Glass Half Full bar now. What if they decide to call the police to check up and make sure they sent a man over? Then he's sprung. Next thing they'll send the cops after him. Slap breaking and entering charges on him. Jeopardize the whole mission. Who's going to finish it off if he gets pinched by the cops? Peter? No damn way.

Marion pulls the Beretta from the hostler, spins around, aims, and fires two shots into the maid's chest. Another two in the landscaper. They didn't get time to let out a scream or even a whimper. Both of them jolted back a little and fall to the ground limp.

They didn't land in the water like he expected. The gunshots still echoing in his ears as he strides to their dead bodies. Their faces frozen with shock. The maid's towel has come loose and is half off her body. The fat rolls around her stomach exposed. Marion pulls a chair over and sits down, staring at the two dead people. Mesmerized.

He's never killed anyone before. He's always wanted to, and for some reason, it's not what he expected. He still feels hollow where he thought he wouldn't. He starts to figure it's because this whole scenario was unexpected. These two people. He really wanted it to be the kidnappers. Bad people who deserved it. He stares at the half naked woman, blood oozing around her flabby corpse. They are employees. They should not have been using the pool to have their dirty sex in. Disrespectful. Deceitful. Yes, if they hadn't of been here drinking wine and fornicating where they shouldn't, this wouldn't have happened to them.

Satisfied with his justification, Marion stands up and holsters the Beretta. He takes one last look at his ill-fated victims and marches steadfast back upstairs into the house, turning the alarm back on the way it was, and locking the back door he came in from. Marion feeling quite confident now. All he has to do is kill the kidnappers. Put a couple of bullets in Peter for good measure. And maybe Ruby.

Marion is in the Tesla driving back down the cobblestone driveway. His hands-free headset on, he talks on the phone to Jillian's assistant, Cassandra.

'Do you know when she'll be available?'

Cassandra is at Vanguard Wine Bar, Upper West Side Manhattan, sipping on a Chilean Carmenere at a table by the back under a framed Bridget Bardot poster. Marion called Jillian but the call was diverted to Cassandra, who told him that she's incapacitated.

'I couldn't tell you I'm afraid. It's a personal affair.'

'Tell her to call me back as soon as she can. I've made some unexpected progress. She'll want to hear it.'

'I'll be sure to pass the message along, Mister Delaney.'

Cassandra hangs up just as she spots her Tinder date coming through the door. Jillian didn't tell her when she was getting back. She took a private jet to the other side of the country. Cassandra's primary instruction is not to tell a soul that she's on her way to, as she put it, 'that faggot ass town in Arizona.'

CHAPTER SEVENTEEN

Knock On Wood

The lit up Plucky's sign grows increasingly distant in the rearview mirror of Rose's mustang. She's got her fresh boxed chicken in a thin plastic bag on the passenger seat. The smell of the chicken getting stronger now. Rose thinks it's time for some cinnamon gum to counter the smell of the deep fried crap. She leans over to the glove box and opens it, reaching in for the pack of gum she knows is in there somewhere. Her hand feeling around, can't quite seem to find it. A pothole in the road makes the car shudder. She looks at the road quickly, doesn't see anything coming, then leans back over to allow better reach into the compartment. All she can feel are registration papers, a drink bottle, the .44 Magnum revolver, some of Winter's make-up stuff. Her fingers fall on the pack of gum. Got it.

BAAAAAWWWWWW. The loud sound of a truck horn. Rose sits bolt upright as headlights flood the cabin of the car, having drifted to the other lane. She instinctively yanks the steering wheel to a hard left and swerves out of the way of an oncoming truck.

The mustang hits the gravel off the road and slides to the side, drifting for a moment as Rose tries desperately to pull the wheel to straighten the car and slams the brakes. It's too late. The mustang's front tires hit a raised embankment and the car careens to the side, the built up speed making it climb the embankment a little more until the combined weight and speed of the car cause it to lose balance and flip over completely.

Rose is banged around a little as the car flips and lands on the roof, sliding across the dirt several yards and comes to a stop. Rose, hanging in her seatbelt upside down, takes a small moment to process what just happened and checks herself for injuries. She's good. Just a little dazed and in shock. She looks up at the rearview mirror, the glass now cracked. Rose looking at her spliced reflection, thinking this isn't good at all. A broken mirror is a stock standard omen for bad luck. Anxiety swelling in her head like someone is blowing a balloon in there. She shakes her head, fighting it off. Not now. Not now. NOT NOW.

Rose plants her hand on the roof and unclips her seatbelt. She grunts as she contorts her body to sit on the roof, upright. She looks around, spots the take-out bag. Chicken and mash has spilled all over the passenger side. Rose takes the near empty plastic bag and shoves as many pieces of fried chicken as she can find into the bag. Rose also grabs the .44 Magnum and shoves it in the bag with the chicken. She pulls the lever to the driver's door and kicks it open with both legs. Rose makes grunting sounds as she climbs out of the car and onto the dirt of the incline.

Rose stands up and stretches, making sure she hasn't pulled a muscle. Chunks of hair stemming out messily from her hair bun. Satisfied, she starts running, plastic bag in hand, across the highway. She's maybe a few miles from the saloon she reckons. Rose hotfoots it across the road, looking over at the truck that nearly collided with her, now pulled over about 20 yards up the road. The driver out of his cabin and starting to walk toward the mustang. He's a silhouette against the rear truck lights. He sees Rose and stops, looking confused as she runs with her bag across the highway and onto the dirt on the other side.

'It's all good man! I'm okay! I'm fine!'

Rose now running in the darkness of the desert in her sandals, feeling the pricks from the odd plant and cactus on her feet and ankles. Rose realizing now that she could have asked that trucker for a ride to the saloon. Too late now, she's built up good traction. The adrenaline kicking in from the post-shock of the accident. She slows to a jog for a while, stops to catch her breath every so often, and keeps running through the desert parallel to the highway, a half mile out. Thinking of her brave Winter. Poor girl, having to wait this long for her to get back. Winter's smiling face giving Rose motivation to keep running.

Rose can see the dark outline of the building as she races toward the saloon.

'Good', she thinks. No new cars outside. No random visitors.

There's two pick-up trucks at the start of the driveway, both reading the 'go away' sign Rose made. The two cars turning and driving back onto the highway. Rose slows her full pelt running into a lazy jog, arms flailing everywhere, catching her breath back. She reaches the back door and wonders why it's open. Rose reaches in the bag of chicken and pulls out the gun. The butt slimy to hold from all the chicken grease it was been marinated in during her little cross-country adventure just now.

'Fuck me,' Rose says under her breath in disbelief.

Rose is now at the pantry staring inside. The Jell-O powder everywhere. Coyote shit and piss. Ripped up paper towels. Looks like a clown exploded in here. Rose turns and dashes through the kitchen and bursts through the swinging doors, coming to a skidding stop next to the end of the bar counter. She drops the bag of chicken at her feet. Her jaw drops. In the middle of the main floor of the saloon is Winter and Dennis tied up, back-to-back on chairs, with duct tape.

'What the ever loving fuck?!'

Winter and Dennis are trying to talk frantically through the duct tape over their mouths. Two strips formed into an 'X'. Rose dashes over to them, shoving the Magnum in the back of her pants, and claws frenziedly at the tape, tearing off the mouth strips first.

Winter lets out a gasp of air. She looks down to Rose's feet. Bloody and scratched up from the desert run.

'Honeybee! Oh my God! Your feet! Those poor little piggies.'

'They're okay. A million scratches, but they're just little ones. I'll clean 'em up and bandage 'em no problem. These little piggys'll be back at the market in no time. What happened here?'

Winter's eyes turn sad. She looks down at her knees as Rose peels tape off them.

'I'm sorry Honeybee. Honestly I am.'

Rose stops a moment to plant a sloppy kiss on Winter's lips. She affectionately rubs the side of Winter's cheek with her thumb.

'Don't you dare be sorry baby. Never.'

Rose rips the tape off both of them, a little hesitant with Dennis. But seeing as though he's dressed like a woman, and no doubt Winter had something to do with it, she obliges. Rose now noticing that the gown and bra exposed underneath are hers. Winter is up, checking to see if there's any damage from the tape on her clothes or affected her nails. Dennis straightening out the gown and fixing the blonde wig on his head.

Rose is grabbing the used tape and rolling it into a ball in her hands, staring at them both. Looking around now at the damage. A chair shattered to bits by what looks like a shotgun blast. Jell-O powder trailing down the hallway by the kitchen. Tables scattered. And the two bathroom doors open. No sign of Ruby.

'You okay, Winter?'

'I'm a little shook up, but otherwise, I'm just dandy.'

'Good. Great.'

Rose flits her eyes to Dennis a moment, then back to Winter.

'Now Sweetpea, wanna tell me what happened here?'

'First you gotta tell me why on earth there was a poor scared coyote locked in the pantry.'

Rose sighs and says, 'I was gonna kill it and skin it.'

'Now why would you do something so mean?'

'Because, Sweetpea, I was gonna give you the coat to make a new outfit or somethin'.'

'You know I would never wear fur from a murdered animal.'

'Yeah, I know. I was gonna tell you a little white porky pie. That it was roadkill I found on the highway.'

'You were gonna lie to me?'

'Just an itsy bitsy little vanilla one.'

'So why didn't you do it?'

'I... just couldn't. I've gone soft or some shit. So I drugged it out while trying to work up the courage. And that courage never came.'

'Awwww, my tough cookie. You did the right thing.'

'Thanks. Now, more importantly, you gonna tell me what the hell happened in here while I was gone?'

'We, uh, got robbed.'

Dennis says, 'Winnie honey, the only person here that got robbed was you. I was just about to show you my Doris Day routine.'

Winter giggles. She blows Dennis an air kiss. He gives her one back. Rose clenches her eyes shut a moment out of agitation. Thinking she just ran over a few miles in the cold dark desert in sandals, cutting up her feet and riddled herself with worry. All for what? To come back to these two playing it cute.

'Okay. I'm gonna skip the part why Dennis here is wearing my underwear, for now. Or how you both came to be tied up. But sugar cake, sweet as you are, if you could enlighten me as to the whereabouts of a mister Reuben Wallace, well that would be even sweeter.'

Winter plays with the curls of her raven hair coyly.

'Nick took him.'

'Nick?'

'Well, more like Nick's girlfriend.'

Rose pounds her fist on a table, shaking the whole thing.

'Nick?!'

Winter's expression turns blank and she cocks her head to the side in a contemplative manner.

'Well, she did save my life first.'

Rose blinks with concern.

'Wait. Save your life?'

Dennis puts his hand limply in the air in front of him.

'Yes, she did save your life. But then she called you a skank.'

'Mmmm, yeah. That wasn't very nice.'

Rose shaking her head erratically, then stares wide eyed at Winter.

'Someone tried to kill you?!'

Winter looks to Dennis, flattening out her creased butt bow.

'What was her name again?'

'Star of the Sea,' Dennis recounts in a mocking tone. He and Winter both giggle.

Rose now looking horrified. The thought of someone trying to kill her sweet little angel.

'Hang on. Just… just hold up. Someone tried to kill y-,' Rose pauses, thinks a moment, then looks through slitted baleful eyes at Winter. 'Who called you a skank?'

'Nick's girlfriend.'

'Nick has a girlfriend?'

'Uh-huh. She's real short and kinda cute. Like an Indian garden gnome.'

Dennis lets out a guffaw.

'Wait, wait, wait. Who exactly has Ruby?'

'Star of the Sea,' Winter and Dennis say at the same time.

'Who the fuck is Star of the Sea?'

'Nick's girlfriend,' they both repeat in tandem.

Rose turns and punches one of the wooden foundation beams.

Winter steps forward, reaching in an imaginary pocket in her skimpy outfit and pretends to take out the imaginary medicine bottle.

'Time for a chill pill Honeybee.'

'Fuck the chill pill, I need some 'shine.'

Rose marches to the bar, hops up, slides across on her butt and lands on the other side. She grabs a bottle of apple moonshine and unscrews the lid. Winter and Dennis watch in silence as Rose knocks back the equivalent of four shots. She wipes her mouth and starts to stride back around the bar.

'Alright Sweetpea. You ready to ride in style?'

'Where we going?'

Rose reaches behind the bar to grab the limo car keys, flinging them at Dennis.

'Heads up big guy.'

Dennis catches the keys.

Rose saying, 'My car is a little outta sorts right now. So we're gonna have to take the limo. You okay to drive Dennis?'

'Like it was my job honey.'

'Good. Cause you're in on this with us now. If you play real nice, I'll throw a little of the cash your way.'

Winter steps forward, hands sassily on hips.

'Dennis gets more than a little cash Honeybee. He's our partner. It goes three ways.'

'Like hell it does.'

Dennis waves his hand at them and arches his neck to look up with his eyes closed.

'Bitch please. We can negotiate this later. Let's go get senior skinny jeans and his pint sized bitch. Time is money, honey.'

Rose glances over and sees Nick's trucker hat still lying on the floor. She strides over and snatches it up, turning to face Winter and Dennis.

'Alright kidlets, let's roll.'

Winter is standing by the TV by the bar and turns the volume up on a news channel, showing a picture of a young handsome man, the anchor saying, '...*police believe one of the alleged suspects from yesterday's robbery at a Chicago bank is Jesse James Sadler, who was pronounced dead nearly twenty-five years ago...*'

Winter staring at the screen with a longing look, completely mesmerized.

'Jesse,' she says with a smile.

Rose behind her now. 'You know that guy?'

'In another life,' Winter says loftily as she plays with a hair curl.

'Come on, we gotta go,' Rose says as she turns the TV off and grabs Winter by the arm.

Dennis at the wheel of the limo cruising down the highway toward Holbrook. Still dressed in the pink robe and wig, the high heels off and lying neatly paired under his driver's seat. Rose is slouched against the window of the passenger seat, one leg up and folded, the foot tucked under the thigh of her other leg. Wearing her scuffed black Doc Martin boots again, having bandaged her feet. The ragged Voodoo Doll in her lap. It's wearing Nick's trucker hat. Rose believing that bringing the doll along might help them find Nick with a little black magic.

Rose is placing two bullets into empty chamber slots in the .44 Magnum. She spins the chamber with her finger for fun, then flicks her wrist, snapping it shut.

'Hey. You got some music or sompthin'?' Rose sticks her thumb out, motioning to the back area behind the black tinted rolled up partition. 'Keep my little gem back there entertained.'

'Hun, I've got just about every kind of music known to man, woman or coyote.'

Dennis plugs a USB in the slot on the car radio. He searches until he finds what he wants. He grins playfully as the chosen song comes on. It's "Knock on Wood" by *Amii Stewart*. They both start singing along in unison.

'It's like thunder. Lightning. The way you love me is frightening!'

After singing a few lines then realizing she can't remember the rest of the lyrics, Rose leans forward, pressing the intercom button.

'You okay back there Sweetpea?'

Winter is in the spacious back compartment, sitting in the rear leather upholstered two-seater. She spots the intercom buzzer on the wall next to her seat and presses her hot pink nail on it, her cherry red lips up against the speaker.

'Peachy keen, jelly bean!'

The interior paneling of the limo is a mix of pine wood and hard black PVC plastic to keep the sound out. A long black leather couch running up the side to the front. Two TV screens at the front, either side of the tinted visor, playing stock market and news channels. Winter has a champagne flute in one hand, pulling out a bottle of Dom Perignon sitting in the refrigerated box in the wet bar filled with scotch and wine glasses.

Winter splays back on the two-seater, kicking her heels in the air with excitement as the Knock on Wood song blasts through the speakers. She leans over and tears the aluminum paper off the top of the bottle exposing the cork. Winter uses one hand to grip the neck of the bottle and one to pull at the cork. She sticks her tongue out her mouth and clenches her eyes shut as she struggles with the cork. She's almost got it out, feeling the cork slowly sliding up.

Pop!

Winter lets out a mousy squeal as the champagne jets from the bottle, then giggles uncontrollably as she tries to control the gushing liquid. She's having a ball.

'Weeeeeeeeeeeeeee!'

She licks her champagne soaked wrists and fills her glass with the crisp bubbly drink, then necks the bottle like a wino.

They drive to the other side of Holbrook, down West Buffalo Street, passing Holbrook High School, turning right onto a dusty dirt road to 13th street, arriving at Nick's parent's house at the end of a cul de sac. Dennis parks at the end of the driveway in the shadows behind a streetlamp. Rose tells Dennis and Winter to wait in the car.

Rose slinks up the driveway to the house, the revolver in the back of her pants. Rose peers around the quiet street then the driveway to

Nick's house. No sign of Nick's car. A sensor light goes off and Rose curses, leaping into the shadows. She waits for a few minutes to see if anyone comes out to investigate. They don't.

Rose continues her tactical approach to the side of the house. She peers in the windows, the first one the living room. She sees two older people in lazy-boy chairs watching TV. Nick's parents, she gathers. The mother wearing a granny floral print nightgown. The father in faded blue striped flannelette PJ's. Rose recognizes him. He's come into The Glass before a few times. Has a quiet drink at the bar and leaves. Staring at Winter the whole time. Rose now thinking this is one of the creeps she's caught taking sneaky photos of her on their phone to jerk it to later. Rose now remembering those thick square glasses and how he keeps pushing them up his nose. Her blood boiling now. Wanting to throw a rock through the window or something. No, focus. Stick to the plan. Find Nick.

Rose pussyfoots around the length of the house, looking in windows. Kitchen. Main bedroom. Sewing room. Nick's room. She can tell by the band posters and guitar.

Rose sighs with dejection. Nick and the girl, Ocean Star or whatever the fuck, are not here. She dashes back to the limo.

They drive around town slowly, checking out the shopping centers first. The Safeway across from the Best Western. The Family Dollar. Hatch's Gas and Market. Checking out the car parks looking for Nick's beat up old yellow Mazda. Not turning up anything.

As they drive down West Hopi Drive again, Rose notices a man running down the street in a very colorful suit. As they grow nearer she thinks it's a woman's suit. And what's this? The man has a body over his shoulder. What looks like a young girl. He's a slightly portly guy, and it looks like he's headed for the motel down the road. What's this man doing running this late at night down the street with a little girl? Rose's eyes widen.

'Pedophile! Get him!'

CHAPTER EIGHTEEN

Uno

Scattered chicken bones lie all over the road. A take-out box from Plucky's lying on its side, some bones still left in it. A few yards away to the side of the road is an empty sweet potato mash container.

Screech.

Car tires come to a sudden stop on the highway. Headlights illuminating the bones and box. The passenger car door to the yellow Mazda creaks open.

Star strides over to the box and picks it up, then the chicken bones one by one, putting them in the box. Star muttering cuss words under her breath the whole time. She peers through the headlights at Nick, sitting in the running car, letting her do all the work. She clenches her jaw and marches over to the mash container and snatches it up, stuffing it in the box. As soon as she's back in the car Nick puts it in motion. Star throws the garbage on the backseat.

'You could have got out and helped me, Nick.'

'I had to keep the car running in case a truck or another car came. It's a main highway Sue, there's always-'

'It's Star of the fucking Sea! How many times do I have to tell you?!'

'Sorry.'

'Why do people have to litter? What, you can't keep that in your car until you get to the next place? You just *have* to get it out of your life right this instance. The planet is dying, everyone knows it. So you just make it worse because you can't be bothered doing what's right. Lazy assholes. Karma will fuck your shit up. Just you wait.'

'Yeah. Karma is a bitch.'

'You're no better Nick.'

'What'd I do?'

'If you drove an environmentally friendly car instead of this gas guzzler, you can have a say on the matter.'

Nick clears his throat, looking out his window a moment, then back to the road.

'I was thinking about getting a Tesla.'

'While that's a nice sentiment, you couldn't afford it.'

Nick wipes his hand through his long hair, staring ahead at the road. Thinking of how he will able to afford it soon enough when he finds that map to the raw gold in the mine. The distraction of handing over their hostage might be his best chance.

'What do you think the Elders are gonna do? With Mister Wallace?'

Star shrugs haphazardly.

'They can tar and feather him for all I care. All we need to-'

Star is jolted forward, slamming into the dashboard from Nick suddenly hitting the brakes.

'What the fuck Nick?!'

'Sorry! I just… this guy here looks like he could use our help.'

Star follows his gaze to the side of the road, where a man in a business suit is walking, holding out his thumb.

Star breathes angrily through her nostrils.

'Are you nuts? There's a guy in the middle of the night in the middle of nowhere, and you want him to ride with us?'

The man is now waving, a big smile on his face. He starts walking toward the car. Nick wondering why Star has her back up like this. She was literally just talking about Karma. And here he is, doing something good.

'He's wearing a suit. A really nice looking one. He doesn't look like any axe murderer I've ever seen.'

Her voice a loud hiss of words. 'He could be a psycho!'

'He's holding a Bible.'

'That's my point!'

Knuckles rapping on Star's window. She looks up to see the big round face of the blonde chubby man in the expensive suit, yelling at them through the closed window.

'Hey there strangers! Mind if I get a lift into town?'

Star hushes her voice at Nick.' Not to mention we have a goddamn hostage in the fucking trunk.'

'He's tied up. And it's only a ten minute drive into town.'

Nick leans forward, giving a thumbs up to him. The man gives him finger guns back. Star rolls her eyes.

Peter opens the stubborn unoiled door with a harsh pull and quickly hops in before these two youths change their mind. As soon as his butt hits the seat and the door slams shut, the car is in motion. Peter rubs his hands together vigorously.

'Holy Mackerel it's getting windy out there.'

'What brings you out here at this time?' asks Nick.

Peter stops rubbing his hands. He needs a good excuse. He can't tell them he works for a major fast food chain and is here to find the missing patriarch and became stranded at the hand of his so-called partner. Marion the Judas.

'I was driving to Phoenix. From Albuquerque. Business thing. My car broke down some ways back. I opened the hood to take a look at the engine, but it's all spaghetti in there to me.'

Peter forces a loud laugh. Nick pretends to laugh as well.

'The name's Peter. Peter Kane. Thanks for stopping. I'm in a hurry so this is just swell.'

'I'm Nick. And this is Sue.' Clenches his eyes shut. 'I mean, Star of the Sea.'

'Star of the Sea? That's an interesting name. Were you, born with it?'

'In a sense, yes. I was born out of my mother's womb as Sue. But I was reborn on the spiritual plain as Star of the Sea.'

The car hit a pothole and everyone bounces in their seats.

Peter furrows his brows, still grinning. 'I see. Good… um… good for you.'

Peter somewhat curious about the meaning of the name, considering there is no ocean even remotely close to here. But decides not to push it. Peter looks around at the interior of the car. A cheap tin box, decades old. Hell, he can even feel the springs poking out. Wait, is that springs? Peter careens to the side and slides his hand under him. No, those aren't springs. He pulls out the Plucky's take out box, now flattened under his weight.

'What the…' Peter looks at the box in horror as a couple of chicken bones fall out and hit his leather shoes. He throws the box at the adjacent back seat window in disgust.

'What the hell!'

Nick looks in the rearview mirror.

'You alright back there?'

'There's leftover food here in the back!'

Peter shifts his pelvis up and to the side, facing the window, so he can use the moonlight to get a better look. His mouth opens in horror as he notices grease from the box and bones have seeped into the fabric of his pants all around his crotch.

'No! Oh Jesus, no. These are seven-hundred-dollar pants.'

Nick's mouth makes that 'yeesh' face. 'Bummer. Sorry man.'

Star turns her head to the side, talking back to Peter.

'It's just cooking oil grease. Some dry cleaning will fix that. Trust me.'

'They're tailored pants. From Italy. No, no, no. I need them now. I need to look professional for...,' Peter stops himself before saying too much to these hippie nitwits. 'Why would you leave this junk in the back of your car?'

'It's just leftover fast food man, get a grip, it'll wash out,' says Star.

'I need them tonight!'

Nick's eyes in the rearview mirror.

'We can swing around. Take you back to your car.'

Star shoots him the eyes of death.

'Or not.'

'No, no, I didn't bring a spare suit. Crap-a-moli!'

Star wriggles with agitation in her seat, straightening up.

'Listen buddy, we did you a favor. So if you want, we can-'

THUMP.

Peter jerks his head to the side.

'What was that?'

'What was what?'

'I heard a noise. Coming from the back.'

THUMP.

'There it is again.'

Nick and Star immediately look at each other, eyes widened. Nick swallows hard.

'It's, ah, the car has a bad rear, um, axle. Been meaning to fix it.'

Peter can't see Nick too well, but his body language has become stiffened. His relaxed grip on the steering wheel has tightened. Peter figuring something fishy is going on.

Star smiles at Nick sweetly.

'Can you pull the car over for just a sec, honey?'

Nick pulls over the side of the road. Star quickly jumps out and dashes to the back of the car. Peter seeing her for the first time, noticing her short height.

The trunk opens, a few moments there is a faint dull crack noise, then the trunk is slammed shut. Star is back in the passenger seat again and the car is in motion.

'We're all good. I fixed the problem.'

'That didn't sound like it came from the car. Sounded more... I don't know..,' Peter trailing off in thought a moment. He instinctively rubs his elbow.

Star says, 'Y'know what? My mom owns a dry cleaner in town. I used to help out after school a lot. I know how to operate the machines. I've got a spare set of keys. We can go there right now and get those pants cleaned. Lickety split. Won't take long at all.'

Peter sighs. 'Fine. But make it quick.'

They drive in silence for a few moments. Star picks her nose and flicks the dried ball of snot at her feet. Nick looks in the rearview mirror again.

'Sorry about the mess.'

'It's happened now, so lets make the best of what we have.'

'I'm gonna trade this car in soon. Thinking of getting a Tesla.'

Peter perks up. 'Nice cars. Good for the environment.'

The streets of downtown Holbrook are bare of life. Nick's yellow Mazda is parked out the front of Helen's Dry Cleaning. Star is peering in the open trunk of the car.

Inside the shop Peter sits on an orange paint chipped stool in his Abercrombie checkered boxers and white tank top a size too small. Star said she may as well clean his whole suit. Peter's plump round stomach jutting out, stretching the fabric and testing its durability. He's looking at the Thunder From Down Under calendar on the wall opposite. The muscular model leaning against a tractor, straw dangling from his sultry smile. Peter low-key jealous of the model and his washboard abs.

Nick is in the back corner sitting at a fold out square plastic table with a deck of Uno cards. He looks at the five remaining cards in his hands. Star's two cards lying face down on the table. She's outside checking on Ruby, making sure he's still breathing. She said she didn't hit him that hard with the tire iron in there. Just a hard tap to shut him up for a bit. Nick looks at her cards impatiently. She said if he peeked at them, he would end up in the trunk with Ruby.

The sound of a little bell jingles as Star comes through the front door. She walks past Peter and takes her seat opposite Nick, adjusting the frayed deck of Uno cards. The cards worn down by the dense moisture of the dry-cleaning machines. Star is down to one card and calls out Uno. Nick drops a "draw 4" card. She flips him off and picks up four more cards. Nick's eyes dart to Peter a moment, then to his car outside, then back to Star. He leans in toward her, lowering his voice, the loud machine noise near them covering their voices from Peter.

'He could wake up any minute.'

'Relax. The old warthog is snoring like a jet engine. He must have farted a storm too, cause it stinks to high heaven in that hot box.'

'Did you have to knock him out?'

'The guy was kicking the trunk door.' She motions to Peter with her head for a second. 'What else was I supposed to do?'

Nick scratches his head.

'I dunno… it's just that… he's old. What if he doesn't wake up?'

'Then we dump his body in the desert and hightail it to Mexico.' She looks away, thinking, then back to her cards. She puts down a "yellow 3". 'Or up north. Canada maybe.'

Nick watching her with dubiety. The way she said that. No hint of joking. Like she would actually do it. Just take to the road, a fugitive of murder. He lays down a "blue 3" card.

'It's cold in Canada.'

'It's hot in Mexico.'

She lays down a "reverse blue" card.

'And besides, who says I want you coming with me? You're a nervous wreck. We wouldn't make it over the border.'

Nick looks at her with a slight pout while he picks up a new card. Ouch.

Star lays down a "blue 8" card. Nick looks at his card. Damn it. He reaches over and picks up a new one from the deck. Star smiles. She lays down a "red 8" card.

'Uno.'

Nick grins. He's got a "red 2" card. Which means he's Uno as well. He looks at her. Her little blue eyes staring eagerly at him, waiting for his next move. Her little button nose sniffs to the left, her freckles moving with it like stirred bowl of Cocoa Pops. Man, she's a cutie. Now he really wants one of her amazing blowjobs. Better let her win. Keep her in high spirits. He reaches over and picks up a card from the deck instead of laying his card down. Star's whole body jitters from excitement as she dramatically slams down a "yellow 8" card.

'Boom bitch! That's how it's done.'

'How much longer do you think?' Peter calls out.

Star walks over to the tangerine colored machine and takes a look at the panel on the side. The needles wavering slightly on the little pressure barometers.

'Twenty minutes, dude.'

Star's phone beeps. She checks it to find a text message from "Bear Claw", it reads; 'Have you been to the secret headquarters tonight?!' Star frowns and begins typing a response.

Peter looks at his watch and sighs openly. His gaze shifting to his paunchy gut looking like a big protruding marshmallow. Now even more depressed. He grabs it on either side and starts jiggling it. Yeah, definitely put on weight this last month he muses. Thinking now that he shouldn't have eaten all that chicken and mash earlier. And those chicken tenders from Safeway before that. And the Burger King before that. He's got to get a hold of his diet. He looks up at the calendar on the wall again.

That chiseled body on the model. Peter imagining how much more seriously people would take him if he lost weight. He's been standing up on stage giving life advice. From a guy who can't control what he eats. No wonder his numbers are down. Maybe he should hit the gym. Even start lifting. Get a body like that guy. Calendar worthy. He touches the crown of his head, where the hair is thinning the most. 'I'll get plugs too', he thinks. Peter wipes the thin glaze of sweat from the side of his face. This room starting to feel like a sauna now.

Nick rises up from the plastic fold-out chair and moseys past Star, on her phone texting, and over to a rack of freshly cleaned garments. He runs his hand along the collection, his fingertips taking in all kinds of materials. He feels lace and stops. He pinches the frilly black lace in his fingers and rubs it, liking the feel of it. He peers closer and sees it is attached to something purple. Nick pushes his hand in further and separates the clothes, pushing them to one side, then the other, revealing a purple corset. Not just any purple corset.

Winter's purple corset.

The one he saw her undress from the other night. His fingers start shaking as they progress across the purple satin, the stitched vine leaf running up the back, up to the lace drawstring. Nick is vividly recalling watching her slowly take the outfit off her perfect body. He swallows a lump in his dry throat. He digs his hand in his pockets. No chocolate. Damn. He licks his lips and closes his eyes. Fantasizing pulling off her fishnets seductively. Nick's fingers trembling as he rubs the satin material in his hand. His eyes snap open.

Star, still texting on her phone, looks up when she hears Nick all of a sudden yell out 'Winter!' She watches with a puzzled expression as Nick rips the corset off the rack, then sprints past Peter almost knocking him off his seat, ramming the glass front door with his shoulder, bursting out onto the street, losing his balance and almost falling over.

'Nick?' Star says quietly as she dashes to the front door.

Star reaches the front cashier's desk and watches Nick slam the driver's door shut. He starts the engine, revs it, and the tires spin to life. The car rockets off down the street. Star simply standing there, dumbfounded.

'Nick?!'

Star rushes out onto the sidewalk, the smell of burnt rubber still lingering in the air. She throws her arms out either side in a pose of helplessness.

'What the actual fuck?!'

The jingle of the bell above the door. Peter comes running out in his boxers and tank top, holding his Bible.

'Where is he going?'

Star sighs and buries her face in her hands, now making the connection between the corset and Nick's sudden exit.

'I… fuck's sake. I think he's gone back to the bar.'

'Why?'

'Because Nick is a horny idiot. That's why.' Star looks to Peter, shaking her head. 'We gotta go after him.'

Peter shrugs. 'I'm not going to any bar. And you're not going anywhere until my clothes are done.'

'No, we have to go now.'

Star pushes past him and marches back into the dry cleaners.

Peter follows her back in, watching as she sorts through the clothes on the rack.

'Hey, what's the rush?'

'He just took something very important. And I need it back.'

She growls under her breath in frustration, sorting hurriedly through the clothes on the men's side.

'What are you looking for?'

'We can't wait until your suit is done. I'm gonna have to put you in something temporary until we get the… ah… the car back.'

Star gives up on the men's clothes and starts with the women's on the other side. Her phone keeps vibrating from someone messaging and trying to call. Star ignoring it.

'I'll wait here,' says Peter.

'You can't.'

'Why?'

'This is my mom's shop. She'll flip out knowing we even came here in the first place. Can't risk it.'

Star reaches a set of clothes. She pulls over one of the little wooden stools and stands on it, unhooking the suit from the rack. She holds it up to the light to get a better look at it. It's a woman's two-piece suit. The polyester material shining a little under the light. A crazy mishmash of pastel colored squares all patched together to assemble a flamboyant outfit. Whoever the old lady is that wears this, she's got the attention of the whole bingo hall. Star holds it out to Peter.

'Put this on.'

Peter stares at the wild suit, the outsides of the pastel squares have a gold tinsel material sewn on.

'Are you kidding me? That's hideous.'

'It's the only thing in your size we got. You've got no choice.'

'I'm sorry little lady, I am not wearing that.'

Star sneers. 'Don't call me little. Or a lady.'

She jumps off the stool, the bottom of the suit dragging on the floor as she carries it to the table in the back where her shoulder bag is hanging on one of the chairs. She digs her arm in, rummages around a moment, then pulls out the .38 pistol. She strides back over to Peter and points the gun at him, holding out the suit with the other hand.

'I deadass don't have time to fuck around bro. Get dressed.'

Peter's eyes nearly pop out of his head. He's never had a gun pointed at him before. Well, once when he was out hunting with Ruby, when he drunkenly pointed his gun and said he would start shooting if he didn't dance like an Irishman. But this is different. Star has a steel-like glare boring into him. The way she's holding the gun means business. Peter swallows hard and sticks his hands in the air like he's being robbed.

'I'm not mugging you, dipshit. Just get in the damn suit.'

She throws it to Peter who fumbles with it when he catches it. His nerves in shock. He stares at Star and the gun while he quickly puts the suit on, watching her the whole time. Star lowers the gun when he finishes dressing. The suit fits him, almost. The waist of the jacket a little tight, his tank top clad gut poking out of the jacket.

Star puts the gun back in the bag and motions for the front door.

'Let's go sassy britches.'

Peter picks the Bible up from the front counter and Star bustles him out the front door, locking it with a mound of keys from her bag.

'How are we going to get to... wherever it is we're going?' says Peter.

Star sighs, looking down both ways of the empty street.

'I haven't thought that far ahead.'

'Hey. I'm staying at a motel. They have a twenty-four-hour reception. Maybe they have spare rentals?'

'I thought you said you were driving from Albuquerque to Phoenix?'

'I, uh, was. I got this far and realized I forgot something. So I decided to get a place here so I could retrieve the... thing.'

'Where are you staying?'

'I'm at the Best Western. Something Inn.'

'Adobe Inn?'

'Yes, that's it.'

'That's only a few blocks from here.'

'You want to go there?'

'Why not. It's the best plan we got right now. And you're right, they might have a rental. Plus, I know the night shift guy. One of my Tribe members. Pete. Or, Valley Snake as the Elders baptized him. If he's on tonight, we might be able to borrow his car or something.'

Peter remembering the little dweeb now. The lackluster attitude. Throwing away Peter's self-help brochure like it was garbage.

'Alright, it's not a great plan but it's our only plan.'

'This way.'

Star is already walking across the street. Peter speed walking to catch up with her. The polyester outfit not keeping the cold night air at bay, making swish noises as he walks. He catches up to Star and tries to keep by her side.

Peter furrows his brows, thinking about what she said just now. 'Lords of Light?' That seems vaguely familiar. He saw that somewhere recently. Oh, the chapel. On the altar.

'Back there, you said Lords of Light. What is that?'

'It's my spiritual tribe. We're on a mission to save the planet.'

'From who?'

Star looks up at him with an impassive glance as they turn a corner onto West Buffalo Street.

'From the corporations raping the land.'

Peter continues looking ahead, not saying anything.

Star says, 'You work for a corporation, don't you?'

'Yes I do. But we are environmentally responsible, I'll have you know.'

'What does that even mean? Like, you recycle and shit. Big deal.'

'No, we use organic products. Mostly. And we support PETA, Greenpeace, and a few others.'

'Just because you donate money to a cause doesn't make you Florence fucking Nightingale. You just deadass do that to look supportive and responsible while you collect your checks and smoke your fat cigars.'

'I don't smoke.'

'Good for you.'

'You people are highly judgmental, you know that?'

'You people?' Star gearing up now, thinking he means either 'short people' or Native people.

'You hippie types. Always on your high horse, putting down anyone who eats meat, or, or, drives a diesel car, or whatever people do that doesn't fit your agenda. And that's easy for you to say, sitting around smoking your marijuana, or dropping your acid and listening to The Grateful Dead.'

'Marijuana,' she scoffs. 'Who even calls it that?'

They turn another corner onto North Sixth Avenue, passing a Mom & Pop hardware store. Ruby's limousine cruises by a few streets away that neither of them sees. Peter glancing at the long black feather dangling from her headband.

'You're a lazy, entitled group of people who use the word "love" like you invented it. You protest about fur coats and the "murderers" who wear them. Yet I see you adorning yourself with animal remains. Hypocrite.'

'Whoa, whoa, whoa, pal, hold the fucking phone. For someone bitching and moaning about others being judgmental, you're pretty fuckin' judgy yourself. You don't know me, what my ethics are. What my plans are. I don't do acid. Yeah, I smoke the ganja, but I don't sit around getting high and worshipping crystals and eating kale like you want to believe. I've got plans. Big plans.'

Star's phone chimes in with a fresh text message. Bear Claw is getting on her nerves now. He's been frantically calling and texting, asking if she knows anyone went to the secret headquarters. And now asking if she took a Bible. She has no idea about any Bible, and why it's so damn important.

Peter chuckles. 'Big plans? You Lord of Light folk are going to, what is it, take back the night?'

Star snaps her head toward him accusingly.

'How do you know about that?'

'I don't. Saw it graffitied like the amateurs you are.'

'Amateurs?' She scoffs. 'You'll see soon enough.' Her voice high and bittersweet. 'In the back of that car is my meal ticket to greater things your pencil pushing ass would never understand.'

'Meal ticket?'

Peter now recalling the thumping sounds in the trunk of the car earlier.

'I'm going to be an Elder after I hand him over. They're the most intelligent people you'll ever meet, and our statement to the world will be astronomical. It'll change-'

Peter stops in his tracks. Cold wind making the stitched gold tinsel on his suit move, the streetlamp above catching it, making it look like he's shimmering.

'Him? You said "him". Him who?'

Star stops a few feet ahead, spinning her sneakers on the pavement to face him.

'A big fat Plucky's coupon I'm going to cash in. And I mean that literally. He's big and fat and farts like a herd of cattle.'

She notices the Bible he's holding again. Shit. Is this the one Bear Claw has been yammering on about?

Peter's eyes widen with realization. He drops the Bible to his feet. He strides to her and grabs her by the shoulders. She looks at his hands on her, then to his face, her expression twisted with confusion and alarm.

'You have Reuben Wallace?!'

Star aggressively pulls away and slaps at his hands on her shoulder. 'Hands off dude.'

He responds by gripping tighter, shaking her.

'You're the kidnappers! Holy Mackerel! It's you the whole time!'

Peter's face red. His cheeks flushed. Eyes bulging. Jaw clenched. Star locks eyes with his. She's becoming very worried. Peter looking to her like a crazed lunatic.

'I said back the fuck off buddy!'

Star grabs his wrists and tries to pull his hands off her. He's shaking her violently now. She suddenly leans her head over and bites down hard on his wrist. Peter cries out and loses his grip on her. Star storms past him toward a lit-up gas station down the road. Peter turns and lunges, grabbing her by the hair and yanking her back. Star squeals as he pulls her back by her greasy brown mop of hair.

'Where is Reuben?! Tell me!'

Star tries to pull free a moment, but he grips another wad of her hair in his other hand. She's got no other choice. Star belts out a bloodcurdling scream. Peter's knee-jerk response is to let go, the sudden release making her lose balance and fall to the sidewalk on her side, landing on her bag. The hard metal gun digging painfully into her rib.

The gun.

She quickly rolls over and scrambles to get her arm inside her bag to get the weapon. Peter now by her side, stooping down to grab her by the shoulder. She wrestles it off and continues going for the gun.

'Hey, hey! We got a little carried away there. We're adults. We can work this out efficiently and calmly. I've got negotiating skills. That's why I'm here, to negot-'

Star takes a huge gulp of air and lets forth an ear drum bursting scream. WHACK! Star is knocked unconscious, and she falls limp to the ground. Peter, in shock, looks at the Bible in his hand. The spine of the book heavy enough to put her brain to sleep.

Peter's breaths becoming faster and shorter. He's panicking. Peter has never knocked anyone out cold before, let alone hit anyone. He's always wanted to know what it feels like. The adrenaline pumping through his arteries now. A sensation he's never felt before, like someone just set off a string of firecrackers in his belly.

Peter licks his lips, eyes wide as he scans the street for witnesses. No one up the street. He whips his head around to look south toward the gas station. A silhouette charily stepping from the gas pumps to the street, peering down this way. Crap. Better get out of here before that person sees him.

Peter looks down at Star lying motionless on the pavement. Her chubby little arms flailed out of her poncho.

Peter notices the silhouette at the gas station is walking this way down the street. He stuffs the Bible in Star's shoulder bag, hanging it over his right shoulder. He shimmies his arms under Star's limp body and hoists her up, then places her over his shoulder so her legs dangle down his front. Her mop of hair trailing down his back.

Peter starts running down the street taking the first corner he can, running down a dark side street, through an alley, down 6th Ave past the Safeway supermarket and out onto West Hopi Drive. He didn't even notice the limousine cruise past him in the opposite direction. Peter heaving and grunting, almost out of breath, using every ounce of his physical being to make it to the motel, just across the road. The white lit up Best Western sign like a heavenly beacon.

Peter reaches the carport to the front reception, and leans forward, gently placing Star on a long wooden seating bench between two tall plants out front. Peter grabs the door handle and pushes hard, bumping his face hard into the glass, his cheek fat flattening and pushing the skin up to contort his eye area. Realizing, once again, that he needs to pull not push. Peter growls and whips the door open, striding to the front desk, his hard leather heels clip-clopping across the light brown ceramic tiles.

Peter reaches the desk where Pete, the night shift worker, is playing a PC game. Pete looks up from the computer, looking Peter up and down in his flashy clothes, thinking this guy just escaped a float in the Rio De Janeiro Carnival.

'May I help you sir?'

Peter doesn't say a word. He maintains vigilant eye contact as he sticks his arm in the shoulder bag, rummages for a moment, then produces the Bible. He slams it down on the polished milky brown and white imitation marble counter. Pete looks at the thick old book and raises his line of sight back up to Peter. His eyes crease with confusion. Peter jams the tip of his finger on top of the book, holding it there for emphasis. Peter's relentless eyes staring into Pete's.

'You're missing this in one of your rooms.'

Pete staring at him back, blinking slowly. 'I... don't...,' Pete now noticing the sweat on Peter's face and neck. Sweat stain patches on parts of the suit. Peter's hands shaking.

'Are you okay man?'

Peter is breathing heavily. He wipes beads of sweat from his face.

'It may not be illegal, but it's a staple. In every hotel and motel.'

A moment as he takes a few weighted breaths.

'You're in charge here. It's up to you... to...,' takes a few more catch-up breaths, 'initiative doesn't grow on trees. You have to plant it. One of my motto's. Do you understand?'

Pete simply stares at him, the blueish tint of light from the computer monitor casting shadows on his face, black rings under his eyes.

Peter takes his finger off the Bible and swipes it from the counter, stuffing it back in the bag. He turns on his heels and marches swiftly back toward the front door, goes to pull the door, remembering in the nick of time that he has to push it, and exits.

Pete watches through the large glass window looking out into the carport as Peter picks up the flaccid little body lying on the bench, puts her over his shoulder, and dashes off toward the rooms. Pete shrugs and resumes his computer game.

Peter makes it to the top of the stairs, heaving his breaths, wondering how this short girl weighs so much. He holds the card on the scanner above the handle. Beep. The scanner lights up green and Peter pushes the door open, slamming it shut once inside. What he didn't see as he entered was the limousine pull up at the bottom of the stairs to the motel room, and a very angry woman in Doc Martins and khaki shorts getting out of the car with a .44 Magnum in her hand.

CHAPTER NINETEEN

Back In 10

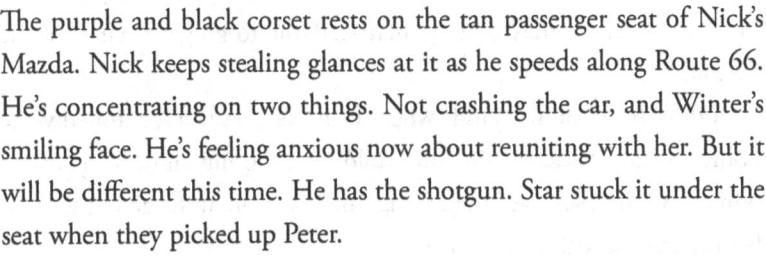

The purple and black corset rests on the tan passenger seat of Nick's Mazda. Nick keeps stealing glances at it as he speeds along Route 66. He's concentrating on two things. Not crashing the car, and Winter's smiling face. He's feeling anxious now about reuniting with her. But it will be different this time. He has the shotgun. Star stuck it under the seat when they picked up Peter.

But now, with a powerful weapon like that, he can point it at Rose and break Winter free of her chains. He'll have to forget about that raw gold in the mine. Probably not even there anyhow. That's alright though, he's been saving up cash for this. Not much, but enough to hit the road for a couple of weeks. Enough to get to New York, where Winter can fulfil her dreams. Nick's not sure how or where they'll live, but they'll survive. He can get a job in a bar or café. Two jobs if need be. Finish up his vet studies while Winter breaks into Broadway. When they both make it big, they can buy a house. A big house. Somewhere modest like Long Island where they can still commute to the city. Then children. Two, one of each gender. Maybe three. Nick starts wondering what they'll name them as he swerves off the highway, past the crudely made sign that reads; "BAR CLOSED UNTIL FURTHER NOTICE", and up the dirt drive to the saloon, slamming on the brakes.

Nick is already out of the car, the headlights still on and pointing at the chained shut front doors. Corset and shotgun clutched in one hand, he dashes up the stairs and peers through the dust laden front windows of the bar, not being able to see much inside because of the heavy black drapes. He notices a splinter of light coming from one of the windows to the left of the porch. Nick tiptoes on the end of the porch, leaning against the rotting wooden rail to look through the small gap in the drapes. He can make out the middle of the room just barely. Enough to see the chairs that Star strapped Winter and Dennis on are now empty. The torn-up duct tape on the floor. They escaped. Or Rose set them free. Doesn't matter. Time to go get what he came for and-

'Drop the weapon. Hands where I can see them,' a low toned voice booms behind Nick, causing him to lose his footing on the edge of the porch. He tumbles over the railing and onto the unforgiving ground below, littered with little stones.

Nick groans, rolling over; little rocks falling out of fresh indents in his skin. The shotgun a few feet away in the dirt. Nick sits bolt upright, looking around frantically for the corset.

'Hey! Don't move.' That low voice again.

Nick looks up as a figure, silhouetted by his headlights, steps over cautiously, pointing what appears to be a gun at him. He can see the man now as he gets closer. Tall, short dark hair, skinny. Thick eyebrows. Nick remains frozen on the ground, staring as the armed man approaches.

'Who are you? What are you doing here?' Marion says, flicking his eyes around suspiciously.

Marion already checked the perimeter when he arrived here about twenty minutes ago. He surveyed the whole building, looking through all the windows and listening for any voices. Surmising there's no one inside, he decided to wait until the kidnappers return, convinced they are operating out of here. Especially with all that used duct tape he saw inside.

'I said, what are you doing here?'

'I-I-I, ah, I used to work here.'

'I ask again, what are you doing here?'

Marion inching the gun closer to Nick's face.

'I didn't do anything! I swear! Winter isn't a part of it either. I just came to get her out of this mess. I love her. I love Winter. It was all Star of the Sea's idea. She's crazy!'

Marion staring at him with a vexed expression, not knowing what this kid means. He loves winter? What's that got to do with anything? Star of the what?

'Are you on drugs boy?'

'No sir.' Nick gulps, sliding back a little on the dirt. 'Are… are you a cop?'

'I'm worse than a police officer, son.'

'Are you with the health inspector?'

'Stand up.'

Nick pushes off the ground and rises up, eyeing Marion and the gun with trepidation. Marion uses the gun to motion toward the Mazda.

'Keep your hands up where I can see 'em.'

Nick raises his hands up and starts to walk to his car, stopping at the hood.

'Eyes front. Hands flat on the car.'

Nick complies and leans forward, planting his palms on the hood, still hot from the overworked engine. Marion steps up behind him, able to talk in his ear at a normal tone. He sticks the barrel of the gun into Nick's lower back, causing him to stiffen.

'You said it wasn't your idea. What was the idea?'

Nick realizes he may have said too much. Maybe this cop, or FBI agent, or whoever he is, doesn't know about Mister Wallace. Could be here to bust Rose on the illegal booze. Oh no, did he just implicate Winter? Nick clenches his eyes shut a moment, disappointed in himself.

'I don't know what you're talking about.'

Marion darts his eyes to the trunk of the car, then to the back of Nick's scruffy head.

'Open the trunk.'

'You got a badge, or something? A piece of paper maybe?'

Marion stamps the butt of his gun into the base of Nick's skull.

'Ow! Man, why did you do that? Police brutality dude.'

'Trunk. Now.'

Nick uses one of his raised hands to rub the back of his head, turning and marching to the back of the car, Marion in tow. They both stop at the back of the yellow car. Nick fumbles in his pockets and finds his keys. He looks at Marion as he sticks the key in the lock, then turns it. The trunk lid slowly rises. Nick stands back and raises both hands again.

Marion cranes his neck to peer into the trunk as it opens. He looks back to Nick, not wavering his stiff aim of the gun at him.

'Where is he?'

'Where's who?'

'Don't play coy. You know damn well who I mean. Where's the old man?'

Nick is breathing heavily, a cacophony of emotions circulating in his head. He dumped Ruby. And he didn't end up stealing the methanol.

So they have nothing to pin on him. Yeah, to hell with this asshole. Nick lowers his hands, a look of defiance on his face.

'Alright chief, here's how it's gonna be. I'm telling you, that I don't know any-'

Marion suddenly steps forward and cracks Nick in the forehead with the gun.

'Ow!'

Marion grabs him by his shirt and pulls him in close.

'Listen you little dipshit. Either you tell me where Reuben Wallace is, or so help me God, I will empty an entire clip into your skull. And I'll enjoy every millisecond of it. Your head will look like a busted cabbage once I'm through. Now. Where. Is. He?'

Nick's eyes are wide with panic and surging terror, and he can't spit the words out any faster.

'Please don't shoot! I'll tell you everything. All of it. I put Mister Wallace at the one place I knew he's be safe!'

The glass doors to the Plucky's restaurant burst open from the force of Ruby's body, tumbling out and onto the cement footpath and rolling out onto the car park asphalt. Ruby groans and rolls over to face the restaurant just as Seth, Frankie and Chester strut to stand just outside the door. Seth out in front, folding his arms, looking down at Ruby with a smug visage. His voice a crude imitation of Ruby's.

'Eat shit like the kind you serve, dick cheese.'

Seth and his cronies burst into laughter. Ruby grunts as he sits up. Patches of black dirt all over his white suit.

'I'm not fuckin' around here! I've been kidnapped. Twice in one friggin' night. They'll come back. Please, I just need to use your phone. I'll be gone, I swear.'

Seth spits on the concrete a few feet away from Ruby, his expression turning sour for a moment, enjoying his revenge.

Ruby says, 'I'll see to it you all go down for this negligence.'

Seth says, 'You're a known drunk. We'll just say you came in here like a madman, waving your arms and threatening us. We had no choice but to eject you, for our safety. There's three against one.'

'You'll pay for this!'

Seth looks to both his cohorts.

'You guys wanna smoke a doob?'

'Hell yeah dawg.'

'Yeah man.'

The three of them unfold their arms and turn, heading back inside. Seth closes and locks the doors with his chunky set of manager's keys. An 'open' sign hanging by strings on the glass door, the Plucky's chicken mascot printed on there, giving the thumbs up. Seth turns it around, so it now has a picture of a clock that says "Back in 10 Minutes". Ruby watches helplessly from the ground as Seth and his cronies meander away out the back.

Ruby struggles to stand, his joints still stiff and sore from being cramped in that car trunk for God knows how long. That skinny bus boy opened the trunk and helped him out of the trunk, down by the Plucky's sign on the side of the highway. He kept saying 'sorry', cutting at the duct tape free, then got back in the car and burned rubber down the road.

He'll think about revenge on everyone involved later. First, get home and change. And a drink. Lord almighty he needs a bourbon. This is the longest he's been without an alcoholic beverage since he can remember.

Ruby clears his throat, letting out a cloud of hot breath into the cold night air. He looks around. The car park is bare except for a Vespa chained up to a light post. A beefy pick-up truck and a Toyota Lancer parked in the staff parking zone to the side of the building. His eyes find a stream of smoke down on the driveway. Coming from a navy blue BMW M4. Ruby immediately shuffles into a half power walk half jog to the car.

Ruby reaches the driver's side of the car and bangs his fist on the tinted window. It startles the man inside, Ned the health inspector. He had stopped to get in a mouthful of fries lathered in the Secret Sauce before he hit the highway back to the Best Western motel.

'Hey! I need a lift. You gotta help me!'

Ned, wearing a standard white hotel robe, fresh droplets of sauce on the lapel, looks up with a mouthful of fries. His eyes wide and full of alarm.

'I'll pay you handsomely, just let me in.' Ruby very paranoid now, looking over his shoulder every few seconds for a Shelby Mustang or a yellow Mazda.

Ned opens the window just a crack, his eyes the only thing Ruby can see.

'I'm not a taxi. Sorry.'

'Come on man, I'm in a cunt of a calamity! I could end up dead. Please! I'll go wherever you go and from there I'll sort it out.'

Ned looks Ruby up and down.

'I was just going back to my motel.'

'Suits me fine.'

'Alright,' says Ned reluctantly. 'Hop on in.'

Ruby dashes around the front of the car to the passenger seat and gets in. Ned takes a plastic bag with two takeout boxes and a medium bucket of chicken and puts it on the console in between the two front seats. When the door slams and Ruby is settled. Ned sets the car in motion, turning onto the highway and taking a right toward town.

'Thanks brother. You're a real life saver. Literally.'

'No problem.'

Ruby's collection of new and old sweat stenches now filling the car. Ned reaches into the take-out bag and fingers the cardboard lid off the bucket.

'Want some chicken?'

Ruby looks down at his father's brand of fried chicken and glowers with contempt at it.

A few minutes after Ned's BMW left the Plucky's car park, the rented Tesla pulls off the highway sharply and speeds up to the front doors of the restaurant. Marion keeps the engine running, and leans over toward Nick, resting his elbow on the passenger seat.

'Don't you move from your seat. You try to run, and then I'll shoot you dead. Do you understand?'

Nick nods his head eagerly. He watches Marion step out of his door with force, his long spindly legs kicking the door all the way open.

Marion strides steadfast to the front doors of the restaurant. He can see the "Back in Ten Minutes" sign on the door as he approaches. He tests the door anyway, but it's locked.

Marion walks up and down the cement footpath surrounding the outlet, stopping to peer through the glass. There's not a person in sight. Marion breaks into a half jog around the building, trying the staff back door. Locked. He can see cars parked in the staff bay, but where are the staff? Marion can't see, but Seth, Frankie and Chester are behind a hill in the near distance taking turns inhaling Mango Kush weed that Frankie brought in.

Marion walks back up to the entrance door and stares in a moment. Marion pounds his fist on the door.

'Hey! Anyone there! It's an emergency goddamit!'

Marion starting to lose his temper now. He pounds on the doors with both fists. He even lays in a kick, the rubber sole of his shoe leaving a smudge mark on the glass.

The sound of tires screeching on the asphalt. Marion whips around to find that the Tesla has reversed to the back of the car park. Marion's quick reflexes kick in and he's already running toward the car before he comprehends what's happening. He grabs the butt of his gun in the holster mid stride. The car leaps into action again and speeds through the car park, down the driveway to the base of the sign, then does a hard right, heading in the direction of Holbrook. Marion slows his run and stops, taking in a few measured breaths. Watching the car's lights disappear into the darkness.

Marion now wondering if Reuben was ever dropped off here at all. This was just a ploy for Nick to escape. Marion realizing he just got outsmarted by a teenager. The rage in his stomach now surging. He's going to kill that little shit.

Marion starts looking around the car park. The pick-up truck and the Toyota Lancer. The Vespa chained to the light pole in the middle of the car park, about 9 yards away. Marion strides over to it and inspects it. He takes the chain in his hand. The links small but tough. He looks the bike over. He opens the seat, which houses a little compartment underneath. A bottle of water and a rag inside. Marion feels on the underside of the seat. And there it is. Stuck there with tape, is a spare key. Marion rips it from its hold. He looks at the chain. No key for that. Oh well. Marion pulls his gun from its holster and puts the barrel right on the chain links. He fires, the shot ringing out in the empty car park. Marion throws the broken chain on the ground, sticks the key in the Vespa, turning it on. He starts to drive, a little awkward at first due to his long legs on the short scooter but manages to steady the balance. Marion cruises down the drive onto the highway in pursuit of Nick.

Nick sitting in the car, watching Marion coming back around the front of the restaurant. He seems flustered and angry. Marion suddenly grabs the doors and shakes them with full force. Marion kicks the door in a fit of rage. Nick thinking, yeah, this man is unhinged. He can't lead him to Winter. He might threaten or hurt her as well. Nick quickly unbuckles his seatbelt and clambers across into the driver's seat. He leans over and pops the glove compartment. There's a remote. He presses the button, and the car silently starts up. Nick puts the car in reverse and floors it to the rear of the carpark. He looks up and sees Marion running toward the car, reaching for his gun. Nick slams the gear into drive and stamps his foot on the pedal, swerving a little but quickly regaining control of the steering. Nick admiring for a moment in the madness, how well this car drives.

The BMW M4 sits in an underpass under an abutment, a truck roaring on Route 66 above. The hood of the car is open. Ruby and Ned peering at the engine.

'Are you sure it's the battery?' asks Ned.

'Did you leave your lights on?'

'I don't know…,' Ned looks at Ruby, his face has a twinge of guilt. 'You know what, I may have. I'm just thinking when I came downstairs at the motel, I was… yeah. I think so.'

Ruby sighs and wipes his hand over his face, pulling his goatee at the end.

'Well, that's your fucking culprit alright. The chicken at Plucky's has more battery in it than this car.'

Ruby slams his fist against the hood lid and meanders toward the back of the car.

'Make yourself useful dick cheese and go see if you can flag down a car. I'm gonna see if there's any jumper cables in the back.'

Ned lingers a moment, somewhat offended, but knowing this jackass is right. He turns and clambers up the cracked cement embankment leading up to the main road. Sporadic bits of grass and weeds fighting their way through the cracks. Ned actually using a clump of grass to stop himself from sliding backward on his brown fluffy slippers. Ned reaches the top, heaving his breaths.

He stands on the side of the highway, a truck and two cars had just gone by on the other side. Ned squints to peer ahead into the darkness. Two headlights, coming right his way. Perfect. He starts flailing his arms, walking forward. The headlights hit him and light him up just as his foot connects with a cactus through the soft slipper. Ned howls in pain and goes to grab his foot, putting him off balance. He falls forward onto the road several feet in front of the car, causing it to slam on the brakes just a few feet shy of his face. The driver is out of the car now. He helps a bewildered Ned up, apologizing profusely. Ned recognizing Nick from The Glass Half Full.

'Hey, you're the bus boy from the saloon bar down the road.'

'I was, but not anymore, thanks to you.'

'Look, I'm sorry about that. But I really need your help right now. I'll pay you.'

'It's no problem. I'm giving back. I need every good deed I can get my hands on. I'm working on my Karma.'

'Good for you. And me, I guess.'

They both get in the Tesla and Nick drives them to the underpass, parking next to the BMW. Both out of the car, Ned guides Nick to the open hood of the car.

Nick says 'So what's the problem? Sorry, I'm in a bit of a hurry.'

'The battery is out of juice. I think I left the lights on during the night.'

'We've all been there,' says Nick as he stares at the engine helplessly.

'Do you have jumper cables?' asks Ned.

Nick glances at the Tesla, having no idea what's in there.

'I, ah, don't know. It's a rental.'

CRACK. A thick burst of blood hits Ned from his face down to his legs with a 'glop' sound. Nick's face frozen with shock, a moment later he falls forward and lands at Ned's feet. Ruby steps out of the shadows brandishing a bloodied tire jack. Bits of Nick's scalp and hair still on the curved tip of the jack. Ned looks down in horror, seeing a dark cloud pooling out of Nick's head.

'Wha... what the hell?!'

Ruby steps forward, peering down at Nick's body. The tire jack clasped firmly in his hand, ready to administer another blow. Ruby quickly realizes that's not going to happen. The pool of blood like a giant puddle around the boy and growing fast.

'I'll call an ambulance,' says Ned.

'Don't bother. Kid's dead as democracy.'

'Why did you do that?!'

'That son of a bitch was one of the one's who kidnapped me. Well, he wasn't the first, but he... anyway, he dropped me at the Plucky's. Maybe the dick cheese had a change of fart.'

Ruby shrugs. Ned looking at him with disbelief, how ambivalent he is to just having killed someone.

Ned kneels down by Nick's side, feeling his pulse on his wrists and neck. After a few moments, Ned rises up, his face full of panic.

'You killed him!'

'Correction, *we* killed him.'

Ruby tosses the tire jack on the road making an echoing clanking sound in the underpass. He walks to the Tesla and pops the trunk. A set of coiled black and red jumper cables are resting to the side.

'You distracted the kidnapper, while I hit him. Self defense. Easy-peasy bosom-squeezy.'

Ruby attaches the metal plated pliers on the BMW's negative battery terminal and clips the other on the metal lining of the car.

Ned shakes his head with an incredulous expression.

'That's not what happened. And I refuse to-'

'You like that chicken, don'cha? The shit you got back there. Big fan huh?'

'I like the Secret Sauce. But I don't see what that's got to do with anything.'

'Well that chicken and the sauce are the brain jizz of my late father. He invented that shit. And it's rightfully mine. I'm about to take the company back, mark my words. Why do you think I've been kidnapped twice in one night? See, you deliver me safely, and I'll clear this mess right up.'

Ruby walks over to him, holding the other end of the jumper cables out for Ned to take.

'So if you want a lifetime supply of that chicken, you'll shut your pie hole, and say whatever I tell you to say. We understand each other, chief?'

Ned stares at the cable ends for a moment. He has been proud in all his sixteen years of public service never having taken a bribe, despite being offered several times. The real burgeoning question is; is it worth turning a blind eye to a murder for a lifetime of free fried chicken?

Ned reaches out and takes the cables and quickly heads to the Tesla to begin hooking the cables up.

A slight tinny buzzing sound can be heard on the highway above, coming from a Vespa being pushed to its mechanical limits.

CHAPTER TWENTY

Bait And Switch

Star of the Sea is limp over Peter's shoulder. Peter uses his foot to slam the motel room door shut. He dashes to the light green two-seater polyester couch and lays her down gently, her hair splaying out and taking up most of the couch.

He accidentally drops the Bible on the floor, and Star's bag slips off his shoulder falling next to the Bible, spilling out her scrapbook. Peter stoops down and shoves the things back into the bag. He didn't see the folded-up map fall out of the Bible when it fell, and blindly stuffs it in the bag with Star's other things.

Peter's hands are shaking. Adrenaline pumping through his core. He dashes over to the nightstand and opens the drawer, placing the Bible in the middle, fussing over it so it looks perfect there in its new little home.

Peter moseys back to the couch. He is looking down at the unconscious girl in her filthy poncho. He is mighty proud of himself, having found and apprehended a criminal. He's a hero.

Peter catches a glimpse of himself in the long mirror on the outside of the bathroom door. Standing there in the ridiculous pastel squares suit. Gold tinsel outlining. Heroes don't look like something Elton John threw up, he considers. His shoulders drop. His mouth guides the rest of his face down into a frown.

Knock-knock-knock. Three raps on the front door. Peter turns around, thinking that might be Marion at the door. He heads toward the door, preparing to give Marion an earful, leaving him on the side of the road like that. As soon as Peter has the door open halfway there's a .44 Magnum revolver in his face.

'Put yer hands up.'

Peter is cross-eyed, staring at the end of the metal barrel, his eyes slowly focusing beyond the barrel to the owner of the gun.

Rose says, 'I said up with the hands, cock waffle!'

Peter immediately puts his hands up.

'I don't have any money.'

'I don't want your money, kiddie rapist,' Rose says with a sneer.

Peter's eyes furrow with confusion. Kiddie rapist? Behind him, the sound of groaning. Rose looks over Peter's shoulder to Star splayed out on the couch, slowly moving to consciousness. She murmurs something, then lolls her head to the side, looking at Rose in the doorway with the gun on Peter. Rose shoves Peter to stammer back a few steps. She steps into the room now, looking to Star with a motherly visage. A thin smile and droopy eyes.

'Hey there sweetie, are you okay?'

Peter's eyes darting between the two of them, hands still raised.

'I don't know what you think is going on here, but I can-'

'Shut your corn muncher, asshole. If you've harmed a hair on this girl's head, I'll blow yours all over that ugly wallpaper.'

Rose now at the couch, squatting down next to Star, caressing the side of her frizzy mane of hair.

'Did that bad man hurt you, sweetie?'

Peter sees something in peripheral vision and turns his head to find a large black man in a pink robe and blonde wig, clutching the hand of a hot woman in 50's pin-up getup.

Winter points at Star with a champagne bottle clutched in her hand.

'Hey. That's the chick who took our chicken man.'

Dennis bursts out a guffaw and says, 'Chicken man.'

The two of them giggle.

Rose looks over at Winter with furrowed brows.

'Sweetpea. What do you mean, took our chicken man?'

'That's Nick's girlfriend.' Winter nonchalantly takes a swing out of the bottle. 'Star of the Sea.'

Rose slowly turns her head back to stare down at Star, a wrathful expression consuming her face. Cheeks starting to go red. Breathing becoming heavier.

'You pointed a gun at my baby girl?'

Star slowly sits up, rubbing the side of her head where she was struck by the Bible. Her eyes flicking over to the doorway, spotting Winter and Dennis, then slowly looking back to Rose. Before she can get out a word, Rose clobbers her over the other side of her head with the butt of the revolver, right next to her left eye. Star flops back into a limp position - out cold.

Dennis steps forward, still holding Winter's hand.

'Rose honey, why did you do that? She can tell us where the fat fuck is.'

Rose takes a deep breath, thinking he's right. She acted too impulsively. But that's what happens when someone messes with her Sweetpea. Rose rises up, gun clenched tightly in her hand, turning to face Peter who still has his hands up. Rose takes slow, deliberate steps over to him, bringing the gun up as she arrives in his personal space. She sticks the barrel of the gun on his plump sweat glistened cheek.

'Where is Reuben Wallace?'

Peter gulps, looking at Winter and Dennis, then the gun, then Rose.

'Her boyfriend drove off with him.'

'Nick?'

'Y-yeah.'

'Fuck!'

Rose sighs and looks at the floor a moment, then back up to Peter.

'Where?'

Peter simply shrugs and shakes his head with an apologetic look. Rose grabs his collar with her other hand and pulls him in so their noses are both touching. Peter feeling and smelling her hot breath, the potent scent of moonshine making him wince a little.

'Where mother fucker, where?!'

'I swear! I don't know! I didn't even know they had him until after he took off. He just yelled "winter!" and ran off. Took the car with Ruby in it and that's the last I know.'

Winter, slouched with her weight on one leg, delivers her trademark beaming smile.

'He went to find me? What a darling he is.'

Rose says 'What do you mean you didn't know they had him? What are you doing here?'

'I'm from Tasty Incorporated. I came to negotiate. For Reuben. Jillian sent me.'

'I told that bitch no cops.'

'I'm not a cop. I'm a lawyer.' Peter blinks, unable to help himself. 'And a life coach. I've written a book, about to write-'

'Who else is with you?'

'A security chief. Advisor. I-I-I'm not sure what he does exactly. He's a contractor for Tasty Incorporated.'

'That's nice. Where the fuck is he?'

'I don't know. He left me on the highway and took off.' His eyes divert to Star, lying unconscious on the couch. 'That's when they stopped to help me. That's all I know. You can have Reuben, I don't care. He's a mean old coot. I don't want to be here, I never wanted to come in the first place!'

Rose looks Peter up and down.

'Why are you dressed... like that?'

Peter opens his mouth but Rose cuts him off.

'Y'know what, fuck it, I don't care,' she looks to Dennis, 'We gotta bounce.'

Rose takes two steps backward, then spins on her boots and strides to the wooden unit housing the TV, modem and cable box. She takes out her Swiss Army knife on her keychain and severs the cords from all of them. Then does the same with the lamp on the bedside table. She grabs padded wooden chair from the desk and drags it over, pointing to the chair for Peter to sit in it. He complies without any contest.

Rose wraps his arms to either side of the chair with the severed wires, doing the same with his calves to the chair legs. Rose marches into the bathroom and reappears with a hand towel, wrapping it around his face and tying it at the back to serve as a gag. Rose, standing in front of him now, stoops down so their faces are level with each other.

'You stay put, 'till I figure out what to do with you. First, I gotta get my prize pig.'

Rose marches over to the couch and picks Star up. She strides to the door and holds Star out for Dennis to take. Dennis lets go of Winter's hand and offers his arms out. He takes her up with ease, her little body draped over his tree trunk arms.

'Nick, the little shit stain he is, prob'ly gone back to the bar. Let's roll.'

Dennis nods and follows Rose as she power walks down the cement walkway to the stairs leading down to the parking lot.

Peter sits helplessly in his chair, looking straight ahead at Winter, still standing just outside the doorway. Champagne bottle loosely dangling from her grip. She's holding onto the metal rail outside, half drunkenly swaying on the spot. Winter brings the bottle up and takes another chug from it, wiping her lips with the back of her hand, smudging some of her red lipstick across one side of her mouth. She smiles through lazy eyes at him, looking his suit up and down.

'I like your duds.' Winter follows that up with a high-pitched giggle.

Dennis appears back in the doorway. He gently places his arms around Winter's little waist and lifts her off her feet, carrying her like a surfboard. She waves at Peter as Dennis closes the door.

Marion pulls into the Best Western motel carpark on the aqua Vespa. His tall bent legs stuck out awkwardly either side. He pulls up in the parking bay under the room he and Peter are staying. Marion shuts the engine off, leaving the key in it. He ascends the stairs and pulls out his room key as he approaches the motel room.

Marion enters and stops mid stride, seeing Peter tied up with appliance wires on the chair. Dressed in the gaudiest suit Marion's ever seen. Okay, deal with that question later. Marion marches over to Peter, pulling at the cords until they rip off. Peter stands up as soon as the last one is off and tugs at his makeshift gag, impatiently pulling it down so it's around his neck.

'Did you see them?!'

'See who?'

'The… people. The muscly woman with the gun. The big black guy in drag. The pin-up girl. They were just here!'

'Drag? Wait, a gun? Why did they have… did you find the kidnappers?'

'You're damn right I did. All of them.'

'How many?'

'Well, there was the first two. The little girl and the boyfriend. Then three others showed up. Pointed a gun in my face asking where Ruby is.'

'Why would they want to know where Ruby is if they kidnapped him?'

'I think there's lots of people who want him, that's why they interrogated me.'

'What did you tell them?'

'Everything I know. Which is nothing.'

'Why are you dressed like that?'

'Why did you leave me at the church?'

'It was a chapel, Lars.'

'For the last time, it's Peter. And why did you leave me at the chapel?'

'Because *Lars*, I didn't have time for whatever shenanigans you were pulling. Breaking into a chapel is absurd when we had a job to do.'

'Well I don't know where you've been, *Marion*, but I had one of the kidnappers in my possession.'

'Well, where are they now?'

'Don't be a smart ass. It's more than you've accomplished.'

'Oh yeah? I had one of them too.'

'Where's he now?'

Peter folds his arms with defiance. Marion's jaw is clenched. Both of them staring each other down. Peter walks past Marion to the bedside drawer between the two beds, opening it dramatically. He points to the Bible inside.

'See that? I put things right.'

Marion flits his eyes down to the book, then back up with an apathetic gaze to Peter.

'You are a fucking idiot.'

Marion turns and walks over to the closet, taking out his weapons case and places it on the bed.

'You and your whole cash grab operation is just as pathetic as your hollow ethics to cover for the fact you are a meaningless corporate whore who no one takes seriously.'

Marion pops the case open and pulls out the M4 carbine assault rifle.

Peter breathes heavily through his nose, fighting back tears.

'You don't know me.'

'I know more than I ever wanted to about you because you won't shut up. You're a validation seeking insect. The only thing that validates you are your parking fees, Lars.'

'My name is Peter!'

Peter suddenly lunges over the bed at Marion, football tackling him to the floor. The gun knocked from Marion's grasp and lands on the carpet a few feet away. Marion tries to free himself of the bear hug around his waist that Peter has him in. The two of them wrestle around on the floor. Peter lets go and lays blind punches into Marion's side and back, wherever he can. Marion pounds his fist on Peter's upper back. Both of them kicking their legs, trying to kick each other and find decent footing at the same time.

Peter pinches Marion in the stomach. Marion growling in pain. Peter's hand finds itself on Marion's chest and pinches his nipple hard. Marion lets out a cry of agony. The two of them looking like young siblings in a brawl. Marion suddenly lands a direct punch to Peter's gut; hard and fast. Peter rolls over on his back, winded, gasping for air. Marion uses this opportunity to grab the duvet on his bed and pull himself up halfway, holding his hand over his chest.

Marion crawls over the bed and swings his legs around to hit the floor on the other side. He leans over and plucks the Bible out of the drawer, and purposefully falls onto his back on the bed, rolling over so his shoes hit the floor on the other side of the bed where Peter is still fighting for oxygen, coughing and spluttering.

Marion drops to his knees and walks on his kneecaps a few feet to where Peter is. He opens the Bible to the middle and tears out a few pages. Marion looks at the verse on the ripped page and reads it out, yelling, 'Joshua, one-nineteen. Have I not commanded you? Be strong and courteous, do not be afraid, do not be discouraged, for your Lord our God will be with you wherever you go!'

Marion scrunches the pages in his fist into a ball and shoves it into Peter's foaming mouth, getting spit all over his long skinny fingers. Peter's hands grappling at Marion's arm, clawing and hitting at him to stop. Peter begins to choke now, looking up through his watering eyes at Marion's determined face, red with rage and exhaustion. Marion's fingers have pushed the ball of paper to the back of Peter's throat. Peter gagging on the paper and struggling to breathe, suddenly blurts out a stream of vomit all over Marion's hand. Marion withdraws his hand in disgust, looking at the chunks of half digested Plucky's chicken. Peter coughs up the ball of Bible paper onto his chest along with another blurt of puke. Marion delivers another hard punch to Peter's stomach, forcing him to cough, splutter, wheeze and gurgle all sorts of bodily fluids all down his front, rolling over so it spills on the carpet next to him.

Marion stands up and strides to the bathroom, turning on the faucet to let the water rinse his hand free of Peter's bile. Marion looks up into the mirror. His face red and sweaty. He lathers his hand with soap and washes them thoroughly, then wipes his hands on his hands on his black trousers. Marion adjusts his loosened tie and straightens his jacket, trying his best to look professional.

In the mirror, Marion can see Peter clawing his way up the duvet to the bed, coughing up spit and vomit, clearing his throat. His plump face red as a beetroot.

'Say whatever you want! It doesn't bother me. You're just a security guard. A fucking desk clerk whose only phrase is "sign here sir".' Peter follows that with a guttural cough.

Marion's face twists with indignation. He is trying so hard to suppress his rage a vein in his forehead protrudes running from his hairline to the top of his left eye. Marion reaches for his Beretta and spins around, whipping the gun from its holster. BANG. Blood and flesh sprays from Peter's head as he jolts backward and thumps on the floor next to the bed; out of sight.

Marion stands there, dumbfounded. He actually shot the annoying jerk. He looks at the gun tightly clasped in his hands, then slowly places it back in the holster. He turns to check his appearance in the mirror again. He turns the tap on and drinks water from his cupped hands, then switches the tap off. Marion rises up to his reflection - to also find Peter's reflection as well. Standing there, about seven feet away in the main room, blood down the left side of his head. Half his ear missing. Blown right off. He's also holding the M4 carbine assault rifle.

'Howdy Pilgrim.'

Marion spins around and reaches for his gun. Bullets from the carbine rip into him, a spray burst of three round point ammunition cuts through Marion's stomach and torso, blood spraying up on the white tiles and mirror behind him. Marion clambers back, arms flailing and hits the wall with his back, then slowly slides down. He lies there in a slouched position, head lolled down. Blood now seeping out the side of his mouth. His white shirt now completely red, soaked with deep intestinal blood.

Peter steps into the bathroom, the rifle in both hands, but his grip on it has sagged. Peter ogling Marion with wide eyes. All that blood. All over the wall like some kind of abstract painting. There's that surge of energy deep in his stomach. Just like before, when he knocked Star out. It's more intense this time. It's not just like some fire crackers being set off. No, it's a lot more than that. Like a Disneyworld fireworks spectacular show. The ones they put on not long before closing time. Boom, boom, boom. A succession of exploding lights in vibrant colors. Peter licks his lips. He's never felt a sensation like this before. Not even close.

Peter is standing over Marion now, looking down at him with a sense of pity. Blood dripping from the bottom of Peter's earlobe to the pastel colored fabric on his shoulder. Peter turns and strides out to the main room. He opens his little travel bag and takes out a steel blue Burberry tie. He rests the gun on the TV desk a moment as he wraps the tie around his head, ensuring the fattest part of the fabric is covering his severed ear. He ties a tight knot on the other side of his head, now wearing the tie as a makeshift headband. Peter picks the carbine up from the table and carries it in one hand, the other he uses to snatch the unopened can of watermelon soda from the bedside table.

Peter steps back in the bathroom. A pungent smell in here now. A gassy, almost metallic kind of smell. Marion still slumped against the bloody wall. Still breathing, though it sounds tough to get those breaths in and out. Peter gently lays the carbine on the porcelain sink. He cracks open the can of soda.

'Here.'

Marion slowly looks up with a dreary visage, looking like it's a struggle to move his neck so he can see the watermelon soda can in Peter's outstretched hand. His throat is bone dry. He lifts his left arm with great difficulty, shaky fingers managing to grasp the can. He almost drops the can as he brings it to his lips, his arm loose and heavy to him. The can finds his lips and he takes a good, long gulp from it.

Peter watches as a mixture of blood and light green bubbly soda runs like a small stream from his mouth onto his blood soaked chest. Marion's fingers lose grip of the can and it falls, rolling to a stop at the bathtub. Marion makes a slurping sound, having trouble swallowing. Then, as if he has just received a new burst of energy, he lolls his head up to rest against the tiles on the wall. Blinking erratically, then closes his eyes a moment. Peter notices a little smile forming. Marion opens his eyes and locks with Peter's.

'I... I can actually taste. First time in... my life... I can taste.' Marion tries to cough, but it comes out a splutter.

'Good for you.' Peter smiles.

Marion coughs weakly.

'Howdy Pilgrim... you got it right.'

'Yeah. Googled John Wayne earlier.'

Marion smacks his lips, the sticky soda still around his mouth and on his chin. He looks away a moment, then looks back up to Peter with an earnest expression. Like a little child asking a question. His eyes drooping. Feeling tired, but curious.

'Is that what watermelon tastes like?'

Marion's eyes slowly flutter closed. He slumps to the side, his body wiping the blood into a fanned red streak across the wall. Marion lies on his side. Dead.

Peter takes a few deep breaths, staring at Marion's deceased body with a flurry of emotions. Killing Marion has opened up something inside Peter. Something profound. He doesn't know what just yet, but he knows he has to hit the open road. A new life awaits. But first, there's matter he needs to take care of.

※

The front door to the Best Western motel reception bursts open. Pete, the night clerk with his Emo haircut and crinkled uniform, stands at the computer monitor, eyes firmly on his phone where he's reading aggressive texts from Bear Claw, asking, no, demanding to know where the Bible is. Saying it's gone from the headquarters. Pete swallows hard, thinking that if someone got a hold of that map, he's in a world of trouble. He doesn't hear Peter storm in because of the headphones blasting garage rock band music into his ears. Peter walks right up the desk wearing his blood stained pastel suit and the tie wrapped around his head. He's also holding the carbine.

Pete looks up at Peter from his phone, eyes erratic.

'Look man, this is not a good time, I've got an emergen-'

Then his heart races again at the sight of the assault rifle.

BOOM.

Pete is yanked back a bullet rips through his chest. He hits the wall behind, a look of shock on his face, then topples forward and falls on the granite tiles; dead within seconds of hitting the ground.

Peter gives himself a stern nod of approval, then turns and marches outside. There's only three vehicles in the parking lot. A white Sudan, an old Lincoln town car, and a 1968 Vespa VLB Sprint.

CHAPTER TWENTY-ONE

COCK-A-DOODLE-FUCKIN-DOO

Desert rats scurry through the low hanging desert mist from agave plant to agave plant, intermittent clouds switching from a pitch black to moon-kissed desert landscape. The limo is parked a stone's throw from Route 66 near a large cactus tree, just outside of Holbrook.

Dennis stands by the cactus, twirling a curl in his blonde wig, looking up at the stars. Winter is behind the cactus, squatting down and emptying her bladder. She's having to hold her thick black panties to one side with her fingers to let the piss out. The copious amount of champagne finally got to her.

Winter squints, peering at the night sky.

'Oh… yeah, wait… okay, I think I see it.'

Dennis points to the sky.

'It's right between those two stars. You can always tell, because it's the brightest one.'

'Venus is a star?'

'No honey, it's a planet. It's the brightest thing in the sky. It outshines all those stars.'

A pause as Winter shimmies her hips. No toilet paper, she's going to have to drip dry.

Dennis says, 'It's also the closest planet to Earth.'

'Huh... so, why don't we go there?'

'To Venus?'

'Yeah, I mean, everyone's sooooo obsessed with little ol' Mars. And that planet is all sandy and boring. Just like here in Arizona. Nobody *wants* to come here. Everybody would rather go to Las Vegas. It's pretty with all them colorful lights. The brightest city in the world.'

Dennis grins.

'You've got a point there Winnie. But, do you know why Venus is the brightest?'

'Nuh-uh.'

'It's the second closest planet to the sun. It's such a hot chemical soup, it makes those clouds thicker than oatmeal, and the sunlight can't get in. So, the light reflects off the clouds like a mirror, and that's why we get to see that little beauty with our own nakie eyes.'

Winter is standing now, adjusting her panties back into place. She rounds the side of the cactus, placing her hand on it for support, completely forgetting all the bristles on it, amazingly managing to miss being pricked by one. Dennis takes her gently by her other wrist, making sure she doesn't trip on a plant or rock on the uneven with those high pumps she's still rocking.

'You sure know a lot of stuff about stars and planets Dennis.'

'I love the night sky. It reminds me there's so much out there, and we're just little ants scurrying around on this little anthill we call Earth.'

Dennis uses his lit-up phone screen to guide them back to the limousine several yards away.

'Some nights, when the old man is passed out in a bourbon coma, I take his big ass telescope up to the billiards room and look into space for hours.'

'And it's lookin' right back at ya.'

They both smile in the dark, not seeing each other's smile, but knowing it's there.

The door to the limo is open. Rose is in the back, sitting on the middle couch running along the side. Star's hemp bag next to her. The map from the Bible has fallen out and is lying on the floor which no one has noticed. Star of the Sea's unconscious body sitting upright on the other side of Rose. Chin resting on her chest. Her hair all frazzled down her front, hiding the neat make up job Winter did.

On the way back through Holbrook from the motel, Winter administered some make up to Star's face. She doused the back eye that Rose gave her with foundation. Winter feeling like her face wasn't balanced out enough, so she gave her some contour to balance out those cheekbones, and some blush to make those adorable little freckles pop. She was about to do her eyes, maybe some mascara to draw away from the heavy foundation, but that's when the sudden need to pee surfaced.

Winter climbs back in the back, the lights inside making her blink to adjust from the darkness outside.

'Come on Sweetpea, we're short on time.'

'I'm sorry. I really needed to go.'

'Don't have any more of that booze. You're a lightweight, and I'm gonna need you focused if we're gonna get Ruby back.'

'Okie-dokey.' Winter closes the door behind her and plonks down on the back sofa. 'Can I have a wee little smoke? It'll calm me.'

Rose holds an impassive gaze on Winter. They can both feel the car sink a little as Dennis lands in the driver's seat.

'Maybe... just a few little puffy-puffs?' Winter bats her lashes.

'A couple of puffs. Then you gotta be a good girl 'till we're paid and on the road.'

'Roger dodger.' Winter follows that up with a salute.

The car engine starts. The music kicks back in on the speakers. A 70's pop song everyone knows but no one knows the singers name comes on. Winter takes a half smoked joint from her little sewn on pocket on her corset and lights it up.

The limo starts moving. Winter looks to Rose with pleading eyes.

'Honeybee?'

'Yeah pork chop?'

'Can we just go? Y'know, like, just drive. Take off outta here.'

Rose is distracted by something out the window.

'Of course darlin', that's the plan. Soon as we get the splash.'

'No, I mean now. No more shenanigans. You and me, we can…'

Hold on, what's this. Rose looking past Winter through the window, spotting some movement in the underpass they are about to drive by. A man in a white bathrobe by the looks of it. And there's a second person. She can make out a portly figure in a white suit. The two of them appearing to be jump starting a car.

Holy mother of Christ. It's Ruby Tuesday.

'Stop the car Dennis! Stop! Now!'

Rose lurches forward to the tinted divider screen and pounds her fist on it, repeating herself.

Dennis slams his foot on the brake just as they are passing the two men. They both look over at the car, Ruby busy winding the jumper cables back up. Both the BMW and the Tesla are running now.

Ned turns around, armed with a cable and a look of confusion as the limo scrunches to a sudden halt on the gravel dusted asphalt. Ruby drops the half wound up cable to the ground, his arms falling loosely to his side, defeated. It's his car, but he knows right away why it's here. For him. Sons of bitches found him.

Rose is out of the back door, revolver in hand and pointing at Ruby before the limo comes to rest on its axles.

'Ruby Tuesday. Ain't you a sight for sore eyes.'

'Stick your sentiment up your ass fuckin' rug muncher.'

Rose noticing the man in the robe, recognizing him immediately as the asshole that shut her bar down.

'Well I'll be damned. How the hell did you end up in this mess?'

Ned swallows hard, racking his brain for words. A word. Any word. All that comes out is a weird sound, almost like a whimper.

Rose shrugs and says 'Well, looks like you're comin' along for the ride.'

'N-n-no. Please. I-I didn't... I was out for a late night snack. I couldn't sleep.'

'Oh really? Maybe 'cause you put two struggling honest working girls outta business?'

Ned's eyes flit to the gun a moment, thinking the word 'honest' doesn't fit here. But he damned well isn't going to say that to this clearly unhinged woman.

Rose sighs, and motions to the limousine using her head.

'Alright, in the car. Both of you.'

Rose steps forward, a flash of light from a cargo truck's headlights on the highway above lighting her up for an instant, the sound of it rushing by almost deafening. Rose stops, her boot sliding a little on the ground from something wet. She looks down. Blood everywhere at her feet. She peers to the side and notices she is standing mere inches from a person's head. A big dark puddle around it. She recognizes that shaggy hair and skinny jeans. She recoils slightly and steps back, looking back up, her eyes darting dubiously between the two men.

'Nick!'

Everyone looks over as Winter approaches the scene, stepping slowly in her heels toward Nick's corpse. Her expression filled with horror. She puts her hand over her mouth and gasps, seeing all the blood. Tears already welling in her doe eyes.

'Oh Nick. No, not him. Not poor Nick.'

Rose switches gun hands from right to left and side steps toward Winter with her free arm ready to console Winter, who is looking up from Nick to Rose, Rose to the gun.

'Enough *Rose*. That's enough. This has gone too far.'

Rose's eyes widen a little with surprise. She can't remember the last time Winter called her Rose. And the way she just said it. With a kind of disdain.

'Sugarcane, you're drunk. Get back in the limousine. Let the grown up handle it.'.

'Fuck you!'

Rose's jaw physically drops. She's never been told to get fucked by Winter. Not even in a joking way.

'What did you say?'

'I'm sick of you treating me like a child. Yeah, I'm not that smart. I'm not as smart as you. I'm a big kid at heart. But you treat me like a child.' The waterworks coming now. Winter's protruded bottom lip quivers as tears run from her eyes. The trail of salty liquid blackened by the mascara. 'A child is someone you tell what to do. Go to your room. Stop talking to that man. Stop flirting with that girl. Pick up after yourself. But I'm a kid. A kid is someone you play with. You never wanna play with me anymore. All you do is treat me like your object. I just wanna be a kid. Play with me like a kid.'

'That sounds like some pedophile shit right there.'

'Oh shut up. I love you. And I know you love me. But you love me more as a possession. Like a liability.'

'Liability? Babycakes, I did this for you, all fo-'

'And for fuck's sake, pick a nickname and stick with it. Sweetpea, Sugarcane, Pork Chop, fucking jam drop cunt sparkles. It drives me crazy!'

'I never called you that last one.'

Dennis is out of the limousine now, stepping past the headlights toward the scene, but stops short, giving the two lovers their space.

Rose steps over Nick's corpse closer to Winter. Both boots now standing in the congealed blood. A tear starting to poke out of her eye. Winter steps over to Rose, now in each other's space. Rose sticks the gun in the back of her belt and gingerly offering her hands out to Winter.

Winter takes a step forward and gently puts her hands under Rose's, interlocking their fingers, having to both hold the gun.

'I know you did it for me. All of this. But you said no one would get hurt. And...,' Winter chokes up, 'Poor Nick. Look at him. He's not gonna cure animals anymore.'

Rose looks down and turns her head to the side, seeing Nick's converse sneakers and the skinny jeans on the ground right behind her. Rose feeling sad. She gave him a hard time because she wanted him to use his head more. Now the contents of his head are all over road.

The song "Total Control" by *The Motels* now coming from the limo speakers. Dennis is smiling to himself. This particular song playing is no accident.

Winter smiles. Rose smiles. They both move into each other. Rose kisses Winter softly, squeezing her finger tighter into Winter's. Rose pulls back, locking eyes with Winter.

'Our song,' says Rose.

'Mm-hmm.' Winter licks her lips. Her smile fades. Her eyes becoming sad again, coming out of the moment. Remembering where they are. And poor Nick.

'Now, this chicken sauce farce is over, understand? Let Mister Wallace go. No more guns. No more violence. Just us.'

Rose turns her head to look at Ruby, standing anxiously nearby. His arms folded and looking pissed. Ned, still holding the jumper cable, staring at the two of them incredulously. Dennis leaning on the hood of the car with his pink robe pulled in tight, enjoying the music. Rose looks back to Winter, moving her lips around tightly, thinking.

After a moment of deliberation, Rose says 'He'll tell the cops.'

Ruby steps forward to chime in.

'I won't. Cross my heart and hope to die. Stick a dry finger in a moist apple pie.' He follows that with what looks like a military salute mixed with the Scouts Honor symbol.

Dennis waves his hand at Ruby.

'Gross.'

Winter gives Rose a hand squeeze of encouragement. Another big truck zooms by above, the high beams lighting them up for an instant.

'Please Honeybee. Let it go.'

Rose stares into Winter's pleading eyes. She feels the cold metal of the gun barrel at the top of her ass crack. She gets a chill up her spine finishing with a tingle in her shoulders. Feeling the cold early morning air seep into her pores. The hairs on her arms standing on end. Reality starting to kick in. She's come this far. In a few hours the bank will be open, the money will be wired, and they'll be out of here. Sure, Nick is dead because of this, but should he die in vain? All this madness for nothing? No, they're too close now.

Rose reaches behind and pulls the gun from her belt, pointing it at Ruby again.

'I'm not letting this sack of chicken shit off so easily. We deserve that money more than he deserves to be rich. And we're only hours away from just that.'

Winter's head drops forward, her bottom lip pouting, disappointed. Another tear rolls down her cheek.

Rose says, 'Then I'm taking you to Broadway baby girl.'

'No you won't.'

Rose grabs her by the wrist aggressively.

'Like hell I won't.'

Winter pulls back.

'Let go of me.'

Rose pulls her back toward her harshly, almost causing Winter to trip on her heels.

'I said let go!'

Dennis pushes off the hood of the limo, his manner defensive, but stays where he is.

'You listen to me,' says Rose in a harsh low tone. 'Don't pull that bratty shit. Not now. Where do you think your nice clothes come from? Huh? Your make up and all those accessories?'

Winter glares at Rose with contempt.

'I'll tell ya where. Me. I run that saloon. You do shit all day except smoke your weed and lie on your sunbed. I'm doin' all the repairs. Makin' the hooch. Sure, you get yer ass out on the floor, make everyone look at it. Bring in business. But honey, don't think for a second I can't hire some other pretty girl to do that. I've supported you all these years, and your dreams. When I say we're outta here, we're outta here. And when I say how it's done, then that's the way it's gonna be done. Because remember where you'd be if it weren't for me. Think long and hard about that abusive sack of shit you'd still be with if it weren't for me. I love you, but damn girl you gotta know what's what once in a while. I'm getting' real tired of having to spell shit out for you.'

One of Winter's nostrils rise with the side of her mouth into a sneer, her gritted teeth showing.

'I'm not going to New York with you. I'll go with Dennis. At least he wouldn't talk to me like I'm stupid.'

Winter yanks her wrist back again. Rose pulls her again. They play tug of war for a moment, Ruby and Ned exchanging precarious glances in the background. Ruby taking small subtle steps back into the shadows.

'Where you think you're going old man?' Dennis calls out as he takes a step in his direction.

Ruby sighs despondently and slumps his body back against the BMW, throwing his hands up helplessly in a dramatic fashion.

Rose and Winter's little scuffle heating up now, both of them pulling and pushing each other. Winter slapping Rose's arm holding the gun. Rose trying to get her other arm around Winter's waist so she can pick her and carry her to the limousine.

Ned standing there in his blood sprayed robe holding the cable, watching everyone with bewilderment.

Rose sticks the gun in the front of her pants this time and uses both hands to grapple at Winter more ferociously, her face growing red from both physical frustration and irritation.

'Stop this Winter God damn it!'

'Fuck YOU!'

Rose suddenly backhands Winter hard across the cheek, the shock of the slap making Winter let go of Rose's arm, falling back onto the unforgiving asphalt in a mess of sprawled limbs.

Dennis jumps into a run to Winter, helping the dazed woman sit upright on the ground. The bow on her head slipped to the side and hanging loosely on her head.

Rose is frozen on the spot, still holding the hand out that slapped Winter. She's staring at it with utter disbelief. Staring at her own hand like it was some kind of alien weapon. Like it was the Devil's own hand. Out of place on her whole body.

Rose looks from her hand to Winter in a daze. She's being pulled up to stand by Dennis, his arms hooked under her armpits. Rose swallows. Tears form in her eyes. Rose can't remember the last time she cried. Properly cried. From physical pain, yes. Emotionally, she's not sure if she's ever wept. She didn't even cry at her parents funeral. But this. This she did not see coming at all. Rose now recalling how she met Winter.

When Rose fled Kentucky after Jumbo Jackie got pinched, she headed for the East Coast thinking there would be a lot more opportunity. After a few stints working as an assistant mechanic in Connecticut, several years in South Carolina as a delivery driver and landscaper, Rose befriended an old man whose hedges she was trimming. Turns out the man, Dale, was dying of lymphatic cancer. No relatives or friends, Dale took to Rose. She would make lemonade and sit on the porch with him. He would tell her stories of the Korean War, his family who died in a car crash, and years working in the mines out west. He bought a property out in Arizona that was going at a good price. A saloon bar outside of Holbrook. He tried his hand at running a bar, but in the end the hot dry temperatures were too much for him. It had been sitting there gathering dust for some years. When Dale died, he left Rose his house and the bar. Rose sold the house and headed out west to use the money to renovate the place.

Rose, not a big fan of flying, took the Amtrak out to Arizona. There was a stopover in Atlanta. Rose was reading the newspaper and sipping a coffee in the train station when she heard a domestic dispute happening a few seating benches over. She ignored at first, until the woman in the couple spoke up. Her voice was like fresh cotton candy to Rose. Then she stood up to look over there properly. And that was the first time she laid eyes on Winter.

The most beautiful thing Rose had ever seen. A perfect figure in a vintage black halter pin-up dress, the bottom of it and the breast section white and black polka dot printed with traces of red. The back of it tied in a bow around her neck. She was pleading with her tall muscular boyfriend to keep it down, to not make a scene in front of all these strangers. He was yelling at her to shut up, calling her demeaning names and pointing threateningly in her face. Rose didn't know this couple, but she could tell this guy wasn't as restrained behind closed doors. That flawless make up on her doll-like face was used to cover up black eyes and swollen lips, Rose was sure of it.

Rose edged closer to the fighting couple. When she was a few yards away, the guy, who the woman called 'Johnny', slapped her hard on the side of her head, forcing her to fall back into the seating bench. The slap so hard Rose could feel it. Rose stormed over there and told Johnny if he hit her one more time, it would be the last time he did. Johnny laughed her off and told her to mind her own business. Rose told him that fighting was her business, and she was keen to come out of retirement. He yelled at her. She pushed him. He pushed back. She gave him a right hook that put him on the ground, out cold. Winter watched on in amazement. Her knight in shining armor. It was whitewashed jeans, a tank top and Croc shoes, but close enough.

Rose held her hand out for Winter and told her if she didn't want to be abused again, she could come with her to Arizona, right now. Help her run a bar she owned but had yet to lay eyes on. Winter felt a surge of improvisation and took Rose's hand. Rose always figured she was asexual until now. She had never been more attracted to anyone in her life. Winter had experimented with girls before but it never quite stuck. Until now. The two of them knowing, in that instant, they were a couple. It just felt right. They never talked about it, they simply accepted it. In the dark train carriage later that night, snuggling into each other, Rose promised Winter one thing.

'Darlin', you won't ever have to worry about being abused no more. You're the safest with me you're ever gonna be. I can promise you that. The day I hit you, is the day I don't deserve you. And if that ever happens, you walk away and don't ask any questions. You understand?'

Winter nodded slowly, looking into her eyes. They kissed, and Winter fell asleep in Rose's lap as the train took them to Arizona.

Rose now looking at her hand, standing in the highway underpass. Ruby and Ned watching as Winter is brought to her feet by the help of Dennis. Winter isn't crying anymore. Her face pale. Dried black mascara stains running down her cheeks. A stoned faced expression. She pats the spot where Rose struck her. With the other hand she rips the bow from her hair and tosses it to the ground.

Rose takes a step toward her with a consoling hand out. Winter holds her arm out, palm in the air signaling for Rose to stop. She does. Tears dripping down her face.

'Sweetpea, I-'

'No.'

Rose swallows the lump in her throat.

Winter takes a deep breath and lets it out slowly, her face full of resolve.

'The day you hit me...'

Rose parts her dry lips to say something but stops herself. Remembering the end of that sentence. The same one she said on the train four years ago. Feeling to Rose like a lifetime ago. But she remembers what she said. And so does Winter.

Without another word, Winter turns on her heels and marches back to the limousine. Dennis gives Rose a look of sadness and pity. He turns and follows Winter to the limo. He climbs in the back and after a few moments reemerges with Star of the Sea in his arms. He gently lays her by the side of the road next to one of the thick foundation pole, placing her weaved shoulder bag next to her. He returns to the limo and hops in the driver's side. Rose watches Winter hop in the back and closes the door.

Rose watching with disappointment and sadness. The last time she'll ever see her Sweetpea. And it's all her fault. She wants to run over there, tear that door off its hinges. Grab her Winter in her arms and carry her home. Put her into bed and turn the fan on. Stick her Pikachu toy in her arms and pull up a chair. Watch her sleep for eight hours straight.

The limousine engine starts. Rose watching helplessly as it drives off up the curved road leading back to the highway.

Ruby adjusts his pants higher above his waist.

'So, um, sorry about all that.'

Rose's voice is flat. Lifeless. She's looking down at Nick's dead body.

'I'm not done with you Ruby Tuesday.'

'Fuck's sake.'

'Why'd you have to kill the kid? Nick was annoying as fuck, but he didn't deserve to die. The kid was gonna heal animals and shit. Do some actual good. Who killed him?'

Rose looking at both of them. Ned quickly raises his arm and points to Ruby.

'It was him, he did it. I was just helping him set up the jumper cables.'

'You God damn snitch,' says Ruby with a sneer to Ned.

'Look, I didn't do anything here except give that man a lift. Can I go now? I won't say anything, I promise.'

Rose turns her head to look at Ned. She raises her arm out and beckons with her index finger for him to come over to her. Ned looks at Ruby, gulps, then drops the jumper cable and ambles over to Rose. As soon as he reaches her, she whips the gun out from her pants and uses the butt of it to slam into Ned's forehead. He hits the ground unconscious.

Ruby sighs. 'Jesus Christ.'

'He'll live.' She motions to the Tesla. 'Get in that car.'

'Where are we going?'

'Wherever the fuck I take you.'

Ruby growls a few curse words under his breath and goes to get in the passenger side.

Rose says, 'In the back.'

Ruby stops, looking at Rose with contempt. Her standing rigidly in the middle of the road eyeing him sharply. Ruby takes a couple of steps back and opens the back door, climbing in.

Rose wedges the gun in the back of her pants and strides over to Star and picks up her limp body. She takes her to Ned's BMW and opens the back door, laying her across the back seat. She drops the shoulder bag on the floor of the back and slams the door.

Rose marches over to Ned's body and hooks her arms under his, dragging him to the BMW. She struggles with his portly body but manages to get him in the passenger seat and arranges him to sit upright in the chair. Rose rounds the car and jumps in the driver's seat. She starts the engine and drives it several yards and parks it, hiding it behind one of the big foundation poles. She cracks the windows a little, in case it gets hot later and no one has found them.

Rose gets out and throws the key as far as she can. It lands in a cluster of plants about fifteen yards away. Rose grabs Nick's ankles and lifts them up, dragging his body behind the pole next to the BMW. A long thick trail of blood leading to where he is. Rose figures it'll be a little while until anyone notices. She arrives at the driver's side of the Tesla and opens the door. Before she gets in, Rose looks out to the desert landscape beyond the road. The first hints of sunlight are emerging on the horizon.

'Cock-a-doodle-fuckin-doo.'

With that, Rose hops in the Tesla and turns the engine on. She drives up the bended road and back onto Route 66.

CHAPTER TWENTY-TWO

A Hen In The Rooster House

Stars are still visible in the violet morning sky, slowly being drowned out by the crisp rays of sunlight creeping their way across the red desert landscape. The Tesla is parked next to The Glass Half Full. Lights still on and two doors wide open. No other cars in the lot. Until a black rental Mercedes cruises past the "BAR CLOSED UNTIL FURTHER NOTICE" sign at the start of the drive way leading to the saloon. The car pulls up slowly on the gravel a few yards from the stairs leading to the front porch. The driver's door opens and two legs swing out, a pair of shiny black calfskin Louboutin stilettos with red soles lands on the dirt.

Jillian hops out of the Mercedes and adjusts her Gucci Butterfly sunglasses on her pointy little nose. Her hair pulled back tight into a neat ponytail. She looks freshly showered, because she is. Jillian managed to squeeze in a shower on the private jet, and a few gin and tonics with her egg whites and salmon. She's dressed in a dark navy blue tightly trimmed power suit, tailored for her petite, yet firm, body. The top has three buttons and a thick collar, popped up, the skirt down to her knees with a long slit running up the side.

Jillian struts toward the saloon stairs, something catching her attention out of her peripheral vision. She detours over a few yards to where a scorpion is scuttling across the dirt. Jillian smiles down at it. Admiring the toughness of this creature, out here in the hot sun during the day, freezing at night. Foraging for food and battling predators. Her smile fades into a sneer. Jillian raises her foot and stamps her Louboutin shoe on the scorpion, twisting her foot left and right several times, feeling the crackling of its shell armor turn to mush in the dirt. She takes a deep breath and resumes her strut toward the saloon.

Jillian ascends the stairs, her thick calf muscles protruding. She gets halfway and stops, looking down at the side of the staircase. She notices a purple corset and a shotgun lying in the dirt. Jillian raises an eyebrow curiously a moment, then continues up the stairs and onto the porch.

The front doors are wide open. The interior a little dark, the black drapes over the window blocking the growing morning sun. The wagon wheel chandelier in the middle is on but no other lights in use. Jillian steps in and delicately removes her sunglasses, waving her other hand in front of her face. A dank smell making her wince. Jillian wondering what the pungent aroma is, settling on alcohol. Cheap, nasty booze, she thinks, looking around the kitsch saloon bar. Paltry decorations, tasteless art and worn furniture. Jillian disgusted by this place. Except the jukebox. She kind of likes the retro music player for a reason she doesn't quite know. She hooks her sunglasses above the top button of her top. She looks to her left where the busted-up pinball machine is. Then over to the far corner where a chair used to be, replaced by a million woodchips. Some action definitely happened in here, Jillian surmises. Confident she found the right place now. That confidence goes full blown a hundred percent when she turns her head to the right and spots Ruby. He's sitting on the small stage, bound to a chair with old oil and grease soaked rope.

Jillian turns to face him with a soft grin one would sport when seeing an old friend.

'Hey Dad.'

'I hate it when you call me that.'

'That's why I said it.'

'How's your mother?'

'Dead.'

'Good for her.'

'Heart attack last year. A cocktail of painkillers did the job I believe.'

'I don't care.'

'I know.' Jillian smiles warmly.

She starts to step slowly in his direction, her heels wobbling a little at first, Jillian not used to the uneven wooden planked floor.

'So, we've all caught up now. How are you? Did they hurt you?'

'Don't worry. I still remember the fuckin' recipe.'

Jillian's voice jolly. 'Great to hear.'

'Get me the hell outta here.'

Jillian pulls at one of the knots above Ruby's bounded wrists. Her long fake nails digging in and doing a good job.

'Oh don't worry, I will. I just want to have a wee little chat with your-'

The two swinging doors to the kitchen burst open and Rose comes charging through, on a mission, eyes focused on a chore at hand, she stops in her tracks when she sees Jillian standing behind Ruby.

'Speak of the Devil and she shall appear.'

Rose remains still, silent.

Jillian unhooks her sunglasses from her top and brings them her face, biting on one end of handle gingerly as she steps down from the stage.

'Might you be the thorn in my side?'

'Might you be the Queen Bee?'

'As I live and breathe.'

Jillian now facing Rose, standing under the wagon wheel lights.

Rose looks her up and down, admiring her taut little body and manicured face.

'I knew you'd be hotter in person.'

Jillian rolls her eyes and says 'Ugh. I knew you were a dike.'

Rose places a hand on the end of the bar and haunches on her tip toes to look through the open front doors, expecting to find a cavalcade of cop cars. All she can see is the Mercedes.

'Are you alone?'

Jillian grandly gestures to herself with a big sweep of her hands from head to toe, like she was the top prize in a big competition.

'Just me.' Jillian now peering around the saloon skeptically. 'Where's your partner in crime?'

'She bailed. She won't be back.'

'Couldn't handle the heat?'

'Something like that.'

'So, it's a she? Am I to assume it's your girlfriend?'

Rose dodges the question and asks her own.

'How did you find me?'

'Good question.'

Jillian folds her sunglasses with one hand and drops them in her handbag. She takes a few steps forward and pulls an upside-down wooden chair off a table, wipes it a few times with her hand, inspects that hand for grime, then sits down daintily, crossing her pantyhose clad legs.

'See, I'm a firm believer of the mantra, "if you need something done, do it yourself". When I got off the phone to you, I sent out Tweedle-Dee and Tweedle-Dumb to come and source things out here, see if they could turn up anything. But I'm not one to leave important matters like this to chance. So, I did my own detective work. I mean, it wasn't exactly CSI type stuff to figure out my own flesh and blood over there is a full blown alcoholic.'

She turns her head casually to speak in Ruby's direction.

'Like father like daughter, am I right daddy dearest?'

Ruby grunts something untoward. Jillian grins and turns to look back at Rose. Hands neatly folded in her lap.

'Anywho, as soon as Peter and Marion left to come here-'

'Peter Kane?' Ruby chimes in, genuinely inquisitive.

'Yup. That ever grinning shit dumpling. Anyway, it doesn't matter. So, while knowing that Reuben drinks his weight in bourbon, I figured I should do some research on all the bars in the vicinity of his home. See if I can turn up anything. I narrowed it down, then I gave the results to a few of my private detectives. They're all good at what they do, I pay for the best. Ex military. Unlike that joker Marion I sent here to deal with you. I had them look into him as well. Turns out the head of security at Duke Security is not who he said he was. He wasn't even in the military at all. I've got more experience playing Call of fucking Duty. The only organization he was a part of was a stint as a mentor figure at the National Guard Youth Foundation. Can you believe that? The guy's a fuckin' glorified Boy Scout. He tried to join the police force years ago, but after a psych evaluation they thought he was too unhinged to wear a badge. So, he does security work and opens his own business. I was right to look into him it turns out. And Peter? The guy's useless. I really wanted him to come here because I knew he'd hate it out here. I thought maybe it would be good for him. Give some life experience to the spineless turd.'

'Wait, hold up. Who are these people? What the fuck does it have to do with anything?'

Jillian shrugs.

'I like telling stories.'

Rose pulls the .44 revolver from the back of her pants and cocks the hammer, holding it up next to her face with a bent elbow in her side.

'My forty-four likes telling stories too. They're real fast, and real fuckin' loud. Get to the point and tell me where my money is.'

Jillian smiles lazily. She reaches in her bag sheepishly and pulls out her big smartphone.

'Let's make something clear. I'm not a fucking idiot. My assistant Cassandra has the location of this bar, and if she doesn't hear from me in twenty minutes, every cop car this side of Arizona will be all up in your ass. Cool?'

Rose uncocks the gun, dropping her arm limply to her side, the gun swinging next to her thigh.

'Yeah, cool.'

'So, as I was saying before I was rudely interrupted, I was particularly interested in this establishment, considering it was the only one in the area which had a woman listed as the proprietor. I sent my guy to look into you, and do you know what I found, Rose?'

Rose doesn't say anything, just breathes angrily through her nose, staring at Jillian apathetically.

'Or, should I say, Katherine?'

Rose can't help widening her eyes a little.

'Katherine Robicheaux, to be exact. He managed to trace Rose Glass back to another establishment in Lexington, Kentucky. Like I said, the man is good, and he got a cleric from the Kentucky Office of Vital Statistics on the line. They did some digging, and do you know what they found?'

Rose places the gun on the end of the bar and walks around to behind the bar, pulling a glass tumbler off a shelf.

'What did they find?'

'They found that there was another Rose Glass, just seven years old. Died of a drowning the previous year the records were updated. They found that a tad bit interesting. So, they have this photo recognition software now. You can put a picture of someone's face, and the software searches all state records, newspapers, school photos, all that jazz. When they stuck your license picture into the software, it struck a partial match. A picture in a newspaper article. About a rich girl from Baton Rouge who absconded her family. Cool little story. I mean, I could've alerted the authorities right then and there. But, I figured I'd have to come meet this chick from money who murdered her brother and disappeared. Movie of the week shit right there.'

Rose, in the middle of pouring a hefty glass of moonshine, stops mid pour. Jillian notices her freezing up. The look of a woman changed right there on her face. Jillian can almost see the blood flow from her face.

'Oh. You didn't know, did you?'

Rose doesn't say anything. She keeps pouring the drink then slams the bottle down on the wooden bench.

'Your brother died two weeks after you disappeared. Complications from head injuries, or some shit like that. The rest of your family pulled the life support.'

Rose chugs the whole glass, some of it spilling out from the sides of her mouth. She slams the glass down and starts pouring another.

Jillian rises up from her chair, picking her small handbag up, hands still clasped together holding the bag as she moseys toward the other end of the bar, one foot deliberately slow in front of the other.

'I get stuck in the office all day, in and out of meetings with clients, lawyers, having to put on a fake smile and laugh at their stupid jokes. Then this happens. Some Southern Bell's parents died. A family squabble and a sister kills a brother. Teenage girl up and vanishes like a black dude on his knocked up baby mama. Never found again. Not until she pops up in a small town in Arizona nearly twenty years later, trying to extort millions from a successful fast food chain. Man, this is some cool ass shit, know what I'm sayin'? Nothing cool ever happens to me. Then you did. So, thanks, I guess. Can I grab one of those drinks? Seems unfair you drinking all by yourself.'

Without looking at Jillian, Rose grabs a thick sturdy short glass from the shelf.

'What's your poison?'

'Whatever's floating your boat there.'

'It's moonshine.'

'Super.'

'It's strong stuff, I make it myself.'

'Even better.'

Rose shrugs and pours Jillian half a glass of peach moonshine. She steps over to the long bar top, Jillian at the other end of it. Rose places the glass on the bar top and pushes it effortlessly, the glass sliding down the bar toward Jillian like from an old movie. The cool bar glass sliding thing. The thick bottom of the glass hitting a small dent in the wood and tips over, spilling moonshine all over the bar. The glass falls off the side and smashes on the floor. Rose stares at the puddle of booze on the bar top, blinking with defeat. She looks over to Jillian, who gives her a big shrug and a comically screwed up face.

'Would've looked cool. 'A' for effort though.'

Rose sighs and grabs another glass from the shelf, filling it with moonshine as she walks down the bar to hand deliver it to Jillian. She takes it and gives her a 'cheers' motion with the glass, then takes a sip. She winces as the alcohol slips down her throat.

'Woo-wee girl. That's some powerful shit. That'll strip the nicotine tar right off my lungs. Day-um.'

Rose meanders back to her glass and takes a gulp out of it. She turns to face Jillian, leaning her hip against the counter.

'So we gonna talk about my money or what?'

Jillian pulls a stool over from a nearby barrel table.

'We will. But first, tell me what you've been up to all these years. I wanna hear all about it.'

Jillian props herself up on the stool, her arms out in front of her on the bar top clutching the glass with both hands like she's in kindergarten about to hear story time.

'There's not much to tell.' Rose sounding irritated now.

'Oh sure there is. You're being humble. Mind if I smoke?'

Jillian already has her hands rifling in her bag, pulling out a pack of Marlboro Lights and a zippo lighter.

Rose strides down toward her, grabbing an old glass ashtray on the way. She plonks it down on the bar top in front of Jillian, who lights up a smoke and blows a huge stream of smoke out the side of her mouth.

'Where did you go after?'

'Lexington. Worked for a sordid lady a while. Went east, did some odd jobs. Met a guy who gave me this bar. That's as up to date as it gets.'

'I don't believe for a second it was that simple. You're a criminal. You've clearly always had it in you. Most crims don't open their careers with murder though. That's impressive.'

'I didn't mean for him to die.'

'Now, see, I'm not so sure about that. I mean, here you are. A kidnapped billionaire in the corner of your bar. A lady sitting in front of you, that you tried to blackmail. Crimes not as big as murder, or manslaughter, whatever you wanna call it. Point is, a leopard can't change its spots.' A pause as Jillian takes in a lungful of smoke, blowing it out of the other side of her mouth. 'That's what they say.'

'Well, they, are full of shit.'

Rose knocks back the rest of her moonshine and is quick to pour another.

'See, thing is, the leopard didn't start out with spots. They looked just like most other big kitty cats. The spots came later. An evolutionary advantage. They found more prey in forests. But their yellow coats made 'em all too visible to those forest creatures. It was when the leopard started using the tricks of light caused by the thick foliage. The sun rays and leaves giving spots of light and dark. The leopard using the mix of light and dark to its advantage. Creepin' in the shadows. Happened so much that their physical appearance was warped over centuries to the stealth master they are now. So a leopard can, and did, change its spots. It's all relative to what your needs are. You know what flamingoes look like right?'

'Yeah, I know what a fucking flamingo looks like.'

'Those pink feathers are no accident. They should be grey. But the shrimp and algae they eat has some funky pigments in 'em. Makes the feathers turn pink.'

'Look at Animal Planet over here.'

'I like animals.'

'So do I. I like eating them. Are we going to sit here all day and talk anecdotes? I came all the way out to this dump to meet a bad ass bitch, and all I'm getting is David fucking Attenborough.'

Jillian ashes angrily into the glass tray.

Rose says 'What I'm tryin' to say is, you can't just paint a picture of someone and tell everyone that's what I look like. I pushed my brother off that balcony because no one else had the balls to. He died? Well, shit. Not my intention. I had to hit the streets and steal to survive. That's when I earned my spots. Now, out here, I was just a grey bird. Until you called, then my appetite changed, so did my feathers. But unlike most criminals, I wasn't doing this for me. I did it for Winter. She turned me into a Flamingo, you might say.'

Jillian blows out smoke, trying to get a ring in the air going, but failing. She blows the rest out in a big ugly cloud.

'Who or what the fuck is Winter? Was that this mysterious partner of yours?'

Rose lowers her head, looking at the floor with dejection.

'She's no one.'

'You two are talkin' so much shit your asshole must be jealous,' says Ruby.

Jillian takes one more drag of the smoke and stubs it out in the ashtray.

'The old cunt has a point. This is going nowhere. I was a little drunk last night. I had all these fantasies of... I guess I thought you were cool in a way. Like, I'd meet you and we'd hit it off. I could even hire you. Be my number two. Go on adventures and start shit. Thelma and Louise kinda stuff. Y'know? But now, I'm a bit more sober and all this is beginning to seem like a waste of time.'

'Fuckin' aye. So how about we get around to talking about my money?'

'Yeah, about that.'

Jillian pushes off the stool to stand, running her palms down her skirt to smooth out the fabric.

'I think it's probably becoming clear to you that it's not going to happen. I mean, now that I have my charming father, and the recipe back, and the name and location of the kidnappers, why the fuck would I give you a dime?'

'We had a deal.'

Jillian bursts out laughing. A moment as Rose watches. Jillian stops and clears her throat. She looks at Rose with furrowed brows, taken aback.

'You're serious, aren't you?'

Rose pours herself another moonshine, giving Jillian a no-nonsense look.

'Wow. You are something else. First you try and rob me by being a dick. That goes south, and now you're asking nicely if you can rob me?'

Ruby clears his throat and chimes in.

'You're both fuckin' thieves. One of you just dresses better.' Ruby makes a deliberate glare at Jillian. 'And the other one I should have squirted down my ex wife's throat instead of her cunny.'

Jillian cocks her head to the side and gives him an overly sweet smile.

'Awww, how sweet.'

Jillian turns to face Rose again.

'Here's what I will do. I'm gonna give you a big, sweet fuck all. No money, honey. But what I will do, is say nothing. I've had to handle way too many scandals recently, and I don't need Plucky's in the headlines again, not for something negative. So, we call it quits, here and now. I take my adorable father to New York, and you figure out what hairbrained scheme you're gonna hatch next. Maybe stay away from kidnapping. Doesn't seem to be your thing. Deal?'

Rose finishes what's left in her glass. Her head all the way back to catch every last drop. She slams the glass down on the bar top, wiping her mouth with the back of her hand.

'Fine. Take him. I didn't think I could turn more gay, but being around that cock thumper convinces me otherwise.'

'Oh, I hear ya.' Jillian brings her glass to her mouth.

Rose rounds the bar to the other side on the main floor.

'But how about I fight you for that money?'

'Excuse me?'

'You heard me. I'll fight ya for it. Not all of it. One million. If I knock you out, I get to have it. You KO me, you just walk outta here with Ruby Tuesday, like nothing ever happened.'

Jillian just stands there, glass in hand, her expression incredulous. She spits out a guffaw, and keeps her mouth open a few moments.

'You're insane.'

'A little.'

'I love it.'

'No guns. Just pure fisty-cuffs. Mono-a-mono. You think you can manage that daddy's girl? Let's see if you're a bee or a wasp.'

'First of all,' Jillian motions to Ruby, 'don't you dare compare me to him.'

Jillian places her glass on the bar top and steps out on the main floor, standing a few yards in front of Rose.

'Secondly, you're on like Donkey Kong.'

Jillian sizing her up now. She's fit as hell, but Jillian reckons she can take her.

Jillian sports a devilish smile, licking her lips with excitement. She's never used her fighting skills on a real opponent before.

Jillian uses her feet to kick her heels off. They both clatter on the wooden floorboards next to her. She picks the shoes up and goes to put them on a nearby table.

Rose points at the table and raises her voice, 'Don't you fuckin' dare.'

Jillian freezes, hovering the shoes mere inches from the table top.

'What?'

'Don't you know puttin' shoes on a table is bad luck?'

'No. I didn't.'

'Well it is.'

Jillian sighs and shakes her head, shifting her arm to place the shoes on a chair.

'You're a fucking weirdo.' Jillian steps over to stand in line with Rose. 'Alright faggot. Let's rumble.'

Jillian raises her fists like she's a pro boxer. Throwing in a few air punches. Psyching herself up.

'We're doing this bare knuckle. No bitch mittens.'

Rose gives Jillian a lopsided grin.

'I prefer no gloves too.'

'I don't give a flying fuck what you prefer.'

'You're turning me on lady.'

Rose assumes the boxer position. One foot in front of the other. Fists raised and bouncing in the air.

'I'm newly single. Sure you don't wanna fuck instead of fight?'

'Fish taco's make me puke.'

'Your loss.'

Jillian grabs the slit in her skirt at the top and rips it to make the slit bigger, coming up to the top of thigh. Jillian locks her fingers together and cracks her knuckles, stepping forward into Rose's space. Eyes locked, they circle each other for a good minute. Jillian sticks out her ass, wincing, then continues to circle. After about ten seconds, Rose's nostril twitches. She smells something, and it's not the pungent alcohol smell. It's something else. Something a lot worse. Rose stops on the spot, fists still raised.

'Did you fart?'

Jillian stops. Her lips are warped, fighting a smile. She's trying to hold back a laugh and can't anymore. She bursts out giggling, putting her hand to her mouth.

'That fuckin' stinks. It's wretched. Like milk left out in the sun for hours.'

Jillian starts laughing boisterously, like it's the funniest thing she's ever heard.

Rose peers at her through the slits of her eyes, not impressed at all.

'Seriously, you're one nasty bitch.'

'Thank you,' Jillian manages to get out between belts of laughter.

Ruby even laughs. Jillian looks over to him through watery eyes, nodding and laughing. The two of them having a father-daughter moment for the first time in a very long time.

Rose shakes her head in disappointment.

'Fucking Christ, man.'

Rose gets back into fight mode and starts circling again. Jillian pulling herself together now, getting down to business and assuming a mirroring fight pose against Rose. It's Rose who goes first, throwing the first punch.

And it's on.

Jillian ducks the jab.

Neither woman sees it, but Ruby has liberated himself of the rope shackles. The two of them too focused on each other as they start to bout. Ruby undoes the main knot binding his wrists, which Jillian started clawing at earlier. He carefully pulls the rope off and drops it to the floor. Ruby creeps along the side of the wall past the draped windows. A floorboard creaks but Jillian and Rose are too busy fixated to notice. Ruby slinks out the front door, down the stairs, and hobbles to the Tesla. He grabs the remote key and presses the engine to life. He grabs the wheel and drives off onto the highway, taking a left toward Holbrook.

Jillian throws a jab at Rose, who weaves aside with ease. Rose throws a few more punches to Jillian's head and misses. A distraction from what Rose really wants to do, which she does next and lands a hard fist in Jillian's side. Jillian careens back, letting out an 'oomph' of air.

Rose comes in for another, doing a duck and weave to the side before springing a punch out again. Jillian was waiting for this exact move and launches an attack on Rose's face, hitting her square in the eye with her knuckles.

Rose jolts back from the punch, a sharp surge of pain linking straight to her brain. 'Nice one', Rose thinks. Jillian smiles, pleased with herself. The smile making Rose lose respect for Jillian; too cocky. Rose pivots forward with a barrage of punches, hard and fast. Body shot, head shot, body shot, head shot, repeat, repeat, faster and faster. Jillian having trouble defending herself from the onslaught, using her wrists to try and block. Some successful, some not. Because of the rapid movements the punches don't land as hard, but Rose is doing some damage. Not just to Jillian's body, but to her ego as well.

When Rose finishes her spree attack out of exhaustion, that's when Jillian takes advantage. She sweeps a perfect right hook into the side of Rose's head, making her see stars a moment and lose balance.

'Damn girl. You're good. That's some Lennox Lewis style shit right there. Where'd you learn to box?'

Jillian uses the moment to two-step forward and uppercut Rose in the chin so hard it sends her crashing into a four-seater table behind,

Rose's weight breaking the wood and sending a mess of table legs and broken wood all over the surrounding floor.

Jillian blows loose strands of hair from her face with her mouth.

'X-Box Kinect, bitch.'

Rose groans and rolls over, preparing to stand, when Jillian takes run up and kicks her hard in the gut. Rose yells out in pain and barrel rolls across the floor, holding her sides.

'You fuckin' asshole!'

'What's your problem, faggot?'

Rose's face red and angry.

'You don't kick people while they're down.'

'You think I'm gonna give you a million bucks that easy? Fuck you.'

Jillian runs at her again to give another kick, but Rose manages to roll out of the way. Jillian's kick meeting thin air. Rose on all fours now, glaring up at Jillian. She pushes her toes onto the floor and springs herself forward, launching at Jillian, tackling her around the waist and charging her backward into the jukebox; Jillian's back crashing into the glass viewing panel. A few pieces of serrated glass stabbing through Jillian's skin and making her squeal through her teeth.

The jukebox kicks into action and starts playing "Together in Electric Dreams" by *Philip Oakey and Giorgio Moroder*. Jillian clasps both fists together and brings them down hard on Rose's head, forcing her to lose her grip on Jillian's waist, stumbling back. Jillian pushes off the jukebox and reaches blindly around her back, pulling out the shards of glass embedded in her. She growls like a dog as Rose comes in for another tackle. Jillian pivots on her feet into a 180-degree spin and avoid the tackle, Rose stopping herself by grabbing the sides of the jukebox.

Rose turns her head just in time to see Jillian's balled fist clock her in the nose with a resounding crack and pop sound. Blood gushes from

Rose's nose. She covers her nose with her hands for a moment, then looks down at her blood-soaked palms. She looks to Jillian, bouncing on the spot with her fists raised. Looking mighty pleased with herself.

Rose roars with anger and clenches her fists, coming at her. She throws punches with both hands, one-two, one-two, one-two. Rose lands a hit on Jillian's cheek, making her lose confidence for a moment, and that's all it takes. Rose goes for the torso and lands two heavy punches into Jillian's rib, cracking the bottom bone. Jillian howls with pain and is knocked into one of the wooden pillars. She sucks in a lungful of air and holds her side. Rose not wanting to lose momentum comes in blazing, fists thumping into Jillian, who flimsily tries to block them.

Jillian is trapped against the pole as Rose pounds into her. Jillian, not knowing what else to do, grabs Rose by the head and leans in, biting her ear lobe. A chunk off the bottom tears off in Jillian's teeth, blood immediately dripping from the fresh wound. Rose lets out a guttural scream. Jillian spits the chunk of flesh to the side, Rose's blood now on her teeth. Jillian lifts her leg out and kicks Rose in the side of her arm, making her lose balance. Jillian socks her again in the other eye. Rose's head jerks back. The pain now being substituted for adrenaline. Rose returns the sentiment and punches Jillian in her right eye. Jillian stumbling backward a few steps. Rose coming in again with the rage of a wounded bull. Rose punches Jillian right in the mouth hearing a crack sound. She delivers a heavy fist into the side of Jillian's head, forcing her to spin to the side and into the nearby wall. Jillian seeing stars a moment, disorientated. She can make out Rose's figure in the haze of concussion.

Rose saying, 'Ready to pack it in Sweetheart?'

Jillian reaches blindly around the wall for something. Anything. The music playing in the background. *"We'll always be together, however far it seems…"*

Rose says, 'I'll let you off the hook, if you wanna just wire me the money now.'

Jillian's hand feeling the felt of a dartboard. Her fingers find the welcoming metal of a dart and she rips it from the board, spinning around and pegs it aimlessly at Rose.

The dart lands right in the center of Rose's left breast with a 'thonk' sound. Rose stops in her tracks and looks down to see the red and black tipped dart jiggling from her boob. She looks back up at Jillian, her expression stunned.

'You got me right in the tit.'

Jillian stands with her back up against the wall, both hands planted on the wooden boards either side of her. Her hair is a frayed mess, strands sticking out all over, looking like a wild animal. Jillian is grunting, catching her breath and her bearings. She's blinking her eyes back to proper sight.

Rose looks down at the dart hanging from her chest.

'Right in the fucking nipple!'

Jillian wipes blood from her mouth and smiles. She's missing a tooth on her upper gum, the third one back from the front tooth. She blurts out a low toned laugh.

'Bullseye.'

Rose rips the dart out with a groan and tosses it irately to the side. Her face full of wrath, wanting to kill this woman now.

Jillian shakes her head rapidly like a wet dog, trying to get rid of the double vision she has. Her sight like she's inside a soap bubble. She starts to see straight again. Rose clenching her fists and coming at her again. Jillian now fueled with the taste of her own blood, pushing off the wall and diving into Rose, the two of them losing balance and crashing into a table behind so they are both lying on top.

Jillian rolls over on the table and starts laying hammer punches into Rose's side. Rose rolls out of the way and grabs Jillian's wrist, stopping the punches. Using her other hand to pull Jillian's hair, making her squeal. They wrestle a moment on the table, Jillian trying to free her fist. Rose rolls over and rises on her knees above Jillian, grabbing the other wrist. Jillian fighting to get free, Rose fighting to hold on. They both fall off the table and land hard on their sides on the floor, knocking wind out of them both. Rose has lost her hold of Jillian's wrists, but is quick to roll over and straddle Jillian, knees either side of her. Rose starts laying in punches to Jillian's upper body and face.

Jillian arches her back on the floor to raise herself a little, then kicks her legs around wildly, bucking like a bronco. Rose keeps hitting her, one of the punches hits her in the nose and busts it. Jillian howls out in pain. She manages to get one leg free and brings it up to Rose's neck, sticking her dirty pantyhose into Rose's mouth and eyes, trying to gouge them with her webbed together toes.

Rose stops punching and grabs Jillian's ankle, then leans in and bites the side of her foot. Jillian lets out a high-pitched scream. She reaches around on the floor for any kind of weapon, her hand finding a broken chair leg. Jillian swings the wooden leg into Rose's head, clubbing the side of her skull. Rose groans and topples to the side.

Jillian rolls the other way and props up on her elbows. So much pain running through different parts of her body she doesn't know where to start. Jillian uses a wooden pillar to help herself stand, clawing her way up, several of her fingernails broken and jagged. She's upstanding now, clutching the pole for dear life, looking over to find Rose using a wooden stool to pull herself to stand. Rose holding the side of her head, disorientated. Jillian staggers over and reaches Rose just as she gets properly upright and kicks her hard in between the legs, her foot landing hard in Rose's groin.

Rose doubles over in agony, wrapping her arms across her lower torso, eyes wide with shock. She drops to her knees. Jillian has a chair in her possession now, holding it by the top, the four legs sticking out in the air. Rose goes to say 'stop', but before she can Jillian crashes the wooden chair on her back, shattering it to pieces. Rose falls forward in a heap, thumping on the floorboards. A new song playing on the broken jukebox, "We Like to Party!" by *The Vengaboys*. An addition to the jukebox administered by Winter, being one of her favorite songs.

Jillian throws the two sticks that used to be part of the chair to the floor. She steps over Rose's body and trips, hitting the floor. Ever resilient, Rose crawls across the floor toward the bar, knocking wooden remnants from broken tables and chairs out of her way. She drags her whole body using the little energy she has left, fingers digging into the clefts between the floorboards. Jillian pulls herself back up onto her knees, then pushes off the floor to stand up, staggering toward the bar. The two women after the same thing.

The .44 revolver still sitting on the corner of the bar.

The music pumping from the jukebox, "*We like to party, we like, we like to party. We like to party, we like, we like to party.*"

Rose is getting her strength back, using more power in her elbows to drag herself in longer and faster. Jillian hobbles on her bitten foot to the bar and plants her hands on it. She uses the edge of the bar as a guide down to the gun. She picks it up just as Rose reaches the bar. She sees Jillian pick up the gun and her spirits sink to the pit of her stomach. Defeated. Rose reaches the bottom of the bar and shimmies her back up to sit upright against it.

Both women are beaten. Their eyes swollen. Blood smeared all around their mouths and nostrils. Rose missing the bottom of her ear lobe. Both their knuckles on either hand blue from constant hammering. Hair frazzled with dried blood on parts of their scalps. They have been fighting dirty and look like it.

Jillian turns and aims the gun at the jukebox. She fires twice, the bullets hitting the main console, causing sparks and stopping the music.

'I fucking hate The Vengaboys.'

Jillian steps like a drunk toward the other end of the bar and grabs her pack of cigarettes and the lighter.

'Game over. I win.'

'That groin shot... that was below the belt, man.'

Jillian limps back to where Rose is propped up against the bar, heaving her breaths. Jillian now standing in front of her, looking down. Gun in hand by her side. Jillian licks her gums, only noticing now she's missing a tooth. She puts a smoke in her mouth and lights it up, dragging that first hit of the cigarette, eyes shut and savoring every second. She exhales a long cloud of smoke and looks down to Rose.

'I'm the CEO of a billion dollar empire. I didn't get to where I am by playing fair. I sold out my own father for fuck's sake. Isn't that right Dad?'

Jillian looks over to see the empty seat on the stage with loose rope at the feet.

'Fuck.'

Jillian turns her attention back to Rose.

'On the plus side there'll be no witnesses.'

Rose winces, hurting to talk.

'Witness to what?'

'To me shooting you out of self defense.'

Her voice high now, mimicking a damsel in distress.

'She went crazy officer. Then she beat me up. I managed to fight back and get the upper hand. I told her to stop, to let me go. But she said she was going to kill me. I had no choice but to shoot her. I didn't mean to kill her officer, I swear!'

Jillian smiles, showing her bloody teeth and the gap where a tooth used to be. She raises the gun and points it at Rose's face. Rose coughs and looks up to Jillian with a wooden expression. Deflated.

Jillian says, 'And after I'm done here, I might go find this partner of yours. Winter, wasn't it?'

Rose holding an impassive glare. Behind that she is hiding her rage.

'Wait. Before you do it. Can I have one of those?'

Rose nods her head to Jillian's hand holding the cigarettes.

Jillian looks at the smokes and then back to Rose, shrugging her shoulders.

'Why the fuck not.'

She tosses the Marlboro Lights pack into Rose's lap.

Rose says, 'Don't forget the light.'

Jillian chucks the lighter, it lands next to the cigarettes.

'You're not gonna smoke a whole one. I haven't got enough time for that. Just a few puffs, okay?'

Rose nods slowly as she picks up the lighter. Jillian's memory has never let her down. She's good at remembering little details. Like when Marion originally told her he was in the Marines, then later saying the Navy Seals. Her gut telling her that his story isn't straight. That's what prompted her to call her private investigators. But now, in this moment, something doesn't feel right. And then it hits her. When she was talking to Rose on the phone last night, she lit up a cigarette, and Rose said something along the lines of "smoking will kill you". Sounding like one of those arrogant assholes on her high horse. Jillian watches as Rose snaps the zippo open.

'Wait. I thought you said you didn't smoke?'

Rose thumbs the little metal wheel igniting the flame. She looks up to Jillian. Her black eye a lot more swollen, the blood on her severed ear lobe drying, and a mischievous smile broadening.

'I don't. But we're about to be smokin'.'

Rose suddenly pitches the lighter a few feet away and it lands on a floorboard that looks wet and damp. That's because Rose tossed kerosene all over the bar ten minutes before Jillian arrived.

Jillian now sniffing the air. Remembering the pungent alcohol smell when she first stepped in here, thinking it was just cheap booze. Jillian watches as the flame from the lighter connects with the floorboard and a 'whoompf' sound as a much bigger flame rises from the floor. Jillian's eyes on the big flame, watching as it snakes across the wooden floor in a trail of kerosene, connecting with other trails of kerosene. The flames spreading quickly across the bar floor, rising into hot streaks zipping all over the floor and now the walls. Jillian looks at the wide open entry doors.

She smirks to herself thinking this is brilliant. She can just waltz out those doors and the whole place will be reduced to ashes, disposing of any evidence. Hell, she can say she was never here in the first place. Jillian noticing now that the trails of flames are converging and heading in the corner room behind the main bar. Jillian's intuition making her feet move down the bar, following the flames. She reaches the end of the bar and peers into the betting room. The flames are ripping through the wooden furniture, to the back of the room where several large metal tins are stacked in the corner. Jillian doesn't know those tins are filled with methanol, but she notices the edge of the big generator outside through the window, just on the other side of the wall from the tins. The flames about to hit the tins, Jillian puts two and two together.

Jillian looks over at Rose, still lying against the bar. She's cackling with laughter, raising one of her arms and gives Jillian the middle finger.

Jillian looks back into the room just as the kerosene flames hit the methanol tins. Her expression dour. Her face full of subdued acceptance.

'Fucking fagg-'

BOOM.

CHAPTER TWENTY-THREE

The Not So Secret Sauce

Large red fire ants are crawling into Nick's gaping mouth. There's a long string of the fire ants, following the trail of blood under the highway in the lonesome underpass. Nick's dead body still lying behind a thick foundation pillar, the BMW parked next to him.

Ned is in the passenger seat, slowly coming back to consciousness. His eyes flickering open. He rubs his forehead where Rose clobbered him with the butt of her gun. He groans and leans forward. He opens his eyes properly and looks around to get his bearings.

Ned shifts in his seat, pulling his blood splattered white bath robe tighter. The cold air from early morning still lingering in the car from the windows partially down. The smell of stale fried chicken. The tub of untouched chicken pieces still sitting in the middle of the passenger and driver's seat. The sun seems to be coming up. Ned wipes his bald skull to his horseshoe ring of hair, wondering now how long he's been out cold. He looks at his watch. Almost an hour and a half, he surmises, give or take. Ned turns his whole body to look behind the car and around it. He can't see any other cars. The bitch who knocked him must have fled with Reuben Wallace.

A loud truck roars by on the highway above.

Ned opens the car door and steps out, his slippers hitting the gravel, looking down as he rises to stand, noticing the ground moving. Ned yelps and jumps back at the sight of the fire ants. He rushes to the back of the car, then stops at the sight of Nick. Ned stares at the body a moment. Eyes closed and mouth agape. Ants beginning to take over his body, crawling in every orifice Ned can see. He looks away, to the back window of this BMW rental. That's when he sees a pair of sneakers dangling over the edge of the backseat.

Ned fumbles around the car to the back door. He opens the door to find Star of the Sea lying across the whole seat, her head next to the adjacent door. Ned looking her head to toe, wearing the woven headband and the dirty poncho. Wondering where on earth she came from. Was she lost, wandering down the highway? Maybe she got cold, saw the car and helped herself. Like Goldilocks. Ned focuses on her face. She looks very young he's thinking. All that baby fat on her cheeks. Ned leans in and lifts up her poncho a bit. She's wearing short shorts and a white crop top underneath. Ned thinking now that with her small, delicate figure, she must be no more than twelve or thirteen. A little older than he likes his girls, but Ned's not necessarily too picky. Not right now at least. She's a fine little specimen this one. Ned licks his lips.

Star's eyes flutter a moment, then they start to open. All she can see at first is the backside of a car seat. She can feel her legs being caressed. A big soft hand is stroking her calf muscles, sliding up the inside of her poncho toward her crotch.

Star raises her head to look over at the source of the wandering hand. It takes her a moment to focus. Her head is a fuzzy mess of concussion. Star's eyesight now returning enough for her to see Ned in his robe stained with blood. His long forehead and big eyes, focused on her legs. His mouth slightly agape, practically drooling.

'What the fuck…' says Star in a croaky voice.

Ned's eyes meet her droopy eyes, and he smiles warmly.

'Shhhh little darling. It's okay, there's nothing to be afraid of.'

'Why are your hands on…'

Star now realizing what's happening. She has no idea of who this is and why she's in this new smelling car, what time it is, or where the hell they are. But she does know one thing; this man is a creep. Star makes a face of utter disgust which quickly clouds into seething anger. She uses all her strength to raise her leg and kick him in the face. It's not a powerful blow, because Star's flimsy kick is all she can muster in her woozy state. Ned's face is pushed to the side as her sneaker mushes his cheek fat. He recovers quickly then looks back to her. His hand still on her thigh, his other hand waggling his index finger at her.

'Now, now, little one. That was naughty.'

He brings his other hand to slide up her leg to meet his other hand.

'And do you know what happens to naughty little girls? They get a spanking.' Ned says that with a mischievous grin.

Ned's hands find the top of her little shorts and he starts to pull at them to get them off her. Star shimmies forward and hits her head on the inside of the car door. Ned grabs her thighs now and pulls her toward him. Star struggles against him, wriggling her hips to try and pull away, so she can sit up straight and open the car door to run. Ned has her legs in a tight grip. Star tries to kick him again, but he has her legs pressed together, so she just bucks her body. She's not making it easy for him, but he's managing to pull her inch by inch closer to him. Star starts grabbing at the door handle, pulling at it but it won't open. Child lock must be on. Ned yanks her roughly to him.

'Come here you little shit!'

She's getting desperate now, reaching around her for anything to use as a weapon. Her hand falls on her shoulder bag on the car floor. She shoves her hand in and feels around a moment, her hand resting on a familiar object. Star quickly rises into a sitting position with her arm outstretched.

'Hey pedophile!'

Ned looks up, his eyes meet the end of the metal barrel of a Colt Viper .38 pistol.

BANG.

A bullet rips through Ned's skull ending his life in seconds. His eyes roll back and he falls backward into the dirt, on top of the bloody patch of contents sprayed from his head. His robe now open, exposing his bloated hairy stomach and flannel boxer shorts.

Star remains in the sitting position a moment. Her vision still distorted a little, she fixates on the smoke from the shot wisp from the barrel of the gun. The inside of her head feeling to Star like shag carpet. She blinks a few times and edges across the seat to look out at her surroundings. She notices the trail of blood leading from the road to the car.

Star jumps out of the car and follows the trail to Nick's corpse, crawling with fire ants. The back of his head has a large split along the skull, the encrusted blood now a dark maroon, bits of dirt and pebbles stuck there from when he was dragged to this spot. Star stands back, staring at the body. She feels a wave of sadness. Star thinking it's sad he died a virgin.

Star starting to feel tired now. Feeling like she needs to sleep. Her resolve telling her she needs to flee this crime scene. Get her head and story together. The only way out is this BMW. She looks through the car for keys. She finds the bucket of fried chicken. Feeling hungry all of a sudden. Star does the unthinkable. She grabs a cold drumstick and bites into it. Chewing, and enjoying the welcome taste of protein. The first time she's eaten meat in a very long time. She finishes the whole thing, throws the bone back in the bucket and grabs another, chowing it down. Star surprised how much she likes this chicken. She feels dizzy again, shaking her head. Must find those keys.

Star checks all through the car. No luck. She dashes to Ned's body and searches his pockets for keys. Nothing. She does the same with Nick. Again, nothing. Her eyesight sketchy from the concussion. Everything looking like slowed down shutter speed when she moves. She searches the area around the car, runs across the road in the underpass. Star runs to the clumps of plants under the highway. She sees a metallic glint coming from a cluster of plants. A set of keys. Bingo. She snatches them up and runs back to the BMW.

Oh right, she's too short to drive this car.

Star pulls the laces out of her sneakers. She finds two thick rocks and ties them to the bottom of her shoes with the laces. Star pulls the driver's seat as far forward as possible. The rocks on her feet just being able to reach the pedals. She starts the engine and drives the car slowly, trying not to run over the two dead bodies lying either side of it. Star drives onto the road and up the bend to the highway.

Ruby speeds down Route 66 in the Tesla. His face sweaty and heart racing. The lights around the odometer flicker. The car jolts a little, then the sound of the engine conking out. Ruby is forced to slow down and pull over to the side of the road. The Tesla already sucked dry to charge the BMW with the jumper cables. The nickel-metal-hydride battery pack has seen way too much use and is on its way out.

Ruby pounds the steering wheel with his fists as the car comes to a stop. A truck roars past followed by a string of cars. Ruby looks up ahead, just making out the Plucky's sign. It's early morning, so there will be people around. Those fuckers who work there can't kick him out again. Too many people to see. Ruby pushes out the driver's door with a series of grunts, and power walks down the highway, holding his thumb out. Cars soaring past. No one wants to give a lift to a sweaty red faced man in a dirty white suit. Ruby keeps his resolve and heads for the Plucky's restaurant.

Star of the Sea is at the wheel of the BMW, stretching her neck to look over the dashboard. Flashes of colors whiz by like a strobe effect, other cars on the road that are a blur to her concussed mind.

She is too focused on the road through her askew vision to notice Rueben Wallace speed walking down the side of the highway as she drives past. She keeps blinking, trying to keep it together. Suddenly a large explosion booms ahead. A ball of flame licks the sky above The Glass Half Full as she almost passes it. Star hits the brakes and veers off the road to stop, realizing she's gone the wrong way, heading out away from Holbrook and not to it. She watches as flames tear through the whole saloon bar, being destroyed in a matter of seconds. The neon glass sign sailing through the air from the rush of explosion and landing in a smoky heap not far from the highway. The whole bar furiously ablaze now. Charcoaled foundations crumbling. Star thinking if there's anyone in there, there's no way they survived that.

Star flicks the car's indicator lever, though the cars coming the other way have all stopped to watch the massive explosion and ensuing bonfire. Star turns the wheel and starts driving back the way she came. Blinking a lot more furiously now, her head feeling lighter by the minute.

The BMW hits a pothole and the car shudders making Star's vision scramble a moment. She shakes her head from side to side. When she looks back to the road she sees a coyote fifteen yards ahead. A black coated coyote. Star panics, not wanting to hit the animal, and sharply pulls the steering wheel to the right.

The car tires hit the gravel and she steers the car along the side of the road, only noticing a shape just in front of her becoming rapidly closer. The car smashes a cactus and the top of it barrels into the windscreen creating a spider-web crack. Another shape coming fast. The shape turning into a fat old man in a white suit. Star hits the brakes, but it's too late. A loud thump sound as the hood of the car catches Ruby and knocks him off his feet, a moment later the front of the car slams into the base of the Plucky's sign pole on the side of the highway. Ruby smashing into the pole with force. Star, not wearing a seatbelt, is sent smashing through the cracked windscreen and lands on the end of the crumpled car hood. Ruby has landed on the bashed up hood as well, knocked out from the violent crash. Blood seeping out of his mouth. Star's pudgy little face is mottled with bits of broken glass embedded in her skin and scalp. Both Star and Ruby lie on the hood of the car, broken and near unconscious. Their bleeding faces mere inches from each other's.

The doors to the Plucky's Chicken Palace Holbrook outlet burst open and night manager Seth comes rushing out, sprinting through the empty car park down the incline to the Pluck's sign where he saw the car slam into the pole from inside. Smoke is pouring out of crumpled hood. He can see two bodies lying on the front of the car facing one another. As Seth arrives to the scene, he recognizes Ruby in his filthy white suit. And another person. A girl. 'Holy shit', thinks Seth. It's that protestor chick always down here with her sign.

Seth cautiously steps closer, waving the steam from the car from his face. He is standing right next to the car now. The girl's eyes are wide open in shock, bits of glass all over her face. Seth dashes around to the other side to see if Ruby is alive. His eyes are open too, staring right into hers. His mouth is moving. Seth steps closer and hears murmuring coming from Ruby's lips. A droning slew of words he can't make out. He's repeating something over and over. She's staring into his face listening to the words through a hazy, ringing head.

A high buzzing sound coming from behind on the highway. Seth turns around to see a man on a Vespa approaching wearing a colorful matching suit. A necktie wrapped around his head. Seth now recognizing the man from last night who came in and asked weird questions, then gave him shit about his uniform. Seth also realizing that the Vespa he's riding, is his.

Peter pulls up at the car crash scene at the Plucky's sign. He looks at the smoke billowing car, the two people on the hood, then to the guy in the Plucky's uniform standing next to it. Peter now recognizing the guy as the manager from last night.

Seth steps forward, pointing angrily at the aqua blue and white Vespa.

'That's my fucking Vespa, asshole!'

Peter glances over at Seth phlegmatically. Remembering now when he was stranded on the side of the road last night and this guy saw him and went by, leaving him in the cold. Peter reaches on the seat behind him and takes out a long instrument wrapped in a business jacket. He unravels the material to expose an M4 carbine assault rifle. Seth's eyes widen as Peter casually gets a grip of the gun in both hands and aims it at him.

BANG.

A bullet punches through Seth's abdomen, sending him flying back and landing into the red Plucky's sign pole with a loud crack. His body slumps down into an upright sitting position, leaning forward, his hands in the space between his legs. Seth lets out his last breath of life and his head sinks down, facing his stomach which is oozing out blood rapidly, all over his red and white Plucky's uniform.

Peter hops off the Vespa and strides over to the BMW. He looks down at Star. Eyes wide and staring at Ruby, who is mumbling through his lips. Ruby's eyes slowly shift to look to Peter, standing there with the assault rifle resting over one shoulder. Ruby noticing the flamboyant outfit he's wearing. The golden tassels glimmering in the sun. Ruby now looking confused. He manages to get one word out between his wheezing breaths.

'Peter?'

Peter brings the rifle up and rests it on his shoulder. His expression serious, looking tough.

'It's Lars.' Peter puffs his chest out with pride. 'Lars Gronholt.'

With that, Lars turns and marches back to the Vespa. He wraps the weapon in the coat again and rests it on the back of the Vespa. Lars hops on the bike and revs the little engine. With a loud buzzing noise, the Vespa hits the road and drives off down the highway. Lars doesn't know where he's going. He will stop at a bank and withdraw a large sum of money, and then, who knows what. He has a new life ahead of him, and for the first time in a long time, he's excited about what's to come. No more manicures. No more lecturing to a small crowd of desperate men. No more Ruby. No more Jillian. Just Lars and the open road.

On the hood of the car, Ruby gurgles a lungful of blood from a ruptured spleen. His last breath slips out and his eyes close. Star still staring at him through wide, traumatized eyes. Her little mouth slightly open, now murmuring like Ruby was.

Ruby's old limousine is cruising up Route 66, heading north out of Holbrook. Dennis is at the wheel, focused on the road ahead. He's wearing a dark chauffeur suit again, no wig or make up. Better to not look out of the ordinary when the police eventually send out information about them.

The bags under his eyes have dried tears in them, having cried in the memory of Karina and Raphael. Dennis had dropped into the old homestead to get a few things for the road and stumbled on the bodies of the maid and landscaper out by the pool. Both of them shot, and Dennis can't figure out who or why anyone would do that. Dennis didn't get to know Raphael too much, but Karina was a nice lady. The soundtrack to Chicago playing on the limo's speakers, lifting his mood a little. Going to the Big Apple with Winter is a new chapter in his book. He'll be able to show Broadway his talents. And Winter's too. It's only up from here.

In the back of the limo is a couple of suitcases filled with Dennis's clothes and odd belongings. He would never leave behind his framed pictures of vintage Hollywood starlets. Or his collection of wigs and heels. And his pages of music and instruments. Dennis also took a few other things. The massive telescope, so he can show Winter the stars he was talking about. He took a few of Ruby's cufflinks, broches, and pendants worth some cash. Something to get started with in New York. He could have taken a lot more of Ruby's valuables, but it only gives the police reason to assume he was part of any murders if he robbed the joint clean. It'll be rough adapting in a new, expensive city. But Dennis is sure they'll make it work somehow.

Winter is standing barefoot on the backseat of the limousine, half her body through the open sunroof. The wind whipping around her as the limo cruises down the highway past oncoming cars and trucks. Her hands are planted on the roof of the car as her bountiful raven hair is carelessly blown around her smiling porcelain face. She's wearing her corset outfit and a long scarf she found at Ruby's, flapping majestically in the wind behind her. For once in a long time, she feels free.

She climbs back into the cabin and shuts the sunroof. She plonks down on one of the couches and considers making a cocktail when she notices something on the floor. She leans over and picks it up. It's a map. Winter opens it and glazes over it. There's a circle around a mining district with instructions next to it. The instructions read; "3rd shaft. 103 feet deep. Blue ribbon."

Winter stares at it, twisting her lips, wondering what this means. The circle on the map is near a small town that they will drive by in thirty miles.

She leans over to the intercom to the driver's cabin and presses the talk button.

'Hey Denny.'

'Yeah Winnie.'

'Mind if we make a pit stop on our way?'

The limousine drives off into the yellow soaked horizon, not far from the state line now.

Star is on a gurney being loaded into the back of an ambulance by two paramedics. Her neck is in a cervical collar brace, she lies stiffly on the little bed with her eyes closed. The rocks taken off her feet. She had passed out on the hood of the car, the ambulance arrived and managed to get her into a stable condition. She heard the paramedics pronounce Ruby dead.

She's half conscious now, mumbling to herself as two paramedics hop in the back with her, laying their jump bags on the floor, and slam the back doors to the ambulance closed. One of them pounds on the front of the cabin. The siren starts up and the ambulance lurches into gear, starting to speed off toward Holbrook.

The two paramedics have Star hooked up to an ECG monitor by clamps on her fingertips. They watch the monitor showing her vital signs. Cords, straps, fluid bags and other life saving equipment swing from the ceiling of the ambulance as it soars through traffic on the highway. One of the paramedics is filling out information on a clipboard. He looks up to his female partner, watching the vitals monitor.

'How's she doing?'

'She's lucky to have minimum internal damage. Her face, neck, shoulders and chest are going to need some work. Lucky for her the windscreen was already cracked, or else she'd be a goner. But she'll pull through.'

They both look down at her on the stretcher, her face full of cuts and chunks of windshield glass. Her mumbling mouth spitting out words. The female paramedic leans down, putting her ear close to Star's mouth, listening for a minute, then she sits back up.

The male paramedic says, 'What's she saying?'

'Three parts this. Four parts that. Paprika. I dunno, I bunch of spices and shit. Sounds like some kind of recipe.' She shrugs. 'Probably just gibberish.'

The two paramedics nod in understanding to each other and go back about their business.

Star's lips stop moving. Her eyes open slightly into little watery slits. A cunning smile starts to creep across her lower face, showing broken teeth. She's just now realized she is the last person on Earth who knows the recipe to The Secret Sauce.

The black coated coyote sits on top of a dirt mound across the road from the Plucky's restaurant, still a bit shaken from almost being hit by a car just before. She watches the growing cavalcade of cars with flashing lights on top approaching the scene, some headed to the huge fire and black smoke down the road. The coyote licks her hairy snout, thinking about the Jell-O, and wondering if she will ever find that delicious, sweet taste ever again.

Epilogue

Winter holds a flashlight aiming it at a clump of rocks that Dennis is pulling apart. There's a blue ribbon tied to a wooden foundation above.

Dennis takes a large rock from the pile and freezes, staring down.

'Winnie honey, bring that light over.'

Winter steps over the course rocky ground in her heels.

Dennis reaches in the pile and, with some grunting, picks up an object.

Winter aims the flashlight at Dennis's hands. Her jaw drops and eyes bolt open.

The light bouncing off the large nugget of pure gold in Dennis's hands. Sparkling yellow tinges all over it as wisps of heavy dust swirl in the light and disappear into the pitch black shadows around them.

The gold is almost as bright as the sparkle in Winter's eyes.

ADAM PATRICK FOSTER

Adam Patrick Foster is a filmmaker and author of novels, produced screenplays, theatre writer and actor, television editor and radio broadcasting contributor, and offers you a twisted tale that will cause shock, laughter, and suspense.